"Russia has always inside an enigma.' E anarchy strangled b sets before us, how ponce state have *given way to the steely grip of an unpolicable one.*

"From the streets and offices of Moscow to the back rooms and bedrooms of New York, Steve penetrates the veils of fear, secrecy, and conspiracy to shine a bright light of understanding. He knows these places and these people: he has been there and seen what has not yet been fully reported. It is an exciting tale, a cautionary one, and an all too human story. As the Russians would say, 'Steve Block has the soul of a novelist.' Unfortunately, he also has the job of lawyer, so he will still go to hell. But at least not before leaving us a damn fine book."

—Peter Tauber

Author of The Last Best Hope and The Sunshine Soldiers; former presidential campaign speechwriter and Saturday Night Live writer

"A true to life primer for anyone contemplating business in the former Soviet Union."

—Nancy Ramsey

Free-lance journalist

"As enlightening as it is entertaining, Kooperativ reveals some of the primary problems Russia faces in its transition to a market economy. Mr. Block's novel is a much needed examination of the social environment that affects Russian-American business relationships."

—Yevgeniy Knizhnikov

U.S. representative of the Primorie Lawyers Association

KOOPERATIV

STEVE BLOCK

KOOPERATIV

A NOVEL

James C. Winston
Publishing Company, Inc.
Trade Division of Winston-Derek Publishers Group, Inc.

TO SOW THE FALLOW SOIL

PUBLISHED BY JAMES C. WINSTON PUBLISHING COMPANY, INC.
Nashville, Tennessee 37205

Library of Congress Catalog Card No: 95-61851
ISBN: 1-55523-771-1

Printed in the United States of America

For Leslie

A Note from the Author

Russians almost invariably have three names—a first name, a patronymic, and a surname.

The first name is rarely used informally because most Russians are called by a diminutive nickname. These nicknames usually end in "ya" or "a" (for example, Pyotr becomes Petya, and Mikhail becomes Misha). More affectionate nicknames are often further derived from the diminutives (for example, Alyona becomes Lyena, Lyenka, or Lyenochka, and Pyotr becomes Petya or Petyenka).

The patronymic (middle name) is derived from the first name of the individual's father, to which men add "ovich" or "evich" and women add "ovna" or "evna." Siblings of the same sex would therefore have the same patronymic. In this story, for example, Oleg's sons Misha and Petya both have the patronymic "Olegovich."

To indicate respect (as in the English "Mr." or "Ms."), the first name and patronymic are used together. Ilya Konstantinovich Lukov would not be referred to as "Mr. Lukov" among Russians, but rather as Ilya Konstantinovich.

Russian surnames differentiate between male and female by adding the letter "a" to the end of women's last names. In the above example, Ilya Konstantinovich's wife and daughters would therefore have the surname "Lukova."

ONE

"You see, Ilya Konstantinovich, this safety latch protects the operator from catching a finger in the shredder's gears. Without it, use of the apparatus is quite dangerous. I have an experienced volunteer running it now, but to be honest with you, I wouldn't want to be up there," explained Misha Grunshteyn loudly over the ululating factory machinery, his eyes filled with the concern of a loyal employee.

Ilya was kneeling beside the shredder, rubbing the back of his bald head. He glanced up at a faded hammer and sickle on the far wall, which he'd somehow neglected to remove in the four years since the fall of the Soviet regime, then leaned closer to Misha. "Turn it off then. Let's not risk the worker's safety." He examined the large oily contraption for a moment and sighed. "If we have to shut down the entire mill, it will cut our production by one fourth. Do you have any suggestions?"

Misha, the chief engineer at the Mosteks factory, shrugged. "Well, I can work late tonight. Maybe it's worth a try to rig something up. But I don't know, Ilya Konstantinovich. This is very old Soviet-made equipment, and there are no spare parts available, especially here in Moscow, because—"

Ilya shook his head at the engineer, smiling to show his gratitude. Misha was a good engineer. A good kid. Ilya was lucky to have found him. "No, no. Don't bother, Misha. Thanks for offering," he said. "We'll just have to go without mill number two until we can get better equipment." Ilya stood with a groan, brushed his knee, and motioned the soiled factory worker to come down from the malfunctioning shredder. "Thank you, Gregori," he said to the man with another gracious smile.

"I'll shut it down, then," said Misha.

Ilya had just nodded at Misha when he was startled by his secretary's excited voice. "Ilya Konstantinovich!" said Lyena breathlessly, obviously having searched for him frantically. "The State Inspector's Office has sent representatives! Two *chinovniki* wish to meet with you immediately!"

Ilya closed his eyes tightly and rolled his head in a futile attempt to ease his tension. "Thank you, Lyena." He opened his eyes, forced a smile, and headed toward Mosteks' business offices in the adjacent building. "I'll be back in a minute, Misha," he said over his shoulder before opening the door. "They're probably here to find something else to tax!" He winked as he left the noisy factory with his secretary.

Ilya Konstantinovich Lukov was a pleasant man. No taller than he was wide, he had a horseshoe of thick grey fuzz encircling his bald, round head. His face bore the imbedded charm of one's kindly uncle—a rather gregarious look, especially for a Russian authority figure. Like many other cooperative chiefs, he rarely bothered with the formality of a suit, or even that of a tie, and the first two buttons of his usually tattered shirt were often unfastened, revealing a frayed undershirt. He seemed like an old giant teddy bear, a *Meeshka*, ragged with age and rough handling, but all the more lovable because of it. He'd tolerated the comparison for years.

But Mosteks' employees greatly respected Ilya Konstantinovich. Most of his staff had worked in other Russian plants before, many in textile production. They appreciated Ilya's obliging treatment and generous salaries, both of which differed radically from what they'd received in state factories. It was unusual for a Russian boss to treat his workers as generously as did Ilya, and his benevolence resulted in the workers' unquestioned loyalty to him and the cooperative. Rarely would a Russian employee agree to operate dangerous machinery as a simple favor to his boss. It was extraordinary for a Russian secretary to become genuinely concerned about a government inquiry. And it was almost unheard of for a Russian engineer to volunteer his overtime labor. The *Meeshka* somehow inspired a work ethic in his employees that generations of communism had only dreamed of. And he took pride in the fact that his maverick business philosophy was paying off.

"The *chinovniki* are in the waiting room," said Lyena, using the Russian word that literally meant "bureaucratic functionary." She accompanied her boss quickly through the corridor.

The two entered the reception area and, when Ilya saw his two visitors, the pleasant charm vanished immediately from his face. He studied the two men for a silent moment and braced himself.

These were no *chinovniki*.

"Lyena, stay out here in the reception area. I'm not to be disturbed for any reason. I'll meet with the gentlemen in my office," Ilya ordered, his voice uncharacteristically stern and restrained. He went through his office door, and the two men followed him in.

A tall, wan man with longish dark hair stood a short distance from Ilya, looking around Ilya's large office. Sizing it up, it seemed. He wore a fashionable black leather jacket of the quality one rarely found on a Russian. He stood silently for a moment, his cold eyes peering down haughtily at the cooperative chairman. "Good day, Ilya Konstantinovich. My name is Svetov," he said with a brief, pretentious bow.

Ilya glanced at the man's dark eyes, which, he decided, could never express joy or sorrow or even fear. They were *zlo*—flagrant evil. Discerning, calculating, maybe even cautious. But they were pure *zlo*.

Ilya forced his own eyes to glance toward the other man, younger and fair-haired, standing a few steps behind and to the left of Svetov. He was huge and ominously silent, yet his eyes were those of an apprentice, observing his mentor's work and storing the lessons for future reference.

Ilya ignored Svetov's hand. "What do you want?" he demanded, sounding distressed despite his attempts to remain firm.

"We are looking forward to establishing a mutually beneficial working relationship with you and your cooperative," said Svetov, his hand still extended.

There was nothing actually threatening about the man's words, or even in his expression or tone. Ilya saw that only the man's eyes were menacing, as if they were two Nazi guards holding the other features of Svetov's face at bay.

"We would like to help your cooperative operate in its most efficient capacity," continued Svetov. "I am in a position to offer you some very useful services, Ilya Konstantinovich."

Ilya continued to ignore the man's feigned politeness and extended hand. He dismissed the ridiculous idea of asking the two men for credentials. He took a deep breath and said, "I am not in need of any of your services, thank you. I am also a very busy man. I do not appreciate your misrepresenting yourselves to my secretary as state officials. Now if you'll please leave my office—"

Ilya headed toward the door to open it, but Svetov's companion quickly moved to block his way. It was an obviously rehearsed maneuver, as if learned in boot camp, and Ilya thought he saw the younger man seek approval with a glance at his boss. The sentry was not as seasoned as was Svetov; he didn't even attempt to disguise his visage with fabricated amiability.

"I said I am not interested in anything you have to offer," repeated Ilya curtly. "Our meeting is over."

"Ilya Konstantinovich, please. Listen to our proposals," said Svetov, now with both hands extended, palms up. "We were not entirely incorrect in identifying ourselves as representatives from the State Inspector's Office." He put his hands in the pockets of his jacket.

Ilya watched Svetov begin to pace about his office arrogantly. The man's head was tilted back slightly, displaying a nauseating vanity.

"As you know," continued Svetov smoothly, "the new Russian government has been taking strict measures to ensure that cooperative and other privatized activities conform to ministry rules and regulations. Inspections are being conducted at all manufacturing facilities and, unfortunately, many are being closed for safety violations." He stopped pacing and looked directly into Ilya's eyes. "I would hate to see your successful enterprise also shut down. It would be such a waste."

Ilya had adjusted to Svetov's style, the effect of the man's feigned compassion heightened by his callous eyes. Ilya knew that Mosteks could not afford to pay protection money to the mafia. It would be the end! He quickly recounted the cooperative's struggling financial situation in his mind, recalling the probable loss of mill number two, and then returned his attention to the colorless man.

"However, I am in a position to prevent such an unfortunate occurrence from happening," continued Svetov. "I have come here today to make my services available to Mosteks." He again raised his opened palms. "Of course we would expect worthy compensation for our efforts on your behalf, Ilya Konstantinovich." He paused and looked up at the ceiling. "You will pay us five percent of Mosteks' gross monthly income. You should have your accountants document the hiring of several dummy employees for official bookkeeping purposes and…"

Ilya felt his face become flush and his breathing deepen as his visitor listed the details. Svetov spoke like a businessman, his proposal well conceived and worded, almost as if the services he was here to offer were legitimate.

Suddenly Ilya took a forceful step toward the man and shouted, "*No!* My cooperative will not be extorted!" He pointed a shaking finger at the two men. "Now, get out before I call the police!"

Svetov wasn't even fazed by Ilya's outburst. Ilya had startled himself more than he had the *mafioznik.*

Svetov gazed at Ilya a short while, then calmly said, "Ilya Konstantinovich, we did not come here to argue with you. You have no choice. If you do not accept our terms, you will simply be put out of business by the end of the week." His attempts to sound congenial had now vanished, along with his revolting smile. Svetov glowered at Ilya, waiting for a response.

The chairman stood staring back. While the *mafioznik* was seasoned at such confrontations, Ilya was not. Of course, Ilya was aware of the widespread extortion and racketeering of successful Russian businesses. All Russian private enterprises were subject to mafia intrusion; he'd known this for years. But he'd never been approached by the mafia himself, probably due to the fact that Mosteks' private enterprise status had never been publicized.

Khuligani, he thought, vicious street criminals with not a drop of moral decency. He would never give in to the mafia, at least not without a fight! He realized that if Mosteks were to survive these *khuligani,* it would have to be with a counterattack. A war was the only thing these people could understand. He quickly formulated a plan.

Ilya momentarily sauntered around his office, a look of rumination upon his face. "I guess it would be unwise of me to bend your stick, wouldn't it?" he asked. "So. If I agree to pay you, am I assured that no state inspection will ever reveal...violations of ministry regulations? And am I also assured that no one else will...offer me similar services?"

"Of course, Ilya Konstantinovich," replied Svetov, his smile returning.

Ilya gave a sigh of concession. "Very well, then. This month Mosteks grossed three hundred seventy million rubles. I will be able to give you five percent of that amount in three days. Please come back this Friday at four o'clock to pick up the payment." He glanced at both *mafiozniki*. Had they fallen for his act?

Svetov continued smiling as he shook Ilya's hand and said, "I knew you were a reasonable businessman, Ilya Konstantinovich, and I'm glad to see that we will be partners. Until Friday."

The chairman held his breath as he showed the two men out.

Ilya sat alone in his office the next morning, supporting his large head in his hands behind the Soviet-made, imitation hard-wood desk. He had called a meeting of Mosteks' directorate, the three board members who governed the cooperative's daily business and manufacturing operations. The other two men were due to arrive any minute.

Ilya looked at the picture of his wife and daughter which stood on the corner of his tilted desk. Russians didn't ordinarily keep family photos at work, but Ilya, who'd been fortunate enough to visit the West several years back, liked the idea. It made his loved ones more a part of his everyday life. He'd often wondered if his dedication to Mosteks had caused him to…well, neglect them a bit. Not give them the full attention they deserved. How had little Aksana, who preferred to be called Ksenya now, grown up so quickly? At least his wife Luba hadn't changed. Strange, he'd always known that he could never have made it without them. It was they who had enabled him to rise through the ranks of the Soviet system and obtain the skills that eventually led to the creation of Mosteks. These two women were the strength of his soul, the essence of his life. But while he knew that his family was financially better off than most people the Lukovs knew, Ilya hoped that his business success hadn't deprived them of something far more important than money.

When the two *mafiozniki* had left yesterday, Ilya had immediately locked his office door behind them, then paced for a few minutes, trying to regain his composure. He remembered looking up at the top shelf of his bookcase where the collection of his father's medals from the Great Patriotic War with Nazi Germany was proudly displayed. They were usually a source of inspiration, a reminder to Ilya of all he stood for. But Ilya had been so shaken that it was nearly ten minutes after the criminals had left before he could even sit down to make the call. And his still trembling hand had needed several tries to dial the number to MVD, the Russian Federation Ministry of Internal Affairs.

He'd been directed to MVD's Department for the Struggle with Organized Crime, where he'd spoken with some paper-pushing bureaucrat named Major Nikita Aleksandrovich Kulishev. "Special Operational Deputy," said Ilya despondently to himself, mocking the cop's official-sounding title.

After describing Svetov's threats to Kulishev, the chairman had expected compassion and a zealous police effort. He'd even wondered how he'd keep the Mosteks plant workers from being upset when police cars suddenly pulled into the parking lot. After all, he'd already done all the dirty work, right? All the MVD had to do was show up on Friday and arrest the *khuligani!*

MVD was familiar with the Gagarinskaya crime organization, the "Gagarintsi," the mafia organization that had threatened Mosteks. Kulishev explained that, as was the case with most local mafia organizations, this group had been named for the territory in which it operated, the Gagarinskaya region of Moscow. Mosteks was located in the industrial region, so it was not surprising to Kulishev that the cooperative had been sought out and approached by the Gagarintsi. And Kulishev had known immediately who Svetov was after hearing Ilya's description of the *mafioznik's* eyes and his black leather jacket.

It sickened Ilya to learn that the mafia clan's title was derived from Yuri Gagarin's name, the first cosmonaut, a true Russian hero. Ilya had immediately become enthusiastic about playing a role in the Gagarintsi's demise. But Ilya's hopes for a quick finish to the ordeal were soon thwarted.

"So. How do we proceed, Major?" asked the chairman after having described his encounter to Kulishev.

"What do you mean?"

Ilya hesitated. "Aren't you going to arrest the *mafiozniki* when they come next Friday? I made an appointment at a specific time so as to make apprehension easy for you."

A brief pause. "I'm afraid not, Ilya Konstantinovich," replied Kulishev.

"What! But what do you mean, Major Kulishev? I'm being assailed by racketeers! Aren't you going to intervene? Isn't that the purpose of your department?"

Kulishev again paused, then said, "Ilya Konstantinovich, our country is besieged by organized crime. We simply do not have the resources to take action in every instance. In your case, there hasn't even been a threat of physical harm. If a corrupt inspector were to shut your facility down on false charges, you would always be able to appeal the matter to the proper authorities."

"But...but this is lunacy!"

"Ilya Konstantinovich, please. There are thousands of instances of mafia organizations having inflicted concrete damage in Moscow alone. They have burned buildings, raped the wives and daughters of resisting private enterprise entrepreneurs, and murdered the employees of businesses such as your own. These are examples of palpable destruction that must command my immediate attention. Now, the Gagarintsi *are* dangerous, and we already have them under investigation for offenses similar to the one they are committing against you. But until they at least threaten you with real violence, my options, I'm afraid, are limited."

As a final blow, MVD had refused even to call the State Inspector's Office to investigate the matter, claiming that to do so would be futile.

Ilya sighed as he recalled the conversation and began plotting his next course of action. He was, after all, a survivor, having used all of his talents and resources to build Mosteks into a successful manufacturing operation. He'd just have to figure something out.

Ilya stood from behind his desk and began pacing impatiently, reminiscing about his efforts in establishing Mosteks. He was a seasoned Soviet businessman, with roots in the "old system"—the centralized communist economy. Not that Ilya ever favored the inept regime. For years he'd secretly believed that the old system was the reason that Russia had failed to develop on a par with the West. There was simply no incentive for anyone, from the highest decision-maker to the lowest plant worker, to produce effectively and efficiently. Business simply could not be productive if accomplishment was not met with reward. Of course Ilya never voiced his discontent during the Khrushchev through Chernenko years. Only now, after Gorbachev and under Yeltsin, was that possible. Still, his frustration with the system was very much intact, and frequent incidents like the one he'd just experienced at MVD served as unpleasant reminders of the problems and frustrations he'd dealt with all his life.

Ilya's desire to beat the system, to show that economic reform in Russia was both feasible and critically necessary, was the guiding force behind his efforts to take advantage of *perestroika*. Seven years earlier, he'd left his prestigious position at the Soviet Ministry of Light Industry, where he'd managed the department overseeing textile production. Ilya immediately entered into discussions with a failing state textile enterprise, one that he knew would soon have to close its doors due to inefficient production if it were not rescued by a competent entrepreneur. After months of planning and calling in favors, the Mosteks cooperative was finally born. It wasn't just an economic venture in which Ilya was sure he'd reap a much-deserved personal benefit, but Mosteks was also to be a demonstration. The cooperative would prove to Russia that only incentive could serve a business's best interests. And thus far, the cooperative had fulfilled both of its missions well.

He looked up at his father's medals. In the center of the display was a large picture of Konstantin Antonovich Lukov, Senior Sergeant, Marksman First Class, killed in action at the Battle of Stalingrad in 1943. The round-faced soldier stood with his chin raised at the remains of a German Panzer. A Russian hero, thought Ilya, a martyr who died for the *rodina,* the Russian Motherland. He was only ten when Papa was killed, but like so many other Russians of the era, Ilya had carried on his father's legacy with a devout love for Russia. His contribution to the rodina would not be with his blood, though he would have gladly given it. Rather, Ilya Konstantinovich Lukov would serve his country by making it a better place in which to live. Like the Nazis, Russia's horrible economic situation could be beaten, and it would have to start with people like him. The battle would have to be fought from the ground up. He felt his own chin rise at the thought.

But the task would be great. None of Ilya's friends and colleagues could understand his motivation to put in sixteen hour days without pay, or to confront the Moscow City Council in order to obtain real estate rights for a factory. They said that the Soviet bureaucracy would make successful private enterprise impossible. "It's a waste of time, Ilya," he'd often heard. "It will never work in Russia! The cooperative movement won't even get off the ground!" But Ilya Konstantinovich Lukov had only smiled at the pessimists and pushed on to create Mosteks.

Indeed, many cooperatives did rather well in the early *perestroika* years. They were the rudiments of free enterprise, the beginning of a Russian free market economy, and cooperatives set the course for Russia's entire economic conversion. Many *kooperatori*, or cooperative entrepreneurs, had even become wealthy through the fruits of their own labors. Ilya was proud that Mosteks was still called a cooperative. Private enterprises formed since the Soviet Union's collapse were given more corporate-sounding names such as "stock societies" or "organizations of limited liability." But a cooperative was a pioneer, a founding father of the Russian free enterprise movement. A cooperative was a part of Russian history.

The movement had been beset with sociological problems, especially in the beginning. For example, *kooperatori* were often scorned by the average Russian, the typical "Ivan Ivanovich" on the street, who'd never witnessed success by his compatriots. Ivan Ivanovich was accustomed to being destitute, but he'd always found comfort in the thought that destitution was his national legacy. The cooperative movement had now eliminated that comfort, and Ivan Ivanovich was now being forced to evaluate himself and discern the reasons why some were wealthy and he was not. The result was often jealousy, and sometimes even violent resentment. Ilya had long wondered if he might someday suffer because of this social phenomenon, or if one of countless other obstacles to successful free enterprise in Russia would someday show him its claws.

Now he was encountering the first such threat. This was the first time that his success had been confirmed by the dark side of Russia's conversion to a market economy. He supposed there was actually some measure of compliment in it. Maybe it was the final proof that things were really coming along. But while the country might be on the right track, he thought, the legacy of the old system would still have to be beaten.

In the meantime, the two other directorate members had arrived, and Ilya told them about the incident with the mafia and his phone call to MVD.

"If we pay the mafia this time, who can say the Gagarintsi won't return next week and demand an even larger percent of our profits?" asked Albert Denisov, the cooperative's general manager and second in command. He was a good deal younger than Ilya, about forty, with thinning black hair and a belly which was starting to catch up with his boss's.

"It's possible," answered Ilya despondently. He noticed that his voice had become hoarse.

"I can assure you that with such a financial strain, we won't last six months," added Andrey Muravyev, Mosteks accountant and treasurer. Andrey was a husky man about Ilya's age, with blond hair and a penchant for American sweatshirts whose logos and expressions he couldn't even read. Today he wore a red one that read "Don't Worry, Be Happy." "From what I've heard," continued Andrey, "the mafia is usually wise enough not to kill the cow it milks. It seems a bit strange that—"

"Gentlemen, gentlemen," interrupted Ilya. "I share your concern, believe me. But first let me explain something." He groaned as he rose from his chair and ambled toward the window. "I was not taken completely by surprise when the racketeers approached me." His smile returned amidst the anxiety in his brow. "Most successful businesses in our country suffer from mafia intrusion. We all know this, and there is rarely anything that can be done about it. But I believe that we have already inadvertently set in motion a means to combat the racketeers."

Albert and Andrey looked up at him in anticipation.

Ilya continued. "As you know, we are finalizing our negotiations with the New York based company Inter-American Industrial Services—'IIS'—to establish a fabric manufacturing joint venture. I believe that the arrangement with IIS will afford us protection from the racketeers."

After a short silence, Andrey asked, "What do you mean?"

"As soon as our joint venture is registered with the authorities, I believe that the mafia will not be so quick to intimidate us. As a participant in an international JV, we will come under the jurisdiction of the Ministry of Foreign Economic Relations and other state agencies of international business. We will receive the attention of a variety of law enforcement bureaus which answer directly to the highest levels of Russian government. I believe that mafia organizations will not wish to expose themselves to their scrutiny."

"But why do you think that other government agencies will be any more effective in combating the racketeers than the MVD?" asked Albert, running a hand through his thin hair.

"International JV's are an important avenue through which the government taxes foreign hard currency," interjected Andrey, nodding his approval. "The ministries are likely to keep a much closer eye on them to assure that the source remains unobstructed."

"So the project with IIS has become far more important, gentlemen," Ilya added. "Of course, protection from the mafia isn't the only reason we have for establishing the JV. We stand to make a lot of money through the arrangement as well." He gave an embarrassed laugh. "It's now imperative that we ensure the JV's establishment."

Ilya walked back to his desk and sat down. "As you know," he continued, "we have a lawyer from IIS coming to visit us this month for negotiations. I want the entire facility in top working order. The lawyer will be treated to the best accommodations we can obtain. I'm going to agree to some of IIS's earlier business demands in order to speed up the JV registration process."

Albert and Andrey regarded the chairman silently for a moment. "What will happen when the *mafiozniki* arrive on Friday?" asked Albert.

Ilya sighed. "I'm going to pay them, my friends. Hopefully they'll be satisfied and leave us alone for the time being." The room again fell silent for a moment while he quickly surveyed his colleagues. "Gentlemen, I'm not happy about it either. But what are we to do?" His colleagues shrugged in unison.

"Obviously our discussion is not to leave this room," added Ilya. "And please, your knowledge of the mafia's activity and our attempts to invoke MVD assistance are also to be kept completely confidential. Do not even advise any of the staff or plant workers of our situation. I'm concerned about our employees' safety."

Ilya paused again. "Albert. Andrusha." He looked at each man separately. "You have both known me for years. I'm sure you know how I feel about giving in to these *khuligani*. I feel violated, like my soul has been punctured, and I can only fight to minimize the damage. But I see no other way out of this."

"Good afternoon, Ilya Konstantinovich," began Svetov. He arrived with the same accomplice, who seemed to be a bit more self-assured this time in his role as muscleman.

Ilya stood silently behind his desk.

"It's a pleasure to see you again," continued the man, his devilish eyes and nauseating smile as penetrating as they'd been the last time. "We are both very busy men, so I think we had best get immediately to the matter at hand." The tall, pale man spoke arrogantly, his hands deep in the pockets of his black leather jacket.

Ilya stood looking at the two criminals. Thoughts of the long battle he'd fought to establish his cooperative—about all Mosteks meant to him, to his employees, and to Russia— stormed his heart. He studied the men whose breed constituted one of the largest threats to the economic survival of his country. With all that lay ahead of Russia, men like Svetov simply could not be tolerated. Ilya felt his expression slowly turn to an uncharacteristic scowl.

"So, Ilya Konstantinovich?" drawled Svetov, apparently undaunted by Ilya's demeanor.

How could he have even considered betraying his principles, his cooperative and its hard-working employees, Russia and the memory of his Papa? What fear had captured his soul? He glanced up at the two men. He saw the huge frame of the nameless presence by the door, then the dark eyes of the man in the black leather jacket. But what could he do now? Ilya waited a second to see which way his instincts would direct him, then felt himself take a brash step toward Svetov. The bodyguard snapped to attention, but Svetov's face remained confidently expressionless.

Ilya pointed a finger at Svetov and spat, "Into the cunt with your mafia! You want money on a blue bordered saucer? Never! I'll not be a victim of your fucking extortion!" His voice grew louder as he continued. "I won't give you a fucking *kopeck!* Now get out of my office! *Fuck your mother!*" Ilya, shocked by his own words, felt himself beginning to pant. He steadied himself by clutching the edge of his desk and waited desperately for Svetov's response.

But as before, Svetov wasn't even fazed. He didn't flinch or even take a deeper breath in response to what might have been a prelude to physical attack. Svetov's fair-haired accomplice also stood stoically, observing and mimicking his superior's manner. "Ilya Konstantinovich, I must urge you to reconsider," said the colorless man calmly, slowly withdrawing his hands from his jacket and crossing them in front of him.

Ilya felt beads of sweat begin to form along his broad forehead, but he knew his scowl responded adequately to Svetov's demand. He thought of the heavy ashtray on his desk, then quickly inspected Svetov's build. Should he try it? Should he hurl the ashtray at the *khuligan,* or better yet, slam it over his head? He could almost feel the satisfying shatter of the *mafioznik's* skull beneath him.

No. Svetov was a rather thin man, but there would be no chance of the chairman overpowering both him and the huge bodyguard. He abandoned the idea and continued to return Svetov's glower.

"Do not disappoint me, Lukov," said the *mafioznik* coldly, abruptly breaking the momentary silence. "You are making a terrible and very costly mistake! Give me the money!" His last words were nearly shouted.

But Ilya stood steadfast, struggling to keep his now heavy breathing from becoming audible. He'd never been a pugnacious sort and had rarely seen confrontation; there was simply no previous experience for him to draw upon for guidance. Was he handling this correctly, or was he being a fool? Was his life in danger at this very second? How did things suddenly get so out of control?

The pale man slowly approached Ilya, who summoned all his courage. Ilya felt his toes curl and dig into the sole of his shoes, as if preparing for a final stand of their own. When Svetov's face was inches from his own, Ilya spoke quietly. "Get out." His voice was so hoarse it was nearly a whisper.

For a long moment, Svetov didn't budge. He then turned and began to pace about the office, looking at Ilya's collection of personal memorabilia, the tributes to his family and his career with the Soviet Ministry of Light Industry. "I can see that you are quite agitated, Ilya Konstantinovich. Afraid, perhaps. But please relax. It is rarely necessary for us to harm *kooperatori*. Of course, I could have your legs broken if I so wished." Svetov turned from the bookcase and went directly to Ilya's desk, where he studied the picture of Luba and Ksenya for a long moment. He gave Ilya that smile again. "Why are you so shaken, Ilya Konstantinovich? Maybe there are others about whom you are concerned?"

Ilya felt his fury rise in his chest but quickly willed himself to disregard the man's comment.

"But again, we seldom use our muscles, Ilya Konstantinovich. Sometimes, but not often. If you fail to honor our agreement, your textile mill will simply be put out of business in a few days. Period."

"Get out!" repeated the chairman, more forcefully this time.

"You will pay, Lukov, or Mosteks will be closed down! And if that doesn't bring you to your senses, then perhaps a few months in a wheelchair will!"

"*Get out!*"

"We'll be meeting again soon, fool," spat Svetov curtly. He then turned and left the room.

"We'll see!" replied Ilya. He was about to savor the feeling of relief when he saw Svetov's cohort lingering at the threshold of his office. This man's thin smile affected him in a way that Svetov's had not. It was somehow less…predictable. Ilya felt a cold knot in his stomach but managed to return the young man's stare. Mercifully, the accomplice then also disappeared through the doorway.

The next week was the longest Ilya Lukov could remember. Every morning the chairman arrived at Mosteks with bloodshot eyes and a furrowed brow. He rarely came out of his office during those seven days, allowing only Albert Denisov, the manager, and Andrey Muravyev, the accountant, to speak with him. And even then only about the most urgent of matters. Ilya's office window afforded him a view of the road that approached the cooperative facility, and every time a car passed by, he was sure it was some team of corrupt, profiteering inspectors coming to find bogus infractions of the state safety code at Mosteks. Then it would only be a matter of time before the factory was shut down.

On each of the seven days, Ilya Lukov was forced to review his principles, asking himself if he was being naïve to think he could simply ignore the strength of Russian corruption and carry on a successful business. Was he digging the ground out from beneath his own feet, as the saying went? The whole damn country was plagued—no, run—by corrupt forces! Who was he to be immune from it all? Maybe he should just pay the Gagarintsi and get on with it!

A skinny bespectacled man of about twenty finally came to the Mosteks facility. He displayed a State Inspector's Office identification and an order compelling Ilya to allow him access to the factory. Ilya wondered why it had taken seven days. Was there a backlog of factories to shut down? Did Russian inefficiency extend to its corrupt forces as well?

"May I ask what gave rise to this inspection?" he asked the man. "Our plant was just examined by your agency not six months ago and was actually commended for its compliance with state safety regulations."

"I was not told why, Ilya Konstantinovich," said the inspector, adjusting his glasses and looking away. The scrawny man's timidity made Ilya feel a bit more confident, but the latter assumed that the former's superiors were behind the inspection and that a debate with the kid would be futile. The inspection itself was a mockery of standard procedure; usually at least three agents with various expertise would inspect a plant the size of Mosteks. But Ilya kept his observations to himself.

As the two walked through the noisy factory, Ilya began to feel almost sorry for the inspector. He silently wondered what circumstances had befallen the kid, how he'd come under the domination of corruption and the likes of Svetov. Like most Russians, Ilya had a keen sense of character and quickly deciphered that the skinny inspector was not an evil young man.

Ilya Konstantinovich Lukov was sitting in his office with the directorate, reviewing the list of apparent infractions the inspector had cited. "Three instances of exposed wiring, insufficient lighting over heavy machinery in mill number four, a malfunctioning safety device on mill one, a worker having been exposed to hazardous cleaning compounds, a ventilation shaft unlawfully closed during operational hours, a worker being forced to labor hours beyond legal restraints." He sighed deeply, then forced a smile. "Sounds awful, doesn't it?" Andrey and Albert remained silent, their eyes expressing the same despair. "I guess it's only a matter of time, gentlemen. We'll probably be shut down by Monday."

Andrey said, "Our only hope is for a quick and successful registration of the joint venture with IIS, Ilya. It's clear that the

Gagarintsi are in firm control of the Inspector's Office, and unless we comply with Svetov's demands, we won't be allowed to operate."

"My thoughts exactly, Andrusha," replied Ilya. "And we have to stay operational long enough to survive. It will be at least several weeks before we're in a position to submit our joint venture documents for registration." He rubbed his tired eyes with both hands and said, almost to himself, "I guess we have no choice but to pay the *khuligani* after all. I apologize for my foolishness in last week's meeting with the criminals."

Suddenly Ilya's head snapped toward the window. He'd caught sight of a Mercedes-Benz on the side of the main road in front of Mosteks. Mercedes were a unique status symbol in Russia; they were rarely seen in the industrial area of Moscow.

Ilya watched as the driver's window lowered electrically and the elbow of a black leather jacket appeared from within the car. Svetov's dark hair was disheveled from the gush of cold wind hitting his face, but his coal black eyes were clearly visible. He smiled at Ilya.

TWO

"How are you Sam? It's good to see you," Davies said with a commanding smile as he shook the young lawyer's hand. Four other IIS big wigs were already assembled in the huge office of Jonathan Davies, President and CEO of Inter-American Industrial Services. They all bore that executive expression of total devotion to the task at hand. Davies probably evokes the same reaction from people on the street, Sam thought as he took his seat on the sofa.

"That's all of us, then. Shall we get started?" continued Davies, verifying the undivided attention of his troops, his voice agreeable but resolute. He sat down behind his huge oak desk, the Empire State Building looming through the window behind him. "I've called you to this meeting, Sam, because I want to involve you in a pivotal company project. Let me give you a little background."

Like the others, Sam Morris gave the CEO his best look of formal attention. The look was a part of the game, a very big part, and Sam gave it because he was prepared to do whatever was necessary to play the game correctly. And win it.

"We've been attempting to develop international operations in some of our smaller divisions," explained Davies. "Our expansion overseas has been a bit slow in comparison with American industry generally, and the IIS board has recently deemed it essential that we spread our wings. The entire conglomerate will be best served if we embark on a course toward making the corporation more transnational in nature, and we wish to—shall we say—start small." Davies raised his arms, extending two fingers on each hand to symbolize quotation marks. He smiled again, only with his lips, which were partially hidden by a thick salt-and-pepper beard. "We have decided that our textile division, Old Virginia Mills, is a prime candidate for overseas expansion." He put his fingertips together and paused a second, his eyes locked on Sam's.

"Yes, sir," responded Sam. Although he knew his concurrence was by no means necessary, Davies was clearly looking for it. Sam squared his shoulders and resumed his business demeanor.

"Now, as you know, Sam, the U.S. has been lagging behind its foreign competitors in the textile manufacturing industry," Davies continued. "The Chinese, Koreans, and Indians, for example, are simply in a much better position to produce than we are. They're able to obtain cheaper labor and materials, which makes competition with them extremely difficult."

Sam, a junior attorney working in IIS's legal office, knew this all too well. Competition from Asia was the main reason that his family's textile business, Old Virginia Mills, had been forced to sell out to IIS, a nationwide conglomerate of small and medium-sized industrial enterprises. He pushed the troubling thought aside.

"European markets are very tough to break in to, but doing so is absolutely essential to our company's long term profitability, Sam," resumed the CEO, shifting in his chair. "Research has recently revealed a very attractive proposition in Europe, and I would like you to see to it that the legalities of the proposal are in order."

All right! thought Sam, making sure he didn't reveal his excitement. Could this be it? The moment he'd been dreaming about for ten years? It was only on very rare occasions that he was even called to meet with the CEO. And here he was about to get a major corporate assignment! In Europe! Or so he hoped, at least. "I see. What kind of proposition is it?" he asked, leaning back on the president's lavish sofa.

"I'll let Ben Kaplan explain the details, Sam, since he has more hands-on familiarity with the project." Davies turned his somber, bearded face toward Benjamin Kaplan, who was sitting in a maroon wingback chair to the right of the CEO's desk. The other men in the office shifted likewise.

"Uh, yes," began Kaplan, IIS's chief acquisitions executive, usually responsible for researching potential new additions to the conglomerate empire. "I was the one who originally conceived the idea and initiated formal contacts with our partners in Moscow."

Moscow? thought Sam, catching a breath in his throat. Russia? Hot damn! Old V's going to Russia! Sam immediately pictured his father and wondered how he would have responded to the news. It was only proper, Sam thought, that Daddy, who'd passed away a few years ago, still helped run Old V. Even if it was only through his son's memories and mental images. Sam exhaled silently and looked down at the oriental rug.

"Labor and materials are available to us very inexpensively in Russia," continued Kaplan in his characteristically shrill voice. "In light of the political developments over the past few years, we feel that there is good opportunity in that country to establish ourselves and thereby gain a foothold in Europe for other projects."

Sam adjusted to Benjamin Kaplan's steadfast gaze. Kaplan was as dedicated as he was industrious, which was no doubt a primary reason why IIS had developed its various holdings so successfully. The acquisitions exec understood the company's needs. And more importantly, he knew how to satisfy those needs. It occurred to Sam that he'd known Kaplan longer than anyone else at IIS, having met him during the negotiations for Old V's sale to the conglomerate.

"I have located a Russian textile enterprise which would like to establish a joint venture with IIS through our Old Virginia division," continued Kaplan. "Basically, we would be providing the Russians with equipment, technology, and marketing skills. They will provide raw materials and labor. The joint venture enterprise will produce a variety of fabrics that will be sold in Western Europe for hard currency."

Old Virginia has arrived! thought Sam, again containing his glee. Why hadn't he thought of it himself? Russia was the up-and-coming place! And Sam Morris was going to bring Old V there! Back there, really, considering that Russia was where it had all started in the first place. "Hard currency?" asked Sam, willing himself back to the meeting. "What do you mean?" He diligently withdrew a yellow legal notepad from his briefcase.

"Well, you have to understand, Sam, that Russian money—the ruble—is extremely unstable. Its value in the world market is not reliable, so it's called a 'soft currency.' Of course, the Russian textile enterprise only has rubles, so it can't just buy our equipment and expertise. Only when fabrics are sold in Western Europe through the joint venture will we receive stable exchange, or hard currency." Kaplan looked away from Sam and smiled wryly. "Or what the Russians call *valuta*, from the English word for 'value.'"

Good boy, Benny. I'm glad to see you have at least a shadow of a sense of humor, Sam thought with a hidden smile as he jotted down notes.

"A Russian joint venture, a 'JV,' must be agreed to in contract by the parties, and then be submitted to the proper Russian authorities for registration before business activities may commence. We want you to see to it that this procedure goes smoothly."

"I see."

"Despite the fact that the formerly Soviet Muslim republics are no longer sending them cheap cotton, the Russians still have sufficient raw materials and low-cost labor. Their problem is that they're lagging behind the West in equipment technology. They have the means to provide a high quality product once quality machinery is in their hands. Fortunately, we are in a position to provide such machinery. The Russians will compensate us for our investment with the proceeds of sales of the product to Western countries. Am I making myself clear?"

Sam was accustomed to ignoring Benjamin's somehow condescending one-liners. The guy didn't mean anything by it—it was just a part of his rather dry nature. "Yes, sir," answered Sam, nodding into his pad as he continued taking notes. "What kind of Russian textile concern is this?"

"The name of it is Mosteks, an acronym from the words 'Moscow' and 'textiles,'" explained Kaplan. "It's what they call a cooperative enterprise, which is a breed of privately held corporations in Russia. The chairman of Mosteks is a man by the name of Ilya Lukov. Mr. Davies met him a number of years ago at a trade convention in Moscow. Ilya used to be fairly high placed in the Soviet Ministry of Light Industry's department dealing with textile production. You'll be speaking with him in a few minutes, as soon as my secretary can get a telephone line through to Russia."

Sam stole a glance at Jonathan Davies, who still sat imperiously behind his overbearing desk. Why had the CEO selected him for this project? He was just a twenty-six-year-old lawyer who hadn't even been at IIS two years. *Hmm.* "What's involved here?" he asked Kaplan.

"We need you to go over to Moscow, probably in about six weeks, to finalize negotiations of the joint venture arrangement."

Yes! Sam reached up and adjusted the knot in his tie, staving off the mirth which might have belied his professional demeanor.

"Mr. Davies and I have already been to Russia twice in pursuit of this project. Your Uncle Ned has spent some time studying the Russian textile industry and has a pretty good grasp of the business issues involved here. Just a few details remain before we can submit our documents to the Russian Ministry of Finance for registration of the JV. You should be able to finalize them while you're over there so that we can get underway with production."

The heads of all five men at the meeting snapped toward Davies when he said, "Meanwhile, during the next few weeks, I want you and Ned to go over the project carefully and make whatever legal preparations are necessary for your trip. But although Ned is somewhat familiar with the textile industry in Russia, he won't have time to attend to the details of this project. That will be your responsibility. And this matter is to remain completely confidential, Sam. Please. No one outside of IIS's New York City office is to learn of it. Clear?"

Sam nodded dutifully. He thought of his uncle, Ned Morris, who'd headed the Old Virginia division of IIS since its acquisition by the conglomerate some three years earlier. Because Ned was the only original Old V principal who was still able to work, he'd been given the position of division chief. But although most IIS execs spoke of "Ned's proven business acumen," Sam had never been able to figure out what the hell his elderly uncle was actually doing at the company. His duties seemed to be limited to passing Davies' orders on to Old V's plant manager. "Where is Ned?" asked Sam. "I haven't been able to reach him all week." The elder Morris was stationed in Newport News, Virginia, where the Old Virginia facility was located. But like all other IIS division heads, he also maintained an office in the New York City headquarters, which he frequently visited.

"I asked him to take a few days off, Sam," answered Davies. "Your Aunt Sylvia told me he hasn't been feeling well lately, and I want him to get his strength back. But he's flying up here this afternoon. You can meet with him then." The compassionate comment, which contrasted with the CEO's stoic disposition, confirmed Sam's belief that Davies' heart was in the right place.

The conference room telephone buzzed, interrupting the conversation. "Mr. Kaplan, I have Mr. Lukov in Moscow on line three," announced a secretary over the intercom.

"Thank you," replied Kaplan, turning toward the speaker-phone. He reached for the phone perched on an antique drop-leaf end table and pushed a button. "Hello, Ilya. How are you?" he asked as he shifted in the wing chair, attempting to sound hospitable and enthusiastic. Sam noted that such qualities were simply not in the exec's character, a fact that made the attempt humorously futile.

"Very well, Ben. Is good to hear your voice," responded Ilya through the hissing and crackling of the overseas connection.

"Ilya, I just wanted to introduce you to one of our attorneys, Samuel Morris, whom we're sending over to meet with you and your colleagues next month."

"Hello, Mr. Morris. We are looking forward to meet you. I am sure you will have pleasant stay in Moscow."

"I'm looking forward to meeting you as well. Please call me Sam."

"And for you I am Ilya. I hope you will find business in Russia quite interesting, Sam." He pronounced it *Sem*. "Our joint venture law has just been revised, and we are not foreseeing any problems in working with your fine company. We are hoping that business matters will be finished quickly so that production may start at soonest possible time."

"I'm sure things will go smoothly."

Kaplan's shrill voice interrupted. "Ilya, Sam will become thoroughly familiar with the project during the next few weeks before he leaves for Moscow. Meanwhile, let us know if there is anything we can do from this end."

Sam ignored the austere exec's compulsion to constantly be on center stage. Humor him, he ordered himself, looking down at the rug again. He could tolerate anyone's quirks now that he had an assignment with Old V in Russia.

"With pleasure," replied Ilya cordially. "And same for us. Please let us know if we may be of assistance."

"'Preciate it," said Sam.

After the meeting concluded, Sam walked briskly down the corridor and straight into Eric Highsmith's office. He gave his friend a smile that said he had great news.

"Okay, what is it this time?" asked Eric, looking up. He was a massive guy, his linebacker's build almost dwarfing the desk beneath him. "Did you get promoted to chief counsel?"

"Not quite, but I might have just as much fun." Sam closed the door.

"All right, let's hear it." Eric dropped his pencil and leaned back in his chair. Both attorneys had begun working at Inter-American Industrial Services immediately after completing law school some two years earlier. Sam had relocated to New York City to accept his first job. Eric, a Brooklynite, had befriended him and taken it upon himself to acclimate the newcomer to big city life.

"You fuckin' hick!" exclaimed Eric after hearing the details. "I can't believe you!" He closed his eyes and shook his head incredulously. "Russia! You're going to have a blast, man!" His Brooklyn accent contrasted sharply with Sam's Virginia drawl.

"Whoa, it's not going to be all fun and games, Eric. I'll have to work my butt off for this one. If I blow it, Jonny will have me out of here faster than quick."

"Fuckin' hick," repeated Eric at Sam's vernacular.

Sam smiled and pointed his finger at Eric. "Damned yankee. I'm going to have to sit down and learn all of Russian joint venture law in about six weeks. Looks like I'll definitely be putting in some overtime."

Eric mimed playing a violin, mashing a bulky cheek against the top of his shoulder. "Aw, too bad, Sammy." He put down the violin and shrugged. "What difference does it make? You put in overtime almost every night, anyway."

Sam wondered when his friend was going to suggest they celebrate his new assignment with a good drunk. One of the things Sam liked about Eric was that he was a "good ole boy," at least as far as such could be found in the north.

"Why do they always pick you, man?" asked Eric, again shaking his head in disbelief. "How come you always get the good stuff around here? They send you away on all the interesting assignments, and all I get are trips to upstate New York."

"I reckon it's my charm and boyish good looks, Highsmith. Doesn't just work with the women, ya know."

Eric rolled his eyes.

"I don't know, to tell you the truth, bud," said Sam, turning serious. "Actually, that's a good question. I mean, this is one of IIS's biggest new projects. It's the start of a whole new corporate policy. And here they are picking some kid lawyer to go handle it by himself. It really doesn't make sense, does it?" He stood and headed toward the door. "Well, just thought I'd let you know."

Eric shook his head briefly, then said, "Well, congratulations, man. We'll definitely have to go down a few to celebrate."

I was hoping you weren't getting slack on me, thought Sam with a smile. Aloud he said, "We'll have to. But right now, I've got to go figure out what makes Russian law work."

Sam left Eric, returned to his office, and closed the door behind him. He sat down at his desk with a deep sigh. "Russia," he said aloud, smiling and leaning back in his chair. "Fantastic." He pulled back the sleeve of his charcoal pinstripe suit jacket to look at his watch. It was a gold Rolex Oyster, given to him by his father shortly before died from complications from a stroke he'd suffered with for the last few years of his life. For a few seconds, Sam watched the unusual sweep of the Rolex's second hand, which sort of quivered as it advanced, as if not quite sure about how it wanted to proceed, but always moving forward nonetheless. He felt the smile fade from his lips. Damned strange that watch's second hand; it was somehow like him, a moving representation of his life. He shook his head and smirked at his own silliness. "Daddy, Daddy," he murmured, wiping a smudge from the Oyster's crystal. Only southern men could get away with calling their fathers that at any age; there was something about the drawl that kept it from sounding uncool. He pulled his jacket sleeve back down.

Grandpa's knee. He'd conjured the vision up, not quite knowing why. It was the only part of Hyman Morris which he remembered vividly, as the old man had passed away when Sam was little more than a toddler. He remembered running to hug his Grandpa, his face colliding with the giant knee, the texture of black wool trousers rubbing his cheek. He'd often sat on that same knee; faced it as he walked on Grandpa's feet; and played with it under the dinner table. It was strange, he thought, that he knew Hyman's face only from photographs and the oil painting in Old Virginia's Newport News conference room.

Sam's grandfather had opened Old Virginia Mills outside Newport News, Virginia shortly after his immigration to that town in the early 1920's. What a success story! It was the American dream in its fullest splendor—the struggling Jewish immigrant who'd come penniless to America from Russia, changed his name from the unpronounceable Mrachnikov, and saved every nickel and dime until his vision became reality. The mills were successful, producing fabrics and yarns which were in increasing demand from America's booming clothing industry. And Hyman Morris had married and raised his three sons in a comfort his own parents could never have even dreamed of.

"Someday, Samuel. Someday soon enough, boychik," Hyman had said when the young boy was upset at not being able to sit at the grownup table for Passover dinner. "Someday you'll run Old Virginia, too, with me and your Daddy and uncles!"

Sam recalled the distant words and again sighed. He'd always wanted to be a part of the Morris legacy. He wanted to carry on where Hyman and then Joseph had left off. Wasn't it only fair to Grandpa that he did? Grandpa had risked everything to come to America to start a new life, all so that his loved ones could lead better lives. Old Virginia was the manifestation of that dream, the symbol of Sam's heritage and the Morris presence in this country. It was what he was supposed to do with his life, wasn't it? Didn't he, as Hyman's only grandchild, owe that much to him? Again, Sam pictured the knee.

After Hyman's death, Old Virginia had continued to run successfully through the sixties and seventies, with Grandpa's picture in the conference room gazing down at his sons as they made the decisions that brought the company growth and prosperity. The three brothers, Albert, Ned, and Sam's father, Joseph, followed Hyman's proven business practices to the last detail under their father's watchful portrait. Sam remembered the feeling of awe that the picture inspired in him, first as a young boy and later as a teenager, when he visited his father at the office.

But the early 1980s saw a turn in the textile industry, when foreign manufacturers entered the scene competitively with their cheap labor, abundant resources, and aggressive sales forces. Success became difficult for smaller American textile concerns. The three brothers struggled to keep Old Virginia alive, cutting their costs and attempting to develop new products, but their efforts were barely adequate. Old Virginia simply didn't have the means to compete with the larger American and foreign facilities.

It was in late 1990 that Sam's Uncle Albert was the victim of a crippling car accident. His mounting health bills forced him to ask his brothers to bail him out financially. It was the beginning of the end. The two brothers were simply in no position to help.

Sam remembered the raging quarrels that ensued and the toll they took on his family when Albert finally sold his interest in the business. Sam was in college at the time and could hear his father's distress over the phone when Sam called home. "Things are fine here, Sam. Just fine," Joseph would tell him flatly. But Sam's worries were always confirmed when Daddy would add, "Have you thought about going to grad school, son?" or "It's always a good idea to have a marketable skill in your pocket, son."

Only the company's acquisition by Inter-American Industrial Services brought any hope of peace. What else could Daddy and Ned have done? he thought, recalling their despondent faces when they announced their decision to the rest of the family. He looked out his window at the Manhattan skyline, shaking the confusion from his belly for the thousandth time. The offer from IIS, a New York City based conglomerate of two dozen different companies, including cement manufacturing, chemical processing, plastics production, lumber, and other industries, had been a blessing. Thank God Davies came along, he told himself, trying to imagine what might have become of Old V and the Morrises without the conglomerate.

But the merger hadn't been easy. Sam recalled his father's depression during the many weeks of negotiations with IIS, the look of defeat in his embittered eyes. Sam was in his first year of law school at the time, having already embarked on a legal career he'd hoped would bring new skills into the next generation of Old Virginia family businessmen. Hell, seeing Daddy's despair had been even more difficult than the thought of never being able to follow in his footsteps. But the acquisition agreement was finally drafted, and everyone was looking forward to getting it over with.

Then came Daddy's stroke, which would render him helpless and soon take his life. Shit. As far as Sam was concerned, his father's death was just another element of the same catastrophe. It was as if his whole family had been programmed to self-destruct at the same time. Sam again pulled back his jacket sleeve and gazed again at the sweeping hand of the Oyster.

Sam was startled out of his reverie by Eric, who was standing in the now open doorway with a stack of documents under one arm. Sam quickly pulled his jacket sleeve back over the watch.

"Yo, Morris!" said Eric. "Some friends of mine are going to the Kamikaze tonight. You want to check it out?"

"'Preciate it, Eric. I don't know. I've got a lot to do with this Russian project. Time's a-wastin.'"

"Come on. We can go late. Do me a favor. That accent of yours helps me with the babes."

Sam smiled, admitting to himself that his slight southern drawl had definitely been an asset in the city.

"Besides, we have some celebrating to do, remember?" added Eric.

"Eric, don't you ever get sick of the Kamikaze? I mean, you go there almost every week to talk the same shit to the same kinds of women for hours on end—"

Eric smiled and shrugged. "It works, sometimes."

"—all along doing shot after shot of that too-sweet stuff until you're so smashed you can't even see straight. Maybe you shouldn't start throwing back kamikazes so early on in the evening, Eric. You don't stand a chance of making time when you're liquored up."

"Fuckin' hick."

Sam laughed and shook his head incredulously. "Damned yankee. Okay, Eric. Let's do it. I could use a good time myself. But I'm not playing the straight guy in your routines tonight, got it?"

"Morris, you can't help but play the straight guy."

Later that afternoon, Sam entered Ned Morris's office and sat down. "Hi, Uncle Ned."

"Hello, my boy. How are ya?"

Sam wondered if his uncle had forgotten they'd agreed to meet not five minutes earlier. The eldest of his grandfather's sons had begun to slow down a bit, which, Sam thought, was probably why the IIS brass really didn't take Ned too seriously anymore. He was over seventy and probably should've retired already. But Sam knew Ned would only leave IIS feet first—the remains of the family business were simply the driving force in his life. Actually, it was all he had. "We were going to discuss the Russian project," Sam reminded him.

"Ah, yes. Benjamin and Jonathan are attemptin' some rather interestin' maneuvers here, aren't they?"

With the way women up North like my accent, you should be beating them off with a stick! thought Sam, smiling to himself. He had always admired his uncle's southern ways.

"Samuel, I have here an English copy of the Russian joint venture legislation. It seems that joint ventures are the primary way in which American corporations and Russian enterprises are doin' business these days...Uh..." He paused and ran a hand through his full head of white hair.

Sam sat patiently, glancing around at Ned's collection of antique memorabilia, which inhabited every available square inch of his New York office. Pictures from the 1930s of the original Old Virginia Mills. A 1950s newspaper clipping of Hyman and his three sons in front of Old V. A swatch of fabric from the mill's first production was framed above his desk. Sam waited for his uncle to continue. Ned had a way of trailing off like this—it had something to do with his short-term memory failure.

"Yeah," he continued. "Now, you're the lawyer, but I've done some readin' on my own. A Russian joint venture is like a private corporation in that it's a distinct, legal personality. It has its own capital and can sue and be sued in courts of law. When IIS and uh—" Ned referred to his notes. "Yeah, Mosteks. When the two form a joint venture, the new entity'll be separate from both its American and Russian parents. IIS and Mosteks'll be equal share-holders in the new entity. A Russian-American joint venture's really a fascinatin' concept, ain't it? I've spent a little time speakin' with experts in the field. These JV's are a clever mechanism to get Western businesses to go over there. Looks like the Russians've come a long way, don't it? I think they can look forward to better times ahead."

He's a nice old man, but God, can he get long-winded! thought Sam. The entire New York City office, probably including the brass, dreaded the times when Ned Morris became chatty.

"I've spoken with Mosteks' chairman and done a little reading myself, Uncle Ned," said Sam, hoping to cut short his uncle's oration.

"Good. Good. Yes. I have the titles of some materials on Russian law and business here. I suggest you read 'em if you can." He passed the list to his nephew. "Keep in mind, Samuel, these Russians are new at Western-style business. They're smart, but inexperienced and too concerned with coverin' their hineys. Many of the concepts and strategies you're used to'll be foreign to them, so you'll have to be patient, see. Don't you see?"

"Yes, I see."

"Oh, by the way. Have ya spoken with your Mom lately? Aunt Sylvia was wonderin' if she'd like to come over to our house for Thanksgivin' down in Newport News."

Sam paused before answering. He was well aware that his mother, Eileen, had been unsure of her role in the Morris family ever since her husband's death. The Morrises, who were Jews, had objected vehemently to Joseph's decision to marry a Catholic. And even while Joe was alive, relations between Eileen and the rest of the family had always been strained. Sam wondered if Uncle Ned was making the gesture of inviting his mother purely out of consideration for his nephew. "I think that would be very nice," he said, figuring she could always claim to have plans if she didn't want to go. "I'm not going to be able to make it down to Virginia for Thanksgiving, but I'm sure Mom would like to go."

"I know it's tough on your Mom, Samuel, what with her husband dead and her only son outta the house. We're gonna do everythin' possible to help her out, see."

Maybe, Sam thought, trying to decipher Ned's expression. But he didn't want to worry about it right now; there was too much else on his mind. "Are they easy to deal with?" he asked. "I mean are the Russians...laid back?"

Ned paused, then said, "Oh, yeah, from what I've heard. Sometimes too much so. They tell me Russians are tardy in everythin' they do, from preparin' documents to meetin' at the theater. I guess you shouldn't make no plans that cut deadlines too close, Samuel. But I believe they're generally very hospitable and quite pleasant to work with. I'm sure you'll have no problem whatsoever." He gave a congenial wink. "You're a Morris, remember?"

"'Preciate it, Uncle Ned. I'll let you know how it goes," replied Sam with a smile before standing to leave.

"Oh, yeah. Samuel, I'm told it's advisable to pack a good supply of peanut butter and cans of tuna fish and such for your stay in Moscow. Even durin' the best of times, Russia can be the culinary disaster area of the world, and you'll at least want somethin' for breakfast in your room."

"Thanks, Uncle Ned. I know about the situation there." He smiled, working his way toward the door.

"You know, we still have family in Russia, Samuel. A brother of your Grandpa's half-sister Gussie."

"That's right!" said Sam, stopping at the door. "I do remember Daddy mentioning we had a relative in Moscow."

"Oh, yeah," said Ned. "Name's Yakov, I believe. Yakov Edelman. They call 'im Yasha. I have his address somewhere at home—I'll get it for ya. He was a dissident in the seventies. A writer, I believe. Upset the Soviet authorities with his writin' so much they wanted to kick his hiney clear outta the country." He gave an old man's belly laugh, shaking in his seat as if it were set on a large spring. "He's probably quite an interestin' fella."

Sam nodded with a smile, then opened the door to leave.

"Samuel."

Sam stopped. "Yes, Uncle Ned?"

"I...just wanted to tell ya somethin' else." He breathed deeply and paused. "Uh, I'm glad they got ya workin' on this for us. I mean...for Ole V. It's important, son. Both my Papa and yours're routin' for ya."

Sam looked into Ned's tired, somehow pleading eyes. What did he mean by that? he wondered. What was bothering him? "Of course, Uncle Ned," he said. "They're both on my mind." He stood silently for a moment, then turned to leave.

"If you have any more questions 'bout the project, Samuel, just lemme know. Anytime at all," he said as Sam closed the door behind him.

THREE

Misha Grunshteyn, Mosteks' chief engineer, had left work early for the day and was on his way to his mother's. Misha was one of relatively few Muscovites privileged enough to own his own car, although the machine was only a Soviet made Zhiguli. The small white sedan was always dirty to the point that it almost looked black, and it was never in completely good repair. Now the damned heater was broken.

Tonight would be a big night. Misha had waited more than ten years for it, an opportunity to bring his family back together, to try to reconcile Mama with his brother Petya. It had been over a decade since their father Oleg had disowned Petya, ordering him never to come to the family's apartment again. Misha had hoped that Papa might be a part of the reconciliation, but that had become impossible when Oleg Grunshteyn had suffered a heart attack and died a few years earlier. As his Papa's memory came into focus, Misha sighed, watching his breath condense in the cold air.

It had been difficult. Mama's health had deteriorated rapidly since her seventieth birthday, her arthritic condition rendering her almost helpless. She probably didn't have long to go; it seemed that elderly people never outlived their spouses very long. Thank God Misha's wife Marina had adopted Mama as her own. Marina had been taking care of the old woman for over a year now, providing a link that kept at least part of the Grunshteyn family intact.

But Marina was also opposed to Misha having anything to do with his elder brother. And how could she feel otherwise? God only knows what kind of propaganda Mama was feeding her about Petya. "What do you see in that *khuligan?*" Marina had asked Misha. "Can't you see how dirty he is? Can't you see what he did to your father?"

Dirty, thought Misha, shaking his head incredulously. Petya was "dirty" because he was a hustler. Because he goes out and makes a life for himself. Because he has always refused to be victimized by an inept system. Because he chooses not to live like Ivan Ivanovich, the typical Russian on the street.

But Misha had long known he would need Marina's support to get Mama to even speak with Petya. Misha and his mother were on good terms, but she still suspected him of participating in Petya's illicit affairs. Only Marina was "pure enough" to have any chance of convincing Mama to give Petya a chance. And he would need Marina to convince his brother to come home in the first place.

Mama hadn't even uttered her eldest son's name in years! When she spoke of "her children," it was always clear she meant only Marina and Misha. But Misha knew the old woman wanted nothing more in life than one last moment of harmony with what was left of her family. And he wanted to give that to her.

"Please, Marinochka," Misha had said, running a hand through his wife's dark, shoulder-length hair. She was a Slavic beauty, with high cheekbones and slightly slanted eyes that revealed the Tatar influence in her ancestry. "If you won't do it for me, please do it for Mama! You know she really wants to see

Petya, even if just for a few minutes. And we don't know how much time she has left!"

"But it will never work, Misha," Marina replied, looking down at their apartment's parquet floor. "She will never agree to see him. You know that." But then she'd looked up at him with eyes that spoke otherwise. Mama needed a chance to be with her firstborn, and Marina knew it. And soon Marina had agreed to go with him to visit Petya.

Misha rubbed his hands together briskly as he waited for the stoplight to change. Checking his appearance in the rearview mirror, he took off his hat and tried to arrange his curly black hair. He thought about his wife again, recalling how scared she'd been about going to Petya's a week earlier, about seeing her estranged brother-in-law for the first time in over a year. After all, Petya could be a rather overbearing figure. He was not as tall as Misha, but he had very broad, muscular shoulders and a loud voice. More importantly, the elder Grunshteyn didn't carry himself like most Russians. He wore his hair in the style of that American magazine, *GeeKoo.* His clothes were always from the West. He never wore a Russian *ushanka* hat. And he seemed so content with life, so complacent.

Misha remembered how he could almost feel his wife's anxiety in the car as they drove to Petya's. She'd sat silently the whole way, looking straight ahead, seeing nothing. When they were ascending the elevator to Petya's floor, she'd stood slightly hunched over, her hands clasped together over her belly, as if she were still shielding herself from the outside cold. And when they'd reached the door to Petya's apartment, she quickly moved to his right so that Petya wouldn't see her first.

"Hi, Misha…" Petya had said, turning away as he opened the door.

But then he had stopped suddenly and turned back toward them. "Marinka! Oh, Marinochka! It's so nice to see you!" He lowered his head to kiss her.

"Hello, Petya," replied Marina, returning the kiss with her lips only.

"Come in! Come in, you two!" said Petya. "Tell me how you've been, Marinochka! How are things? Oh, it's been so long!"

"Very well," she answered, glancing at Misha, who smiled at her reassuringly.

"You look so beautiful, Marinka! You haven't changed a bit! I want to hear all about what you've been up to! Has little brother been treating you well?"

Misha saw her nod timidly. "How do you like this apartment, Marina?" he asked her. "It must be twice the size of ours. And Petya lives alone in it! Can you believe that? Come here. I want to show you something." He took her by the hand and led her quickly down the hallway into Petya's bedroom. "Wouldn't you love to have one of these?"

Marina poked at the waterbed inquisitively for a moment. "What's it for?" she asked softly.

"What's it for?" interrupted Petya from behind. "Why, Marinochka, it's only the most comfortable bed in the world!" He lay down. "See? Ah! Would you like to try?"

"No," she replied, looking away.

"Oh, come on, Marinka. You'll love it. I might even get one for you and Misha! Now, lie down here and try it out!"

"Petya, no," she said.

Oh Marina, thought Misha as he put the Zhiguli in gear and drove through the intersection. He supposed she'd been brave, although her concerns about his brother were obviously ridiculous. He knew she'd been intimidated by the boxes of Western electronic equipment that lined the walls of Petya's apartment. Petya made a lot of money selling the valuable contraband. What was he supposed to do? Just give it all up because his sister-in-law found it objectionable? Petya had been as nice and understanding to her as he possibly could, Misha thought. He'd behaved like a polite, solid man.

"I'm glad you two came today," said Petya with a proud smile, his arms crossed in front of his massive chest. "You can help me celebrate my sale this morning. Won't you join me for some French Cognac?"

"What did you sell?" asked Misha.

"Oh, just a color laser printer," replied Petya with a dismissive wave of his hand.

But Misha knew that his brother had probably made a profit of a million rubles on the sale. And Petya made it sound so damned simple! He probably bought the printer for a few million rubles from someone travelling abroad, who had bought it for a few thousand dollars. Everybody makes a killing!

The three moved into the dining room and sat around Petya's exquisite, Finnish-made dining table, and Petya filled Misha in on the details of the sale. Misha saw that Marina had been uncomfortably silent for some time, so after a few minutes and two shots of cognac, he decided to get to the point of their visit. "We have a proposition for you, Petya," he announced with an enthusiastic smile.

Petya smiled back, then reached over to his sister-in-law and pinched her cheek. "That's my little brother, Marinka. Always with a mind for profit. And they say I'm the Grunshteyn with all the business sense."

Misha saw Marina's discomfort increase with Petya's gesture. "It's not really business, Petya," he said. "It really has more to do with—you know—our family." Misha felt his eyes reflexively leave his brother's. He always dreaded the confrontation that might result from serious discussions with Petya. Especially when the topic was the Grunshteyn family. Petya sat across the table, his broad, confident shoulders juxtaposed against his brotherly smile. The combination was ominously confusing.

Misha forced himself to look back into his brother's eyes, which he knew resembled his own. He said, "Marina and I think it's time for you to come home, Petya. To visit Mama."

Petya's smile melted away, and his face assumed its serious mien, the expression usually reserved for business matters. He exhaled, interlocked his fingers in front of him, and said, "Misha, little brother, you know it would never work. It's been too long. Mama is too old to change her opinions of me. It would be a waste of time and might even upset her."

Misha pulled into the parking lot of Mama's huge monolithic apartment building, wondering how he'd ever gotten Petya to change his mind. He remembered presenting his arguments of family love, of obligation to one's parents, and of how important it was to them as brothers, all while Petya sat in silent rumination. But a moment later Petya had simply shrugged and nodded.

Why? Misha wondered. Was it because Petya's love for Mama was stronger than his pride and resentment for what Papa had done to him? Was it just a gesture to his younger brother and sister-in-law? But it wasn't so important why Petya had agreed to come to Mama's, Misha decided. It was more important that Misha do everything possible to make the reconciliation work. It was hard for him to even conceive what his mother and brother would be like together, what they would say to each other, how they would interact. He pulled into a parking space, still wondering if there was any chance at all for renewed harmony in the Grunshteyn family.

Misha was in his mother's tiny communal apartment, pacing nervously in a tight circle as he waited for his brother to arrive. It was a one-room flat that joined three other apartments in a hallway leading to a shared kitchen and bathroom. Marina was with Mama in the sleeping area, which consisted of a bed in the far right corner separated from the rest of the room by a section of floral fabric hanging from the ceiling.

He picked up an old picture of his father from the shabby wooden dresser. It had been taken several years before Oleg's death, but the old man's declining health could clearly be seen in his eyes. What a terrible life he had led! Other pictures of Oleg, mostly of him in uniform, hung on the wall over the dresser in a futile attempt to cover the apartment's yellowing wallpaper. Misha again looked at the soldier's eyes and thought about the stories his Papa had often told him. How Oleg was actually one of the lucky ones, escaping death through the sanctuary of a prison camp.

Oleg Grunshteyn had been among the Soviet forces to push westward into Hitler's Germany, making him witness to the horrors of Nazism. He was aghast at the unfathomable atrocities he'd observed at Auschwitz and other Nazi death camps. Having helped liberate humanity of such an evil, he'd thought that the world would become a different, more righteous, more humane place. A world that would certainly welcome the truth.

But in this, Oleg Yosefovich Grunshteyn was terribly mistaken. The Jewish soldier who'd endured incredible hardships in the name of Mother Russia—who'd risked his life in defense of the Hammer and Sickle and fought desperately to make the world a better place—returned home not a Jewish soldier, but a Jew. He hadn't conceived that such merciless persecution in his homeland would be possible after the horrors the Soviet people had endured at the hands of the Nazis.

Oleg decided to promulgate his observations of the holocaust. One autumn day in 1947, he approached the Soviet writer's union seeking permission to write a book detailing his experiences. The next day he was arrested. After a mock trial, the Jewish soldier was sent to a Siberian labor camp where he spent the next six years of his life. It had been Stalin's decree that the Jewish holocaust would not be publicized in the Soviet Union, and Oleg had unwittingly been in violation of that order. And although Khrushchev's de-Stalinization reforms later freed Oleg Grunshteyn, the KGB's scrutiny would haunt him for the rest of his days.

Misha's reverie was suddenly interrupted by the door buzzer. Marina, in her nicest dress, came running from behind the floral cloth. She glanced at Misha, who quickly put down Papa's picture.

He nodded at her and silently took a deep breath.

She opened the door.

There stood Petya, dressed in a foreign-made sport jacket, holding a wrapped box in one hand and a bouquet of roses in the other. Misha watched a smile appear on his wife's face as she looked Petya over. "Come in, Petya," she said softly, lifting her head to kiss his cheek. "You look so nice."

"Does Mama know I'm here?" asked Petya, his voice lowered.

"No," replied Marina. "We didn't think it a good idea to fore-warn her. She's sleeping now. I'll go wake her." She ran back behind the sheet of fabric.

Misha examined his older brother's jacket, wondering how much money, *valuta*, it had cost. He'd always envied Petya's social successes, his contacts, his reputation. The elder Grun-shteyn's triumphs with women were almost legendary in their social circles, among their friends. Misha, of course, had never objected when others referred to him simply as "Petya's little brother."

Petya had begun ten years earlier as a *fartsovshchik*, a black marketeer who preyed on foreign tourists by purchasing their blue jeans or trading currency with them. The title itself was comically apt; it was Russianized slang from the English "for sale," adding *shchik* to suggest "one who does."

At that time, Misha was studying to be an engineer at the Baumanskiy Institute. It had been quite a feat for him to enroll at the prestigious institute, especially with a Jewish name like Grunshteyn. But prestige, he'd soon learned, was the only thing that an engineering degree promised in the 1980s. It certainly didn't offer any financial advantages.

He remembered how Petya had convinced him to try "doing business" with him for the first time. "You see, little brother," he'd said, "while you are sitting in your engineering classes at Baumanskiy, struggling to learn a craft that will pay you a few hundred rubles a month, I am out making thousands of rubles every week," Petya had said. "What's the point of your struggling, Misha? Every Russian earns a little extra 'on the left,' so why shouldn't one devote all his efforts to making good money from foreigners?"

And Petya, even at that young age, had been entirely correct. It was true that no Soviet job paid more than a pittance of a salary on which it was impossible to do much more than subsist. It was also true that the overwhelming majority of the Russian population engaged in some form of black market commerce to earn supplemental income.

And who was the victim in this business? No one. Unless you counted the state itself, which few would do. Petya had offered to train Misha, to introduce him to his contacts and show him how to approach foreigners.

Why should I miss out? Misha remembered asking himself. Why should I live like the peasants?

"But what if you go up to someone who is really with the KGB?" was the younger Grunshteyn's first question. "I hope you're careful, Petya. Maybe you should only do business with women and teenage foreigners. They're less likely to—"

"Misha, Misha. Never teach father how to fuck," interrupted Petya, waving his finger. "I am the master of business with tourists. And besides, would I do anything that could possibly get my little brother into trouble? Of course not. You know I'll take good care of you!"

He'd been persuasive. After all, Petya had never once been troubled by the KGB. And anyway, the authorities couldn't possibly apprehend even a fraction of the people who were soaking foreigners.

Petya said, "Misha, everyone who wants to get ahead in life is doing it. It's no sin! Who is harmed? Comrade Brezhnev?"

47

Misha remembered answering the question with a silent smile, and the next day he'd brought an English textbook with him to engineering class. Learning the language would be the first step, he'd decided. He had to be able to communicate with the foreigners. To get them to trust him. Misha remembered ignoring his bombastic instructor's lecture. He'd been too preoccupied to pay attention to how auxiliary generators work. To do business with foreigners, he'd have to know how they think. Like many Russians, Misha had taken English in secondary school, and he cursed himself for not having studied the language more diligently.

Misha remembered placing the English language textbook on his lap under cover of the table. *How do you do? Very well, and you? I can't complain. What beautiful weather we have today, Mr. Smith. Yes indeed, Mr. Jones.* He'd had to suppress a laugh. If he was going to learn English, real English, it wouldn't be with this damned book. He'd have to spend time with Petya, listening to rock 'n' roll albums, reading American novels, and just speaking the language. He'd have to meet English speaking foreigners and—

"Grunshteyn! I asked you a question, which you will kindly answer!"

Misha almost jerked his head as he recalled being caught by the instructor. He smiled at Petya, who stood holding the flowers and wrapped package. He strained to hear Mama and Marina talking behind the floral fabric. There was an unfamiliar nervousness in his brother's eyes, almost as if the latter were a fifteen-year-old waiting for his first date. A long minute passed before Marina's whispers were interrupted by the sound of an old woman's scream.

"No! No, no, no, no!" wailed Mama's scratchy voice. "I'll not have that poisonous monster in my home! Get him out! Get him out now!"

Misha ran back behind the fabric to find Marina comforting his distressed mother on the bed. "But Mamochka, your firstborn son just wants to talk," he said. "Please at least have a look at him. He wants to make peace! He just wants to be with his Mama!"

Petya was standing against the wall near pictures of Oleg when the three emerged nearly half an hour later. Mama was supported on both sides by her youngest son and daughter-in-law.

"They have convinced me to greet you," said the old woman. "It was against my wishes, but your brother and sister-in-law implored me. I am here for their sake. Why have you come here, Pyotr?" Misha felt her shaking slightly as she clung desperately to his arm.

"Why, to see you, Mamochka. I want to be part of our family again. Look! I've brought you presents!"

She looked at him for a moment with incredulous eyes, then said, "You wish to make up for the years of suffering you caused me and your dear father with a bouquet of roses?"

Petya smiled patiently and said, "Mamochka, I just want to become your son again."

Misha and Marina glanced at each other simultaneously. Petya now bore the same expression he did when selling Western electronics on the black market. The same demeanor as when he was showing Marina his waterbed a week earlier. Misha feared that his efforts to reconcile the family had been in vain after all. He hung his head and grit his teeth, still listening anxiously.

"Mama, I'm your son!" continued Petya. "You wrapped me in swaddling clothes! You nursed and weaned me! I sat at this table for twenty years and had my meals! Doesn't any of this mean anything to you? How can you kick your son out of his home when he comes with a gesture of love?"

Misha saw Mama look at Petya pensively. A twinge of hope passed through him. She released her grip from his arm and slowly approached her firstborn, her obese body and arthritis making her step an unstable hobble. The old woman touched Petya's cheek, and her eyes filled with tearful confusion. "But I fear I no longer know you, Petya."

Tell her you've quit the business, Petya! thought Misha. Just tell her! Maybe there was a chance after all!

"I have a present for you, Mama," said Petya, renewing his smile. He gave her the gift-wrapped box and lay the flowers on the dresser.

Mama set the box on a small table, still flustered by the unexpected encounter, her struggle apparent in her wrinkled eyes. No one in the small apartment said a word.

Petya smiled confidently as he watched her unwrap the gift. She tore at the paper and cardboard clumsily, her arthritic hands unable to firmly grasp the wrapping. Soon the box revealed something unfamiliar to the old woman. She lifted it with shaking hands from the box and turned it upside down. It was some kind of appliance, Misha saw, though he wasn't quite sure what it was himself. Mama stood staring at the machine for a moment, then gasped through her opened mouth. She'd seen "General Electric" displayed across the container, the English words causing an almost visible shock to descend her unsteady back. She raised the electric coffee maker above her head with a painful yelp, then shattered it on the floor.

"*Mama, no!*" shouted Misha, gaping widely. "Look what you've done! Are you crazy?" He looked at Marina, who was also clearly dumbstruck, standing speechlessly with a hand over her mouth.

"Get out of my home, Pyotr!" said the old woman, struggling to push him toward the door. I should have known you'd never change! You are not my son! I can only pray that God will steer my other children away from you!"

Misha felt his mouth go dry as he watched the exchange. "Do you know what most people would do to get a coffee maker like this?" he screamed at his mother, steadying himself against the dresser. "How could you refuse such a gift from your son!" Misha watched Petya quickly leave the apartment without another word. He then bent to examine the broken coffee maker as Marina embraced his mother and led her back behind the fabric.

"So this couple wants a divorce," said Petya, savoring the attention of his company. "But both spouses want custody of their only offspring. So they take the matter to court, where the judge asks the two spouses separately why they think they deserve to have the child. Understand?"

The table nodded collectively.

Petya pitched his voice to sound like a nagging wife. "'I should get the child,' says the wife. 'After all, Your Honor, I had to carry him for nine months. I had to eat for two and bear the pain of pregnancy. I had to go through labor and give birth. Therefore, I feel that I deserve to take the child.'"

Petya deepened his voice and squared his shoulders dramatically. "The husband approaches the judge and says, 'Your Honor, if I go to a newspaper dispenser and deposit my fifty kopecks, to whom does the newspaper belong, to me or to the machine?'"

The table burst into laughter at Petya's joke. He smiled himself, looking at each guest individually, obviously enjoying the spotlight. They were in the exclusive Arturio Italian restaurant, packed with foreigners and a few Russians who had the means to pay two hundred thousand rubles for a meal. Misha saw the well dressed diners, so un-Russian in their presence, momentarily divert their attention to his table's outburst.

He felt exalted, stately, to be in such opulent surroundings and company. He glanced at Petya, who was still relishing the credit for the anecdote. This was his brother, Pyotr Olegovich Grunshteyn, who had risen from the ranks of the Ivan Ivanoviches to sit at the center of attention in the Arturio restaurant! Misha watched as Petya raised his glass to toast with his friends, all of whom wore the satisfied expression of a happy life. These were hustlers. And wasn't that what life was all about? Hustling? He knew that the hustlers had obtained their means illicitly. But this is a cruel world, he justified, and if you don't go for it yourself, you are doomed to eat with Ivan Ivanovich for the rest of your life.

Misha looked at the women seated intermittently among the hustlers. They wore European clothes and makeup. Their expressions were ones of happy deference. Yes, deference. That's what women want. A man to whom they can defer with security. That's what makes women happy. And to make women attracted to you, you have to make them feel comfortable relying on you to take care of them. They have to be able to defer to you.

Oh, Mama, he thought. Dear, sweet Mama. How I wish we could be close! I would love to share my insights with you, but you would never understand. I would love for you to be proud of me, but you would condemn me for my ideas. How I would love to buy you nice clothes and good food, but you would see them only as the fruits of wrongdoing. What a pity it is that you are so pure, so unwilling to accept what is presented to you without objection—

"How is the new car heater, Misha?" asked Petya.

"America!" answered the younger Grunshteyn. Petya had used his *blat*, or connections with people in high places, to enable Misha to get his Zhiguli fixed without waiting the usual several weeks for a mechanic. He'd also paid the five-hundred-thousand ruble fee.

Petya said, "Good, little brother. I don't know how anyone could get along without a car heater." He looked around at his friends and watched them all shrug their concurrence.

"Thank you for getting it fixed, Petya," said Misha reverently. He marveled as he noticed several women doting on him after the short exchange with his brother. There was interest in their eyes.

He could tell he was being considered attractive. They were trying to decide if they would feel comfortable deferring to him.

"Here's to little brother's repaired car," said Petya, raising his shot glass of vodka, beckoning the other hustlers to do likewise. "May it be the locomotive for much future profit!"

The hustlers clamored, endorsing the libation.

After dinner, Misha drove Petya home. "Thanks for the ride, little brother. Thank God you have the car, so you can take care of me when I'm drunk!" added a tipsy Petya before opening the car door.

"It's my pleasure," replied Misha.

"Poor, poor Mama," lamented Petya. "What a shame she's deteriorated so. You know what I think her problem is? She's just too old-fashioned. Obviously Papa's experiences influenced her, but she's still living under Stalin!"

"Well, Petya, I think many of our countrymen are like that. Russians by nature are xenophobic. Mama's sons are the exception in not being like her."

Petya was obviously not in the mood for sociology, and Misha watched his brother's facial expression make its familiar switch, jovial to somber, despite the jaded eyes. "Can you make a pick-up for me tomorrow, Misha? I'm sorry to ask, but none of our usual couriers are available. Our relationship with this company is new, and we want to establish ourselves as serious."

"What time?" Although Misha had been at Mosteks for several years now and had risen to chief engineer, he still had to be careful. Getting time off from a profit-seeking organization was more difficult than was the case with state jobs. The *kooperatori* had long ago discovered that "time is money."

"Tomorrow at fourteen hours," answered Petya.

Good, thought Misha. Right at lunchtime. He agreed to run the errand.

Petya gave Misha instructions. His face then went back to its more gregarious mode. "So how are things at Mosteks?"

Misha pointed his thumb upward. "As usual."

"Good," said Petya pensively. "Very good, little brother." And he left Misha in his Zhiguli.

FOUR

New York City's Kamikaze Bar was an Upper East Side watering hole catering to the area's large population of young professionals. It was known both for its namesake—a shooter consisting primarily of several liquors—and its large dance floor, which was overlooked by a comical mural portraying a drunken Zero pilot clutching a shot glass.

Sam and Eric entered the noisy, half-lit room and headed toward the bar, scanning the room as they went. Enough women in attendance. Indeed, enough good-looking ones. Music—okay, maybe a bit too loud. All in all, the evaluation was above average.

"What are you having?" asked Eric.

"Just a brew," replied Sam.

But most of Kamikaze's denizens were imbibing a bit more heavily in celebration of the coming weekend. Eric gave a mock look of disappointment and said, "Come on, man, let's party! Loosen up, man! Russia'll still be there tomorrow!"

Sam smiled. "It better be. The way things are going over there—"

"Hey, look," interrupted Eric, pushing his palms out. "No worrying about shop while we're recovering from shop, all right? Leave it in the office. Let's go meet some babes! Why're you always so uptight about your career, man? There's more to life than getting ahead."

"There's more to life than getting head, Eric."

"Come on. You need to realign your priorities a little bit, Sam. Now, lighten up and have a drink. Loosen that tie and wipe that heavy look off your face." With no further discussion, he ordered two kamikaze shooters.

Sam smiled and leaned back against the wall, again scanning the bar crowd, thinking about how his southern courtesy and mild manner seemed to set him apart up here. He kept his dark hair short, and, regardless of the day of the week, he was always clean-shaven. He knew he was "the southern boy next door," despite the slight aquiline dip on the end of his nose.

"Lots of good butt in here, huh?" said Eric with his characteristic naughty smile, his bulky cheeks rising with his eyes. He gave Sam his drink.

"Seems to be, stud," said Sam, smiling back, forcing himself into a more jovial mood. "You're a good commentator. We need you on Sixty Minutes. Now, what are you going to do with it all?" He raised his shot glass to Eric, who tapped it with his own.

"What am I gonna do? I'll show you what I'm gonna do." Eric glanced around the immediate vicinity, then quickly drank his shot. "Hi, how ya doing?" he asked an attractive woman ambling in his direction.

"Hi," she replied mechanically, walking past without pausing.

"She's sweet on you, Eric," whispered Sam, suppressing a smile. "Has to have you." He drank his kamikaze.

"Don't I recognize you from somewhere?" asked Eric to another shapely female.

"That's the oldest one in the book, Eric. Now, don't ask her if she'd hold it against you if you told her she had a nice body."

They watched the woman turn away coldly. Sam laughed. "She's already fantasizing about you, Eric," he teased. "Just playing hard to get."

Sam watched his friend get shot down a few more times, reading humorous significance into the drunken fighter pilot on the wall. When Eric's routine became monotonous, he asked, "Ready for another, Eric? I'll buy this time." He turned toward the bar.

The bartender presented two shot glasses, and the men again prepared to inhale liquor. "Cheers!" said Sam as he poured the kamikaze down his throat, the fiery cold shot warming his belly. "Woo!" he squealed. "Kick-ass!"

"Fuckin' hick."

"You yankees just don't know how to enjoy a good shot—"

"Careful, Morris," whispered Eric, his eyes darting around the room surreptitiously. "You're a lone rebel in a room full of at least a hundred yankees."

"Least it's a fair fight," said Sam, shrugging his shoulders.

Eric laughed, shaking his head. "Tell you what. Why don't we take advantage of that southern charm of yours? Why don't you talk a little louder so we can make some time in here?"

Sam rolled his eyes. "Look Eric. What's the point of this? Don't you ever wear out? Doesn't the singles bar scene ever get old for you?"

"Definitely. Especially when it's going as bad as it is tonight. But you've got to play, Sam. That's the way it is. You don't go for it, you ain't getting it."

"You think so, huh?"

"I know so. Hey, women don't come after you, man. You've got to go to them."

"But there's ways of meeting them besides those worn-out one-liners."

Eric looked around him, spotted something, someone, then said, "Yo, Sam, I'll be back in a minute."

Sam stood alone by the bar, contemplating the New York City singles scene. The bullshit, games, and pretentiousness were among the worst parts of living here, he decided. He sighed as he looked across the pell-mell of the dance floor at a red light swinging to and fro from the ceiling. The colored sphere briefly illuminated various groups of people dancing or standing and chatting. He remembered a bumper sticker he'd seen somewhere that read "Dating in New York: It's not an adventure, it's a job!"

It was just ironic that he played the game so damned well.

He looked up to scan the crowd again, to see who might be out there. Well, you never know, he decided, fixing his tie. He strained to see through the dimly lit, smokey haze which filled—

"Beat it, motherfucker! If I see you again, I'm gonna kick your motherfuckin' ass! Now get out of here!"

Two jerks right beside Sam, both wearing dress shirts and suit pants but no jackets or ties, were about to go at it. Sam didn't think he wanted to be standing around when it happened, but it was too crowded for him to move easily away.

"Oh yeah? Make me."

Yep, they were definitely going at it. He backed as far away as he could, bumping into someone behind him.

Jerk number one shoved jerk number two in the chest, pushing him back, but number two just widened his eyes and deepened his scowl. Bad idea, thought Sam. Number two was twice the size of one. Sam tried to nudge through the rubbernecking crowd. Before it was too late.

Just then number one came crashing into Sam, having been quite audibly slammed in the mouth by number two. He brought Sam to the floor with him.

"Cut it out!" yelled Sam, his heart suddenly pounding. But he instantly regretted saying anything. He didn't want to get involved the slightest bit with these assholes.

He looked around and saw that the crowd had quickly moved apart, leaving the two jerks and Sam in the middle of a small clearing. Number one jumped to his feet, ripping the fabric of his pants, and lunged back at number two. He balled a fist and tried to throw it, but found his arm locked in the crux of two's elbow.

Oh shit! thought Sam again as he saw number two set up to punch. He tried to roll on his side to get out of the way, but there was no time. Number one again came crashing down onto him.

Sam jumped to his feet, poised and ready, his heart pounding in his chest. Who did these idiots think they were? But what should he do? What could he do? He felt like he'd just lost a fight without an opponent. In front of a crowd of people.

He wanted to do something, at least say something, but he had no idea what. Or even to whom, for that matter.

Before the action could continue, a huge bouncer came and broke the two jerks up and dragged them away, leaving Sam alone with his frustration and anger. No one in the bar seemed to notice that he was even there, or that he'd just been knocked to the floor.

He cursed again, brushed himself off and went looking for Eric. Forget it, he told himself. It ain't worth it. And he thought he felt a little better.

Eric, whose immense body made him easy to spot in a crowd, hadn't noticed the ruckus. When he'd left Sam, he must have spotted the chick he was talking with now. He was standing by the bar with her, leaning down to hear her speak, handing her a drink, carrying on about something.

Good for him. Sam walked to the other side of the bar, sighed, and found a metal post to lean on while contemplating leaving.

He strained to manage a clearer view of the dance floor. Through the bobbing heads he noticed three young women standing together against a far wall. They were scoping the premises, waving their hands as they spoke, talking with each other unintelligibly.

Two well-dressed men with impish expressions on their otherwise young, upwardly mobile faces approached the women. Sam watched the interaction, trying to decipher the women's reactions through the sporadic lighting.

Suddenly, the entire room was flooded by bright light from a globe above the dance floor, and Sam saw a disheartened look of frustration appear on the face of one of the three young women. She was an attractive, tallish girl with shoulder-length brown hair and a rather swarthy complexion. She responded to the would-be wooers. A minute later, the two men abandoned their effort and her frustrated demeanor. A moment later, Sam saw her sling her purse over her shoulder and head toward the coat check.

"Hey! Watch it!" Sam heard as he pushed his way through a group of partyers.

"Sorry," he replied over a snicker, then proceeded to wind his way through the club. He'd started toward the woman almost reflexively, without a clue as to what he'd do if he caught up with her. He struggled to keep his eye on her as he meandered through the crowd, apologizing for his running into people as he went.

What are you doing, Morris? he asked himself.

A waitress with a tray full of drinks stepped in front of him, and he had to stop for a moment to let her by. Then he lost sight of the tallish woman when some huge gweedo blocked his view.

What's the point of this? he asked himself.

The woman was now at the coat check, reaching into her purse for a tip. She'd be out in a few seconds…

Just what do you have in mind, stud? Huh?

She had her coat on now and was turning to leave—

"Wait!" said Sam. A bit too loudly.

He'd startled her. She peered at him with a look of semi-confusion that soon sharpened into irritation. She was clearly thinking, *Not another one!*

"I'm sorry," Sam said, lowering his voice. He hesitated, not knowing what to do next. He saw that the woman was now waiting impatiently. "I..."

She raised her brow and leaned forward slightly, as if to say, Yes, asshole?

"I was just standing on the other side of the bar. I saw you and I thought..."

She was still giving him that look.

"...that I'd really like to meet you." He waited to see just how big a fool he'd made of himself. He wondered if she'd be subtle about shooting him down or come up with some witty retort. Some women seemed to enjoy shattering male egos. But what difference did it make? He hadn't come to the bar to meet women. After she left, he'd never see her again anyway. It was an advantage to living in New York City. Besides, she was probably just some bimbo who—

But suddenly the woman's face brightened, grabbing Sam's full attention.

"That's very nice," she said genuinely, a beautiful smile spreading across her full lips. "My name's Stacy."

"Hi. I'm Sam. Sam Morris." He extended his hand to his new acquaintance, who accepted it graciously.

"It's nice to meet you, Sam," she replied, but not at all mechanically. The smile was still on her pretty face, accentuated by her lively brown eyes.

"Why were you leaving?" he asked, absorbing the energy from her smile.

"I don't know. I'm a little tired. I had to work late last night." She shrugged. "I guess I'm just not up for a bar tonight."

Her candor was attractive—no, it was an incredible turn-on. "Yeah, I know what you mean. I've been buried with work, too. What do you do?" He knew it wasn't great. But since the conversation had been sparked by a no-nonsense approach, why not maintain its earnestness?

"I work in the fashion district. I formulate print designs for D. Hobgoode," she said, nodding her head as she spoke. A lot of New York women seemed to have the habit.

But where's your wad of chewing gum? thought Sam, recalling a fashion district stereotype. He trapped a smile, glad he was finally loosening up.

"Times are bad in the industry, and I'm just trying to keep my head above water," continued Stacy. "It takes a lot of work."

"Some of my business has hit hard times, too."

"Everyone's has. What do you do?"

"I'm, uh, I'm a lawyer." He hesitated before admitting his profession.

"What firm are you with?"

"I work in-house at an industrial conglomerate." That's right, Morris, bore her to death.

"Oh," Stacy uttered, unsuccessfully feigning enthusiasm.

Sam laughed intentionally. "It's not as dull as it sounds, Stacy. I get a lot of travel."

"Really? Where have you been?"

He'd engaged her. Half the battle. Now for the second step. "How do you take your coffee?" he asked in a curious tone, raising his eyebrows intentionally too high.

"My coffee? Why? What's that got to do with where you've traveled?"

Sam shrugged. "So I'll know how to order for you at the coffee shop. The one down the block." What are you doing, Morris?

"Wait a minute," said Stacy, turning her head with a confused but coquettish smile. "I didn't say—"

You are going to have coffee with me! "You want to know where I've traveled to, right?"

"Where's your accent from?"

"I'll tell you that, too. At the coffee shop."

Stacy smiled again and raised her chin, giving him a look that said, Okay, I'm challenged.

Time to close the deal. "You are spontaneous, aren't you, Stacy?"

"Let's go for one quick cup of coffee, Sam," she said, nodding and still smiling. "You're an interesting guy."

He exhaled slowly and turned to follow her out.

The two left Kamikaze and walked silently around the corner. When they reached a small diner, Sam quickly opened the door for Stacy in an almost caricature fashion, standing aside and showing her the way in with a wave of his hand.

"I thought you were from the south," she said. "Southern guys are always such gentlemen. Are most New York women you know used to being pampered like this?"

"What do you mean?" asked Sam. They followed a waiter to a booth by the window and sat down.

"Well, women everywhere like to be spoiled. But most New York guys aren't like that."

She gave "aren't" two syllables, a pronunciation unique to New York women. She was looking at him earnestly, waiting for a reply.

"You reckon I should act more like a northern boy?" he asked, smiling, exaggerating the drawl a bit. "Let y'all carry your own suitcases?"

"Are you surprised I came here with you?" asked Stacy, ignoring the question. She picked up a menu.

"No. Should I be?"

"Maybe."

"Are you surprised you left with me?"

She shrugged and said, "No." Her eyes went to the menu. "Maybe."

She was either flirting with him or into head games. Sam wondered if he could fall for her. And if they'd be taking him away in a straight jacket six months from now if he did. He felt his eyes close for a second in angry response to his own thoughts. What's the matter with you, Morris? "Maybe? Are you afraid I might attack you?"

"No. It's nothing like that. Remember though—this is New York City. I'm not supposed to trust anyone. Where are you from, anyway?"

"Virginia. All my life until I moved here two years ago."

"You've lived in one place all your life? You must love your job, then, with the travel and all. Where have you traveled to? You owe me an answer to that one, remember?"

"Mostly down south and to the midwest. The company owns plants in those regions." He cleared his throat. He picked up his menu and opened it.

"I see."

"I'm going to Russia next month."

"Russia? Really?"

"We're developing—" Sam stopped himself when he remembered Davies' directive that the project be kept secret. "It should be interesting."

Stacy nodded, reading his concern, and looked away. "I'm impressed. It must be pretty exciting to be on the cutting edge of world relations."

Sam paused a moment. "You're...impressed with that?" he asked finally.

"Of course! It's cool, Sam. I mean, who would've thought twenty minutes ago that I'd be having coffee with a southern transplant who jet-sets out to Moscow for business?"

"It's really not that glamorous, Stacy—at least not from what I've seen so far."

They were quiet for a moment, both looking at their menus. Finally Sam said, "You must get some excitement in the fashion district, too. Talk about glamorous—"

"No, not really. Nothing like what you're doing. I like it though. I've always loved clothes."

Stacy lowered her menu as she spoke, and Sam's eyes glanced downward to quickly inspect the top half of her slim but lithe body. Her cashmere sweater defined shapely breasts that momentarily distracted him, but he willed himself back to the conversation. "What exactly do you do at Hobgoode?"

"I design patterns that are transferred onto fabric." She leaned forward and put her elbow on the table as she spoke, supporting her cheek with the palm of her hand. "I'm half-artist, half-businesswoman, I guess." She spoke in a near whisper, with interested eyes. Without warning.

"So, you're...creative." Somehow his words also came out in a lowered voice. He found his eyes meeting hers.

"Sometimes," she said. "Not as creative as you seem to be, though."

Sam was quiet for a long moment, wondering what she'd meant, but then he noticed the waitress standing beside the table. "Oh. I'm sorry. Two coffees, please. Oh, would you like coffee, Stacy?" He laughed nervously.

"Please."

"Is that all?" asked the waitress.

"That's all for now," said Sam, hoping that the diversion would end the tone of their conversation. And that it wouldn't. He searched for something else to tell the waitress, unsuccessfully.

"What I mean is, you have one hell of an approach," Stacy continued after the waitress had left. "So tell me. Why did you want to meet me back at Kamikaze?"

"Why? Are you fishing for a compliment?"

"Absolutely."

"Well, to be totally honest with you, I really don't know. I wish I did."

Stacy looked up at the ceiling for a moment, then said, "Interesting."

Sam began toying with his spoon and had to suppress taking a deep breath. A moment of introspection passed through him, but he still couldn't find an answer to her question.

"Do the girls ever ask the guys out in Virginia?" asked Stacy.

"Uh...Sometimes. Not as often as here, though."

"Could this curious northern girl possibly get her new southern acquaintance to join her for dinner sometime this weekend?"

Sam smiled. "I reckon we could work something out."

FIVE

Ilya Lukov and Andrey Muravyev, Mosteks' accountant, were sitting uncomfortably close to each other in the back seat of a Lada sedan, on their way to a meeting with a representative of the Ministry of Finance of the Russian Federation. "MinFin," as it was called, was responsible for registering international joint ventures and licensing them to proceed with their business plans. Ilya's hopes of establishing a joint venture with IIS as a defense to the Gagarintsi depended on his ability to get MinFin to expedite his JV application.

"Corruption will be Russia's doom, Andrusha," said Ilya despondently, shaking his head. Ilya had agreed to meet with Svetov tomorrow—to fork over millions of rubles in protection money—and he was wondering how he'd handle himself with the *khuligan*. As expected, the State Inspector's Office had issued a mere warning to Mosteks only two days after Ilya had capitulated to the Gagarintsi's demands. "If the authorities don't soon take steps against organized crime, the reforms will never come to fruition," he said. "Nearly ten years of progress will go out the window."

Muravyev nodded sympathetically. "Maybe it's just part of our initiation into the real world, Ilya. We've now tasted the evils of a free society."

"Over there, Pasha," said Ilya to the driver. He pointed to the main entrance of the large grey Ministry building. Pasha parked diagonally along the curb.

I'm afraid we've more than just tasted the evils, my friend, thought Ilya, concealing the significance he attached to Andrey's remark. We're actually becoming a part of them. But what else can we do? Is it better not to strive for success? Would it be better for men like us to quit? He groaned as he negotiated his large belly out of the small car.

"Good morning Borya," said Ilya, following Muravyev into the small fourth floor office. Ilya extended his hand heartily to the bureaucrat, who rose from behind his battered metal desk to accept it.

"It's nice to see you again, Ilya," said Boris Antonovich Shturkin, a MinFin JV registration officer. He was as hefty a man as was Ilya, with thinning black hair combed back. Protocol dictated that he wear a suit, but it was clear Boris wasn't comfortable in formal attire. His jacket sleeves were too short, and his belt buckle was for some reason always off-center. Boris presented a pack of Marlboros to his visitors, both of whom withdrew a cigarette with a brief, gracious bow before sitting down. "How are things at Mosteks?" Boris asked. "I hear you're doing well."

"Very well," said the chairman, hoping that his face wouldn't reveal otherwise. It was always important that the ministries be confident that the cooperative was in good working order.

"I'm glad to hear that," said Boris enthusiastically. Ilya and Boris had been acquainted for several years, since the days when Ilya was a ranking officer at the Ministry of Light Industry. Ilya was greatly esteemed in Moscow's business circles, especially since the success of Mosteks. "What can I do for you, my friend?" asked Boris with a smile.

"As I explained to you last month, the Mosteks board of directors has decided to broaden our cooperative's horizons," said Ilya. "We have nearly completed negotiations with a large American company to create a joint venture. A lawyer from the firm is expected in a couple of weeks to complete our negotiations. With Western technological resources, we expect to perhaps double our output by next year. I'd like you to meet our accountant and bookkeeper, Andrey Muravyev. He has completed a study on Mosteks' expected output." Ilya shifted uncomfortably in his chair to watch the other two rise halfway to shake hands, wondering how he'd done with the opening remarks. If Boris knew anything about the textile industry, he should be able to figure out that Ilya's increased production estimates were far too low. But that wasn't the Ministry of Finance's business.

"I see," said Boris, sitting back down, his interest piqued. "And as I remember, you would like the JV to be registered…as soon as possible," he added, nodding his large head both at Ilya and at Andrey.

Boris remembered the proposed project damned well, Ilya knew. How could he forget? By subtly demanding a bribe when the chairman had first approached him last week, Boris was obviously taking a calculated risk. Mosteks had probably been the only thing on his mind for days.

"This is the purpose of today's meeting," said the accountant. He handed Boris a folder containing graphs and information detailing the JV's business plan.

Boris quickly skimmed the contents of the folder and placed it on his desk. He looked first at Andrey, then at Ilya, then uncomfortably at the wall to his left. "Like I told you, Ilya, Min-Fin has a backlog of JV's awaiting registration," he said.

A comment of that nature was expected, Ilya thought. It was like a form of protocol, an obligatory step in the scenario. "We are aware of the problems, Borya, but are hopeful and confident you will be able to…circumvent them," he replied, feeling a bit odd for going along with the game. After all, Ilya had already explained his proposal to Boris.

Boris sat silently, clearly trying to contain his eagerness to hear what Mosteks was prepared to pay him. Ilya watched as the *chinovnik* rose to see that his office door was safely closed.

"We will pay you ten for your assurances that a joint venture between Mosteks and Inter-American Industrial Services will be registered by MinFin within five days of our submission of the necessary documentation and that we'll have no problems obtaining a license to do business at Mosteks' existing location," said Ilya in a lowered voice. The room was uncomfortably silent for a long moment, and Ilya wondered if he'd broken some rule of etiquette of crooked city government officials. He forced a smile and waited for Boris's response.

Boris laughed nervously and shook his head, confused. "Ilya, my friend, you know the state of affairs better than that. Your proposed joint venture would be a rather large-scale effort involving possibly millions of dollars in foreign investment. A review of such an application would normally require a rather drawn-out process." He lowered his voice and looked at the far wall behind Andrey. "To guarantee registration in short time would be worth far, far more than ten million rubles. I cannot even consider your offer."

"Borya, Borya!" said Ilya with a feigned laugh as he rose from his seat and approached the official. "When I said we were prepared to pay you ten, I wasn't referring to millions of rubles! I had thousands of dollars in mind, my friend! Surely you wouldn't expect anything less for the kind of favor we're seeking here!" He reached over to pat Boris's broad back affectionately and was relieved when a grin slowly appeared on the *chinovnik's* face. At least half of Boris's teeth were gold, and Ilya watched with glee as more and more shiny metal become visible. The chairman gestured to Andrey, who quickly handed Boris an envelope. "And here is the first fifty percent of your fee."

Boris quickly flipped through the green bills inside, then stood. "Ilya, my friend. It will be an honor and privilege to support you in a project of this magnitude and importance." He shook Ilya's hand fervently, then opened a file cabinet and removed a bottle of vodka and three shot glasses, his mouth shining gold all the while.

While Boris was filling the glasses, Ilya, again in a lowered voice, said, "Of course, our agreement will ensure us there will be no problems with the JV's registration, at least from MinFin, correct?" He waited apprehensively for Boris's reaction, hoping he hadn't stepped over a line.

Boris looked up at the chairman, the gold momentarily hidden behind now-closed lips. "I don't foresee any problems, Ilya," he said, shaking his head seriously. "But to make sure, perhaps I should attend one or two of your meetings with the American lawyer, just to be sure he doesn't propose something problematic."

"You are kind to offer, Borya," replied Ilya, relieved. "I know that you are quite busy and attendance at such negotiation meetings by government officials is not usual procedure. Thank you very much. I'll have my secretary call you with our meeting schedule."

The three Russian men toasted and drank their shots. It wasn't just a celebration of their having reached an agreement—it was a confirmation of it as well, the final signing on the dotted line. Obviously they couldn't commit the illegal agreement to paper, but by consuming vodka together, the men had obligated themselves in spirit—an even more binding gesture.

"To our agreement," said Ilya with another forced smile before tossing back the liquor. The evils of a free society, he thought, glancing at Andrey. He wanted a second shot.

Again the three men shook hands, and Muravyev explained the details of how the remainder of Boris's "fee" would be transferred.

The two Mosteks directors finally left. Boris saw his visitors out cordially and promptly returned the vodka to its hiding place. He sat behind his dented metal desk and let out a deep, satisfying sigh.

Boris reached for the receipt confirming deposit of his salary last month, balled the paper up, and threw it in the waste basket. Ninety thousand rubles, he thought, shaking his head incredulously. About twenty-five dollars. He had an acquaintance or two who actually lived—no, subsisted—on such a pittance. They were the dedicated civil servants who seemed to have found happiness without money. Maybe they were fools, maybe heroes, maybe even both. Boris didn't quite know. Anyway, it was irrelevant.

Of course there had always been perquisites for city government officials: visits to state-owned *dachas*, use of government facilities and property, and sometimes even state-sponsored travel. But none of this made up for the lifestyle to which their salaries doomed them. "Straight" officials rarely had nice apartments or personal cars, ate well, or provided well for their families. The money wasn't nearly enough.

So Boris had no sense of wrongdoing or guilt, although he knew what he'd just accepted was strictly illegal and would carry the stiffest penalties if discovered by the police. He'd provided a necessary service and was being duly compensated for his efforts. Boris had been with MinFin for twenty-two years—he'd paid his dues. He deserved the profit he was about to receive.

And who was hurt? he asked himself. Of course he knew the old arguments—that society would be the victim of his actions. But really, how much would society suffer by his receiving a little *valuta* for expediting the registration of a joint venture? He picked up a copy of the latest study on the economic crisis that enslaved the country. The current depression was as harsh to the people as the czars had been to the serfs! Shortages of everything in Russia were so acute that they couldn't even be accurately measured. He flipped through the report. Shouldn't he be rewarded for helping to establish an enterprise that might alleviate Russia's suffering? Wasn't it in line with the laws of economics?

Yes, Boris Antonovich Shturkin had made it this time. It was his right, he thought, as a lifelong servant of the people, to finally benefit from his efforts. He'd brought home the big prize—*valuta*. Dollars, real money, and plenty of it. It could be used to purchase anything in Moscow. He leafed through the greenbacks once more and briefly fantasized about how he might spend them.

Boris had his large overcoat on and was preparing to don his Russian *ushanka* hat when he heard a knock. The department secretary's head appeared through the doorway. "Your two o'clock appointment is here, Boris Antonovich," the stocky young woman said meekly.

"What meeting? I don't have anything else scheduled this afternoon," he said, confused. He'd just decided to take the rest of the day off.

"There's nothing on my calendar for you either, Boris Antonovich, but these two men insist you are expecting them."

Suddenly he realized who the visitors were. Not now! he thought. He sighed, took off his overcoat and threw it over his chair. "Show them in, Marya."

Boris first caught a glimpse of Svetov's black leather jacket, then of the *mafioznik's* colorless face. He took a step backward as the Gagarinets walked into the office.

"Boris Antonovich, it's so nice to see you again. I apologize for being so scarce, but I've been tremendously busy," said Svetov.

Boris smiled, but no words, not even platitudes, came to his mouth. It was an effort for him to maintain his composure, but he managed to accept Svetov's extended hand and shake it silently.

In the past, Boris had always found it relatively easy to play the mafia's game. He'd been receiving visits from Svetov and his underlings for several years now. But after the meeting with Mosteks, Boris didn't relish the reminder of his relationship with the mob. The risk was no longer justified. But it couldn't be avoided.

"I've come personally to bring you this month's fee for your services, Boris Antonovich," said Svetov. He took a small package out of his jacket and handed it to the bureaucrat. "Two hundred thousand rubles exactly," he added with a smile.

But Boris knew there was more to the man's visit. He'd been on "retainer" with the Gagarintsi for two years now, receiving a monthly emolument to be ready if they ever needed his services. It had been an easy arrangement; he'd been called on only twice during that time, and then only to run very minor errands. But even on those two occasions, Svetov had sent young mafia recruits to deliver the assignment. And they never came to his office. He wondered desperately why Svetov had come in person, taking the added risk of showing up in a Ministry building. "Thank you," Boris replied as he took the package and put it in his desk drawer.

"Boris Antonovich," began Svetov, placing his hands into the pockets of his jacket, "if it is not too much of an inconvenience, we were wondering if you might be able to do a favor for us. It will be a very small effort and would help our organization greatly."

Boris waited silently to hear Svetov's favor. He was familiar with the mafia style; what was forthcoming would be an order.

"A textile manufacturing cooperative we have dealings with seems intent on creating a joint venture with a large American company," continued Svetov with a slight but intimidating smile. "Of course, the cooperative will need to be approved by your Ministry and granted a license for international business.

We understand you might be the reviewing officer for such an application, or that you could see to it that you are." He took a step forward. "We'd like you to make sure that…this joint venture is not registered. Given our country's harsh economic situation at present, it seems unlikely that MinFin would sanction a joint venture that intends to export domestically manufactured fabrics, correct?"

"What is the cooperative?" asked Boris, looking at the handle of the drawer containing the five thousand dollars.

"I believe you are familiar with it. The chairman, Ilya Konstantinovich Lukov, is an old acquaintance of yours. Mosteks."

The sound of the cooperative's name jolted Boris, causing his head to snap backward slightly. "Mosteks," he repeated, nodding.

"So you are familiar. I take it that Ilya Konstantinovich has already made application. We reached you as quickly as possible. Has MinFin taken any action, Boris Antonovich?"

He sighed before answering, looking down at the floor. "None. We just received their documents today." His voice had instantly become hoarse and dry.

"Good, Boris Antonovich. So I can assume there will be no problems?"

"There will be no problems."

"Boris Antonovich, you look a little weak. Are you feeling all right? I hope our request isn't unreasonable or doesn't pose any inconvenience to you." He sounded genuinely concerned about Boris's health, though the latter wasn't taken in.

"I'm fine," replied Boris, breathing deeply. "Your request is no problem. The Mosteks joint venture will not be registered."

"Very good, then. We thank you for your cooperation and look forward to maintaining a mutually beneficial relationship with you." He turned to leave, then stopped and thought a moment. "Boris Antonovich, did Lukov mention to you how far Mosteks has proceeded toward its proposed joint venture? What steps has it taken, do you know?"

Boris stopped his head from jolting back again, just in time. He wanted a moment to think about how he would answer the question, but he was afraid that any hesitation would be noticeable. "An...American lawyer is coming in two weeks to...finalize...negotiations." His voice trailed off as he realized what he was doing. His eyes turned back to the floor. He pictured Andy Griffith from episodes of Matlock he'd seen dubbed on Russian television—the actor's face beaten to a pulp.

"Did the chairman mention where the lawyer would be staying in Moscow?" Svetov's voice was polite as ever, but his harsh features expressed another bearing.

Boris pushed the haunting guilt from his head. "No," he replied, looking quickly up at Svetov, then back to his shoes.

"Will the lawyer be traveling alone?"

"I...don't know."

"Excuse me, Boris Antonovich?"

"I don't know," he repeated. And I don't know how big he is or whether he'll be carrying a weapon to defend himself, he added to himself, gritting his teeth. He tried to picture what the lawyer might look like, again drawing from images he remembered from American television. What kind of man was he helping to endanger?

Svetov stood silently for a short while, his hands in the pockets of his jacket. "Thank you, Boris Antonovich, you've been most helpful. But please, should you hear anything more about the American, give us a ring." Svetov smiled and patted Boris affectionately on the back before leaving through the door.

Boris returned to his desk and withdrew the thick envelope Ilya had given him not an hour earlier. He opened it and withdrew the leafy notes, fondling them, inspecting their texture, as he counted them. There were exactly fifty one hundred dollar bills there, more *valuta* than he'd ever seen before. He sighed and looked up at the ceiling, then slammed down his palm. The slap on the metal desk reverberated throughout the small office, and Boris was worried that Marya, the secretary, might become concerned.

He rose from his chair, locked the office door, and went to the file cabinet. He opened it and removed the bottle of vodka and a shot glass.

SIX

Sam Morris was crouched over his desk, reading a reference manual entitled *Legal Aspects of Trade and Investment in the Former Soviet Union*. His was always the neatest office in IIS's legal department—the other five in-house attorneys often kidded him about his fanatic attention to orderliness and detail. His bookshelves were arranged with books systematically lined in descending order of height, and every item on his desk was currently in use. His top shirt button was always fastened, and the knot in his tie was always tight. Sam didn't think the resulting image really befitted his true character, and he knew he probably seemed a bit anal to his officemates. But the hell with it! After all, he'd come to this city to get a job done, and he remembered that his grandfather Hyman had credited Old Virginia's successes to meticulous organization and unwavering personal commitment.

Sam was supporting his head with one arm propped up on his desk when the door suddenly opened.

"Don't fall in there, dude."

He looked up to see Eric's immense body standing in the office doorway.

"How's the Russian project coming?"

Sam dropped his pencil, actually welcoming the break. "Smooooth as Stoly vodka, bud. Cool as an autumn night in Moscow." He shrugged. "Some of it can get pretty complicated, but it's basically no prob."

"How long before you go over?"

"The Russians just postponed it for some reason, so I have another two weeks. I think I've got everything under control. I'm just wondering what it's going to be like over there. You reckon they'll have another revolution with tanks rolling down Main Street Moscow while Sam Morris happens to be visiting?" He leaned back in his chair with his hands behind his head and yawned through a smile.

"No way. If you have any affect on the Russkies, they'll be better organized than Amish barn raisers by the time you leave."

"You think so, huh?"

"And they'll probably dress like 'em too," added Eric over a chuckle.

Sam tugged on his tie. "You don't like the way I dress, boy?"

"Sure I do. Makes my wardrobe look hip. Now, let's go get some lunch."

Sam smiled and checked his Rolex. "It is lunchtime already. Yeah, let's go eat, bud."

The two left IIS's offices, descended forty floors in the elevator, and exited the skyscraper. The midtown area was replete with various restaurants, but the two lawyers had a handful of favorite lunch spots. This time they picked a small sandwich shop nearby.

"My group ski house in Vermont starts in two weeks," said Eric, pouring ketchup onto his hamburger. "Can't wait. I bought a half-share in a cabin near Mount Snow, so I go up every other weekend through the end of the ski season. They've already got thirteen inches of packed powder up there."

"Sounds like lots of fun, Eric."

"Fuckin' hick. What would you know about skiing?"

Sam lifted his chin. "Hey, we have skiing down in Virginia. I've even been a couple of times."

"I bet the only thing you'd be good for on a hill is picking up babes. Maybe I should invite you up to help me out in that department."

"Here he goes again."

"How are you and Stacy doing, anyway?"

"We've been out three or four times." Sam nonchalantly turned his attention to a bite of his tuna sandwich. "She's a neat girl. Easy to communicate with, y'know? I might spend some time with her."

"Have you gotten anything off her yet?"

Sam stopped chewing and glared across the table at Eric. "None of your goddam business, asshole."

"Woo, I hit a nerve that time. Hope I didn't start a second civil war with that one."

Sam rolled his eyes. "I'm into her. I think. She's not just some piece of ass, Eric."

"You think you're into her?"

Sam silently took another bite of his sandwich.

"She better be one hot catch, the way you stranded me at Kamikaze the night you met her." Eric smiled, then bit into his burger.

"Shit happens," said Sam with an embarrassed smile.

"You can bring her up to my group house one weekend if you want. Does she ski?"

"Oh, yeah. She's real athletic. She jogs, works out in a health club, lots of stuff. She's into horseback riding in Central Park. She gets out and does stuff, know what I mean? Makes a life for herself. That's one of the things I like about her."

"Yeah, I know what you mean. I can't deal with women who don't enjoy life."

"She's also into her career, though. She's not just some bimbo. She's ambitious and..." Sam stopped his rambling and took another bite of his sandwich.

"Stacy seems nice," said Eric. "She's good-looking, too. I'm glad you met her."

Sam nodded modestly. "I'm taking her out tonight, as a matter of fact."

Early that evening, Sam ran his finger down a list of names on the intercom buzzer. He finally located the button next to "Werner, Stacy" and pressed it.

"Sam?" buzzed Stacy's voice through the intercom.

"Yep."

"Just a sec." The security system in Stacy's walk-up brownstone apartment building required her to identify callers before opening the electronically controlled door downstairs. She lived in a part of town called Chelsea, a good distance from Sam's upper east side neighborhood. Sam had heard that fifteen years ago it would've been considered dangerous for a single woman to live in the lower west side area. But Chelsea was now home to scores of young professionals.

The front door buzzed open and Sam entered. As he ascended the stairs to Stacy's apartment, he wondered if the system really was secure. This was, after all, New York City.

"How ya doin'!" Stacy's smile greeted him through her partially opened apartment door.

"Oh, can't complain." Sam planted a kiss on her olive cheek, drawing in a whiff of her delicately floral scent as he did. It was the first time he'd been in Stacy's small apartment, and he took a second to look it over. It was a one-bedroom, decorated with contemporary but inexpensive furniture. The walls were colorfully embellished with framed poster prints, and an antique wooden trunk served as a coffee table before a red leather couch.

A life-sized poster of James Dean hung on the far wall. Nice place. "Where are we going for supper?" he asked.

Stacy crossed her arms. "I have a plan, Sam Morris," she said. "I'm going to cook you dinner. Right here at Cafe Werner." She took his jacket and hung it in the closet. "It'll be fun, y'know? Creative. I mean, when was the last time you ate a home-cooked meal?"

Still savoring the lingering sensation in his nose, Sam watched as she turned around and strutted into the apartment's small kitchen. She was wearing tight brown jeans that outlined the swell of her behind perfectly. She'd acted cheerfully, as if she were really glad to see him, but somehow Sam had immediately guessed that she wasn't totally at ease. Her eyes weren't as lively as usual, the smile came only from her lips. She was tense, as if something were on her mind. "I can count the times I've eaten home-cooked food in New York on one hand," he answered, playing along.

"See? You could use it. I'll cook pasta, okay? Do you like pasta? With cream sauce and shrimp? I can cook as fast as we could go out, and we'll still have time for the movie. Okay?"

But Stacy! he thought. Single New York City women aren't supposed to be cooks! This should be interesting. "Sure," he said enthusiastically. He'd just turned to follow her into the kitchen when he heard the sound of crashing pots and pans.

"Shit!" he heard Stacy yell.

Sam ran into the kitchen. "What happened? Are you all right?"

She was standing before a pile of metal cooking utensils, a burning look of frustration across her face. She put a hand to her mouth and closed her eyes.

"Are you all right?" he repeated, walking toward her slowly. "What's the matter?" He looked at Stacy for a second, wondering if she'd be ready to open up to him about what was on her mind. She was a New Yorker, a city girl, and they usually needed time. Who could blame them?

He slowly put his hands on her shoulders, then around her, and stroked her hair lightly. She hesitated before accepting his gesture, at first without looking at him, then meeting his eyes warmly. It was the first time she'd said or done something revealing, showing a possible weakness, and Sam found himself savoring the unexpected intimacy of the moment. The New York women he'd dated were usually so damned guarded during the first few weeks, watching everything they said and did. They even had a name for it, the "good behavior" period, which could last for months.

"I'm sorry, Sam. Just give me a minute, okay?" she said with a nervous laugh, fighting tears. "I just had a really rotten day at work."

"Sure," he said softly, then quickly cleaned up the metal heap on the floor, replacing the utensils in the cabinet. When he'd finished, he gave her a smile. "Well, Stacy, if you're willing to trust me, I reckon I could help you cook. At least I could try," he said in a livelier tone. Onions and peppers were on the counter. "Here. Let me cut these suckers up."

Stacy smiled. "Why are you so nice, Sam?"

"Gotta be. Otherwise, I wouldn't have a shot with a gal like you."

"So tell me about this catastrophe at work," said Sam as he ground pepper onto his pasta.

"Oh, it wasn't really that big a deal," she answered over a sigh, her wistful voice and expression contrary to her words. "It's not even worth discussing."

"Are you sure?" He glanced back into the kitchen where she'd dropped the pots and pans. "I'd hate to see you with something that was worth discussing. Why don't you tell me about it?"

Stacy smiled. "Well, sales are down, that's all."

"You must take your job pretty seriously."

She gave a quiet laugh and rolled her eyes. "Okay, there is a little more to it."

Sam took a sip of wine and looked into her eyes, which had brightened up a bit.

"Danette, the head stylist in my studio, quit yesterday. She was the one who actually ran the fabric design department, where I work. Now the raging office scuttlebutt is over who's going to replace her."

"You must be up for consideration. With the amount of time you put in and all."

She shook her head. "No, I doubt it. There are others who've been with Hobgoode for six and seven years. They'd be way ahead of me. It's real competitive. And I think a few girls have been kind of offering to…service the partner in charge for a promotion." She smiled at her own phraseology, apparently having decided she knew Sam well enough to use it, then shoved a forkful of noodles into her mouth, to shut herself up.

Sam smiled back and picked out the most suitable of several different responses. "Is the partner a doity ol' man?" he asked.

She nodded her head, raising her eyebrows into a bawdy but playful expression.

This gal's a lot more fun than I thought, Sam decided. He took another sip of wine, glad to see her mood was improving.

"Many women have ascended the Hobgoode ranks by 'working under Colby,'" said Stacy. "That's what they call it. Sick, huh?"

Sam laughed and nodded his agreement.

"It's incredible how many women will do that," she continued over another mouthful of noodles. "It's so gross. I mean, my career is very important to me. Really. But how could you live with yourself after doing something so slimy? You'd be surprised at how much of that is going on, Sam. I don't know. If I make it in this business, I guess it'll have to be the old-fashioned way."

Sam watched Stacy's breasts rise as she heaved a sigh. They were a firm and round pair, with a hint of her nipples protruding through her thin silk blouse. "I wouldn't want to be successful any other way," he said, forcing himself back to the conversation.

"Are you looking forward to going to Russia?" she asked.

"Oh, yeah. Can't wait." She was waiting eagerly for the details. "It's a lot of fun, working with the Russians and all. I'm kind of looking at it as a way to get my name established at the company. If this thing flies, Old Virginia will be in the news. And the brass will have to credit me for it. And what's more important—"

Stacy shifted, looking at him expectantly.

"Ah, you don't want to hear all this, Stacy." He dropped his fork on his plate.

"No, Sam. Really, I do. Tell me."

Sam breathed deeply. What are you doing, Morris? "Well, it would carry on my family legacy. If I do something that furthers Old Virginia, even though the company doesn't actually belong to the Morris family anymore, somehow I'll feel like I've done my duty to my...to my grandfather." He glanced at her and rolled his eyes. "I'm sorry, Stacy. You don't have to listen to this stuff."

She was silent for a moment, then said, "Well, first of all, I think it's a fascinating project, Sam. I mean, how many people can say they've even been to Russia, and here you are going off to do business there. But the connection with your family makes it even better. Special, y'know?"

Sam smiled and said, "Really?" He watched her nod, her smile filling her face. Then quickly, almost reflexively, he glanced behind him at James Dean. It was somehow a flash of male bonding, a fleeting respite from the energy that filled the table between him and the woman. He savored the twinge the moment had given him, then reached for the wine bottle to fill their glasses.

"I got some good news from Russia yesterday. The chairman of the Russian cooperative called and postponed my trip for two weeks."

"That's good. At least you won't have to rush to get ready for it."

"You're right. But that's not why it's good news." He looked into her eyes. "Now I have more time to wine and dine a certain beautiful woman in Chelsea."

Stacy smiled and said, "I'll drink to that." She raised her glass to meet Sam's.

They sipped and Sam, remembering their plans to go to a movie, said, "Oh, what time's it getting to be?"

"We have a little time." She tilted her head. "Would you like to retire into the parlor for a last glass of wine?" she asked in a haughty English accent.

Sam smiled as he looked behind him at the apartment's small living area. "But of course," he said, then stood and reached to clear the table.

"Oh, don't worry about it," said Stacy, smiling. "You can take a break from being the southern gentleman for a while. I never do dishes right after a meal, it ruins the memory of the food." She walked across the room and sat on the couch.

Sam sat next to her and filled her glass with wine, although it hardly needed it. After a moment, he said, "Dinner was delicious."

"I'm glad you enjoyed it."

"Fixing supper at home was a great idea."

"I know."

Her voice was lowered. Uh-oh. "You're a cheap date. I'll have to take you out more often."

She smiled silently in return.

"Cafe Werner, huh?"

Stacy remained quiet. Sam looked into her eyes, gauging their reply, then reached to take the full wine glass from her hand and lower it to the trunk. He leaned forward and kissed her, putting his arms around her shoulders.

Sam was savoring the sweet taste of wine on her unexpectedly nimble tongue when Stacy startled him with a sudden deep breath. The tenderness of the moment vanished immediately and Sam felt his lips impulsively push more tightly onto hers. She moved closer toward him, pressing her breasts against his chest, tugging slightly at the hair on the back of his head, her tongue becoming a boomerang spinning throughout his mouth. Soon she was breathing in short melodious gasps from her throat, her torrid sounds, taste, and feel charging Sam with bolts of flaming passion.

A moment later, she lowered her head to invade his neck with hungry pecking kisses, pausing every few seconds to take in another musical breath. Sam felt the cool air against the wetness on his neck; he wrapped his right arm around her back and clutched her blouse, as if the silk were the reins on some unfamiliar colt.

He lowered her as gently as possible, his eyes locked in hers, until her head was on the armrest of the couch. She was still breathing deeply, her heart pounding almost visibly in her chest, her nipples now clearly discernible through the blouse. A shiny glimmer covered her forehead. He touched her lips with his forefinger and said in a lowered voice, "I'll bet that movie'll be playing for months. How 'bout let's see it another night?"

She nodded and leaned to whisper into his ear. "Do you want to stay at Cafe Werner for dessert?"

Sam was taken aback, both by the invitation itself and her cavalier spontaneity.

But it was time to make the decision. Now. It didn't take him long. His head lowered to kiss her lips.

Soon he was unbuttoning her blouse, slowly at first, keeping control over himself...then suddenly in haste, the reins no longer in his hands. He nearly gasped when he removed her bra, revealing shapely round breasts that rose and fell in rhythm with her breaths. Sam looked up and saw that Stacy's pretty brown eyes were now locked on some invisible sight in the ceiling. He again pressed his lips onto hers.

Suddenly, Stacy crawled out from under his weight and rolled on top of him, all in one quick motion. She gingerly spread herself out along the length of his body until her chest was centered right above his head, her breasts just skimming both of his cheeks, her elbows propping her up and pinning down his shoulders, her hips straddling him right over his crotch. She swayed her body left and right, brushing his face lightly, and Sam felt the slight roughness of her hardened nipples as they skimmed his cheeks and nose. He tried twice to take them into his mouth, but Stacy would not allow it. Instead, she lowered her chest a bit further and began to massage his face, both hands pressing her breasts into the contours of his eyes and nose, slowly at first, then faster and harder. He didn't mind having to breath through his mouth.

Sam realized his feet were tapping the armrest on the other end of the sofa. They were the only parts of his body Stacy hadn't pinned down—no, he could bend his knees up a little, too. What did she have in mind? What was she going to do next? Shouldn't he be...doing something? For her?

He couldn't decide what to focus his increasingly ecstatic thoughts on. He wanted to get her pants off, his pants off...Both! And now, right now! Her hips began grinding into him, slowly but firmly, causing the small of his back to arch slightly upwards. He opened an eye, only to have it forced closed again. "You're...you're smothering me!" he finally said, immediately regretting it.

Stacy quickly sat up, her long brown hair disheveled as she looked down at him, her lips pursed, her brow unfamiliarly but delightfully knitted.

He looked up at her, over her smooth belly and between those perfect mounds, until he met her eyes. They almost looked savage now, completely transformed from the long-lashed, dainty brown globes he'd first noticed a few weeks ago. What was this woman all about?

"But don't stop," he said, his voice suddenly hoarse. "Who needs air?"

He'd meant it only half-jovially, but they both laughed as Stacy lowered her body back onto him.

"Whatya thinking?" asked Stacy flirtatiously. She was naked, glimmering from a trace of perspiration along her olive skin. She sat on the coffee table, smiling provocatively down at Sam.

"Just about how full of surprises you are," he answered, his hands crossed behind his head on the sofa. His clothes were strewn on the floor, mixed with hers.

"What do you mean?"

"Oh, a bunch of stuff."

"Like how did a nice Jewish girl like me get to be so wild in bed? Or rather on the couch."

Sam nodded and smiled. "Among other things."

"Tell me what else."

Sam hesitated. "Like how you fix a mean pasta." He sat up and joined her on the trunk to massage her neck. "And how you keep such a nice apartment—"

"And a few other things, probably a lot more interesting, that you don't want to tell me about. At least not yet. Right?"

He ceded by tilting his head and raising his brow.

Stacy breathed deeply. "Okay. But while you're thinking about all these wonderful surprises, and about when you might finally open up to me, would you like to spend the night?"

It would be inconvenient because in the morning he'd have to travel from Stacy's Chelsea apartment, located in the lower western part of the city, to his upper east side apartment, shower and dress, and then make it back to midtown in time for work. But then he saw Stacy's smile. And those eyes. "Set the alarm for six," he said.

And James Dean seemed to approve.

SEVEN

Misha entered the two-bedroom apartment he shared with his wife Marina. The flat was posh by Moscow standards; similar space was often shared by two or more families. Like most Muscovite apartments, it had a narrow foyer with pegs on the near wall for hanging overcoats. A selection of slippers rested on the floor beneath the coats, as Russians preferred not to wear their rugged shoes inside. The parquet floor was partially covered by an impressive oriental rug. A brown sofa, somewhat in need of new cushions, faced a wooden wall unit displaying books and knick-knacks.

"How was work, Misha?" asked Marina as her husband walked into the living room.

"Things are going well," he answered. Of course Misha would never delve into the details of Mosteks' machinery problems with his wife. It wasn't proper to trouble a woman with a man's concerns.

"That's good," she said, continuing to peel potatoes in the small kitchen. Most methods of food preparation were still primitive in Russia; utensils and appliances readily available in the

West were in short supply. Now Marina was working arduously with an old knife.

Misha sat down on the sofa and sighed as he relaxed. "Would you bring me some tea, Marinochka?" He knew his wife had seen the anxious look on his face and that his day clearly hadn't been so mundane. He waited for her to pamper him.

"Here it is," she said with a hospitable smile, bringing him a cup of hot tea. "Would you like some sausage before dinner?"

"No, thank you," he replied, then silently returned to the kitchen.

After she'd arranged the plates and silverware, Marina joined her husband at the table. "I heard some interesting chatter today," she began with a smile.

"Really? What?" asked Misha with renewed zeal. He loved good gossip.

"Liusya's been screwing—"

"The Moscow representative of the Hatsiushu Trading Company," he interrupted with an impish smile. Misha prided himself on his network of gossip informants. "He's been buying her French clothes on his trips abroad."

"How did you know?"

"Every affair in Moscow eventually lands on my friends' tongues, Marinka," replied Misha with a swagger.

"I think it's terrible," said Marina, shrugging. "I barely have any girlfriends who don't sleep with men for the wrong reasons. They all think it's their lot in life to use their bodies to be happy."

Obviously the issue was more serious to Marina than her contrived expression revealed. "Times are difficult now, Marina."

Her face turned despondent. "But Liusya has been doing this for years!" she cried. "She says her marriage with Vasya is just for status, children, and an apartment. She thinks that when I get older, I'll be the same way. 'Like all other Muscovite women,' she says."

"Marina. Marinochka. You know that's not true! Our circumstances are not like those of most Muscovites, right? Don't you worry. We'll never have the problems Liusya and Vasya have."

"'And whom am I hurting?' Liusya told me. 'Vasya will never find out and so will never care.'"

Misha rose from the table and walked over to stand behind Marina. He put his hands lightly on her shoulders. "I promise you our love will never disintegrate like Vasya and Liusya's, Marinka." He leaned down and kissed her cheek. "You have nothing to worry about. As they say, 'Water couldn't get between us.' And it never will."

"You think so?"

"I know so, dear."

Marina smiled up at Misha and took his hand warmly. "What else do you know?"

"I know that you make an excellent baked chicken," he replied, smiling back at her. "May I have some now?"

She reached for the chicken as Misha returned to his seat. When his wife leaned over to serve him the food she'd prepared, he was struck by her beauty for the thousandth time. Misha's fingers went reflexively to her head and ran through her dark hair. He marveled when she pressed his hand to her cheek, her pretty, somewhat slanted eyes closing for a moment as she toyed with his thumb.

"The farmers' market has been getting fresh vegetables lately," said Marina, sitting back down. "Would you like me to buy some eggplant and squash tomorrow?"

"That sounds wonderful. Do you need money?" Misha reached for his wallet and handed her a ten-thousand-ruble note before she could answer. Most Russian couples were struggling on two salaries just to keep food on the table. And they lived in splendor on his income alone! Only the nagging realization that he was deceiving Marina kept his spirits from lifting him to the ceiling.

"Why don't we go there together!" she suggested, taking the money and putting it on the table. "Tomorrow. It's so fun to walk around the market on Saturdays!"

"You've got a deal, my dear." How lucky he was to have such a life! he reminded himself. Of course it was risky for him to be involved with his elder brother's "business," but wouldn't any Russian take advantage of such a lucrative relationship? Life in Russia was too hard for high morals! And after all, he wasn't doing anything dirty. All he was doing was a little snooping around at a factory, then telling Petya about what he saw and heard. Anyone would do the same for the kind of money Misha was making.

"We haven't spent a whole weekend together in months, Misha. It will be so much fun, don't you think?" asked Marina.

He looked into her beautiful eyes. They were trusting and caring. Innocent.

But then he felt his own eyes tear away from them. "Of course, Marinochka," he said. "We'll have a great time together."

They had met a year earlier at the twentieth birthday party of a common acquaintance, Nina Kochenko. Nina's parents, with whom she lived, had been on vacation in Odessa. It was therefore convenient to have the party at the Kochenko apartment, a rare treat for young Muscovites.

Misha, who was a friend of Nina's older brother, had come to the party with a selection of American videocassettes for the birthday girl to choose from for a party viewing. He knew that younger women always enjoyed his films.

Misha noticed Marina as soon as he entered the room. He was immediately attracted to her enticing figure and slightly Asian eyes. The woman simply exuded warmth and a beautiful soul. He couldn't wait to make her acquaintance. She was sitting alone on one end of the sofa, behaving like a lady, her legs

crossed in front of her. He could tell she wasn't one of those bois-
terous types, the kind no real man would be interested in. At
least for longer than one night. There were perhaps ten other
girls at the party, but his attention was locked on Marina.

He put down the videocassettes and made his way over to
the sofa. He sat down next to her, giving her a friendly greeting
as he made himself comfortable. She was a modest girl, meek
and reserved, as a woman should be.

Soon, Nina and another girl brought out several trays with
plates of sliced sausage and cheese and bottles of chilled vodka.
They placed a tray on the coffee table in front of the sofa, and
Misha immediately took it upon himself to serve refreshments to
the other guests. He lined up a dozen shot glasses, filled each
one separately, and handed the first one to Marina.

"Will you join me in saluting Nina's birthday?" he asked flirtatiously.

"Of course," she replied softly, taking the glass.

Misha smiled at her, then stood to dispense the rest of the
glasses and make a toast. "My friends, please, my friends! May I
have your attention, please? It is time that we recognize our
guest, or should I say hostess, of honor!"

The small group chuckled. Marina, however, was looking at
Misha fixedly.

"There comes a time when charming little girls, with their
prankish little ways, must pass away from us. Their delightful
innocence and curiosity will have charmed us quite enough—"

"Boo! Boo!" interrupted two male partyers, again eliciting
the group's laughter.

"Buccaneers! Please! Please do not take from this young
woman's moment! This is quite a monumental event! Treat our
lady of honor with respect!"

"Why do that? We're supposed to be helping her celebrate!"
someone interjected. The group again responded with raucous
laughter.

"My friends. Please. I must insist. We are here to witness this young woman's reaching a landmark year in her young life. Now at the age of twenty, she can no longer claim teenage naïveté—"

As he spoke, Misha found himself impulsively glancing at Marina, checking to be sure she was enjoying his performance. He knew women were always most attracted to the man at the center of attention. Was this one?

"—with us tonight," he continued. "Yes, we have lost our charming little girl. Yes, the mischievous but loveable little brat is gone forever. But, my friends, I believe the loss was worth it. For just look what we have gained!" He extended a hand to Nina. "May I have the honor, ladies and gentlemen, of introducing to you Moscow's brightest new flame, Russia's shiniest new star, a dazzling young woman for all men to behold in awe. My dear friends, will you join me in drinking to Nina on the special occasion of her twentieth birthday!"

The group cheered, then raised their glasses and swallowed the vodka. A brief silence followed as the partyers took bites of sausage and cheese to extinguish the fire in their throats.

A moment later, Misha returned to the sofa and sat down next to Marina. "Everyone's growing up," he said with mock disgust in his voice. "It's a shame isn't it?" He smiled and rolled his eyes. "I guess it does beat the alternative!"

Marina laughed. "I think so."

She was bashful by nature, but Misha saw that she definitely wanted to converse with him.

"Nina still looks young, though," she said over her shyness. "That's what's important."

"She still looks beautiful, which is what's most important. It must be a requirement for the women in her circle." Misha smiled as he watched the woman blush at his compliment. "I seem to have driven you into red paint, and I don't even know your name," he said. "How inconsiderate of me. My name's Misha. What's yours?" He offered her one of his Marlboros.

"Marina." She accepted the cigarette. "I'm often in red paint with handsome boys."

"Well, since you joined me in toasting to Nina's birthday, perhaps I might be so lucky as to drink with you to our acquaintance."

She looked at Misha and said, "You're quite a toastmaster. I'm sure Nina never had a finer birthday toast."

"I think she deserves it. She's such a nice girl. I'm like family to her," he said, filling Marina's glass with vodka. "Here's to our acquaintance."

"It's a pleasure," she replied with a smile before swallowing the liquor. Her head shook slightly, prompting her to reach for a piece of sausage to clear her palate. A moment later she said, "I like your tee shirt." Her eyes were still watering from the shot, but there was interest in them nonetheless.

"Thank you. It's Meeky Moos," said Misha in English, pitching his voice to sound like the Disney character. "I love American cartoons. They have so much personality. Especially Micky..."

He spent nearly the entire party with Marina. There was something special about her. She was attractive and well behaved, as were many Russian girls, but Marina also had an agreeable, easy quality about her. He could tell that she would be sympathetically supportive to her man, instead of demanding and pushy. She would act the way a woman should.

That night, Misha asked Marina out for the first time, marveling when she accepted nervously but enthusiastically. They were instantly comfortable with each other, enjoying each other's company as they became better acquainted. Their dates consisted of long walks, of dinners in nice restaurants, and small parties with their mutual friends.

But as the two grew closer, an obstacle typically found in relationships among young Muscovites soon emerged. Misha was visiting Marina, who lived in a small apartment with her parents and brother, when Misha became amorous and made his first advances toward her. "Oh, how I want you, Marina," he said passionately. "I want to make love to you this minute!"

"Misha, stop," she replied sternly, removing his hand from inside her dress. "My parents are here, and you'll wake them up! It's just not possible here." She glanced behind her at the bedroom door to see if her family had heard the noise.

"But where, Marina? Where can we be alone?"

"I don't know. But it can't be here. Not now."

It was a problem. There was really nowhere for the couple to be intimate. Misha couldn't invite her to his family's flat for the same reasons. Petya was afraid to have unknown visitors in his grandiose apartment. The situation was tremendously frustrating for the young couple and, as a result, the two often found themselves driving to deserted lots to make love in the back seat of Misha's car.

It was during one such assignation that mere inconvenience turned into near disaster. Misha and Marina were in the back of the Zhiguli, heads in one seat, feet in the other, both awkwardly restricted by unfastened, half-lowered, half-raised garments. It was a battle of love and affection against the elements, of libido versus the chilly Moscow air. Misha felt Marina's cold nose pressed through his opened shirt into his chest, warming itself to him. His hands were doing the same under her blouse to the heat of her back.

He sat up to better position himself. There was never a completely comfortable position in the back seat of the sedan, but he'd learned a few tricks over the years and knew how to make the best use of the confined space. He just had to move his left knee down a little—

A man was standing outside, looking in.

He was a few meters away, so it was hard for Misha to make him out, but it was definitely a grown man. Not just some mischievous teenager. He was clearly trying to see what was going on inside the car.

Misha slammed his palm onto the door lock above Marina's head, then lunged to grab his overcoat from the front passenger seat. He threw the coat over Marina's partially exposed body and saw the man almost simultaneously rush toward the car and reach for the door handle. He was a monster, at least two meters tall and probably weighing a hundred twenty kilos. The kind of mugger who didn't need weapons or an accomplice.

"What is it, Misha?" asked Marina anxiously.

She'd just sat up to look around when the man's foot came crashing through the window of the right front door. Misha, who was kneeling on the floor of the back seat, quickly leaned to open the back left door, but he lost his balance and missed the handle. He'd just moved to try again when the man reached over and grabbed the back of his collar, yanking him backward, ripping his shirt.

He pulled Misha's entire body between the two front seats, closer to his large head and torso. "Give it," he said in the gruff accent of some lower region republic, his words visible in the freezing air. The man's harsh features confirmed this was not his first mugging.

Misha felt like he was trapped under water. He could barely move—his knees wouldn't bend because of his lowered pants, and his head was locked by the man's grasp of his ripped shirt. Misha was struggling to take in the icy air, his now bare chest heaving with each breath. The sounds of Marina's terror were all he could hear.

"Give it!" repeated the thug, spraying spit over Misha's face. "Give me your money and passports, or I break your face!"

"I'll give it to you," Misha managed over gulps of air.

The man released Misha's collar and pushed him backward onto the seat next to Marina.

"Our...our...money is in the inside pockets of this," said Misha, pointing to the overcoat which Marina held around her.

"Give it."

Marina's eyes were anxious and desperate, but she slowly gave the coat to Misha, gathering her unbuttoned blouse around her as she did. Misha forced himself to ignore her pitiful whimpering and keep his wits. Was he shivering from the cold or from fear? Probably both. But no matter. He reached into the coat and pulled out his billfold.

The man was looking at Marina, a slight smile visible in the corners of his thin lips. She looked down. Misha extended the wallet to him, thankfully getting his attention.

"Passports," said the man curtly after snatching the billfold.

Misha reached back into the overcoat and withdrew his document folder.

The man had moved his head, trying to see Marina's lowered face. When he saw Misha hand him the passport, he looked back up to grab it. "Hers! Where is the woman's passport and money?"

Misha reached back into the overcoat, turning it slowly to the other side. He felt the *pushka*, the cartridge-loaded gas pistol that had become so prevalent during the last few years in crime-ridden Moscow. Almost everyone he knew carried them now. Many had had the occasion to use them against the assorted punks, thieves, and muggers who roamed Moscow, day and night. But he'd never actually fired his gun since Petya had given it to him a year earlier. Was it a good idea to do this? An untried defense in a dangerous situation?

The man was still leaning forward, trying to look up at Marina. He reached over with a finger and touched her chin, causing her to gasp.

Misha grasped the butt of the *pushka* firmly.

The man looked over at him, his finger now fondling Marina's cheek. "You, get out," he ordered.

Misha looked at Marina, then began sliding left toward the door. When the man began to climb into the back seat, Misha took a deep breath, snapped out the *pushka,* pointed it a few centimeters from the man's face, and closed his eyes. Would it make a noise? Would the pistol recoil? Was Marina a safe distance away?

He pulled the trigger. It gave easily, followed by the sound of hissing spray.

The man's scream drowned out the hiss.

Misha grabbed Marina's arm and dragged her with him through the left back door, checking to be sure she was all right. She was hysterical but unharmed. He glanced behind him as he pulled up his trousers and began to run. The man was wailing, rolling on the ground beside the car in agony.

Marina was ahead of him, running steadily, apparently in good control of herself. She was fine, thank God. Misha looked behind him again and saw the Zhiguli. His car. His fucking car. He stopped running.

"Run, Marina!" he yelled. "I'll catch up with you later!" He turned around and walked back toward the car. And the thug.

He drew his *pushka*, holding it in front of him, ready to use it again. Ready to take pleasure in causing the thug to suffer more. He looked down at the slime on the ground below him, the *svoloch,* and poised to kick the man's face. To break it, he thought, just as the mugger had threatened to do to him. But Marina suddenly came running up from behind.

"No, Misha!" she said through her tears and panting, grabbing his arm. "Let's just get out of here! Let's just go! Please!"

Misha turned to embrace her. He did want to break the man's face, just to make a point, but not as much as he wanted to take care of Marina. To relieve her suffering and see her happy. The *svoloch* would have to get his from somebody else.

Seeing that it was safe, the two got into Misha's damaged Zhiguli and drove to Marina's parent's apartment.

Marina calmed down over the next hour or so, although she was still visibly distraught from the ordeal. They sat on the sofa, holding hands.

"This is ridiculous," said Misha. We can't even have a place to be a man and woman without being attacked! We're living like scums."

"I'm sorry, Misha," replied Marina, hanging her head.

Misha sighed shamefully. "Oh, Marina. I'm sorry. It's not your fault. You don't have to apologize." He kissed her lightly and watched her expression change as she smiled timidly. "You're not happy living in this tiny apartment with three others, are you?"

"Of course not. Are you happy living with your family?"

An answer wasn't necessary. Misha said, "The only way we could live decently would be to get married, Marinka. We could get an apartment easily if we were a couple. We could live like real people. Do you know that?"

Marina's face grew bright, the remains of her anxiety forgotten, her slanted eyes becoming almost round. "Do you think we should get married?" she asked softly.

"It's probably a good idea."

She paused, then asked, "Do...do you love me, Misha?"

Misha leaned his head back against the sofa. He had long considered that marriage to a foreign woman would be the most prudent course for him. By doing so, he could move to the West and escape the hardships of Russian life. He could utilize his professional skills and talents and excel as an individual. Misha had access to many foreigners through his brother's connections, so meeting a Western woman wouldn't be difficult.

Would marrying Marina thwart some future opportunity? After all, he was only twenty-six years old. Plenty of other Russian women would be available if he decided to marry later. Was he a fool to forego these others by getting married now? What would Petya do? Surely he wouldn't marry a Russian woman at so young an age!

Misha gazed into Marina's solemn eyes, which waited anxiously for an answer. She was a good woman. He was sure that she'd be a good wife. What a beautiful soul she had! And she wasn't a complainer. She didn't constantly make demands. She was definitely pretty enough and could make life comfortable for him. Besides, he could always get divorced if marriage proved too limiting.

Misha thought of how violated he'd felt when the mugger had touched Marina's chin. As if the grimy finger were puncturing his soul. He thought of how unbearable it would have been to him if she'd been harmed. "Yes, Marinka," he said finally. "I love you very much."

After dinner, Misha led Marina back to their bedroom and began to undress. Following his cue, she silently stepped out of her skirt and took off her blouse. When they were both naked, he raised his hand to her, bidding her to join him on the small, creaky bed.

"Oh, how I love you so, Misha!" she whispered into his ear as they embraced.

How fortunate he was to be with such a loyal and dutiful woman! Misha looked down at her Eastern features and soon lost himself to a presage of the pleasure he knew she'd soon bring him.

Marina lay on her back and allowed Misha to fondle her small breasts. She performed attentively, ready to help him in whatever he enjoyed most. She followed his lead, obliging him, servicing his lust, periodically repositioning herself so as to indulge his passionate interests. Occasionally she'd reveal a twinge of her own excitement and diffidently caress his neck, chest, or shoulders.

Soon Misha lowered his hand and began to stroke her. He waited anxiously until she was ready to accommodate him, then plunged into her, savoring the ensuing sensation. Both found his accelerated thrusts delightful.

I will always make you happy, Marina, thought Misha. You deserve a wonderful life. He soon exploded into a burst of pleasure, then kissed her lightly on the neck, and rolled over.

Misha awoke the next morning to see Marina holding a tray containing two teacups and a plate of sliced cheese and sausage. "Would you like breakfast?" she asked.

"Oh, Marina, you're so nice! Of course I'd like breakfast! Won't you join me?"

The telephone rang just as she sat down next to him on the bed. Misha leaned forward to answer.

"Yes."

"Hello, little brother. This is Petya. How are you?"

The unexpected sound of his brother's voice unnerved Misha. Usually weekends were days off; Petya seldom called him to do work on days when Misha wouldn't be at the Mosteks factory. "I'm okay. What's the matter?"

"I have an assignment for you. I need you to come to my apartment immediately."

Misha sat up, trying to contain his apprehension. The mere fact that Petya had said "assignment" rather than "favor" meant that the matter was more serious than usual. He glanced at Marina to see if she suspected it was Petya. "Now?"

"I'm sorry, little brother. It's terribly important. It involves the American lawyer who's coming next week to Moscow to work on a joint venture with Mosteks. I don't want to discuss it further on the phone."

Again Misha looked down at Marina. "I'll be there in half an hour." He replaced the receiver and sighed.

"Who was that?" asked Marina.

Her eyes penetrated him with a look of confused concern. She'd lain down on her back, resting her head on his thigh. She was the picture of feminine innocence. Misha touched the smooth skin of her cheek, then looked at the ceiling and said, "I have to go to work. I'll be back as soon as possible." He lifted her head and stood to dress, unable to look at her again.

"But it's Saturday, Misha," said Marina. "What about the market? You promised we could go shopping."

"I'm sorry, Marina. Maybe we can go later this afternoon if I finish in time. I'll try to call you." He grabbed a slice of sausage and quickly walked out the door.

EIGHT

"I would just like to confirm that you do indeed have an inspector by that name," said Ilya Lukov, clutching the telephone tightly. "Could you please verify that a Vladimir Igorovich Yablokov is employed by your agency? He's a thin young man in glasses. He inspected the textile manufacturing cooperative Mosteks one week ago."

"A minute," was the curt reply. Most Russian clerks have no concept of being courteous with the public, Ilya thought grumpily. And why should they? There had never been any incentive for them to be polite. A moment later the abrupt voice returned. "It is confirmed."

Ilya replaced the receiver when he heard the line disconnect and leaned forward in his desk chair to rub his tired eyes. But what did the word of some clerk in an obviously corrupt governmental agency mean? There was no telling who else in the State Inspector's Office was owned by the Gagarintsi; maybe the gruff voice with which he'd just spoken belonged to some corrupt administrator as well.

Ilya looked around his office. It was a mess. He'd been too occupied with the problems the Gagarintsi had brought him to straighten it, and somehow he just couldn't allow his secretary Lyena to clean up for him. He didn't want anyone to have access to his private effects. The office contained too much of his personal history, of his soul.

He looked at the pictures of his wife and daughter on the corner of his desk, then picked up the one of his little girl, Ksenya. Actually she wasn't so little anymore; it had been over seven years since the picture was taken, and she was now almost twenty. Ksenya had been one of the biggest reasons he'd decided to have a go at the burgeoning Soviet private sector. Why should his beautiful, intelligent, well behaved daughter be subject to the brutal lifestyle of the Russian order? She certainly deserved more than a ministerial official could ever give her. It would take an unusually successful entrepreneur to beat the age-old Russian/Soviet system, but if anyone could beat that system, he knew it was himself.

He checked his watch. It was fifteen minutes before his tormentors were due to arrive. Svetov had called Ilya the day before and asked him—no, *advised* him of today's meeting. And despite Svetov's polite language, it was clear there was no refusing the appointment.

A paper sack lay under the desk on the floor by Ilya's feet. It contained the first monthly payment to the mafia. Ilya nudged the bag with his foot and felt its heavy weight. Mosteks would fold in a few months under such a burden; the cooperative couldn't raise its prices enough to absorb the loss. But more importantly, Ilya Lukov could never tolerate criminals controlling Mosteks.

He felt lightheaded, his stomach swirling in anguish at the thought of the upcoming meeting. On several occasions he'd fantasized about getting tough with the *khuligan,* of even taking a knife and cutting his throat, but the chairman knew this was impossible. It was simply not in his character. Lukov was a man of order, of the system. And as much as he wanted to beat that system through Mosteks, he was still a product of the system, whatever its form might be at a given moment. And the system made no allowances for vigilante justice.

Through the window, Ilya saw the Mercedes pull into Mosteks' parking lot. Svetov quickly emerged, his black leather jacket closed tightly against the cold air. The large bodyguard followed him out of the car. Unlike his companion, Svetov did not wear an *ushanka* hat. The handsome leather jacket was definitely inadequate for a Russian winter, but the *mafioznik* probably considered *ushankas* and bulky overcoats "too Russian" for his image.

Svetov had a tall, lanky physique, but his gait was overwhelmingly contemptuous and arrogant. His spine was so straight he almost seemed to be leaning backward. He was *nagliy*, a harsh and imperious individual with no concern for his peers.

Ilya stroked the glass that covered Ksenya's photograph, then replaced the picture on the corner of his desk, facing the far right side of the room. He simply had to position it out of sight of the men who would soon be standing before him.

"Good day, Ilya Konstantinovich," began Svetov, crossing suddenly into Ilya's office. The chairman had directed Lyena to leave her station outside his office and to let the visitors pass directly in.

"Good day," replied Ilya from behind his desk, making an effort to appear busy and at ease. He glanced up at Svetov's companion, who again stood silently by the door.

Svetov asked, "And how are things in the textile business?"

"Very well, thank you." He picked up the paper sack from under his desk and handed it to the wan man.

"Thank you." Svetov took the bag and paused, apparently analyzing Ilya's expression. "In the future, I will rarely come personally to pick up my organization's fees from Mosteks.

Occasionally I may do so…just for a friendly visit." He gave that familiar nauseating smile. "Is that okay, Ilya Konstantinovich?"

Ilya managed to nod silently, wondering if Svetov knew about the joint venture with IIS. Of course not. How could he possibly know? He looked down at an opened notebook on his desk.

From the corner of his eye, Ilya saw Svetov again analyzing Ilya's facial reaction. It soon became clear that the mafioznik was not satisfied with the chairman's non-verbal acquiescence. "You know, Ilya Konstantinovich, we do not have to cooperate on such strained terms. Soon you will come to realize that I am providing you with a necessary service." He extended his hands, palms up, and smiled again.

"Necessary to whom?" asked Ilya firmly, then immediately regretted the question. He had earlier decided against even a hint of confrontation with the *khuligan*. Besides, it delayed Svetov's departure.

"Ah, Ilya Konstantinovich. Why must you make your life so difficult? Don't you, among all other people, realize how business works in Russia?"

Ilya felt the ill-advised words flow from his mouth almost reflexively: "I know that with *khuligani* like you, Russia stands no chance of surviving the mess it's now in. Your breed is the worst kind of scoundrel, Svetov. You victimize your own people as an entire nationality."

Svetov placed the paper sack in an empty chair and began to slowly pace around the office. He stopped and breathed deeply, looking up at the bookcase. "You know, Ilya Konstantinovich, sometimes I think people like me are mistreated by society. Unjustly condemned, understand?"

Ilya felt a familiar chill descend his back as he watched the man take liberties with his office. Svetov removed a plaque from the bookcase, examined it briefly, then replaced it upside-down. He resumed his haughty pacing, and Ilya braced himself for what would follow.

Svetov stopped pacing and looked across the desk into the chairman's eyes. "Take my friend Roma here, for example." He pointed over his shoulder at his silent accomplice, who stood like a statue by the door, never removing his cold stare from Ilya. "Last month, Roma was accused by the police of raping the wife of a cooperative chairman, just like yourself." Svetov paused, then turned and began pacing again. "Raping her! Can you believe that? Of course it was all a terrible misunderstanding. The poor victim, beaten as she was, cleared everything up. After considering the matter, she told the police that she had not been attacked after all, and that she really didn't remember what had happened."

Ilya glanced at Ksenya, then quickly returned his attention to Svetov.

"And of course you've heard of Vsevolod Ulanov, the kooperator who was successful with his recipe for...what was it called, Roma? Ah yes, Bird's Milk pastries, yes. It was terribly unfortunate that he misidentified a close friend of mine as the man who had broken his legs, putting him in the hospital for two months. Of course the matter was resolved when Ulanov retracted his statement to the police."

Suddenly, Svetov dashed around the desk toward Ilya and leaned down forcefully, his face only a few inches from the chairman's. Ilya trapped a yelp in his throat and forced himself to look back up at Svetov. He tried not to focus on his tormentor's eyes—to do so might unnerve him. Instead, he concentrated on a mole in the *mafioznik's* eyebrow. Nonetheless, Ilya felt a bead of perspiration break and flow down his temple.

"What do you think, Ilya Konstantinovich? Don't you agree that we are poorly treated by our countrymen, given the invaluable services we provide them? Don't you agree that we should be given more respect?"

"I have paid you in accordance with our agreement," said Ilya. "There is nothing else that you have asked me—"

"Roma says you have quite a beautiful daughter, Ilya Konstantinovich," interrupted Svetov. "I see that it's true. Is that Ksenya, Ilya Konstantinovich?" He reached over the desk and brought the photograph to his face. "Roma said he might like to meet her some day. It would be convenient; she lives not far from him, on Varshavskaya Street. Right?" He shoved the picture at Ilya.

Ilya silently took the photograph and turned it face down on his desk. A breath escaped from him in an audible wheeze.

Svetov turned his threatening gaze into Ilya's eyes. "Oh, don't worry, Ilya Konstantinovich. We Gagarintsi have a policy of never dating our clients. As long as they are clients, of course." He broke the gaze long enough to share a chuckle with his companion, then looked back at the chairman.

"We will cooperate with you on friendly terms," said Ilya shakily before allowing himself to break Svetov's renewed stare. "Hopefully our relationship will...continue to be mutually beneficial."

"Good, Ilya Konstantinovich. So it will not be necessary for me to point out that we are prepared to take whatever action necessary, against whatever individuals necessary, to preserve our agreement. Is that correct?"

"That is correct."

"Against any individuals, Ilya Konstantinovich, including Americans. Understand?"

Ilya nodded.

"Good. Very good. I hope you have a good week, Ilya Konstantinovich. A good month." Svetov smiled and patted Ilya on the shoulder. "I'm glad to see we're off to such a good start." He then nodded at his mute companion, and the two disappeared through the doorway.

Misha could tell something was wrong. It wasn't just the rarity of having been invited to go to lunch with the cooperative's chairman at the Firefly restaurant; Ilya had brought him along on several occasions in the past. But this time Lyena, the secretary, was along as well. This time it was in the middle of a crisis with the factory's equipment, when the chief engineer was most needed by the workers. And this time Ilya Konstantinovich's huge forehead was furrowed in deep, wrinkled lines. But Misha had a feeling he knew exactly what was on the boss's mind.

It was clear that Lyena was confused as well. Misha couldn't remember ever seeing a staff worker invited to Firefly, especially a woman. She sat silently as the two men conversed about everything from Yeltsin's reforms to the weather. About everything, it seemed, except Mosteks.

After they'd finished their meal, Ilya fell silent. Misha waited in anticipation, knowing the purpose of the lunch would soon come to light. He hated seeing his boss so distressed; it had been Ilya who'd personally hired him out of a large pool of graduates of the Baumanskiy Engineering Institute several years earlier, then promoted him to chief engineer when the former one retired. And Ilya had been very good to Misha ever since.

Ilya looked down at his hands on the table. "I haven't told you two this," he started, "but we were approached by racketeers last week." He looked up at his employees with an almost guilty look. "They demanded five percent of Mosteks' gross monthly earnings in exchange for protection from other mafia clans and a guarantee that the State Inspector's Office would not shut us down."

Misha looked at his boss with a forced expression of surprise, while Lyena toyed with what remained of her ice cream. Both were silent. Ilya explained the details without looking at his audience.

When the chairman had finished, Misha glanced at Lyena and could see that Ilya Konstantinovich's painful revelation had upset her. He didn't know the secretary well, but he assumed she held the same high regard for Ilya Konstantinovich that he did. The chairman was good to all of his employees—his personal secretary probably enjoyed as good a treatment as anyone. Misha could see that Lyena wanted to comfort the chairman, to somehow repay him for all he'd done for her, but it was obvious that she was powerless to do so. It made Misha's belly tighten with guilt.

Misha raised his brow and said, "Well, Ilya Konstantinovich, it's no secret that most successful private enterprises have experienced harassment by the mafia. What do the others do?"

"That is the reason for my calling you here today. I am actually confident we will be able to defend ourselves efficiently, Misha. However, what I am about to tell you is to remain completely secret, understand?"

The two nodded silently.

"Last week I decided to submit to the demands of the mafia, at least for the time being. It is the only means by which Mosteks can possibly stay afloat." He ruefully cast his eyes downward and sighed. "Please be assured this is just a temporary measure," he added.

Ilya summoned his two employees to lean closer toward him, then lowered his voice. "Mosteks is in the final phases of negotiating a joint venture with an American company. We hope to get the JV registered shortly. This has been kept secret from everyone except the Mosteks directorate until now for business reasons. You see, we believe that an American investment of Western-made equipment will make us the leading private textile manufacturer in the Russian Federation." He paused again, then leaned farther forward. "But we also believe that law enforcement authorities will undertake to keep a closer eye on us as a hard-currency-producing JV enterprise."

Misha glanced at Lyena, who was still silent. He sought comfort in her face, some expression or communication which would somehow lighten his own predicament. But nothing was there.

"The reason being," continued Ilya, interrupting Misha's thoughts, "that a cooperative is merely a legal entity. A joint venture, however, is a creature of legislation. There is every reason to believe the authorities will take decisive action against threats to a JV. Especially one that involves an American company, because the new government won't want to risk bad international press.

"But in order for the joint venture to help us, it must be registered immediately. The strain that the mafia has imposed on Mosteks cannot be tolerated for long. I think we can have our documents prepared and ready for submission to the Ministry of Finance by the end of the month. In order to expedite registration, I have decided to be very flexible in ceding business points to the Americans during our upcoming negotiations."

Misha again looked at Lyena, who clearly had never been privy to such talk from her boss. He wondered what it meant to her as a female to be hearing this. The secretary was an intelligent woman, far smarter than most, and unusually well spoken. She was pretty—the fruits of her well salaried position at Mosteks were manifested in her nice clothing and Western cosmetics. Misha had always noticed her and found her attractive. Unlike Marina, she was full-figured. Still, somehow she wasn't exactly his type. She was too...independent.

"So we'll either emerge with extreme success, or be completely destroyed," concluded Ilya, raising his palms in an attempt at humor.

"What happens next?" asked Misha before looking down at his empty plate.

"IIS, our joint venture partner, has arranged to send one of its lawyers to Moscow to finalize the JV agreement. His name is Sam Morris. He was due to arrive last Monday, but because of our unexpected troubles, I was forced to reschedule his trip. The last-minute cancellation must have been inconvenient for the American, but we obviously couldn't have him here when our facility may have been shut down. We changed his arrival date to tomorrow."

It suddenly occurred to Misha why he'd been summoned to the meeting as he watched the chairman turn his full attention toward him.

"Misha, I want you to take personal charge of the American's stay in Moscow," said Ilya. "Lyena will assist you. I have chosen you two because you both speak English and are approximately the American's age. You are sufficiently familiar with Mosteks to discuss business with the American when formal meetings are not in session. We are going to provide him with the finest available hotel accommodations. Lyena, you will see to restaurant reservations and other entertainment. It is essential that the American be as comfortable as possible during his week in Moscow. I'm sorry I couldn't give you more advance warning, but I'm sure you can understand the need to minimize the risk of information falling into the wrong hands."

"I understand," replied Misha.

"Mosteks will pay for all expenses," added Ilya. "You should keep track of what you spend, so that you can be reimbursed."

"Should I reserve a Chaika limousine?" asked Lyena. It was the first thing she'd said in over an hour.

Ilya hesitated before answering. "No. I don't think so, Lyena. Chaikas attract a lot of attention. We want him to have a good time, but we should be low-key about it under the circumstances. You have a car, right, Misha?"

"Yes."

"Then you should chauffeur as well. I'll give you his flight and hotel information this afternoon. Let me know if there are any problems. And let me underscore one thing. It is absolutely essential that this entire matter be kept top-secret. No one, including other Mosteks employees, is to learn about these discussions. We don't want the mafia to find out about our plan until the last possible minute. Otherwise they'll understand what we are up to and may try to prevent the joint venture's registration. I have reason to believe that the criminals are aware that an American is coming to visit us, but hopefully they haven't yet learned of our intentions. Is this clear?"

Misha nodded, still looking at the plate in front of him.

"Good. Shall we get back to work, then?" Ilya slid back his chair and stood. The others did likewise.

Lyena excused herself to go to the ladies' room, and the two men went to the coat check. Misha was buttoning his coat when the chairman approached him and placed an affectionate hand on his shoulder.

He still couldn't look at his boss.

"Misha," whispered Ilya. "Uh, when I said I wanted you to show the American a good time, I, uh, meant it." He winked. "Drink some *vodochka* with the Yank. Show him we Russians know how to live it up. I've reviewed his passport and the visa support information that we get in order to issue a foreign business invitation. He's single." Ilya winked again.

Misha smiled genuinely and looked his boss in the eyes. "You've come to the right man, Ilya Konstantinovich."

"You see, Misha, I'm used to dealing with middle-aged businessmen. Sam Morris is your age. He's probably not interested in spending six evenings at the Opera and Moscow Philharmonic. I think we are more likely to get better results during our business meetings with a foreigner who is enjoying himself here. It's a basic principle of international business. Understand?"

"I understand," said Misha. Again, he found himself smiling.

NINE

"Do you have everything together?" asked Stacy from the living room of Sam's apartment. She was watching television while he packed for his trip to Moscow.

"I reckon," answered Sam from the bedroom, arranging socks in a suitcase on the bed. "I've got the warmest clothes in my extensive wardrobe in this bag."

Stacy appeared in the bedroom doorway. "All right, Morris. Time for inspection!" She looked at the mound of shirts, socks, underwear, and ties that lay heaped in the suitcase. "You can't be serious," she said incredulously. "You're not going to smush all those clothes together for a nine-hour flight, and then wear them seven days, are you?" She slapped her sides and gave a mock sigh, then walked to the bed and dumped out the suitcase.

"Hey!"

"You obviously don't know the first thing about packing, Morris."

"What's the matter? It looked pretty good to me," said Sam, throwing clothes back into the suitcase. "Socks don't wrinkle."

Stacy put her hands on her hips and watched him for a moment, then said, "Morris, if you don't let me pack that thing right, then..." She lowered her voice. "Then I'm just going to have to hurt you."

Sam stopped and returned Stacy's smile. "Promise?"

She pushed him aside, then bent over the bed and began packing the clothes. Sam was astounded; she seemed to be picking up, folding, and arranging each item in the suitcase, all in one motion.

"I don't know how men can live without women to take care of them. I can't believe the way you were going to travel! And you don't even care that—"

"All right Stacy. You're right. I don't know how I'd make it without you. 'Preciate it." He stifled a laugh, still marveling at her packing skills. "But no one sees a wrinkled undershirt."

"And what is this? Five pairs of underwear? Morris! Can't you count? You're going for seven days. How can you be so meticulous about your job and such a slob at home? And don't you ever pair your socks?"

When Stacy bent over the bed to resume packing, Sam tiptoed toward her, leaned over her from behind, and pulled her on top of the open suitcase with him.

"How do you know if—Sam! What are you doing?"

He lifted her sweatshirt.

"Come on, Sam. We don't have time for this. Really. You have...to finish...packing."

She dropped a handful of socks, closed her eyes, and leaned forward to meet his lips. A moment later, Sam lowered his head to kiss her neck, waiting eagerly for her now-familiar first deep breath. When it came, he pushed the half-full suitcase onto the floor, then lifted Stacy completely onto the bed.

"What time is Eric supposed to pick you up?" she asked breathlessly.

*   *   *   *   *

"Just a second, Eric. He'll be right down," said Stacy into the intercom. She walked back into the bedroom, pulling on her sweatshirt. "Are you dressed, Sam? He's waiting down on the sidewalk."

"Relax. He'll wait." Sam carried his luggage from the bedroom to the front door, then grabbed his micro-cassette recorder from the table and stuffed it into the breast pocket of his suit jacket.

"Sam, wait a minute," said Stacy, shaking her head. "Uh-uh. If you carry that thing with you, the Russians are going to think you're a spy. Here." She reached into his pocket and took out the tape recorder. "Give it to me. It'll be a good first step."

"What?"

"It's mine now."

"No, Stacy, I need it. I might have to record ideas for later on."

"Sam, don't be ridiculous." She stepped backward to prevent him from grabbing the recorder from her. "I'm not letting you out of this apartment with it. You can forget it."

Sam stopped when he saw that she was serious. "What's the big deal?"

"It's for your own good, Sam. I have to do something to keep you from driving yourself nuts! Eventually you'll go off the deep end if you stay so uptight about your work. I'm sure you'll have no problems getting along without a friggin' tape recorder in Russia. It'll be right here when you get back, okay?"

"Is this our first fight?" asked Sam, smiling.

"No. I'm saving our maiden tiff for when you've mellowed out." She looked up at him a moment, then put her arms around his neck and kissed him.

"But what if some revolutionary idea about the textile business occurs to me while I'm waiting in line for toilet paper in Moscow?" he asked between pecks on Stacy's puckered lips.

"You don't need to bring home any ideas except ones about me," she whispered, kissing him again. "And hopefully you'll remember those without any tape recorder."

Was she the one? he wondered, pulling Stacy toward him for a goodbye hug. She was a terrific woman. Pretty, smart, energetic, the works. Although, he supposed, he wished she were a little more mysterious. A little more unpredictable and adventurous. True, she'd been an unexpectedly fantastic lover. The sex had been amazing! But that had been the last surprise he could remember from Stacy in the three months they'd been dating. He wondered if he'd get tired of her with time and eventually crave other stimulation.

He stroked her hair for a second, then backed away, looking into her lively brown eyes. But everybody feels that way with women, don't they? Why should he be any different?

But then again, wasn't it rather early to even be having such concerns?

He'd have to think this over. Maybe it was good he was going away now. He kissed her once more and said, "See you soon, Stacy."

"Oh, am I nervous. Airplanes are so dangerous. I hope you don't crash or run into terrorists, Sammy. Did you hear about that crash in Iowa last week? Now, I want you to call me as soon as you get to Moscow, Sammy. I'll be waiting by the phone. I've made some peanut butter sandwiches for you in case you get hungry on the trip. Now, promise me, Sammy. Promise me you'll eat well in Russia. You're so skinny, we'll soon have to put rocks in your pockets to keep you from blowing away." Eric's voice was pitched to sound like an old lady's as he accompanied Sam through the airport terminal.

Sam smiled and rolled his eyes at Eric, who was effortlessly carrying Sam's suitcase on his massive shoulder. "Where's my shovel?" he said.

"And I want you to give cousin Yeltsy a great big hug for me," continued Eric. "If you see Uncle Gorby, give him one, too.

Now, give Grandma a kiss…" He made a smooching sound near Sam's face.

"I'd hate to have to embarrass you in front of everyone in this airport."

Sam's gate was located in a special facility at JFK Airport that Delta Airlines used for its flights to Moscow. Delta had a joint venture with Aeroflot, the Russian airline. Sam had read about it while preparing for his trip.

He'd anticipated an uncrowded flight, mostly tourists and perhaps a few Babushkas going back home. The terminal was packed, however, mostly with Russians, all noisily contending for a place in line to the registration counter. "I guess there is money to be made in doing business with the Russkies," he said to Eric, noting Delta's apparent success.

"So you have no excuses, country boy. Now, go out and make us some." Eric quickly looked around him. "It doesn't look like your trip's going to be much fun, though. I haven't seen a decent-looking Russian chick yet. But don't worry," he added. "If there's one babe in all of Russia, Sam Morris will find her. And not even know it."

Most of the Russian passengers stood next to carts stacked high with electronic products. Computers, printers, fax machines, stereo components, all sorts of things Sam had heard were in short supply in Russia. The registration area almost looked like a Sony warehouse.

The two got in line behind a family of Russians proudly attired in their new Western clothing. As Sam and Eric got closer to the counter, they heard squabbles disrupting between Russians attempting to check bulky boxes and airline officials enforcing weight and size limitations.

"Give the lady your ticket, country boy," said Eric.

"Non-smoking, aisle, please," said Sam.

The agent punched into her computer, barely acknowledging Sam's presence. "No available," she said in a monotonic Russian accent. She glared at Sam over the counter, then thrust a board-ing pass at him.

"This is best available in non-smoking," she announced sternly. There was no further discussion about it. Sam glanced at Eric, then shook his head and walked off. Clearly the concept of good customer service hadn't yet made it to the Russian airline industry.

"Well, I guess this is it, dude," said Eric when the two had reached the gate. "Have a good time. Do a shot of Stoly for your friend back in the office. Don't forget to write." He shook hands with Sam before turning to leave the airport.

"'Preciate it, Eric. See you soon, bud."

Sam groaned in his seat. Someone was shaking him. "Deener?"

"Sir, deener?"

He'd apparently dosed off soon after take-off. He struggled to bring the Russian flight attendant into view and soon saw a chunky blonde holding a tray covered by aluminum foil. Her stolid demeanor struck Sam; the offer of dinner sounded more like an accusation.

"Uh, sure," he managed. He pulled down the tray table, although he hardly looked forward to airplane food.

An elderly man sitting next to him was already devouring his dinner. The meal included something vaguely resembling baked chicken resting on a bed of fluorescent orange carrots. "Is it good?" asked Sam doubtfully, wondering if the old timer spoke English. A conversation might ease the hardship of the nine-hour flight.

"Quite good," said the old man in a heavy Russian accent. He spoke without a break in his chewing.

"I just can't get into this stuff," said Sam, surveying his tray disdainfully.

"I understand," said the Russian, glancing at Sam. He took a napkin and wiped his fingers clean as he savored his last mouthful of chicken. "But for me is good."

"Really?"

"My friend, I cannot bring myself to complain about food. You see, there have been twice in my life when I and my loved ones starve. I nearly was killed trying to bring food into Leningrad during siege of world war. I remember once having feeling of joy when I caught rat to eat." He laughed wryly. "No, my friend. To me, all food is tasty."

"Oh." Sam was embarrassed. He remained silent for a moment, searching for something innocuous to say. "Did you enjoy your stay in the States?" He tried the chicken.

"Very much so. I am grateful for opportunity to visit America. A great country. Many beautiful sights. I one month visit my daughter in Brooklyn." The old man smiled heartily.

"That's great. How does she like New York?"

"I think she is happier there than she was in Saint Petersburg. There are problems for her, of course. Is difficult for her and husband to get good work. They not used to American life. But at least there is enough food and big apartment."

"Did you get a chance to do any shopping?"

"Oh, yes, yes. I bought some very interesting souvenirs."

"Electronics, right?"

"Electronics? No," replied the Russian, shaking his head. "Electronics not souvenirs, they business. My son buy walkmans and VCR. But that only for business." He took a bite of cupcake.

"What do you mean?" asked Sam, examining his roll.

"This is your first trip to Russia, my friend?" inquired the man, smiling.

"Yes," said Sam. He was embarrassed again, feeling novice.

"Many of Russians you saw in airport with electronics buy them for self. Such things not available in our country. At least not easily available with such good quality. But because there no good electronics in Russia, is also possible to sell them for very high price on black market there. For example, VCR which cost two hundred dollars in States might taking three hundred thousand rubles in Russia. Is very good business.

"Sometimes is even possible to find buyers willing to pay hard currency, or what we call *valuta,* for such products. There may be someone ready to pay thousand dollars for that VCR in Saint Petersburg. This, of course, is best business.

"Such is the thinking in our country now, my friend. Everything is business, business, business."

Sam thought Russia sounded like the market in Jerusalem, which he'd visited a few years earlier. Nothing but bustling "businessmen" all over the place, trying to make a sale. "But how do you get the hard currency to buy the electronics in the first place?" he asked curiously over a bite of carrots.

"Many Russian visitors having relatives in America who helping them to buy this equipment. They realize that a few such things can make life much easier for Russian citizen. But many Russians have acquired *valuta* through previous business themselves."

"I was really amazed. Just about everyone on this flight had a cart full of electronics."

"It is big reason to come to West, my friend. Getting invitation, visa, air ticket all very difficult right now in Russia. Trip to United States very dear. I am fortunate to have succeeded."

"I'm glad you had a good trip."

The old man paused. "Is ironic, you know? All along we Russians wanting ability to travel to West. It was like dream. We prayed for better leaders, better government. Finally Comrade Gorbachev is general secretary and we having permission to see West. But Comrade Gorbachev also bringing such bad times, such economic crisis, that we have too many other problems to enjoy our new freedom. *Glasnost* and *perestroika* bring Russia closer to rest of world, but I think Russian people not yet ready for this. Freedom not enough. They wanting what rest of world have, but they not knowing how to work to get it. Russian people have not yet learned to associate work with reward. You will see this when you are in Moscow."

Sounds like a wonderful place to bring Old Virginia Mills, thought Sam. Old V had failed with good workers in the States. "So the situation is pretty bad now?" He took a mouthful of chicken.

"Worse than you can imagine, my friend. Shortages of everything. Not that we haven't suffered bad times before. We have. But difference is that now we have had glimpse of real world. New regime allowing us to express our discontent and do something about it. And I think we will do something, something terrible, unless Yeltsin does soon.

"And so. What brings you to Russia, my friend?"

"It's a business trip. I'm going to negotiate a joint venture with a cooperative in Moscow." I hope, Sam added to himself.

"I see," he said slowly, nodding his head.

"Are you familiar with cooperatives?"

"Of course. They are first free enterprise in my country. Best products and services in Russia coming from private business."

"Really?" Finally some good news. Sam reached for his dessert and set it in front of him.

"Of course. They were beginning of new market system." He leaned closer to Sam and lowered his voice. "And I think they are final proof that capitalism is really best system. But private enterprise not enjoying good reputation with Russian people, my friend," continued the old man, shaking his head to emphasize the point. "They often too greedy. Many of them corrupt. I recommend you to be careful in your business."

"What do you mean?"

"Many *kooperatori* think they have right to be wealthy at expense of rest of Russian people. They buying up food and other materials and holding them long enough for prices to go up. Then resell for profit. They running stores and restaurants only for foreigners in order to get *valuta*. And many businesses paying bribes to our government and foreign companies to get advantages. Some involved with mafia. You must to be very careful with them." He raised his forefinger.

Careful, thought Sam. One always had to be careful—there was too much that could always go wrong. He pictured his grandfather. But how careful had Hyman been when coming over to America without a penny in his pocket and opening his own company? He must have just gone for it, right? Made it work. No guts, no glory. But then again, Sam realized, Hyman Morris really didn't have anything to lose, either.

Sam awoke to the thud of the 747's controlled collision with the runway. To his fatigued surprise, the passengers spontaneously began applauding and cheering. He looked out the window and saw an embankment of snow at least eight feet high on the side of the runway. We must've sidetracked into Siberia! he thought. The flight had exhausted him. He rubbed his eyes and yawned, trying to regain his coherence.

As he and the other passengers filed out of the cabin, Sam detected the harsh smell of Russian tobacco that permeated Sheremetyevo Airport. It lingered throughout the passport control area and, he would soon realize, throughout most of Moscow.

Sheremetyevo was a vast warehouse-like structure with rather low ceilings covered by netted swirls of copper tubing. It was darker and quieter than any airport Sam had seen before. There was no sense of voyage excitement among the mostly Russian travelers; no feeling of impending or recently visited adventure. There were only a few advertisements on the distant walls, which added to the building's storage-depot effect, and few services typically found in large airports.

Sam approached a soldier in a small booth who examined his passport and visa. He was momentarily alarmed when the official, who couldn't have been more than eighteen, scrutinized his photograph, carefully comparing it with Sam's face. He was relieved when the soldier stamped and passed his documents back to him under the glass.

Sam made his way through customs, then pushed his luggage cart through the doors leading into the airport's main chamber. A sign with my name, a sign with my name, he thought, recalling Benjamin Kaplan's instructions. A Mosteks rep was supposed to meet him. Wait a minute. Will the sign be in English?

"Tocksi? Tocksi? Tocksi?" called a hundred frantic cab drivers. He shook his head at them, ignoring their importunate gestures.

Sam continued his search for the sign, heading toward a less crowded area in the main terminal. No one seemed to be happy in Sheremetyevo, he thought. He saw an older man screaming unintelligibly with three stone-faced men in uniform surrounded by unaffected passersby. A frail old lady was struggling with an overloaded cart, ignoring protests from people she ran into. People looked angry, lost, confused, sad, uncertain—there were at least a dozen unpleasant descriptions that would accurately describe the airport's denizens. Was this a presage of what he would experience during his week in Moscow?

Finally he saw it. A tall, rather thin man about Sam's age with dark curly hair, holding a sign reading *Sam Morris, Inter-American Industrial Services*. It was a sight from heaven. Sam sighed in relief and impetuously left his baggage cart to head toward his contact, hoping that the man spoke English.

"Hello, Sam. Welcome to Moscow," said the Russian with a pleasant smile, alleviating Sam's language concerns. The man didn't fit the stereotype of the burly, big-faced Russian in a fur coat. Rather, he looked almost Mediterranean and was wearing an Adidas pullover. His features didn't portray the oppressed Russian soul Sam had expected to see in everyone he met in Moscow. In fact, this first Russian acquaintance actually looked and sounded quite friendly.

"Hi!" he responded gleefully. "Boy, am I glad to see you! I was wondering what I'd do if no one was here to meet me!"

"My name is Misha, and this is Lyena. We are from Mosteks." The two Russians were casually dressed, both wearing blue jeans, in contrast to Sam's pin stripe suit.

He looked at the woman and had to suppress his reaction to her radiance. Not beautiful—but damn, she didn't have to be. Her sharply descending eyebrows gave her a confident look of experienced maturity, an understanding of life beyond her twenty-two or so years. Full red lips, even fuller than Stacy's. Unfortunately, she was wearing a bulky overcoat, which precluded further investigation. "It's nice to meet you." He shook hands with Misha, then turned to Lyena and smiled. She didn't seem to expect the attention and smiled silently in return. "Uh, I left my bags over there."

When the three exited the building and headed toward the passenger loading area, Sam got his first taste of the biting Russian winter. Countless needles speared his skin, causing him to reflexively lower his head, the freezing air momentarily blinding him. Russia gave new meaning to the word *cold*. "Woo!" he uttered as he plodded forward, his hands crossed in front of his bent body.

Sam then caught his first whiff of Russian automobile exhaust, a stench far more disagreeable than what he was used to, even in New York City. The combination of the two unpleasant sensations made him consider running back into the airport, but he willed himself to follow the Russians, holding his breath until they'd reached open air.

Misha pushed the luggage cart up to a small white sedan, though the car was so filthy Sam could barely discern its true color. Misha quickly loaded Sam's things into the trunk, then opened the back door for—what was her name?—Lyena. The two men then climbed in the front.

"So how you feeling, Sam?" asked Misha, turning on the car's heater. Like Ilya, Misha pronounced it *Sem*.

"Pretty tired. It was a tough flight. What time is it here, any-way?" He warmed his hands to the heat vents and prepared for his first sights of Moscow.

"Here is three-thirty in afternoon. For you is seven-thirty in morning," said Misha, smiling as he pulled out of the airport. "But is important for you to stay up today in order to get used to new time."

"I hope I can stay up," replied Sam, jokingly. He noticed a collection of cassette tapes in the open glove compartment. Pink Floyd, The Stones, Rod Stewart, Bad Company—the Russian had a taste for classic rock. Sam was glad Misha was his age.

"You will live at Hotel Novgorod, Sam," said Misha. "It is not very best hotel in Moscow, but is located near center. You will like it there. Is nice place."

"Super. I could use a comfortable hotel after that flight."

"Unfortunately, there is shortage of good hotel space in Moscow now. We were lucky to get room for you there. We had hoped to accommodate you even in five-star hotel, but Novgorod was all that is available."

"Oh, no problem," said Sam, smiling. He thought Misha kind for being concerned. "All I need is a room with a bed and a hot shower." He turned his head toward the woman in the back seat. "Do you speak English?"

"Yes," she replied meekly.

Sam watched her remove her gloves, then begin to unbutton her coat to the warming air. "What do you do at Mosteks?" he asked, waiting to check out her figure. From what he'd read and heard, Sam had expected Russian women to be built like gorillas.

"I am secretary for…for Mr. Lukov," she said softly. "Misha is chief engineer."

Sam quickly turned around after he'd caught an energizing glimpse of her ample curves. "I see."

"Lyena and I taking care of you during your stay in Moscow," added Misha. "Your official guides and translators."

"I'm looking forward to it."

As they entered Moscow's city limits, Sam saw several dilapidated billboards on a few buildings, apparently displaying slogans promoting the old communist regime. "What does that say?" he asked, pointing to the inside out and backward cyrillic writing.

"Glory to Communist Party of Soviet Union," answered Misha, simpering. "But nobody reading those signs, Sam. We never reading them even when they were all over city. Not many such signs left anymore, thanks to God. They are bullshit."

Sam laughed, wondering if Misha would have said the same thing ten years ago to someone he'd just met. Probably, he decided. He already knew he'd get along well with the Russian.

As they traveled along the major thoroughfares, Sam noted the sharp contrast between the enormous monolithic highrises on Moscow's outskirts and the ornate buff-colored buildings in the old part of town. The former looked like the battered public housing works outside New York City, though much more shoddily constructed. They were painted in grotesque blue red and green colors. The buildings in the center of town were poorly maintained as well, but they portrayed architectural taste with their ornate arches and baroque doorways. The worst problem he saw with the downtown buildings was that too many of them were of the same mustard color. Statues and monuments were abundant, providing a sense of history and culture to the otherwise bleak city.

Sam had expected to see little advertising in the city, few trade emblems and logos associated with stores and restaurants. But he didn't realize how much their absence would detract from a city's spirit. The bare buildings and roadsides left Moscow with few contrasting designs and colors.

Only the nondescript automobiles added assorted color to the city. Against the drab urban setting, Moscow's cars almost looked like rides in an arcade. They were all small sedans, mostly Soviet models Sam had never seen before. Enormous yellow buses that bent in the middle to accommodate turns stopped intermittently along dirty roadsides to pick up and discharge passengers. Trolley buses, the first he'd ever seen, moved along tracks in the center of streets, powered by electricity from wires which netted the sky above intersections. All vehicles seemed to be filthy; he wondered if the Russians had gotten around to discovering carwashes yet.

And then there were the people, plodding along sidewalks, drudging relentlessly through the grey snow. They wore mismatched plaids, favoring bright colors. Round elderly women with colorful kerchiefs on their heads, oblivious or impervious to the cold, carried bags over their hunched shoulders. Men wearing fur *ushanka* hats queued up outside stores. Sam noted that they all bore the same expression as the Russians he'd seen in the airports, a look of determination and tenacity, a look of survival.

Did they know their once-mighty Soviet Union had disintegrated? That while still the source of much of the six o'clock news, their country had changed from Eastern menace to a land of desperation? As the people went about their routines, they seemed unaware, or at least unaffected, by the fact that the mighty bear was starving.

The car pulled up to Hotel Novgorod, and Misha unloaded the trunk. The three then went inside to check in at the registration desk. A rush of odors met Sam's nose as they entered: a chemical stench, probably from some form of cleaning compound; the now familiar Russian tobacco; and the body odor of the clustered hotel patrons. Again, he forced himself to ignore it.

The scene in the hotel's lobby was similar to the one he'd encountered at the airport. Frenetic confusion. People trying to get things. Dissatisfaction and complaining. The lobby was large and dark; again there was no sense of adventure to being there. The cracked green paint on the walls looked more like Sam's public grammar school than a place trying to attract guests and make them comfortable. There were no advertisements offering services or boasting of delights the hotel offered.

But unlike Sheremetyevo, there were very few Russians in the hotel. In fact, there seemed to be none who weren't hotel employees. Hotel Novgorod was apparently for foreigners only—the guests were apparently foreign businessmen. Not American, but definitely businessmen; Asian, Indian, European, and a few Sam couldn't classify. They were all clad in suits and carrying briefcases. There were very few women.

At the wooden registration desk, Misha spoke briefly with an expressionless clerk, then turned to Sam. "Please give me your passport and visa, Sam."

"What?"

"I must give to hotel for registration. You getting them back in few days."

"Wait a minute, Misha," said Sam over a nervous laugh. "I'd rather not be without my passport—I usually keep my travel documents with me when I'm overseas. What do they need it for?"

"Is normal procedure. They must stamp your visa to confirm that you staying in hotel."

"But suppose I get in some kind of trouble and can't prove who I am?"

"Don't worry, Sam. We taking care of you." Misha put his arm around Sam's shoulders affectionately and pulled the American close to him. "Anyway, you getting hotel registration card for identification. This is procedure in Russia." Misha extended his free hand to receive the documents.

Sam was struck by Misha's affection. The arm around his back and the nearness of Misha's face to his own were new to him; he'd rarely had a male friend, let alone a new acquaintance, make such gestures. Sam reluctantly complied with Misha's request and gave him his documents.

"Is okay," said Misha, smiling reassuringly. "We are your partners and friends. We taking good care of you."

They left the desk and headed toward the main entrance of the hotel, where an elderly uniformed doorman was standing guard, checking the guests' registration cards before allowing passage. Misha approached the doorman and began explaining something to him in Russian. Sam could tell that Misha's efforts, whatever they were, were unsuccessful by the way the doorman kept shaking his head defiantly.

Misha said, "Sam, I am sorry. They not permit Lyena and me to escort you to your room. One must show hotel card to doorman to pass. So I am afraid we must part now."

"Really? Why won't they let you in?"

"Russian citizens still not allowed in international hotel," replied Misha, rolling his eyes.

"Okay, I guess. No problem," replied Sam, confused. "So what's the plan for later on?"

"Here is few hundred thousand rubles in case you must to buy something. You should not need more. Mosteks paying for all your expenses in Moscow."

"'Preciate it, Misha." He looked at the large colorful notes before stuffing them in his pocket.

"Now you will unpack and rest. We have reservation for dinner at eight o'clock. I picking you up at seven-thirty on lobby. Good?"

"See you at seven-thirty. Lyena, it was nice to meet you. I'll see you later," said Sam with more than a diplomatic smile. He was wondering why Lyena had been so silent—she didn't seem to be introverted by nature. She carried herself too confidently, too perceptively. She was too keen an individual to be one of those shy types. There was something interesting about her, something exciting and terribly sexy. He could just feel it.

He watched his hosts leave the hotel, then stepped into the lift with his suitcase, briefcase, and travel bag. He felt numb. First I'll get out of this monkey suit, he thought. Then a nice hot shower and a nap.

When he reached his floor, Sam walked down the long corridor, dragging his luggage behind him, until he found his room. He opened the door and switched on the light.

"You gotta be kidding!" he said aloud.

The bed was no more than three feet wide and held a rubber mattress barely two inches thick. He dropped his bags and quickly walked into the bathroom. When he turned on the light, a dozen cockroaches scampered to cover.

"I can't believe this!" he muttered, shaking his head.

The rusty tub contained a plastic hand-held shower nozzle on a hose that extended maybe two feet. There was no shower curtain. The plastic toilet, with its pull string flusher, was equally primitive.

Sam wearily returned to the bedroom, stripped, and carefully collapsed onto the narrow bed.

"Where's your sense of humor, Morris?" he asked aloud. "Besides, you used to love to go camping." He smiled as he closed his eyes.

TEN

Mikhail Olegovich Grunshteyn looked at the red plastic telephone that sat on an end table near the couch. Touchtone hadn't yet made it to Russia, and Misha knew that the cheap Soviet-made phones looked like children's toys by Western standards. He'd have to replace it soon with an import. He usually waited until late at night to call Petya, when Marina was safely asleep in the bedroom, but fortunately she had gone to Mama's for dinner. He glanced at the clock in the wooden wall unit. 6:00 P.M. Tonight he had to meet the American for dinner and might not be back until too late to call his brother. Misha reached for the receiver, grasped it slowly, but then left it in its cradle.

He stood up from the couch and began to pace around the apartment. It was nothing like Petya's palace, but the place was far nicer than the small flats of most young Muscovite couples. It was in a good location, in a nice building. There were real pictures on the walls, quality furniture, a VCR, and stereo. Compared to most, he was living in splendor.

But it was mostly the fruit of his work for Petya.

What was he supposed to do? Just give it all up? He wondered how much Marina really knew. She wasn't stupid—far from it. He'd told her that his salary at Mosteks was about twice what it really was, but even that exaggeration couldn't possibly account for the means to such luxury. She'd catch on soon.

Petya, Petya, he thought with a sigh as he collapsed back onto the couch. Misha thought about how he'd first been taken by his brother's persuasion to try the black market some eight years ago. He was wearing a Mickey Mouse tee shirt, the same one he'd had on the night he met Marina. Of course he never told her it had been a gift from Petya eight years ago to make him look more Western, more *kul,* when making his first approach to American tourists.

The colors on Mickey's face were now faded, and there were small holes under the arms. Things had changed so much since those days! But his brother had been so skillful a black marketeer even at that young age. First, you have to "befriend" your target. It had been the first thing Petya had taught Misha. Make her trust you. It was like trying to get laid.

He pulled the front of his tee shirt upward to better see Mickey. Petya had been such a good *fartsovshchik* that it all seemed so easy, so obviously natural…

…"Now put on this tee shirt, little brother. It's important. You'll develop a feeling for why with time. There. You look *kul,* Misha," said Petya. They had met, as per Petya's instructions, in the metro entrance across from the Galactica Hotel. Misha rolled up the shirt he'd just replaced and stuffed it into Petya's knapsack. He smiled as he left the metro for the adventure that awaited him, pretending to ignore passersby as they stared at his colorful tee shirt.

The enormous hotel, which attracted mostly tourists, was the ideal site for *fartsovshchik* business in the early 1980s. "You'll get all the foreign *tiolki,*" continued the elder Grunshteyn, referring to young women with the slang word that literally meant "heifer."

Again, Misha smiled. He almost felt Western. Why should I live like these miserable souls? he thought, looking at the Ivan Ivanoviches on the street.

Petya had scheduled their approach to Galactica perfectly. Breakfast had just been served in the hotel cafeteria, so the tourists would soon be emerging from the building to board their buses. *Fartsovshchiki* often gave a standard five ruble bribe to hotel doormen to be allowed passage, but Petya saw no reason to risk entering the building. Instead, he directed Misha to join him on a bench near the front of the hotel.

"We'll wait here until I spot a good prospect," said Petya to a heedful Misha.

Shortly, a group of giddy American high school students came out of Galactica. Hearing their English, Petya immediately stood and headed toward them. "Let's go," he whispered, tapping Misha's knee. Misha got up and followed.

"Hello," said Petya to a group of four teenage girls assembled on the sidewalk.

The girls turned attentively toward the Grunshteyns. "Hi," one teenager replied coquettishly.

"I'm Peter, and this is my brother Michael." Petya's command of colloquial English was impressive; he almost sounded like Steve McQueen!

"*Ochen' priyatno!*" The flirtatious girl greeted them in broken Russian.

"Oh! Do you speak Russian?" asked Petya, his eyes effectively feigning enthusiastic surprise.

"A little. We're here with our Russian language class. It's like a class field trip, y'know?" The girls giggled collectively.

"Well, I'm glad you speak some Russian, because my brother's English is not so good yet. What's your name?"

"Cindy."

Misha listened to the conversation silently, absorbing Petya's tact and style. He noted his brother's delightful smile and its effect on the young girls. The conversation continued for several minutes, with Misha discerning what he could. Why hadn't he taken that damned English class seriously?

"So, we meet tomorrow at nine o'clock at Pushkin monument, right?" asked Petya, looking at each of the girls separately.

"Right on!" replied one of the girls.

"I'm glad, too! Oh, and by the way, Cindy, before you leave. Since we are friends and I'm going to show you Moscow, let me do you favor right now." He leaned down to speak in a lowered voice, his playful expression remarkably similar to those on the girls' faces. "Is not necessary to purchase rubles in hotel at such high rates. There is better way than this. I can give you three rubles for dollar! Right now! You could spend money in Moscow like water! Would you like to change some money with me?"

"I don't know, Cindy," interrupted a leery, bespectacled girl. "Mr. Danzig told us not to trade any money on the street. We could get in trouble."

"Come on!" interjected Petya, rolling his eyes and laughing. "You won't get caught, I promise! Is no big deal. Everyone doing it here. And besides, do you really want your dollars to go to Soviet state so it can provide armaments to Cuba? Is useful politically to trade money with Russian friend instead of with Soviet state bank."

"That's true," replied the brainy teenager, apparently contemplating what she'd read about world politics. "Cuba is the largest threat to the United States in the Western hemisphere, receiving all of its military support from the Soviet Union."

Petya stole a wink at his brother, as if to say, *Am I good or what?* Misha was impressed. He had thought that Western behavior couldn't be comprehended, let alone predicted. He watched Petya exchange several hundred rubles for the greenbacks—seeing the *valuta* pass to his brother caused a twinge of excitement to course through him. He was actually seeing real business being transacted before his very eyes. Why had he been so afraid of this for so long? It was so simple!

And who got hurt? thought Misha as he picked up the red plastic receiver. Petya always used to ask that question. Maybe things were different now, but was it really Misha's business what Petya and the Gagarintsi did with the information he supplied them with? He dialed Petya's number.

But people could get hurt now, it occurred to him. And Ilya Konstantinovich was among those who might be in danger. Not to mention the American, who seemed like such a nice guy—

"Yes. Yes? Is anyone there?"

"Hi Petya. It's me, Misha."

"Hello, little brother."

Misha paused, then said, "I have some information for you. It's, uh, not very important. I could call you tomorrow if you're busy."

"It's okay, little brother. I'm free. What has my favorite scout learned?"

"It's nothing, Petya. I don't even know any details. Maybe I should just—"

"What *is* it?"

Misha breathed deeply. "Mosteks is proceeding with its negotiations for a joint venture with IIS. Ilya Konst—Lukov doesn't seem to be aware of any problems with...getting everything he needs to set up the JV." He was sure Petya understood.

Petya was silent for a moment, then said, "Of course that's important little brother! You've done very well! You can expect an extra hundred thousand rubles this month. Or shall we say two hundred, if you'll promise to take my lovely sister-in-law to dinner."

"Thank you, Petya." He closed his eyes.

"But tell me. Has the American lawyer arrived yet?"

Misha felt his mouth go dry. "No, Petya. He...was delayed. He comes...tomorrow. I...think."

"I see."

"But what difference does it make, Petyenka? You said the Gagarintsi would never approach a foreigner, you would never have to."

"Of course, little brother. We just like to keep an eye on these things, that's all."

Misha was silent.

"This is quite early for you to be calling, little brother. Is everything okay? Why didn't you wait until later?"

Again Misha paused. "I...I just thought you should hear the news as soon as possible."

Misha and Sam arrived at the Lovesong restaurant, where Misha had arranged a *tusovka,* a small social gathering. Sam thought it nice that Misha had invited several of his friends to a welcoming dinner for him. He was looking forward to seeing what the Russian was like in his niche.

Sam and Misha entered the restaurant and gave their overcoats to the wardrobe attendant. The maitre d' led them to a large round table covered by a white tablecloth and arranged with plates of various sliced appetizers. It displayed several bottles of a clear liquid with red and gold labels. Vodka, Sam decided. Now he felt like he was in Russia.

"For once, I am on time for *tusovka,* and my friends are late!" said Misha, throwing his arms into the air.

Sam was smiling at Misha's gesture when he noticed Lyena by the wardrobe, handing her coat to an expressionless attendant. She hadn't seen him yet, so he took a moment to check her out. What a bod, he thought. She filled out her pink skirt and floral blouse perfectly, a slight jiggle in her curves with every step. Sam stood silently as Misha greeted her, then did so himself.

The three sat, and Sam took a look around the restaurant. The large dining room was ornately decorated with intricate gold-colored trim against maroon wallpaper. The all-male wait staff wore tuxedos and seemed to perform quite professionally. Sam was impressed; he'd expected a much harsher reception into the land of shortages and economic disaster.

One by one, Misha's friends arrived and filled the table. First came two young women dressed in sequined pullovers and wearing a bit too much makeup—one brunette, the other with hair bleached to the point of colorlessness. Shortly afterward, a pleasant, intellectual-looking man of about thirty-five, sporting a blonde mustache and more casually dressed in brown trousers and a rugby shirt, sat down. Later, a couple arrived—the man, in his early thirties with longish hair, wore an ill-fitting sportcoat, and the woman, a bit younger and wearing a red dress, was at least trying to look fashionable.

Misha greeted his guests as they arrived, kissing each of them, male or female, with equal affection. Sam noted the Russians' genuine delight at seeing each other. He would have thought they were dear friends meeting after a long separation had Misha not explained that all of the guests belonged to the same social circle which met regularly in *tusovka.*

Misha introduced each of the Russians to Sam courteously, explaining a quick thing or two about each guest. The group was quite interesting and eclectic. The first two women were actresses, the man with the blonde mustache was a magazine editor. The couple were a computer engineer and his wife.

Sam experimented with the various hors d'oeuvres on the table. They were a good icebreaker for conversation, and the Russians were eager to explain each dish in cultural detail. Sam had never tried tongue and pickled garlic, but he enjoyed the culinary experimentation.

"So. Please allow me to make toast to arrival of our new friend from America," said Misha congenially as he rose from his chair, silencing the group's banter. Lyena translated into Russian for the guests, while one of the men poured vodka into eight shot glasses and distributed them.

"We finding ourselves at beginning of new era," continued Misha. "A time when world may rest peaceful, not distracted by arguments from hostile super-nations. A time when we may direct our efforts to cooperation and brotherly love."

Was this a joke? Sam thought. Some kind of satire? Or was Misha really that sappy? He suppressed a smile as he imagined how his friends in New York or Virginia would react if he stood up at a table and started a speech like that.

"Now we are able to be friends with whomever in world we choosing without worry about political differences or mistrust. We are free to be people, as we were meant to be.

"Sam Morris has come to us to help celebrate this new era. Will you, my Russian friends, raise your glass to help welcome our guest? Here's to meeting our new friend from America."

The group clinked glasses enthusiastically, and Sam saw several Russians smile at him. They were being genuine and hospitable. The smiles were real. Sam regretted his initial thoughts about the toast and tapped his glass against Misha's, smiling appreciatively. It was actually rather nice, he decided. He marveled as the entire group, including the women, effortlessly downed eight vodka shots in one gulp. No one even flinched at the alcohol, and the group emerged from behind its glasses with frolicsome faces.

"Thank you, Misha," said Sam after drinking his shot. "That was very nice. I'm looking forward to my stay in Moscow." He reached for a glass of mineral water to clear his blazing palate.

"Do you have any hobbies, Misha?" asked Sam as the other guests returned to their appetizers.

"Sure. I like American films. And rock 'n' roll. Through these I learning English."

"Your English is great."

"Thank you," replied Misha. He smiled wryly.

"What's the matter?"

"You see, Sam, foreigners never telling my brother that his English good. This because his English really very excellent. I hope someday foreigners not telling me my English good, too. Then I will know I have a good language." He shrugged.

Sam thought about it for a second, then nodded. "Makes sense."

"Soon I hope to visit America and see place that creates such wonderful arts," said Misha, forking a slice of pickled tongue.

"We'll definitely stay in touch. I'll show you around when you make it over."

"Will be nice," replied Misha, smiling and nodding enthusiastically.

They talked about New York City for a while, about themselves and their interests, then about the politicians, Russian and American, who'd made their meeting possible. Sam couldn't remember hitting it off with a new acquaintance so quickly; not since he was a young boy had he seen such instantaneous simpatico. He was looking forward to getting to know the Russian.

After another shot, Sam turned his attention to his right, where Lyena sat. The vodka had loosened him up. "You've been awfully quiet, Lyena. Tell me about yourself," he said, wondering if he was pronouncing her name correctly. He'd been waiting all evening for the woman to invigorate; it would apparently be up to him if they were going to chat. He looked at her expectantly.

"In two words?" she answered.

As she looked at him, Sam again noticed how exotically appealing her eyes were. The descending dark brows gave her gaze a penetrating effect he felt well below his belly. "Well...you can use five, six, maybe even seven if necessary." He wondered if his expression matched his intentionally light-hearted tone.

"I am sorry. This is just Russian saying, Sam," she said over a laugh. "Of course, I may need more than two words to tell you about me."

"How did you hook up with—uh, start working for Mosteks?" He realized that her English wasn't as proficient as Misha's.

"My father friend of Ilya Konstantinovich, Mosteks' boss. He get me job."

"Do you like it?"

Lyena smiled, nodding enthusiastically. "Is best job ever." She rubbed her thumb and first two fingers together. "Is wonderful place to work," she continued. "Very nice people. I already working there year."

She gave Sam one of those smiles that reminded him of Stacy. "It's nice to enjoy the people you work with," he said.

"What are your first impressions of Moscow?" asked Lyena. She was being hospitable, but Sam felt there was far more to it than that. There was absolutely nothing pretentious about Lyena's bearing; when she asked questions, even simple ones, it was because she was genuinely interested in the answer. She'd never heard of a "good behavior period."

He found her curiosity about him invigorating; it was the most genuine of complements. He looked into her piercing brown eyes and found himself having to force his attention back to the conversation. "It's a nice town," he said. "I'm looking forward to spending some time here."

"I am glad."

"I really wasn't expecting such friendly, sociable people."

"Why not?"

"Oh, I don't know. I guess because back home the media, the newspapers and television and all, portray Russia as a very bleak, unhappy place to live in. All we hear about are the shortages, overcrowding, cold winters, and domestic strife. I was actually a tiny bit apprehensive about coming here." He was surprised at the frankness of his own answer. Her candor was contagious, it seemed.

"There are problems here, Sam. You just not seen them yet and—"

146

"Oh, I'm sure there are problems, Lyena," he interrupted, not to look naïve. "Life is problems. But it seems that y'all know how to make do with what you've got."

"Is from necessity, I think." "Sure. Of course. But isn't everything?" Sam returned to the plate of mushrooms he'd ordered for dinner and took a bite.

"Is your impression that Russians are like Americans?" asked Lyena with that same genuine curiosity.

"Good question. I haven't been here long enough to decide, but I think all people are alike, don't you?" He shifted in his seat, leaning a bit closer to her. "I mean, we all have the same emotions, right? I think it's just a question of what we value."

"Many peoples say Russians and Americans much alike. I not know enough Americans to decide. Maybe we answering this question together at end of your week here."

Sam nodded his agreement to the idea enthusiastically. The bonding effect of her proposal was exciting; he now had something to look forward to with her.

"I think you will learn much about our country," continued Lyena, raising her glass. "And I think you will have many new impressions about Russian people."

Sam touched her glass with his own. "I'm looking forward to it," he said before gulping down the vodka with her.

"So how you like first evening in Russia, Sam?" asked Misha. He put the Zhiguli in gear and pulled out of the parking lot.

Sam smiled. "Very much. 'Preciate it, Misha."

Misha took a moment, apparently to decipher Sam's unfamiliar vernacular, then said, "Soon you will be real Russian, Sam. Full of Russian soul. I think you will love Moscow."

"You know what I'd like to do sometime during my stay, Misha? I'd like to go to a soccer, uh, football match. Russians are supposed to be fantastic players. I've heard a lot about them."

"Is no problem. Usually winter not right season, but there are Russians who always playing. You play?"

"Oh, yeah. I was a goal keeper most of my career, but I hurt my leg in college and had to quit. I still play sometimes in Central Park, though."

Suddenly, Misha made a sharp right turn, causing the Zhiguli's tires to screech. Sam held on to his seat. What the hell was going on? He looked behind them, saw nothing, then turned to Misha anxiously.

"So sorry, Sam," said Misha. "I almost miss turn." A few seconds later, he slowed down and parked next to a playing field. It was a dark evening, but the city lights adequately illuminated two soccer goals. The field had been cleared of snow recently, although a thick frost still covered the grass. Misha turned off the engine and said, "I have ball in trunk. Shall we play?"

"What?" said Sam, his mouth wide open.

"I play left wing for many years in youth, Sam. Soviets not allow me to travel with my team abroad to play with foreigners. You will be my first Western opponent. Will be nice for me."

"Are you kidding, Misha?"

Clearly, he wasn't.

"It's gotta be ten below out there. And look!" He tugged at his suit jacket. "This ain't exactly athletic wear. Besides, I'm jet lagged out. I couldn't play for shit right now!" He smiled incredulously.

Misha shrugged and turned on the engine. "So sorry, my friend. I not realizing you just amateur. Maybe sometime we go watch real Russian players—"

"Wait a minute," said Sam in a lowered voice. He paused and half-closed his eyes, forming an unyielding expression. "Is this some kind of challenge?"

Misha shifted toward Sam and said, "My friend, you may take off jacket and be in no worse than my clothes, right? Cold will be same problem for both of us, no? And because is now midnight Moscow time, your body only have afternoon New

York time. Jet lag your advantage here, Sam." He shrugged and turned to face forward. "But if you too scared to play Russian…"

Sam impetuously removed his jacket and tie and threw them in the back seat, then reached over and cut the engine. "Get the ball, Russky. Twenty bucks *valuta* says I can block two out of three of your shots from fifteen meters." He watched Misha give a spirited smile, then silently get out of the car. After a moment, Sam joined him in the icy air. He forced himself to ignore the cold's immediate penetration, allowing his face to show only rugged determination.

As he took the field, Sam wondered how long the battered goals had been standing. The one he chose to defend apparently was once a white metal structure, but it was now warped and brownish-red from rust. The crossbar had become detached, jutting up above the left upright, and the net was ripped and tattered. He took his position in front of the goal, rubbing his hands briskly together. "Come on!" he yelled.

He'd played soccer in high school and one season in college at the University of Virginia. Nine years had passed since his last block for an organized team, but he felt his dormant competitive juices slowly emerging. He enjoyed reacquainting himself with the feeling, a blast from the past, a rare taste of his carefree youth. It was novel for him to center his grit on something besides his damned career, even if for just a moment, and in foreign surroundings. IIS isn't the only game in town, he told himself, a smile coming to his now-shivering lips.

"Ready when you are!" It occurred to him how little he'd been urgently tested since college, apart from the pervasive calls of Old Virginia and IIS. At UVA, the pressing challenge of blocking shots had come weekly with every match. He remembered the way his competitive hunger used to burn. In college, a blocked shot, especially a tough one, would ensure his good standing with the coach, win him the admiration of his teammates, and ignite the heady applause of the crowd. It would bring the praises of his parents and friends, and the thrill of personal achievement. It turned women on. But most of all, it was payback for the endless training. Little of that satisfaction was present, even in his grandest successes at work.

Now he could almost hear the crowd of UVA soccer fans as he positioned himself to defend his goal.

Misha set the ball on the ground, then stood a few feet to the side and back of it. The two men were perfectly still, visibly exhaling in the cold air. Their eyes locked for a long moment, then Misha's body bowed slightly in preparation to lunge. As Misha executed his move, Sam took a last glance at the Russian's look of determination, the same one he'd often seen in the faces of his college opponents. Sam bent his knees in anticipation. In one motion, Misha charged and kicked the black and white sphere, hurtling it toward the bottom right side of the goal.

Sam responded instinctively and moved to dive to the right. He leaned and prepared to spring, to propel his entire body from his cleats.

Now!

But he had no cleats.

Before he could thrust, he felt his dress shoes slip on the frosty grass. He fell to the ground, his hands still properly extended in front of him, landing only a few feet from where he'd started.

"Oy!" yelled Misha as the ball rolled inside the holey net. He ran to Sam, helped him up, and brushed the ice from his shirt and pants. "My friend not consider conditions before making his play. Are you okay, Sam?"

"Just warming up, Misha," replied Sam over his deep breathing. "Besides, I had to make it sporting by giving you a freebie, right? Let's go again, Russky!"

Again, Misha looked confused at the English colloquialisms. He picked up the ball and went back to set up for the second shot.

Sam's entire body was now shivering. He looked at Misha, who was lining up, then kicked away the frost around his feet. He again bent his knees slightly, but now his eyes were focused on the black and white sphere.

Misha kicked. This time the ball flew toward the upper left side of the goal. Too high, thought Sam immediately, relieved. It would sail over the crossbar. He didn't even move. He turned his head to see by how far his opponent had missed, then saw the ball land in the net behind him and roll back toward his foot. The shot had been perfectly directed under the detached crossbar.

"No fair!" said Sam loudly, walking out to meet Misha, palms up. "The crossbar's broken! You wouldn't have made that in a regulation goal! It would have landed in the friggin' parking lot!"

Misha smiled and strutted toward Sam like a peacock. "I never say this is regulation goal, Sam." He put his arm around Sam's shoulders. "In Russia we have saying: 'One must press all the pedals' when there is need for something important. Is necessary in life to make use of all one's advantages." He picked up the ball and headed with Sam toward the car.

Sam closed his eyes and turned his head, conceding defeat. "I guess you got it, bud." He accepted Misha's outstretched hand and shook it.

"And I press all the pedals here because this was very important, Sam," continued the Russian, returning the ball to the trunk. "You see, I could not let fucking Yankee beat me in football."

"What did you just call me!"

ELEVEN

Sam stood in the lobby of Mosteks' business office, waiting with Misha to meet with the cooperative's directorate. Despite Ned's warnings about Russian tardiness, Misha had picked him up at Hotel Novgorod promptly at nine o'clock that morning.

The lobby was a small sitting room beset with wooden benches and several wall posters portraying the Mosteks factory. An austere depiction of Lenin's face, still vaguely visible through a recent coat of paint, looked down at Sam from across the room. The face was somehow belligerent, ready to lead the masses against the forces of some terrible enemy toward utopia. Sam wondered briefly what or who those oppressive forces were supposed to have been.

He was exhausted. The time difference had kept him up until five o'clock that morning. His slight hangover didn't help matters, either, although Moscow's sub-zero weather had perked him up a bit. He groomed his hair in his window reflection, then looked out at the snow-covered parking lot. He wondered what Mr. Lukov would look like—

"Hello, Sam! So nice to meet you!" said Ilya cheerfully, startling Sam from behind. He shook the American's hand heartily with both of his own. "I hope your flight was pleasant."

"As go nine hour flights, I guess it wasn't bad," he answered, returning Ilya's smile. Sam took an instant liking to the chairman, although Ilya was shaking his hand a bit too heartily and a bit too long.

"And your accommodations? We doing best we can. Unfortunately, situation very bad in Moscow with hotels," said Ilya, finally releasing Sam's hand.

"Hotel Novgorod is a very nice place," said Sam. "And Misha has been taking good care of me."

"Good, good," said Ilya, nodding his large head hospitably and still smiling. "Shall we go to conference room then? Please follow me."

Sam glanced back at Misha as the three men proceeded down a corridor. Misha raised his brow to Sam hospitably, but somehow the Russian seemed more reserved than he'd been the evening before. He wasn't as jovial as he'd been at dinner or on the soccer field. But Sam figured that Misha was just being professional in front of his boss. Why shouldn't Russians have duel identities, like Americans and probably everyone else in the world?

Ilya led Sam into the conference room. A large green linoleum table occupied the majority of the space, which was illuminated only by sunlight struggling to pass through two grimy windows. On the yellowing walls hung more posters, calendar and advertisement placards obviously meant to fill blank wall spaces. That familiar tobacco pungency flooded Sam's nose as he set his briefcase on the table and wondered if the flimsy chairs would collapse under his weight. He'd begun to realize that almost all floors in Moscow were wooden and usually parquet, as was the slightly warped one on which he now stood.

"I would now like to introduce you to rest of your partners, Sam."

Ilya went around the table introducing the businessmen. The two other Mosteks directorate members were there. The chairman explained that Boris Shturkin of the Ministry of Finance was present "to see to issues regarding registration of the JV." Sam greeted the men, each of whom rose and gave a slight bow from the head as they shook his hand.

When he turned to take his place at the table, Sam noticed Lyena standing silently behind him in the corner. He felt his face invigorate. If she was suffering from the after-effects of last night's *tusovka,* it wasn't apparent. In fact, she looked pretty damned hot. "Hi Ly—" he began.

But she'd quickly turned away. Almost the same way those women had responded to Eric Highsmith's obnoxious come-ons in the Kamikaze Bar. What was wrong? he wondered. She'd expressed no affinity for him whatsoever, as though they'd never even met, let alone had that deep discussion the evening before. He kept looking at her for a moment, then sighed and forced himself to put aside his confusion and disappointment. There was work to be done.

He quickly surveyed the four men, all of whom wore indistinct grayish or brownish suits with mismatched shirts and ties. There was a noticeable lack of differentiating self-expression about their clothing, hairstyles, even about their postures and expressions. It was difficult to determine almost anything about their individuality. They were pleasant, however, friendly and hospitable, and Sam felt welcome in their midst. He looked forward to getting started.

"Sam," began Ilya with Misha translating into Russian for the other men. "Today we devoting meeting to our acquaintance. I am hopeful your seven-day schedule in Moscow will not be fully needed for our negotiations, and that you will soon be able to relax and enjoy as Misha and Lyena showing you beautiful sights of Moscow. I believe we will be able to come to full agreement after only few good meetings. Today we becoming friends.

Tomorrow we will, as Russians say, 'get to where the dog is buried,' and start our business agenda."

Sam was silent for a moment, wondering if he'd missed something. He'd wondered how the joint venture's myriad details could be handled within the allotted seven days. But he nodded diplomatically and said, "I'm sure our business will run smoothly."

Shortly, Lyena left the room for a moment, then returned with a tray containing hot tea and sugar cookies. She poured tea into glasses resting in ornate metal holders and distributed the refreshments dutifully, never uttering a sound.

The entire group, except Sam, simultaneously lit up cigarettes. A rush of grey smoke flooded the air, confirming the source of the stench Sam had first noticed in the room. He quickly inhaled a few clean breaths.

"Your company enjoys fine reputation as leader in American industry. We are fortunate to have been chosen as your partner," continued Ilya. "We look forward to honor and privilege of working with your reputable staff in mutually beneficial joint venture. IIS offers Mosteks much appreciated entrée into world of Russian business."

Sam was no longer surprised at Russian conviviality. Apparently, there was little difference between opening business remarks and dinner toasts in Russia. "I speak for the entire staff at IIS in seconding your optimism," he said, trying his own hand. "We too look forward to a prosperous relationship." As Misha translated his remarks into Russian, Sam stole another glance at Lyena. She still refused to meet his gaze. Again, he ignored his disappointment and returned to the linoleum table.

"These are trying times, both in America and in our country," said Ilya. "But the best of businessmen can survive and flourish under any conditions. Is now our responsibility to show that we are the best of businessmen. Is my great honor and pleasure to welcome you, Sam Morris, to our city of Moscow. Please accept this gift from your partners at Mosteks." He handed Sam a small black lacquer box decoratively painted with a picture of a troika plowing through a snowy field. "This is traditional Russian *palekh* box," continued the chairman. "They are collected all over world for their splendid beauty and fine detail. We hoping you will keep box in your home in America as reminder of your friends in Moscow."

Sam looked at the box, turning it over in his hand. It was an incredible work of art. He tried to decide where in his apartment he might display it. "Thanks very much, Ilya."

Ilya said, "As you know, Sam, we have met already with IIS representatives. Our negotiations have been very promising. Since my last meeting with your respected president, Mr. Jonathan Davies, we making good progress in clearing obstacles to our joint venture. In few days time, I think there will be great cause for celebration." Ilya cast Sam another genial smile. "And so. Does our American guest and partner have any questions before we explaining to him latest Mosteks accomplishments?"

Sam returned Ilya's smile. "I don't think so, Ilya, not yet. I'd like to arrange a tour of your manufacturing facility, though. Do you think Misha could show me around, maybe sometime tomorrow morning?"

Something happened. Ilya's cheery mien, the amiable tilt in his head and his pleasant smile, had instantly disappeared. Sam wondered what was wrong. Had he said something? Had he broken some unfamiliar rule of Russian etiquette?

Ilya cleared his throat and reached for his glass of tea. He took a sip and laughed nervously. "You wearing such a nice suit, Sam," he said. "It might get soiled in our factory."

The group chuckled at Ilya's remark after Misha translated it. "But a dirty suit will be proof to my boss that I'm not too soft a lawyer," replied Sam. It was all he could think of. He felt relief when Misha's translation of his comment elicited more Russian laughter.

"Very well, Sam," said Ilya after a moment, looking down at his notepad and shrugging. "Misha showing you factory tomorrow morning." It almost sounded like a concession.

The introductory meeting lasted a couple of hours while Sam and the Russians became better acquainted and discussed their two companies. He was feeling his way around the Mosteks officers, making mental notes as to how Russians conducted business. Only that Shturkin guy, from the Ministry of whatever, looked out of place. Shturkin was silent during the entire meeting, but he seemed to be paying very close attention. Why should a man like that even be in on meetings, especially at this stage of the game? Sam would have thought the guy was KGB if the organization hadn't been disbanded.

Around noon, Sam saw Lyena trying to catch her boss's eye. Ilya turned to her.

"Ilya Konstantinovich," she said, "your lunch reservation is in half hour. I believe the drivers have arrived."

Sam wondered why she'd spoken in English, but was grateful she had. He assumed it was out of consideration for him.

Ilya said something back to her, but in Russian. Although Sam couldn't understand it, he was struck by the chairman's tone of voice, which was somewhere between slightly flirtatious and like the one a parent would use to a young child.

Ilya then rose from behind the table and spoke again in English. "And now, Sam, we treating you to traditional Russian lunch. We will be dining at fine restaurant called 'Firefly.' You will see that good lunch always necessary prelude to successful business in Russia."

The group began donning scarves, hats, and heavy overcoats in a process which took fully five minutes. Ilya removed Sam's overcoat from the closet and held it open for him. As Sam slipped into the coat, he wondered if he was getting the royal treatment or if overly abundant graciousness was the norm in this country.

But Lyena, Sam saw, hadn't prepared for the Russian winter. He thought better than to inquire, especially after he saw her glance at him and, for the third time, quickly turn away.

Misha was watching Sam button his navy blue overcoat. It was really nice, probably cost him over five hundred dollars. Misha had learned a few things about American fashion through catalogs Petya's friends had brought back from New York. Sam's clothes were conservatively old-fashioned, but not cheap. He wondered what Sam was like in the States. What kind of food he ate and the liquor he drank. Did Americans really drink beer to get drunk? It's so heavy! Sam was a handsome guy, the American *tiolki* must be all over him. There were probably many sides to the New Yorker from Virginia, far more than Misha had perceived already. He smiled as he recalled Sam's futile dive on the icy football field the evening before. Was this the same guy who'd been so serious and businesslike during this morning's boring meeting? Misha looked forward to drinking vodka with him, to sharing dirty jokes and talking more about football. And about life.

Misha had just followed Sam out of the conference room for lunch when he heard Ilya, still inside, whispering something. He was probably in with Boris Shturkin; Misha hadn't seen the MinFin *chinovnik* come out.

"…the joint venture with IIS…be registered as soon as possible…have our own reasons…"

Misha felt a stinging jolt descend his back. His assignment from Petya and the Gagarintsi suddenly focused in his mind, and he quickly put his back to the corridor wall outside the conference room door. He closed his eyes and stifled a deep breath.

Petya came into view, his amiable face smiling as he handed Misha a paper sack of rubles. Misha could almost feel his elder brother's arm around his shoulders.

"...everything must be done as soon as possible..."

Misha's head reflexively jerked to the right. Now he saw Marina, then Mama, and finally Papa, each of whom were glaring at him with the same imploring expression. "Can't you see how dirty he is, Misha?" They were Marina's words, but Mama's voice.

Misha opened his eyes and shook the ghosts out of his head. He had to complete his assignment, or else...who knows how Petya might react! What about the monthly payments on which he, and Marina, depended?

"...that's what you're paying me for..."

Anyway, he could decide later. Right? Maybe he wouldn't actually tell Petya what he learned here. Maybe something would happen to make it all irrelevant anyway. But he had to have the option. It couldn't hurt just to know what the men inside were discussing, could it?

He quickly checked to see that Sam had already proceeded down the hallway with the other men, then inched his way closer to the conference room doorway. The hallway was empty, and Misha held his breath to better hear the mumbled discussion inside. Something was being placed on the linoleum table, probably an envelope or a paper bag.

"And we'll deliver the remaining twenty-five percent through...think it's safer...especially with valuta..."

Misha moved still closer toward the half-opened door.

"Five thousand dollars is enough to raise some eyebrows if it's noticed..." It was definitely Shturkin's gruff voice whispering— Misha had heard the chinovnik before. He quickly withdrew a small pad from inside his coat and began jotting down notes.

"What are you writing?" he heard, his head snapping up on its own. It was Sam! He'd left with the others but must have turned back when he saw that Misha wasn't behind him.

Misha stifled a gasp and said, "Oh, just few notes about things for factory. I just now remember and not want to forget,

Sam." He smiled at the American, glad the latter couldn't read his Russian writing.

"I know what you mean," replied Sam. "I usually carry a microcassette recorder wherever I go. You have to catch your thoughts when you get them, otherwise you might lose them forever, huh?"

Misha laughed nervously, then stuffed the notepad back into his pocket. He put a hand on Sam's shoulder, directing him to continue down the hall. "Shall we have lunch?" he asked, stealing a last glance at the conference room door.

Misha had been to Firefly several times. It was a classy businessman's restaurant by reputation, although its ambience was the same as Lovesong's, where he'd taken Sam the evening before. As usual, a reserved table loaded with appetizers awaited them. Misha smiled when Sam first gaped at, then tried to ignore, the three bottles of vodka. Apparently Americans weren't used to Russian-style business lunches.

The group sat down around the table, still warming to the restaurant's heat. Misha took a seat next to Sam and served him sliced cheeses and meats.

"I recognize these hors d'oeuvres," said Sam. "We had just about every one of them at supper last night."

"Is good. You are already master of Russian food." Again Misha smiled at Sam's attempts to hide his confusion. The American was a pleasant guy.

Andrey Muravyev, Mosteks' bookkeeper, had stood and was filling six shot glasses with vodka. Misha noticed that under the accountant's jacket was a green sweatshirt displaying the American adage *The One Who Dies With The Most Toys Wins*. He made a mental note to ask Sam what the expression was supposed to mean; he was sure Andrey had no idea. He was glad he'd met this American. It would be fun to discuss such things with him.

"My friends and colleagues. May I take this opportunity to welcome our partner from United States," began Muravyev.

Misha mindlessly translated the toast into English for Sam. But his thoughts were centered on Boris Shturkin, who sat silently across the table, clumsily stuffing slices of cheese into his mouth. Like a pig. Misha wondered what kind of trouble he might bring the *chinovnik,* how the Gagarintsi would approach Shturkin if they knew he was cooperating with Mosteks. But then he wondered if that trouble might extend to Sam as well. Forget it, he told himself. Petya had promised him that Sam wouldn't be touched.

"...I have never been to United States. But one not need see America to know she is a great country. Is unfortunate that our two countries for so long expended such great treasure in support of mistrust and fear..." repeated Misha, continuing his translation.

Sam was looking at Muravyev, apparently engaged by the toast. But what might happen to an American if Petya's superior, that jerk Svetov, felt threatened by a possible Mosteks/IIS JV? Sam was just an innocent bystander. Would Svetov try to squelch the joint venture by attacking a foreigner? Probably not, Misha decided, assuring himself. It had happened before, he'd heard, but the Gagarintsi had less risky ways of handling such problems.

"...my friends, will you please join me in saluting arrival of representative from America, with whom it is our honor to embark on this new order?"

Muravyev bowed slightly before gulping down his vodka with a loud sigh. Sam swallowed his shot as well.

The lunch continued well into late afternoon with toasts from Ilya and Albert Denisov. Shturkin was still silent, though Misha saw the *chinovnik* didn't have any problem drinking with the group. What a *svoloch,* a slime ball, Misha thought as he ate a piece of bread covered with caviar. He pushed the troubling thought aside and said in English, "And now I would like to make a toast."

"Hang on a second, Misha," said Sam in a lowered voice, leaning closer.

"What is matter, Sam," asked Misha. "Let's celebrate our partnership!"

"Isn't anyone else getting a little...buzzed here?" he whispered. "We've had four shots already. How are we going to discuss business this afternoon if we're all liquored up?"

"Business, business," said Misha in mock disgust, waving his hand. "Everything in order, Sam. No more business today. We having plenty of time tomorrow."

Sam looked at the ceiling and said, "Beam me up, Scotty."

"Please drink with me, my friend! Drink!" said the Russian, wondering who Scotty was.

Sam did, and soon seemed on the verge of passing out. Misha wrapped an arm around him and put more food on his plate. "Here Sam. Eat. You will feel better. Would you maybe like coffee?"

Sam nodded his befuddled head. "M—Maybe that's a good idea. 'Preciate it, Misha."

"My father say is *mitzvah* to help drunk friend. I'm always taking his advice with foreigners," said Misha, smiling.

"I guess us foreigners can't drink like you Russkies."

"Not even as well as our women. I will take you to hotel soon," said Misha, still amused by Sam's low tolerance. "You are jet lagged and need peaceful night to recover your strength."

"Good idea, bud," said Sam. "I can't remember the last time I got this drunk in the middle of the afternoon. I'm embarrassed to be—"

"No, no, Sam. No be embarrassed. Is very Russian to have good lunch with friends. Plenty time to being serious later. Relax, my friend! No worry."

After lunch, Boris returned to his small office at the Ministry of Finance. "Hello, Marya," he said with a blithe smile, passing his secretary in the reception area. He raised his hand to open his office door, then stopped.

A man had stood from the couch next to Marya's desk, where he'd apparently been waiting for Boris. The man wasn't familiar, but his presence was nonetheless commanding. His expression was one of control, of domination, but set among somehow boyish features. Maybe Boris had seen his eyes somewhere before.

"Boris Antonovich?" said the man, extending a muscular arm to shake hands.

Boris recognized the feigned reverence, and his vodka-induced euphoria seemed to melt away instantly. He nodded, still wondering why he recognized the eyes. "Please come in," he said.

The two crossed into Boris's office. Boris closed the door and sat down, not taking off his coat. The second installment from Mosteks was in the breast pocket and might be visible. He offered a chair to his unexpected visitor. "What can I do for you?"

"We were wondering if you might be able to provide us with some information," said the man. "We're confused about a certain matter involving the Mosteks cooperative."

Boris shifted in his seat nervously. He was about to inquire as to who "we" were, just as a matter of course, but decided against it. Why did they keep coming to his office? "I was visited just last week by—"

"By Svetov, yes, I know," interrupted the man, his voice stern. "You told him there would be no problems in your seeing to the cooperative's failure to register a joint venture with MinFin."

Boris waited for the man to continue. Had he met him before? Maybe with Svetov somewhere? Those eyes!

"But Mosteks seems to be proceeding with its plans for a joint venture nonetheless," continued the man. "Ilya Lukov doesn't seem to realize there are any problems. He met with an attorney from an American company this morning."

Boris sat silently, struggling to meet the man's gaze.

"Have you encountered any difficulties with Mosteks? Have you advised the cooperative that the Ministry of Finance will be unable to register its JV, Boris Antonovich?"

"Not yet," said Boris, clearing his throat. "The decision wouldn't normally be given until after formal application has been made. Lukov probably assumes all is in order and is therefore proceeding. But we will notify Mosteks of MinFin's decision as soon as we receive its JV documentation." He tried to give an assuring, businesslike smile, but saw that the man was unaffected.

"Boris Antonovich, we would prefer that you advise Lukov immediately of MinFin's position. We would rather not have to concern ourselves with the matter any longer. Agreed?"

Boris shrugged and nodded his large head, then looked down at his desk. The man obviously knew about this morning's meeting, so he very well might know Boris had attended it. But maybe the Gagarintsi didn't know. Hopefully they didn't. "The joint venture will not be registered. I'll advise Lukov as soon as possible," said Boris, breaking the man's stare. He watched with relief as the man quickly stood and walked to the door.

"Very good, Boris Antonovich." The man gave a smile that seemed almost genuine, in sharp contrast to Svetov, whose face wasn't capable of forming pleasant expressions. But somehow this man's smile was even more ominous than his cohort's fixed scowl. "We'll be in touch," he said before disappearing through the doorway.

Boris rubbed his face briskly with both hands, then stood to lock the door behind the Gagarinets. He opened his desk drawer and removed the envelope containing five thousand dollars, to which he added the five from the breast pocket of his coat. He thumbed through the bills a moment, then impulsively clutched them to his chest.

The Mosteks joint venture simply had to fail.

But how could he manage to keep the *valuta?*

TWELVE

After lunch, Misha drove Sam back to Hotel Novgorod. When Sam went up to his room, he was scarcely aware of the shoddy accommodations; the combination of alcohol and jet lag had left him too murky to care. It was only about four o'clock in the afternoon, but it was pitch dark outside, and he was ready to crash.

First he had a call to make. He found the number in his appointment book, picked up the phone, and dialed. "Hello? Hello? Is this Yakov Edelman?" asked Sam, trying to interpret an unintelligible voice on the other end. "Do you speak English?" Nothing but Russian chatter.

Sam instinctively did what he knew most Americans do when speaking to a non-Anglophile—what he'd told himself on several occasions he wouldn't do. He began speaking loudly and curtly: "This is Samuel Morris! I am Yakov Edelman's nephew from the United—uh, from America! I—"

"Ah! Sorry, sorry!" interrupted the voice. "Yes, I do speak English! This is Yasha Edelman at your service. Please do forgive me. And how is it that you are my nephew?"

"I'm your sister Gussie's great nephew, so I reckon I'm yours, too. She was—uh, my grandfather Hyman's half-sister, I think. I've come to Moscow for a week on business, and I'd like to meet you."

"I see, I see. We'll most definitely meet, then. Most definitely, my nephew," replied the voice enthusiastically. "And how is Gussie?"

"She's doing fine. She lives in a retirement home in Virginia."

"Very good, very good. This is such a pleasant surprise for me. When would you like to meet, my nephew?"

"I'll have some time late tomorrow afternoon. Is that all right?"

"Yes, yes. That will be quite convenient. I look forward to meeting you, Sam Morris."

"Where do you live? Can you give me your address?"

Yasha paused. "Uh, no, no. It's not convenient for you to come directly here. Instead, we'll do as follows: Meet me under the Mayakovsky statue. Anyone can tell you where it is. Is five o'clock suitable?"

"Yes, that's fine. Mayakovsky statue. I'll see you at five tomorrow." He wrote it down.

"Wait, Sam, just a second, please. Briefly tell Uncle what his nephew looks like."

Sam smiled, thinking they could have missed meeting because they didn't recognize each other. "I'm six feet tall, with short brown hair, and I'll be wearing a suit and dark blue overcoat. What about you?"

"I'm an old man. You'll recognize me."

Sam smiled again. "Are you a tall old man or a short one?"

"I am one meter sixty-three. Figure it out, my nephew."

The two laughed and bade each other farewell.

Sam awoke groggily in the narrow hotel bed and strained his head upward to see his travel alarm clock on the dresser. Two o'clock in the morning. He sighed when he saw he'd passed out fully dressed.

He stood up and tumbled into the bathroom, his legs still a bit wobbly from the alcohol. He splashed cold water on his face, brushed his teeth, and took off the suit.

But when he got back into bed, Sam couldn't sleep. He sat up and tried reading. Then he paced, his mind sifting through the afternoon's meeting at Mosteks and wondering about Lyena's strange behavior. And about how everyone he'd met in Moscow had been so nice, although not completely understandable. But the urge to sleep simply would not come. So he gave up, got dressed, and headed downstairs for the hotel bar.

The bar's red door was next to the elevator on the first floor. Nightclub Operating for Foreign Hard Currency Only read a nearby sign. Russian apartheid, Sam thought. A country which discriminates against the overwhelming majority of its citizens. Their crime: having only their nation's official exchange.

He entered the dimly lit nightclub and began his reflexive barroom survey. It was unexpectedly crowded. Foreign men, mostly middle-aged and somewhat surly, were scattered through-out, drinking and smoking around tables. He'd have to let his eyes adjust to the lighting before checking out the women.

Beer! There were Heineken bottles on some of the tables, and Sam immediately started for the bar to buy one. Something to wash away the memory of two days of massive vodka consumption.

He walked past carousing tables on his way, coming closer to some of the club's patrons. All wore strangely serious expres-sions. They somehow seemed too anxious and concerned to be night-lifers, more contemplative than fun-loving. Many of the men looked shifty, their wily eyes almost intimidating to look at. There were several women at the tables as well, all with com-placent looks on their overly made-up faces.

Sam reached the bar, leaned against it, and ordered a Heineken. A blonde in a very low-cut dress was standing next to him, her gaudy make-up highlighted by sparkling glitter around the eyes. She looked at him without expression, with almost the same look as the airline agent at JFK, and Sam winked, just to see her response. This is a bar, right? he told himself, wondering what line Eric might have tried.

Unexpectedly, the woman immediately came closer to him, her face still unaffected and expressionless. "Zhenya," she said nonchalantly, rolling her head and taking an exaggerated puff on her tilted cigarette.

"Uh, sorry, I don't speak Russian," replied Sam politely, looking away. He hadn't expected the encounter and wasn't sure he felt like chatting. He paid for his beer, took a long swallow, and again scanned the bar.

"Is my name," she said, her voice rather whiny. "Zhenya. You American?"

"Yes."

"What business?" She took another drag on the cigarette.

"I'm a lawyer. I work in-house for an industrial conglomerate." He'd hoped the answer might confuse her and scare her off, but Zhenya stood fast, looking back at him.

"Is your first time in Moscow?" she asked.

"Yes," said Sam. "Is your first time?" He wasn't trying to entertain the woman; he just couldn't take her seriously.

But Zhenya didn't respond. She kept her serious expression and continued talking and smoking: "You from New York, right? All American lawyers from New York."

"Good guess."

"No guess. I know. But I am afraid of SPID. Men from New York have SPID."

"You're afraid of what?"

"SPID. How you say? Sorry, I not can say in English. Just a minute." The woman walked a few feet toward another female of her ilk and conferred momentarily. A few seconds later they both came back to where Sam was standing.

"AIDS," said the newcomer. "SPID is Russian word for AIDS. Have you ever sleep with man?"

"What?"

"Is important to learn if you have AIDS before Zhenya having business with you."

Sam looked up at the ceiling, nodding to himself, then took another glance around the bar. Most of the female population of the nightclub was clearly out to "do it" for money. Why hadn't he seen that from the beginning? "Excuse me," he said finally with a straight face, then headed toward the restroom, checking behind him to make sure that Zhenya and her partner weren't following.

American Standard, Sam read as he relieved himself into the urinal. What a nice little reminder of the comforts of home, even if for just a few seconds. The john had clearly been around since before perestroika, and Sam laughed at the thought of communists buying American toilets to piss in.

He was washing his hands when he heard a voice behind him. "Don't screw the one with the blonde hair, mate." There was an accent there, but not Russian. Sam turned around to see a short, grey haired man in a three piece suit. English, Sam decided. He was a friendly looking bloke, a welcome contrast to most of the bar's other patrons.

"You know, Zhenyer. She's bad news, I say," continued the Brit. "In fact, you shouldn't fuck any of them, if you know what's good for you."

"I wasn't fixing to fuck any of them. Why pay when there's so much out there for free?" said Sam, joining the Brit's humorous tone.

"An analysis of that caliber merits a drink, mate. And I'm buying. Would you care to join me?"

"Sure," said Sam.

"Earle's my name. Francis Earle. Yours?"

"Sam Morris," he answered, accepting Francis's hand.

They left the restroom, and Francis joined Sam at a table. The Brit sighed as he sat down, crouching confidently in his seat, then signalled a waiter to bring two of his usual. "Your first time here, ay?"

"Why does everyone ask me that?"

"It's pretty obvious. A look on your face, I guess. Been here several times m'self. I keep tabs on me company's Moscow office. One gets to know what's going on after a bit."

"Why is Zhenya bad news?" asked Sam.

"They're all whores, mate. Prostitutes. And not the kind you might be used to. Oh, some are sweet enough girls. But they won't suck your dick and be on their merry way, that's for sure."

Sam laughed. "I figured out that they're prostitutes. But what do you mean? Why wouldn't they be on their merry way?" He sipped his beer.

Francis took a surreptitious glance around the bar, then said, "You see that man over there? The one in the brown overcoat in the corner? He's with the police. The new police. Used to be KGB. Oh, he's not a cloak-and-dagger spy out of a John LeCarré novel. What he is, mate," the Brit leaned closer to Sam and lowered his voice, "is a pimp!" He suppressed a high-pitched chuckle.

Sam waited for the details.

"You see, Russian subjects are not allowed to enter international hotels like this one. But most of the women in here are indeed Russian. I found out the hard way how they manage to get in. I'll tell you."

He leaned closer. "One night about a year ago I picked up a beautiful young lass in this very bar. Wonderful round tits. But I'd had a bit too much to drink and wasn't quite thinking right at the time. We agreed on fifty quid in our oral contract for oral services." He raised his brow over another chuckle. "Anyway, I took her up to me room and shagged both our brains out. Oh, was she marvelous!" He paused a moment, apparently reliving the memory.

"But then I passed out. The combination of cunt and cocktail was a bit too much for me, see. When I was your age, mate, I could go all night, but not anymore. Time does that, you know. Anyway, I didn't awaken until morning, and when I did, I was alone. I was all alone.

"The fucking whore had gone through everything in the room! She'd been through me briefcase, me suits, even me bloody toiletries! Nothing was missing, mind you, but it was clear she'd taken full inventory. Know what I mean?

"So this is how it works, Sam. Whores are given permission by the police to do their business, their lucrative valuter business, in the international hotels. The police, for their end of the bargain, expect the girls to spy on foreign businessmen and report back to them. In another words, the police are pimps and the whores are spies!"

Sam sat dumfounded. "And the johns are all foreign businessmen?" he asked.

"Most are blokes like you and I, mate." Francis took a look around and lowered his voice to a whisper. "But the rest of the men here are mafiosos. Russian and foreign. You see, the only bars in Moscow worth visiting work for hard currency only. And most Russians who have access to valuter are organized criminals."

"I'm partying with prostitutes and mafiosi?" said Sam, too loudly.

"Shh!" said the Brit, again looking around. "And Francis Earle, a most decent of human beings."

Sam shook his head incredulously and took another sip of beer.

"Just don't fuck any prostitutes, mate, and you'll do fine, here. I assure you."

"'Preciate the tip, Francis."

"Not at all. Well, it's time for this Saxon to retire." The Brit struggled to his feet and reached into his breast pocket. "Here's me card. Pleasure meeting you, mate. Give us a ring next time you're in."

"I will. And thanks for the beer."

The two shook hands, and Francis Earle left the bar.

Sam stayed at the table, toying with the label on his Heineken. Zhenya was still standing in the same place by the bar, looking around the club, looking available. Despite her gaudiness, she was actually rather pretty, he decided. Just painted up too damned much. All of the Russian whores were trying to be sexy á la the West, with their patently un-Russian clothes, make-up, and carriage. But there was something about them that was pathetically just show. He couldn't decide if these women were even more pitiful than American hookers.

Sam wondered what Stacy might look like if she'd been raised in Russia, what it would be like to meet her here. He'd only been in Moscow two days, but he hadn't seen a single female with the zest of his girlfriend. Stacy didn't even have to try to be appealing. He pictured her lively eyes and beautiful smile, then her voluptuous body in its naked splendor. What an incredible presence she was with that spirited voice. How alive she made him feel!

He just wished there were something...mysterious in her character. Then she'd be perfect. With Stacy, what you got is what you saw, although what he saw and got was incredible. Those eyes were ravishing, but there was nothing cryptic about them. Stacy definitely wasn't boring, far from it. But he wanted something to explore. He knew what she wanted out of life, out of him, and how she intended to go after both. There just wasn't anything to be curious about. He missed the challenge of solving an unpredictable woman's puzzle, of learning what makes her tick. He missed being really curious.

Sam turned his attention to the dance floor. The Brit's words had made it almost discomfiting to watch the frolicking partyers, the mafiosi, the whores, and the philandering foreign business-men. He remembered his agreement with Lyena that they com-pare Russians and Americans after his week in Moscow. He already had a few interesting things to point out, and he was looking forward to telling her about them. In fact, he decided, he couldn't friggin' wait!

"Hello, little brother! How are things? Please sit! Would you like coffee or tea? I have some of the finest French roast here," said Petya, rising from the table to greet Misha. He grabbed a chair and pulled it up to the table next to his own.

Misha looked at the other man seated in Petya's dining room. He'd met Svetov on several occasions. He was the one with the black leather jacket, who always seemed so damned threatening, so...*nagliy*. Misha usually had trouble remembering the names of Petya's friends, but he'd never had a problem with this one. He nodded at the wan man, accepted his handshake silently, and sat down.

"So, I hear you have something for us," continued Petya, pouring a cup of coffee. "What brings my little brother to me?"

"It's just something I picked up at work today. Probably nothing important." He lifted his cup for a sip, again glancing at Svetov. The man sat patiently, authoritatively, as if he were a judge presiding over a courtroom. "I really just came by to visit."

"It's always nice to see you, Mishenka," said Petya, smiling cheerfully. "And how is Marina?"

"She's fine. Very well, actually. She says hello."

"Give her a hug for me. Soon we'll all have to get together again. Our last meeting was under such unpleasant circumstances. But anyway, what do you have for us?" Misha breathed deeply, then took out his pad to find the notes from the conversation he'd overheard in the Mosteks conference room. "It's really nothing, Petya, I shouldn't even bother you about it." He took another sip of coffee.

"Let us decide that," said Svetov. "Please," he added, softening his tone.

Misha saw that Petya was also waiting eagerly. But why did the Gagarintsi consider Misha's snooping so critical? Weren't they powerful enough to do what they wanted regardless of the cooperative's actions? He glanced at his notes, which were scribbled on one page. There was a pencil swipe from the last word where he'd quickly moved to hide his spying from Sam.

Sam. Even if the Gagarintsi were having problems with Mosteks, would they ever touch an American? Petya had said he'd never hurt anyone, especially a foreigner. But why—

"Are you all right, little brother?"

Misha quickly closed the pad. "Two of my assistant engineers have taken sick. I can't fix malfunctioning equipment without them, and Mosteks' output may suffer as a result. I just thought you might like to know the cooperative's profits this month may be lower than expected."

Misha stole another glance at the guy in the leather jacket. There was something there, some barely detectable facial movement indicating his deep consideration of the matter. Could Svetov tell there was more on Misha's mind? Misha quickly looked away, again reaching for his cup. When he saw it was empty, he put it back down.

Petya put his arm around Misha affectionately and said, "Very good, little brother. You do your job so well! Let me get you more coffee. Perhaps we—"

"How are the negotiations going with the American?" interrupted Svetov tersely.

Misha was taken aback by Svetov's impertinence. He'd rarely seen anyone treat Petya rudely, especially in Petya's own home. Who were these damned Gagarintsi? With whom had Petya taken up? Svetov was waiting for an answer. "The negotiations just got started," Misha answered. "Yesterday's meeting was mostly introductions. I think—"

"When are they scheduled to meet next?" interrupted Svetov again.

Misha glanced at Petya, who was refilling his coffee cup. Silently. "Tomorrow morning."

Svetov thought a moment, then turned to Petya and asked, "How did Shturkin act when you saw him today at MinFin?"

Petya looked at Svetov with a rare hint of weakness. A look of discomfort Misha hadn't seen on his brother's face in years. And Petya's uneasiness added to his own.

"Everything seems to be fine," replied Petya in a lowered voice. "The Ministry just hasn't had an opportunity to make an official communication to Lukov yet." His tone was more than just respectful, it was somehow…obedient.

"Where is your telephone, Petya?" asked Svetov, rising from his seat. Petya pointed to the living room, where the wan man went to make a call.

"He's such a diligent businessman," said Petya, shaking the apprehension from his face and voice with a deep breath. "He will definitely rise to the top some day, little brother. When you first told us about Mosteks' planned joint venture, he went to see Lukov within an hour. He certainly doesn't waste time suntanning! We're working on several projects together. He's quite good."

Misha was about to ask more about Svetov, to perhaps learn where his brother had met the man, when he looked down and saw Petya flipping through a stack of photographs on the table. They were of a small apartment building which was at least fifty years old. The more ornate brick architecture had been abandoned by the Soviets after World War II as *inefficient* and *costly*. "What are those?" he asked.

"Oh, just part of one of our projects. Unfortunately we have a misbehaving client." Petya stopped flipping through the pictures when he came to a picture of a young woman descending the building's steps. He studied it for a moment and put it in a separate pile.

Petya looked up at Misha and twitched an eyebrow, causing a chill to descend the latter's spine. Misha knew the Russian mafia's tactics, how the families of businessmen who refused to be shaken down were routinely brutalized. What is going on here? he wondered anxiously. What does Petya have in mind for that girl? Misha reflexively turned his head when he felt his breathing accelerate, bringing Svetov, who sat on the couch in the living room, into his view. The man was bent slightly forward, his arm propped up on a knee. He was speaking quietly on the phone, his face coldly undisturbed.

"You're not going to hurt her, are you, Petya?" Misha hadn't planned to ask the question; the words just came out on their own. He turned to look at Petya, slowly realizing the gravity of his impetuous inquiry.

Petya's expression became contemplative for a moment. He gave a nervous chuckle, then said, "I'm not going to do anything to her, Misha. Do you really think I'd do that sort of thing?"

Misha could almost feel the color leave his face. "You told me that no one would ever get hurt, Petya!"

"Little brother, little brother. She'll be fine! Besides, it will be good for her. She's too old to be a virgin."

Misha tried, but could not control his heavy breathing. What should he say?

Nothing. Go home, think about it, decide later. It was always the best plan.

But again the words came out by themselves, only this time they were nearly a yell: "You *said* that no one would ever get—"

"I'm afraid I must ask you to leave, Misha," interrupted Svetov, returning to the dining room. "I hope you're not offended, but there are things Petya and I must discuss alone."

Misha was panting now, looking first at his brother, then at Svetov. He was about to tell Svetov to go to the prick, but figured he'd let Petya say it for him. Petya would never allow some fucking stranger to kick his little brother out of his apartment.

But Petya sat silently, looking up at Misha with only a hint of trepidation in his eyes. "I'll call you this evening, little brother," he said finally. "Thank you very much. Here's payment for your services." Petya then extended an envelope to Misha.

Misha stood looking at his brother for a moment. He felt his legs start to leave, but before he could take the first step, his hand had snatched the envelope. Only then did he stomp toward the front door.

He was about to turn the handle when he heard Svetov's *nagliy* voice once more: "Was that all you had to tell us, Misha? Was there anything else besides the sick factory workers?"

Misha opened the door and stepped outside. "That was all," he said, never looking back at the men inside. He closed the door behind him and headed toward his Zhiguli.

THIRTEEN

Sam stood in the lobby of Hotel Novgorod, looking through the window at the front parking lot, waiting for Misha's car to pull up. Two stocky old women, their heads wrapped in colorful kerchiefs, were busily sweeping snow from the hotel's front steps. Their cheeks were red from the cold, but somehow the *babushkas* seemed unaware of the elements, as if they were seals or walruses or something.

This morning Sam was scheduled to tour the Mosteks factory. He was curious as to what the Russian facility would be like. He'd seen pictures of West European mills before, most of which more or less resembled those in the States. But the Soviet-made Mosteks equipment was probably old and obsolete, too say the least. The Russkies had never exactly been world leaders in textile technology.

He watched the two *babushkas* team their strength to sweep under a ledge. Sam had to stop himself from running out to offer them a hand. They didn't seem to expect, or even need, male assistance. Who was he to interfere with someone else's culture?

Instead, he turned and began pacing, looking around the hotel's lackluster lobby. Why hadn't Ilya been keen on showing him the factory? he wondered. The man had almost dropped his glass of tea when Sam had suggested it. Was there something in the plant he didn't want IIS to know about? What the hell could be hidden in a friggin' factory? The Russians should have been eager to show him what equipment they needed. Was Ilya just embarrassed about something?

Sam shook his head and dismissed the concern. Maybe he just hadn't acclimated to the strange new environment yet. Russia to him had always been the setting for spy novels and the looming global threat on Nightline. Maybe a Russian would feel the same way in Newport News, Virginia. Besides, if there was any danger, Misha would know about it.

He thought about his new friend and wondered what he was all about. Misha looked happier than the Russians on the street; he was better dressed, in better shape, and his face didn't bear that look of challenged endurance, of survival over unpleasant circumstances. Grunshteyn was not a Slavic name, it was probably Jewish. But weren't Russian Jews supposed to be particularly oppressed people? Was the Grunshteyn family somehow privileged? How had Misha grown up, and what was his life really like?

Finally Sam saw the filthy Zhiguli sedan arrive. He left the hotel, took a last look at the steadfast *babushka* sweepers, and quickly got into the car. "Good morning," he said to Misha.

"So sorry I'm late, Sam. I had to prepare factory for your visit. All is now in order."

"Can't wait," said Sam, warming his hands to the car's heater.

The Zhiguli left the hotel lot, entered a two-lane thoroughfare, and began weaving around the morning traffic toward Moscow's Gagarinskaya district. It was usually about a half-hour drive, but Sam could see that rush hour traffic would make it longer. "So tell me about the Grunshteyns," he said. "Do you have brothers and sisters?"

Misha paused before answering. "Yes." He glanced at Sam inquisitively, then added, "One brother."

When it was clear the question hadn't broken the ice, Sam said, "I'm an only child." A moment later he added, "My grandfather immigrated from Russia. He was a Russian Jew."

Misha's expression eased. "You are Jew? I am fifty-fifty Jew."

"I figured," said Sam. "Your name doesn't sound like one out of *War and Peace*. Besides, you used a Jewish word yesterday at lunch. Remember? You said it was a *mitzvah* to take care of a drunk friend."

"I remember. My father was Jew. He die few years ago."

"Sorry to hear that. I'm actually half Jewish, too."

Misha looked baffled.

"Is that surprising?" Sam asked.

"No. Is just that I think of you as American. That is your nationality. But I know there is different understanding of such things in America."

"Judaism is a religion."

"Of course, Sam. But here it is much more. It is nationality as well. You see, every citizen of Russian Federation having nationality. Most, of course, are Russian, but there are over hundred nationalities in all. Jews having own separate nationality." He tapped the dashboard with the side of his hand.

"Does it make a difference?" asked Sam.

"Big difference, my friend. For one thing, nationality written in passport for identification to authorities." He reached across Sam's knees, opened the glove box and removed his red passport. "We always carrying this."

"Does your passport say 'Jew' in it?"

"No. Mine say 'Russian.' My Mama is Russian, and parents have choice of children's nationality. Russian better because there are often unpublished quotas for Jews in education and jobs."

Sam was taken aback by Misha's explanation. It was his first personal contact with institutional anti-Semitism, his first interaction with a real victim. Of course he'd heard and read about the bigotry that Russian Jews suffered, but countless faceless victims couldn't do what a single acquaintance could. A person whose face and personality was familiar. Sam considered making some remark to voice his feelings, but the expressions which came to mind seemed trivial.

"More importantly," continued Misha, "if one ever get in trouble with authorities and passport say 'Jew,' he get in worse trouble. But my passport not fooling anybody, Sam. Grunshteyn is very Jewish name. Is pity my father was Jew and not mother, understand?" He smiled ruefully. "Do you follow Jewish religion?"

"A little bit. Not as much anymore. My father, who also passed away a few years ago, was my Jewish parent, too. It's not like I've ever regularly gone to synagogue, though. What about you?"

"I guess am interested in religion. But is difficult to be observant Jew here, especially when having serious career." He shrugged his shoulders. "Maybe someday I pay more attention to Jewish religion. My Papa would have liked it."

"Is the anti-Semitism getting any better in Russia?"

Misha shook his head. "Worse. There always been people who hate Jews here, but they used to be quiet. Now they come out. Organizations formed with plan to get rid of Jews. They even planning pogroms, like in nineteenth century. Is very scary. Even for half-Jews."

Sam felt sorry for Misha, and very lucky he hadn't been born in Moscow. The worst anti-Semitic affront he'd ever encountered was nothing compared to this.

"One thing happen to me was when I was in middle school— how you say—high school. When I was soccer player. Anti-Semitic trainer not allow me to travel to France with team. He give my wing position to other boy, who was awful player. Hopefully, my Papa tell me, this will be most horrible experience with anti-Semitism I ever have."

"Why do you think it's so bad here?" asked Sam. He looked through the window at Muscovites milling about the streets and sidewalks.

"I think is very easy for people to blame others for their own troubles and unhappiness. Unfortunately, there many unhappy people in Russia. Life very difficult here, as you may see, Sam. I think is natural to look for someone to accuse."

"They're called a scapegoat in English. The people who get unfairly blamed."

Misha nodded his head. "You are lucky things not so bad in America. People not needing scapegoat."

Sam was about to agree, but kept quiet instead, watching the unfamiliar surroundings pass by.

"Are you married?" asked Misha after a brief silence.

"No. Are you?"

Misha displayed a thin gold wedding band on his right ring finger.

Sam smiled. "You have it on the wrong hand, don't you bud?"

"No, my friend. Is Americans who wearing ring on wrong hand." He smiled back.

"How long have you been married?"

"Six months. To wonderful woman. You will see that women in Russia are best, Sam. They have wonderful spirit. I will make you introduction to Russian girl, tonight maybe." He looked at Sam enthusiastically.

"I have a girlfriend, sort of, at home. Sort of."

"Ah. Thanks God she at home and not here, my friend." Misha gave a naughty smile. "Is important to have second women. I have several."

"Didn't you just say you just got hitched? Married?"

"To wonderful woman."

"And you're already thinking about screwing around with others?"

"What thinking? Doing!"

Sam sat silently. He was going to joke at Misha's decadence, but decided against it. Relationships in Russia might differ from those back home, but were surely no less complicated or difficult. Hell, they were probably far more difficult, as tough as life seemed to be here. He briefly wondered how the absence of material comforts might affect his own attitude toward women and fidelity.

Sam was looking straight ahead when he saw a man dressed in a bluish gray overcoat and hat suddenly step into the street, pointing a white stick directly at Misha. Sam had noticed that militiamen were stationed on almost every intersection in Moscow, eyeing traffic from enclosed booths raised some twenty feet from the ground. Like hawks waiting to dive on unsuspecting field mice. Misha pulled over to the side of the road.

"What's wrong?" Sam asked, looking back at the cop. "Were you speeding?"

"I'll tell you right now," replied Misha, shrugging and raising his brow as if to say, "no big deal." He got out of the car with his passport and ran back to meet the militiaman.

In less than half a minute, Misha had returned and the two were on their way.

"Well?" asked Sam.

Misha laughed. "My car is filthy. Five hundred rubles to Comrade Traffic Cop for letting me know this." He laughed.

"You mean you just paid a bribe to a cop? To ignore your dirty car?"

Misha shrugged. "As you Americans say, 'is the cost of doing business.'"

Misha slowed down as the Mosteks building came into view. Sam instantly recalled Lyena, picturing her captivating eyes and curvaceous body, wondering if she'd be there. And whether she'd at least say hello and share a moment with him this time. He was glad he hadn't joked about Misha's "second women."

Thankfully, Misha parked in a space right in front of the factory's entrance. When he got out of the car, Sam immediately smelled the industrial chemicals used in fabric production. They were probably being inefficiently or improperly contained. But he ignored the odor and rushed inside to escape the cold.

Ilya and Albert Denisov, Mosteks' manager, were waiting in the building's foyer, both dressed in the same clothes they'd had on the day before. But although they wore hospitable smiles, Sam thought their expressions were slightly anxious.

"Good morning, Sam. How you sleeping last night?" asked Ilya. He spoke as if he couldn't even hear the blaring factory noise, which resounded through a metal door behind him leading into the plant.

"Unfortunately not too well," said Sam. "I've never been much good with jet lag. Hopefully I'll be set on Moscow time tomorrow."

"I hope so, my friend. As you requested, we now showing you our facility. Like I said, it probably not be so interesting for you. Maybe you just have quick look and relax for rest of today."

Ilya conversed momentarily with Albert in Russian. The chairman wasn't being as jovial as the day before—something was clearly on his mind. Mellow out, Ilya, thought Sam. What do you think I came to Moscow for, the vodka? What's in that damned factory?

A moment later, Ilya turned his attention back to Sam and said, "Misha giving you tour of plant now. Albert and I meeting with you later. If there is anything you need, Lyena will be at your service."

Sam smiled at Ilya's choice of words, then started to follow Misha into the factory. He'd looked around and was about to ask where Lyena was when she suddenly appeared through a side door in the foyer.

Sam stopped short. Lyena wore a black skirt and green mohair sweater, both of which revealed her shape nicely. Very nicely. She had seen Sam first and given him a half smile, then looked back at Misha with that same bland expression she'd had on all morning yesterday. But Sam felt his lungs fill with air nonetheless.

"Shall we go into production facility?" asked Misha, pointing the way with a wave of his hand.

"How are you, Lyena?" said Sam, adjusting his tie.

"I'm fine, Sam," she said.

He was about to continue, but Misha had just opened the metal door, letting in the full force of the plant's deafening noise. Sam would have to wait until later to follow up, but at least she'd spoken to him.

The Mosteks facility consisted of a main chamber containing four spinning mill processing lines, with passages leading into smaller chambers. The facility's machinery was operated by diligent workers, at least half of whom, to Sam's surprise, were middle-aged and elderly women.

Their faces were large and round, their heads draped with multicolored kerchiefs that clashed with their patterned dresses. They worked single-mindedly, apparently having no problem pushing large carts of finished fabric and positioning heavy machinery components. Sam almost offered to help, but again caught himself. Like the women sweeping at Hotel Novgorod, these didn't seem to need, or want, any assistance. Indeed, they hardly even noticed him. Maybe he was just a victim of sexist conditioning, he thought.

Sam immediately recognized that the operation was very primitive by Western standards, employing antiquated techniques that were inefficient in both manpower and machinery. The equipment was poorly maintained, the result of having too few proper spare parts, and couldn't possibly last for long-term operations. Labor was obviously cheap and easy to come by here, which was probably why Davies and Kaplan had chosen the Russian cooperative for a partner. Sam just wondered if his boss knew exactly how obsolete Mosteks' production lines were.

He stopped by a cotton sorter, which rocked precariously as its sifters turned. "That thing's going to collapse any minute, Misha," he said impetuously, then regretted it. He remembered that Misha was in charge of the equipment here and was probably proud that it was working at all.

Misha shrugged. "Hopefully we will be able to fix it soon."

Misha explained Mosteks' manufacturing scheme as the three walked through the plant. Occasionally Sam tried asking questions of Lyena, who seemed a little more relaxed than she'd been with Ilya and the rest of the Mosteks big wigs. Still, she was rather quiet and meek, answering his inquiries only with short answers.

But Sam just knew she wasn't this timid by nature. No way! She carried herself too damned confidently, even when she tried to appear reserved. He looked at her for a moment as they walked along, waiting for her to catch sight of him. She finally did. Was there something there in those uncommon eyes? Some hint of a fondness for him? Sam promised himself he would find out, sooner or later. But he couldn't allow himself to be preoccupied with her now.

Later in the tour, Sam saw that one of the mills was not operational at all. He asked Misha why it was out.

Safety latch mechanism on press malfunctioning," answered Misha. "Is too dangerous to work it. This is also on list of machinery we must to replace."

"But this is a Soviet model. Can't you get replacement parts for it here?"

"There are shortages of everything in Russia, Sam, even industrial replacement parts. Besides, this mill fifty years old. We obtained it from Ministry of Light Industry because they were preparing to sell it for scrap metal. Is time to acquire new mill with updated technology."

"What about your other equipment? I can see it's still functional, but how much of it is reliable? Is it all that old?"

"Some of it, yes. Is reliable, but only to produce substandard product. This is another reason we needing IIS help. Shall we move along?"

Sam noticed that the workers were ignoring them, which also seemed strange. Surely they didn't see foreigners touring their plant very often. Perhaps they'd been instructed by the directorate to work especially hard today.

"This is chemical preparation department," said Misha as the three entered a smaller chamber. "Chemical treatments taking place in these tanks."

Sam was relieved to escape the pounding noise of the main room, but as he'd suspected, the chemicals in the treatment area were improperly contained, causing his eyes to water painfully. He rubbed them and said, "One thing we've got to put on the equipment contribution list is more saturation tanks, so you and your workers won't have to breathe these fumes. They can be dangerous after long-term exposure."

"It will be nice," said Lyena, unexpectedly.

She looked at Sam, trying, perhaps, to tell him something. She wanted to say more, Sam thought, but for some reason had caught herself and decided against it. "It will be much easier on the staff," he said, looking under her sloping eyebrows, hoping she would continue. But Lyena only gave him a faint smile before turning away.

Damn it, why was she acting this way? Was she afraid he might somehow get her in trouble?

Sam had left his guides to use the restroom and was returning to meet them in Misha's small office. He had to pass mill number one on the way through the plant, where several of Mosteks' employees were busily operating machinery.

He approached a scraggly-looking worker loading carts of finished fiber. The man's face was blackened by machinery oil, allowing only his determined blue eyes to shine through.

"Hi," said Sam over the noise of the factory, smiling genially. "Do you speak English?"

The man stared at him blankly.

"American. I'm an American. Business man," he said, poking himself in the chest, trying to be jovial.

But the worker abruptly turned and walked away. Sam thought he'd detected a hint of fear in the worker's eyes, but he shrugged and continued toward Misha's office.

A few steps later, he encountered a female employee sweeping bits of fabric from around a raking machine. She was a pleasant-looking lady, her body almost a perfect beach ball, her rosy red cheeks matching the kerchief wrapped around her head. She was humming pleasantly under the blaring machinery.

"Hi. I'm Sam." He smiled and extended his hand to the woman.

The *babushka's* pleasant expression immediately melted into one of trepidation and she hobbled away behind the raker. Sam was sure of it this time. He'd definitely seen fear, momentary anxiety, in the woman's face. What was her problem?

"Hey! What's the matter?" he called, following her around the contraption. "I'm not the bogeyman! Come back!"

The woman had stopped running and was standing there looking at him, still wide-eyed. He held out his hand, palm up. "What's the matter, ma'am?" He took one step toward her, and the woman scurried away behind another machine.

He stood there a moment, confused. Why was she so frightened? What was going on?

Just then, he heard a shriek through the blaring factory noise. It almost sounded like the screech of a car slamming on breaks. Some half-century-old piece of machinery finally collapsing, Sam figured.

Eeeee! He heard it again.

No. It wasn't mechanical. He began running in between several sorting machines, looking left and right, searching for the source of the shrill noise. Searching for the woman. His heart began to race.

Eeeee!

He was getting close, the sound was nearer. He turned around and ran between two other machines.

There was the woman, the back of her floral print dress caught in the exposed gears of a fabric roller. It was pulling her up and back. Into the engine. The shrill noises had been her screams.

Sam threw off his overcoat and ran to the woman. He tried to pull the back of her dress out of the machine, but it wouldn't give. He couldn't reach behind her without getting his hands caught in the teeth of the gears. "How do you turn it off?" he yelled, his heart now pounding in his chest. "Where are the controls?"

The woman only screamed in response, her left hand pushing against the machine, trying desperately to keep herself from being sucked into the gears.

"Help! Help!" yelled Sam, twisting around, looking for someone, anyone, who could turn the machine off. But he knew that no one would hear him through the factory noise.

Sam ran around the fabric roller, then climbed on top of it, stepping on a wooden block that had apparently been put there for that purpose. On top of the machine was a set of controls, some of which were labeled.

He rubbed at the words under the buttons and knobs, clearing off dirt and oil, trying to find the off switch. Which one? Which one? Which one? he thought frantically. Only then did he realize that the words were all written in Russian.

He looked down at the woman and saw that her feet were off the ground. Tears were streaming down her face, and her shrieks were now continuous. She was trying to say something, perhaps a prayer, while frantically crossing her chest with her free hand.

"Help! Help!" cried Sam, pushing every button and pulling every knob on the control panel. But nothing he tried would stop the contraption.

He jumped down from the machine and ran around to its opposite side. A cover panel was loosely held up by a makeshift piece of metal, perhaps an unfolded clothes hanger. Sam forced the panel open and found several wires, all leading into the engine of the machine.

He reached to grab them. To pull them out.

Suddenly he snatched his hand back. If these were live wires, they would fry him!

Eeeee!

Sam had to do something. He closed his eyes, reached back in, and grabbed a fistful of bundled electrical works. He held his breath. He pulled.

Nothing. They wouldn't give.

Eeeee!

He pulled again, this time with all his strength.

Some of the wires came out in his hand. But had anything happened? Was the woman still caught in the engine? There was too much factory noise to tell if the fabric roller had shut down.

She was still wailing, he heard. But the sound was different now. She was crying, mumbling something to herself.

Sam ran around to the other side of the machine, to the woman. She was still trapped, her dress still caught in the silenced gears. But there was no blood. She was all right. The roller was off. Thank God. He took a moment to catch his breath. "It's okay, ma'am," he said. "I'm going to get you down."

He reached behind her to release her dress, but the woman suddenly pushed him back, nearly knocking him down, yelling something at him though her tears. She was admonishing him, blaming him for what had happened.

"I'm sorry, ma'am. I just wanted to talk to you, that's all. I'm sorry. I—"

Just then, the blue-eyed male worker Sam had spoken to earlier came running up. He was standing there, maybe twenty feet away, with some unfamiliar tool in his hand. He looked at his coworker, then at Sam, then back at the woman. He took a step forward, then stopped. He looked back at Sam.

"She's okay," said Sam. "We just have to get her down." He moved toward the man, who flinched and stepped back, as if he were considering running away.

Sam stopped, stood still. "Okay. I'm sorry. Please come take care of her," he said. "Help me get her down."

Finally, the man complied and helped free the woman. When she was loose, she ran away as fast as her legs would carry her. Sam waved at the confused male worker to show his thanks, then picked up his overcoat and walked off in the other direction.

He paused and looked around the chamber for the woman. She'd disappeared. He saw only other busy workers. To his consternation, they, too, immediately looked away from him when he attempted to meet their eyes. "What the hell is going on here?" he demanded, then quickly headed back toward Misha's office.

"Your problems are worse than you thought," he said as he entered Misha's small, cluttered cubicle. He fixed his hair and cleared a bit of grime from his hands. He explained what had happened, trying to keep his voice calm, trying not to sound frazzled.

Misha was quiet as he listened, his brow knitted in an uncharacteristically disturbed expression. Lyena, who was also in the office, began tidying up, pretending not to be involved in the conversation.

Misha said, "I will check the fabric roller and the upset worker right now, Sam. I am sorry for this. Is not your fault for wishing conversation with worker. I am grateful for your help." He looked down.

Sam was confused. Was that it? One of his workers was almost ground into sausage, and he's just a little embarrassed about it all! Sam sighed, looking through the window at the dilapidated Mosteks machinery. But then, what else could Misha say or do? This probably wasn't the first time something like this had happened here. What would he do in Misha's shoes? Sam patted Misha on the shoulder. "Thanks. But tell me something. Why are your workers so anti-social? So shy? You would've thought I was KGB or something for trying to be friendly."

Misha shrugged his shoulders. "I not know. Maybe they thinking you from State Inspector's Office, Sam. They might fear you checking them."

Boris Shturkin sat behind his warped metal desk, drumming his fingers and looking around his small office. He had long wished for better office accommodations, but knew there was little hope of improvement. The ministries couldn't stay within their budgets even without worrying about their employees' amenities.

Only a few weeks ago it had seemed that a financial break was in his grasp, but now he was agonizing over what he'd gotten himself into. He'd saved all of the *valuta* he'd received from Mosteks, taking it out every morning from his locked drawer just to fondle it. Damn! There was simply no way he could disobey Svetov's orders and risk a confrontation with the Gagarintsi. He just hoped like hell that nothing would go awry with his plan and alert Lukov.

Finally the telephone rang, and Boris lifted the receiver on the first ring. "I'm listening to you," he said in bureaucratic fashion.

A gruff voice replied, "Begov Street, in front of building number 27, thirty minutes." The line went dead.

Boris quickly stood from behind the battered desk, put on his overcoat and hat, and left the MinFin building.

He didn't even know the man's name. After Svetov's first visit regarding the Mosteks JV, Boris had spoken with another

MinFin employee, a friend of his who'd been in a similar dilemma with the mafia a few months earlier. He'd asked his colleague for suggestions, and the latter had told him whom to contact. Only after the unnamed Gagarinets had come, the one with the familiar eyes, had he found the courage to call.

The man was short and stocky. His eyes blinked rarely. It was cold out, very cold, but the man seemed overly bundled-up nonetheless. Only his eyes and nose were visible through the layers of brown wool and fur.

How had Boris managed to involve himself with a thug like this? How was it that so many government officials were making a fortune through international business without a hitch, and he had 'stepped into a blind alley' by taking up with the wrong mafia? He shook the thug's powerful hand while looking at the icy sidewalk.

"Shall we walk, Boris Antonovich?" said the man. "It will be safer that way."

The suggestion wouldn't have bothered Boris ten years ago, before *glasnost,* when all Soviets watched everything they said, wherever they said it. But now, secrecy only highlighted the depravity of what he was doing. Nonetheless, he followed the man's cue and began to walk down the sidewalk.

"Our common acquaintance has told me you are 'in the cat's soup,'" said the man, his tone businesslike and affable, not unlike Svetov's. "That you have a problem with a cooperative that wants to register a joint venture."

Boris realized he would have to tell the hood everything about his situation. He looked up at the grey sky and said, "That's correct. I would like you to see that the cooperative does not continue with its efforts to form a JV." He spoke quickly, never looking at his audience.

"I am happy to be of assistance," replied the man. "But aren't you in the perfect position to see to that yourself?"

Boris explained to the thug how Ilya Lukov had paid him *valuta* to see to MinFin's registration of the JV, and how he was now unable to deliver. And that he didn't want to have to return the dollars. "If Mosteks abandons the project on its own, I can always claim that I've kept my end of the bargain," he said, still speaking quickly, but in a lowered voice. "Then, Lukov couldn't demand that I return the dollars to him." It seemed so shameful, so heinous, when explained out loud, especially to the likes of his present company. Perhaps that was because Boris didn't have the luxury of adding the cliché, "And who gets hurt?"

"How far has Mosteks gotten in its negotiations with the American company?" asked the thug. He was obviously seasoned at such conversations, walking along confidently, looking straight ahead, aware of everything going on around him. The man's massive body never shifted under his bulky overcoat; it seemed that only his lips and legs moved at all. Boris couldn't tell how old the man was; he could have been anywhere from thirty to sixty, his lined face and covered head revealing few features.

Boris told him about Sam Morris, who was in Moscow for another five days to complete the JV negotiations. He answered the thug's questions about the American, becoming more anxious with each inquiry, wondering if he was making a terrible mistake.

"In which hotel is the American lawyer staying? What is his schedule?"

What did this man have in mind? Boris wondered anxiously as he answered the questions mechanically. Why was he asking these things? Maybe Boris didn't want to know.

"Are there other Americans with him? Has Morris met with any other governmental agencies?"

Boris wanted to object, to make some stand that would convince at least himself that he was a decent man despite all this. But he couldn't. The hood was his only hope. He had to rely on him.

"How big is the American? Does he look like a sportsman? Does he seem strong?"

Boris stopped walking, silent, looking at the grayish snow on the sidewalk.

"Boris Antonovich?"

He thought of his family, of his wife and son, who hadn't left Moscow in five years. They hadn't eaten in a nice restaurant in months and were in need of new clothes. He was tired of his eighty-year-old mother having to wait in line at the market for hours to buy thin chickens. There was nothing for him and his loved ones to look forward to, no hope of something to improve their lives. He'd waited too damned long. He sighed and turned his gaze to the grey sky.

In Russia, every man must fend for himself! Boris didn't know what the thug might do to Sam Morris to thwart the JV; hopefully the American wouldn't be hurt too badly. But there was simply no alternative. "He doesn't seem to be a physical threat," Boris said, having turned to look straight into the man's eyes. "I don't think that's a concern."

The thug nodded.

"As per your terms, I will pay you two thousand dollars—half now, and half when Lukov advises me that the Mosteks joint venture is no longer pending," concluded Boris. He removed a stack of green bills from his coat pocket and handed it to the nameless man.

The thug took the money and quickly stuffed it into his coat. He looked at Boris and said, "It seems that times are bad for you, Boris Antonovich."

Again, Boris met the unblinking eyes. "Aren't they for us all?"

FOURTEEN

It was only three o'clock in the afternoon, but it was already dusk in Moscow. Sam was in a small park on Tverskaya Street, pacing beneath the huge monument to Vladimir Mayakovsky, the famous poet of the 1917 revolution. Tverskaya, Sam had learned, was the historic Russian name of the thoroughfare renamed from the communist "Gorky Street."

The statue stood stoically, impervious to the cold and bitter wind that tortured Sam. He checked his Rolex for the tenth time while he walked to and fro, again recalling Ned's words about Russian tardiness. He promised himself he'd never arrange a meeting with a Russian outdoors again.

Finally, a diminutive man staggered into view, his wobbly, short-stepped gait reminding Sam of a penguin's. The old man was both scholarly and amiable in his mien. He wore a white goatee which, Sam decided, befitted his personality, even though he hadn't even met him yet. As the man came closer, Sam saw that his clumsy walk was accentuated by an awkward dependence on a walking cane, the top of which he clutched in a closed fist. With each quick step, the old man swung his elbow outward to keep his balance.

"Hello, my nephew. Uncle Yasha at your service," he said, shaking Sam's hand warmly with both of his own, which required Yasha to hold his chipped cane under one arm. "Ah-hah! My nephew has the distinctive nose of a Mrachnikov—uh, of a Morris, as it now is. Anyway, he need not further demonstrate his identity."

"I've heard that all my life," replied Sam. He found himself instantly enjoying his uncle's spirit.

"And so. Now we shall go to Uncle Yasha's luxurious apartment, replete with English antique furniture and Van Gogh paintings. My butler will be happy to prepare you the finest veal for lunch," joked the old timer, waving his arms as he spoke.

"Sounds exquisite," said Sam. He picked up his briefcase and followed Yasha into the nearby metro entrance.

The two descended a long escalator into the Mayakovsky station. Sam's first use of the Moscow metro was exciting. The clean, ornately decorated hall was a splendid contrast to the grime of New York City's subway. Paintings depicting Russian achievements during the 1930s adorned the ceilings. Gone were the cracked tiles he was accustomed to ignoring in the New York system. There was no litter or tattered walls, and the metro ran orderly and efficiently.

"How have you been eating, my nephew?" asked Yasha, following Sam into a subway car.

"Not badly. I brought some things with me for breakfast in my hotel room, and my company's partners have been taking me to nice restaurants."

"Good. I'd hate for my nephew to starve on his visit to see me!" Yasha laughed playfully, reaching up to pinch Sam's cheek.

Sam was looking around at the other metro passengers when the train accelerated, and he had to grab an overhead bar to keep from stumbling. He saw that the riders all had sullen, downcast faces, except for the few who'd apparently caught sight of his suit. Those stared directly at him, as if they were criticizing him for having the nerve to be riding their metro in such attire. Sam returned one man's gawk momentarily, but diverted his eyes to avoid what might have become a confrontation.

Yasha had noticed the exchange. "Look at his shoes, next time," whispered the old man, winking amiably.

"What?"

"Next time someone gives you the eyeball like that, just look at his or her shoes. They'll stop every time. Most Russians are very discontent with their shoes, and if they see you've noticed them, they'll become self-conscious. They're staring because they envy you and don't know how to live with their dissatisfaction. It's all psychological, you see." Yasha again winked to confirm the tip.

"'Preciate it," Sam whispered back.

They arrived at Yasha's station, left the metro—again by way of a long escalator—and walked along a snow-covered path toward the Edelman apartment. "You know, there's so many little tricks to getting around in Moscow, Uncle Yasha," said Sam. "I could live here for years and not figure it all out."

"Oh, yes. I'm sure it must be quite confusing for a young newcomer. It's baffling even for an old man who's lived here all his life! And Russian mentality is especially confusing now, because we're in a time of transition, you see. We're trying to get our bearings straight."

"How do you speak English so well? You hardly have any accent!"

"I'm an old man. One can learn very much in eighty-one years, my nephew."

"Come on. There's lots of eighty-one-year-old Russians who don't speak perfect English."

"But they haven't spent their lives reading underground Western literature and having secret meetings with foreign writers, young Sam. English is just one thing that seeps in after decades of such a life."

They entered the dark, musty foyer of Yasha's huge apartment building and boarded a broom-closet-sized elevator that ran through the center of a winding cement staircase. The lift rose precariously, its mechanical noise reminding Sam of the sounds at Mosteks.

The elevator stopped with a jolting thud, and the two men squeezed their way out. Sam followed Yasha down a chipped concrete hallway to his uncle's apartment. Yasha put his finger to his lips, advising Sam to be silent, then opened the door.

"You didn't know that visiting an uncle could be such an adventure, did you?" he said after safely closing the door behind Sam.

"What's the big secret?" asked Sam, still speaking in a hushed voice.

"It's just not a good idea for the neighbors to know who's visiting me, my nephew. No big deal. Like something out of an old Russian spy novel, eh?" He gave Sam his now-familiar wink. "And before I forget. Don't call me again from your hotel room. Just as a precaution. If we ever agree to meet in the future, assume the rendezvous will be in the same place as today. You needn't mention the Mayakovsky statue over the phone."

The two removed their overcoats and hung them on wall pegs in the entranceway. Following Yasha's cue, Sam stepped out of his shoes and put on one of several pairs of slippers.

Had he not been familiar with New York City flats, Sam would have immediately noted how small the Edelman apartment was. The floors were, of course, wooden parquet and the walls were covered with an old orange-yellow wallpaper that was hidden by furniture and as many pictures as possible. The living room was lined with overloaded bookshelves; a frayed green sofa and a small wooden table with chairs filled the floor space. A manuscript, apparently being edited, lay spread out on the table. Sam couldn't imagine what the place might have looked like brand new.

He was surprised when Yasha suddenly began speaking out loud in Russian. Soon, a short elderly woman appeared from the kitchen, her kind grey eyes a perfect match for Yasha's amiable face. She carried a tray of hot tea and slices of cake.

Yasha said, "This is my wife Lilli, Sam. I'm afraid she doesn't speak much English, but she's been waiting anxiously to meet you."

Sam approached the woman and bent down to kiss her cheek. "It's a pleasure to meet you, Aunt Lilli," he said slowly.

Lilli smiled and said something to Yasha, who promptly translated. "We should sit in the living room, nephew. Aunt Lilli has some delicious treats for us."

Sam followed his uncle and joined him at the small table, warming his hands to the radiator. "What are you writing?" he asked.

"Oh, nothing special. Just some thoughts on the impending Russian revolution, that's all," answered Yasha with a wave of his hand. He gathered up the manuscript and placed it on the floor.

"Sounds pretty profound to me. Is everyone writing books about an impending revolution?"

"A few are, especially in my writers' association. But nobody's reading what we write, so who cares?" He laughed. "These days it's difficult to get such things published and distributed in Russia, you see."

"I heard you upset the Soviet government a few years back with one of your books."

Yasha laughed again. "Yes, thank God. I'd hate to think those bastards would ever like anything I wrote."

"What did you write?"

"Oh, just some anti-Soviet rhetoric about government mistreatment of Jews during the early 1960s," he answered. "Strange how touchy the Party was in those days."

Sam laughed. "You must've been a real hell-raiser back then. Weren't you at all afraid of getting in trouble?"

"Getting in trouble? Young Sam, I was always in trouble. Still am, even under the new regime. It's just a matter of how much and with whom!" He rolled his eyes.

Sam shook his head incredulously, still smiling. "It doesn't look like you've let up any, Uncle Yasha. But it must be easier to write like that now than it was thirty years ago."

"Yes, I guess you could say that. But the biggest advantage is that now there are more people willing to express their thoughts. More with whom I can commiserate. And with so many people running their mouths, they can't keep up with us all."

Sam wasn't sure who "they" were, but he figured Yasha would tell him soon enough. It was clear the old man was one of those enigmatic conversationalists, and Sam thought it would be fun to play along. "You're not worried about anything?" he asked.

"Oh, no, young Sam." Yasha's face became serious. "I never worry. Life's far too short for that. Be concerned, yes. I've spent a lifetime being concerned. But I do what I can and then go home to my lovely wife. My conscience is always clear. The world will just have to take it from there." He picked up a slice of the honey cake Lilli had placed on the table and stuffed it clumsily into his mouth. "Eat! Eat!" he ordered Sam, crumbs falling from his goatee. "How should I face Gussie if she finds out Uncle didn't feed his nephew when he visited?"

Sam joined Yasha in having a slice of cake, glad to have met his interesting and entertaining relative. He was looking forward to getting to know the old timer. "What kind of writers' association do you belong to?" he asked.

"It's called the SS." Yasha remained expressionless for a moment, but upon seeing Sam's confusion, burst into laughter. "No, no, my nephew," he said, placing a hand affectionately on Sam's. "Our namesake is not the *Schutzstaffel*. The Russian phrase *sila slova* means 'power of the word.' We chose that as the name of our association.

"We banded together a few years ago to try to push the limits of *glasnost* to the point of true expressive freedom. We thought that Gorbachev's policies were just a start, see. Sila Slova is a group of quarrelsome old men like myself out to make one final stand before it's too late. Before the uncertainties of the revolution come to bear."

"Why are you so sure there's going to be a revolution?" asked Sam. "Aren't the people happy with Yeltsin's policies and the reforms he's set in motion?"

"You will see, my nephew. A week in Moscow is quite enough to comprehend the impasses our society has reached. You will see everything," said the old-timer, nodding his head assuredly.

Yasha breathed deeply and assumed a didactic demeanor, propping his elbow on the table and supporting his white-haired chin in his hand. The posture was probably one of his favorites, thought Sam, and he braced for what would probably be a lengthy exposé.

"Remember the man who stared at you in the metro? That was a fine example of the symptoms of our impasse. The man saw your nice clothes and almost felt threatened by your presence! Why? Because he knew he could never have such niceties. And why did he feel this way? Because Russians have no sense of an ability to better themselves. No tradition of associating hard work with improvement in their lifestyle. They believe it is their legacy to live difficult lives without the pleasures that other people enjoy.

"You see, nephew, throughout our history, we've been forced to struggle just to—what do you Americans say?—make ends meet. Survive. There has never been much of a spirit of fruit-bearing effort and labor in Russia.

"And now, with our exposure to the West, Russians are resentfully envious of foreign traditions through which other peoples have been able to flourish. Russian xenophobia has finally come home to roost."

"So what's next?" asked Sam, shrugging.

Yasha shrugged back. "Russia must adopt new values. It's as simple as that. From the top to the bottom. From the highest governmental official to the lowliest village peasant. We must first recognize the obstacle, and then we must surmount it. It will surely be a long and difficult process, but it can be done." The old man pointed a finger at the ceiling as he made the point, then reached for a sip of tea.

"But why, then, is there going to be a revolution? A revolution implies quick change. If the process must necessarily be long, don't you mean evolution?"

Yasha shook his head, slowly and resolutely, his eyes tightly closed. He looked well versed at defending his points of view. "A revolution will come sooner because of misallocation of power and influence. You see, the Russian government doesn't function efficiently in serving its people. With few exceptions, only the corrupt can prosper here. It's a great tragedy, and one that can be remedied only by immediate and direct response. Corruption is simply an acute symptom of the larger problem I was describing earlier. Only after a revolution can we begin to tackle our most fundamental sociological problems. The revolution will not cure that larger problem, but it will be a necessary first step, a precursor to its demise."

"But I thought that with the new government and free enterprise initiatives, a new order was already under way."

"Gorbachev and Yeltsin, bless their souls, have revealed our underlying social problems. But their reforms and policies have been a miserable failure so far, and our economy is in shambles. Is this because Gorby's ideas were inept? Is Mr. Yeltsin's vision only pie in the sky? I don't think so. The problem is that the people must be reformed before policy revisions can ever work. And corruption must first be weeded out of the system before we can get a start."

206

Sam looked at his uncle and again considered how good it was to have met him. Yasha was family, from Grandpa Hyman's generation. He wondered what Old Virginia Mills might have been like if Yasha had immigrated to the States with Hyman and helped run the business.

He was family. So shouldn't he be given a chance to make a contribution to the family business? He could probably be very useful, what with his profound understanding of Russian society. He'd certainly want to help out. Sam recalled Davies' order that the joint venture with Mosteks be kept secret. But what could one old man in Moscow possibly do to jeopardize the project or IIS's interests? And shouldn't Sam be able to exercise his own judgment to some extent? He was a lawyer, after all. "Let me tell you some history, Uncle Yasha," he said, watching the old-timer lean forward, eyes attentive. Sam told him about Old Virginia Mills, about Hyman's life and what had happened to the family business after his death. Then he described Old V's merger with IIS.

The old man sat silently, occasionally nodding his head as he absorbed Sam's story.

When Sam had finished, Yasha shifted in his seat and said, "Now tell Uncle more about your business in Moscow."

Sam sighed deeply, again dismissing Davies' order. "I'm working on a joint venture with a cooperative," he said. "Do you know about international joint ventures?"

"Oh, yes, my nephew. You'd be hard-pressed to find a Russian who didn't. But tell me. What is the cooperative like? Do you know much about its management?"

Sam quickly recounted his first two days with Mosteks. "Actually, the chairman has been a little strange lately. He definitely has a healthy entrepreneurial mentality, though. And the other officers don't seem to be the lazy types you were describing."

"What's the name of the cooperative you're dealing with?"

"Mosteks."

Yasha turned his pensive gaze toward the ceiling.

"Do you know it?" asked Sam, sipping his tea.

"No. I don't think so. But, nephew, take some sage advice from your old uncle: Be wary of Mosteks. Of any private enterprise here. Although they may operate in the spirit of capitalism, that is often the only spirit they have. Many successful businesses have proven to be quite unscrupulous. They often believe that it is best to take profits now, even at a partner's expense, rather than risk possible future complications. *Be careful.*" Yasha emphasized the last two words by pounding the table on each syllable.

Sam was quiet for a moment. Had he missed something about Mosteks? Was the cooperative just trying to rip off IIS? And thereby Old Virginia? Was there more to Ilya's strange behavior regarding Sam's tour of the factory? Ilya seemed like a nice enough guy, but—

"Tell me, young Sam," continued Yasha, interrupting Sam's rumination. "Have you noticed any unusual activities from Russian government agencies with respect to the JV?"

Sam thought a moment, then shook his head. "No. The JV law doesn't make sense sometimes, but I think I have a good grasp of it. I haven't actually met anyone from the government at all. At least so far."

"Good," said Yasha. "Perhaps you should keep an eye—"

"Wait a minute," interrupted Sam. "There was one guy who attended our first meeting. He was from...is it called MinFin? The Ministry of Finance?"

Yasha nodded.

"I never did figure out what he was all about. And he was acting pretty strange during the meeting and at lunch. Never said a word, but kept looking at me like he didn't trust me or something."

Yasha sat quietly, stroking his goatee, his brow wrinkled in introspection.

"Do you think he might somehow be a problem?" asked Sam.

"Well, I suppose I can sometimes be a bit overly suspicious, my nephew. But I don't see why MinFin would attend JV business meetings, especially in the negotiations stage. It seems rather odd to me."

Sam felt himself breath deeply. What the hell was going on here? What was that Shturkin character doing at the meeting? Sam recalled the plant workers who'd been so afraid of him, afraid enough to almost get chewed up by a machine rather than say hello to him. What was that all about? Wouldn't Misha know what was going on at Mosteks and warn him if something was wrong?

And what the hell was going on with Lyena?

"Ah, my nephew," said Yasha. "You must forgive me. It's so easy to ignite my fire. I didn't mean to have you over here for a lecture on the problems of Russian business. Don't worry too much about Mosteks. Anything of importance will by necessity come to light sooner or later. Right? Here. Have some more." He poured Sam another cup of tea. "Would you care to play a game of chess?"

"Uh, sure. I'm not much good at it, but I'll give it a shot." He tried to push his concerns out of his mind. Yasha was right. If there was a problem, Sam would find out about it soon enough. But he made a mental note to inquire about Shturkin.

"Do you play often, nephew?" asked Yasha.

"Rarely." Sam figured that Yasha would probably need ten moves to beat him in chess, but it would be an interesting experience to give the Russian national pastime a try. "Tell me more about Russian private enterprise, Uncle Yasha." He smiled. "Something positive, maybe."

Yasha had set up the chess board and now moved a pawn forward. "The private sector, of course, is the most important of our new reforms. And despite their widespread corruption, cooperatives were the first successful efforts at free enterprise here. I think cooperatives and other private enterprise provide Russians with a rare opportunity to shape their own lives." He followed Sam's thoughtful chess moves immediately with his own, snapping up and placing pieces in one fell swoop, seemingly without attention to strategy. "This goes for their employees as well as the owners. The owners take risks and receive personal rewards for their success. But because they also suffer for their failures, they must by necessity command a new work ethic of their employees. A work ethic more typical in the West, which rewards good labor and is intolerant of inefficiency."

Sam found it difficult to concentrate on both Yasha and the chess game. He made his moves impetuously so as not to lag behind while trying to digest what he was hearing.

Lilli had been sitting silently on the sofa throughout the conversation, her hands on her lap. She hadn't seemed to notice the oddity of her husband's simultaneous oration and rapid chess playing.

But a short while later, Sam noticed irritation appear on the woman's lined face. She stood up from the sofa and approached the two men, apparently waiting for an opportune moment to interrupt.

"The private sector corruption I was speaking of earlier is a natural result of the interaction of Russian society with those willing to take initiative," continued Yasha. "I believe—"

Suddenly, Lilli broke in. Sam couldn't understand the Russian words her piqued voice spoke, but it was clear she was coming down hard on Yasha. He almost pitied his uncle, who shuddered at his wife's reproach like a boy seventy-five years his junior. Yasha immediately, almost comically, shut up.

"Please forgiving Uncle Yasha," uttered Lilli. "He always too much philosopher."

She probably wouldn't have understood a plea from Sam to allow Yasha to continue, so he decided not to object.

Yasha cleared his throat and said, "Well, nephew. Perhaps we shall continue our little discussion some other time. Right now, Aunt Lilli would like to hear about our relatives in America. Tell us about yourself, young Sam." He struggled to regain the composure he'd lost at his wife's rebuke. "But before you begin," he whispered, moving a rook into place, "checkmate."

FIFTEEN

The next morning, Misha again picked Sam up in front of Hotel Novgorod. But as the Zhiguli pulled out, Sam realized they weren't headed in the direction of the Mosteks facility. "Where're we going?" he asked.

"Meeting not at cooperative this morning, Sam. We meeting at old union headquarters instead."

"What for?"

Misha shrugged his shoulders nonchalantly, looking straight ahead. "I not know."

Just what Sam needed to hear. He'd spent all of last night mulling over what Yasha had told him about Russian private enterprise. Why had the whole project been fraught with changes in plan? he wondered. Every time he turned around, something was rescheduled, or they hit an unexpected snafu, and it had started before he'd even left New York, when Ilya had postponed his trip! He tried to shake it off. This trip was supposed to be his big chance, he reminded himself. An opportunity to show Davies and Kaplan his mettle, to make him a real player with Old V.

He saw the buff-colored buildings when they approached downtown Moscow. There were no answers in the city's sights, only more questions. What was this place all about? What made it work? What should he know that he didn't?

Sam was scheduled to call IIS today to give the brass a progress report. He considered conveying his uneasiness to Davies. If something went wrong, it would probably be Sam's ass. Maybe he should cover it while he still could.

But no. The boss had sent him here to do a job, to work out the JV's problems. Crying home to Mommy wouldn't show anyone how sharp he was. And besides, nothing concrete had happened to indicate that Mosteks wasn't on the level. Wait and see what develops before saying anything, he decided. He looked across at Misha. At least he had a reliable friend in him.

They pulled up to a large granite building located on a downtown thoroughfare, where Misha parked diagonally. As with most streets in Moscow, there were no gutters to allay the accumulation of black, slushy snow. Sam stepped into a muddy quagmire when he got out of the car and cursed as the cold wetness saturated his shoes. He kicked out water with each step on his way into the building.

"Good morning, Sam," said Ilya with his familiar sanguine smile, greeting Sam by a conference room door. "Let me take your coat."

The same assemblage of Russians were already seated around a long, narrow conference table in the center of the room. The union building's meeting room was nicer than the one at Mosteks; the table was real wood, and paneling covered the walls. As Sam looked around the room, he saw that only Lyena and that Boris Shturkin guy were missing. The Mosteks team seemed more prepared for the negotiations than before—the Russians almost looked fortified. As if the group were prepared to defend itself against an attack. "How are you?" asked Sam cheerfully, feeling them out. He watched the men nod and give silent smiles at his greeting.

"I am sorry about necessity to change meeting's location, Sam," said Ilya. "We believe it wise to keep meetings secret. There are people who thinking we are scheduled to meet at Mosteks again this morning."

Sam ignored the remark's connotation and added it to his list of odd observations. "No problem whatsoever," he responded congenially. He just wanted to finally get down to business. It was his turn to take control and make some real progress. If his mission were to be a success, he had to show his stuff now. He inhaled deeply and prepared to meet the Russians head-on.

"Gentlemen," he began, with Misha's voice translating behind him, "there are a number of issues I am unclear about. I think it prudent to address them now, at the outset." He referred to documents Ilya had sent him before he'd left New York that listed Mosteks' conditions for forming the joint venture. "I have a list here of various photocopying, fax, telex, and computer equipment you have requested that IIS provide the JV. In light of the large investment my company must make in actual production equipment, I believe this to be somewhat excessive. Could you explain why you think it should be our obligation to furnish such machinery?" He held up a document and pointed to the relevant portion.

"We, uh—" began Ilya, clearing his throat nervously. "We felt that presence of this sophisticated equipment would substantiate our JV, Sam." He looked around at each of his colleagues apprehensively before hiding his face behind his teacup.

Sam said, "But Ilya, the expense involved in—"

"We are prepared to omit the request," interrupted the chairman, taking a second nervous sip of tea.

Sam was quiet for a long moment. He'd prepared responses to a variety of possible arguments on the issue, the notes for which waited on the table in front of him. He'd even been prepared to compromise somewhat. *Hmm.*

The Mosteks team sat patiently, waiting for Sam to proceed. After the pause, he flipped through his yellow notepad to another point and asked Ilya about the necessity of certain high-dollar spinning equipment. Less expensive machinery was available. "Given that your equipment compilation request will probably have to be revamped in light of the current state of the Mosteks facility, IIS will probably prefer to avoid the most expensive machinery. Do you agree that this is reasonable?"

Following Misha's translation, all three directorate members nodded, saying, "*da, da.*"

Again Sam paused, still hiding his confusion at Mosteks' instant, unquestioning acquiescence. The Russians looked up at him, waiting for him to proceed, each with that same defensive look of anticipation.

The meeting continued for a few hours, Ilya assuaging Sam's concerns in every instance. Issues Sam had expected to spend days resolving were handled in minutes. And the Russians never put anything on the table themselves.

He'd finished his prepared list. He looked around at Ilya and the Mosteks directorate, then turned to take a quick glance at Misha. Maybe a little prodding was in order. "I have a question," he said, closing his notepad, "mostly for my own edification. I did a good deal of research as to how Russian joint ventures are constructed. As I understand it, MinFin's role in a JV's creation is quite limited. Its only function is to register the JV after submission by the parties of the necessary documentation. Why then did Boris Shturkin attend yesterday's meeting?"

Ilya shrugged his shoulders nervously and leaned to exchange whispers with Andrey. Sam wondered why he didn't just speak with his colleague under the cloak of the Russian language. Perhaps it was just a surviving habit of the former Soviet bureaucrat. Finally the chairman shrugged, gave Sam his congenial smile and said, "We wishing to make sure no problems arising with registration, Sam." Ilya glanced at Albert and Andrey, then put out his cigarette in the ashtray. "Why you worrying about such things, Sam? This is Mosteks' concern under our agreement."

"Just curious," answered Sam, still considering the answer. Another item for the oddities list. He glanced at Misha, hoping to glean something from his expression, but saw his friend was wearing his professionally detached look, that second personality that Sam had noted earlier. "Do you expect any problems?" he asked, raising his palms.

Ilya shook his head and said, "Nyuh-uh," then lit up another cigarette.

The room fell silent again, while Sam sat looking at the wooden panel on the far wall. There was more to this story, obviously. But Ilya's explanation made sense, so what else could he do?

Shortly, Ilya's smile returned, though it seemed a bit reserved. "Like I said, Sam, it seem that we have come to quick agreement as to majority of your concerns. I think we having documents ready for submission to authorities in next couple of days."

"It seems so," said Sam, trying to smile back diplomatically. He looked around the table, studying the Mosteks team. They were pondering something with each other—some secret agenda to which he had no access. The uncertain tone of the meeting sharply contrasted the words. Surely the Russians saw this, too.

"So, Sam. Lyena will now accompany you to international telephone station for your scheduled call to Mr. Davies," continued Ilya, still smiling, now with noticeable beads of sweat along his broad brow. He checked his watch. "In five minutes she is meeting you downstairs in lobby. Telephone connection with America can be made quickly at station instead of several hours it would take from Mosteks or hotel."

Sam forced himself to look down at the table for a second— he didn't want the businessmen to detect even a hint of a non-professional concern on his face. But the mere thought of spending time alone with the captivating Lyena had charged him. Finally he had a chance to be with her, to possibly pick up where he'd left off a few days ago. Would she be more at ease with him alone? He'd consider his apprehensions about this strange business meeting later.

The men simultaneously stood from the table, this time without the lively chatter Sam had witnessed at the end of the first meeting. Even Misha was uncharacteristically quiet. Had Sam done something wrong, perhaps by asking about Shturkin? He wanted to find out; somehow he knew it was important. But right now his mind was elsewhere.

Sam and Lyena walked into the international telephone/telegraph station on Tverskaya Street, not far from the Mayakovsky monument. It was a large, crowded room, filled mostly with people sitting on wooded benches, looking detached. To the right was a counter manned by apathetic clerks taking orders from a queue of customers. The plaster walls were lined with rows of phone booths, primitive-looking glass enclosures with wooden frames, each marked by a number. The only attempts at decor in the room were the metal wall sculptures depicting boats, planes, trains, and what seemed to be a spaceship. A loudspeaker summoned callers to the proper cubicle when their international connections were ready.

A wave of envious, glowering eyes assaulted Sam as he entered the room in his Western suit, complete with Bally shoes and leather gloves. He remembered Yasha's advice and quickly directed his gaze at the Russians' footwear. The silent assault was immediately repelled. The two got in line.

Lyena said, "Don't be worried."

She speaks at last! "About what? I'm not worried."

"Yes, Sam. You worried. Is easy to see."

Sam had almost forgotten how damned perceptive she was. He'd been trying to seem unaffected since they'd met in the lobby of the union building. He'd extended a businesslike hand to her, thanking her formerly for escorting him to the international

telephone station. Put the ball in her court. But it had been difficult pushing his fascination with her to the back of his mind. "I
just want the project to go well, that's all," he said.

"You worry much about work. Is good. Important to take
career seriously."

"So what else have you figured out about me?" asked Sam
through a nervous laugh.

Lyena gave an unfamiliar, playful smile. "I know you like my
boops."

Sam looked at the floor like a little boy caught with his hand
in the cookie jar. He'd thought his glances had been inconspicu-
ous. "Boobs," he said.

"Is okay, Sam. No be shameful. Is compliment for me. Thank
you," replied Lyena, her smile confident now.

"You're welcome," said Sam, now really wondering what
else she might have picked up about him. She'd been so damned
quiet since they'd first met, but maybe she'd been watching and
observing him all along. The thought was unsettling, but somehow mysteriously enchanting as well. "Why don't you talk,
Lyena?" he asked. "I mean, when you're with Mosteks people.
How come you act so shy when you obviously aren't?"

"Not shy," she said, looking away from him.

"I know you're not shy. That's what I mean. So why are you
so quiet most of the time?"

"Not shy," she repeated, and turned toward the clerk. It was
their turn to order phone calls.

Sam watched Lyena give the necessary information to place
the overseas calls. Why was she so intent on evading him? What
was going on behind those eyes?

A moment later, she turned from the clerk and said, "Will be
twenty minutes until first call. Second call few minutes after. We
sitting on bench until announce your name. Good?"

Sam nodded and followed her to two vacant seats in the
waiting area, where she withdrew a cigarette from a pack and lit

up. Lyena didn't offer Sam one. She'd apparently deduced he didn't have the habit.

"Do all Russians smoke?" asked Sam. He knew it was trite, but nothing else had come to mind.

"Most. Why you not?"

"I don't know. I just never have. Besides, it's not fashionable to smoke in the States anymore." He looked at her flirtatiously and added, "Kissing a smoker is like licking an ashtray."

"But if kisser also ashtray, he never notice," she replied with a shrug.

Sam laughed. "But cigarettes aren't good for you, Lyena."

"Here we have saying, Sam. 'He who not smoke and drink, die healthy.'" She smiled playfully before taking another drag.

Sam again laughed at Lyena's simplistic conviction. "Are you married?" he asked.

"No. Divorced just recently. You?"

"No," he said, shaking his head.

"You have girlfriend?"

Sam hesitated. "No," he answered, turning his head away from her, not quite sure what had made him lie.

"You seem like type to have girlfriend," she replied. "I think you have one soon."

Sam heard the hissing of the overseas connection and was struck by the intermittent buzzing sound of the American ring tone, which differed from the high-pitched hum of Russian phones. There were many innocuous differences between Russia and America, most of which, Sam decided, were apparent only when brought into contrast.

He'd forgotten which of the two calls he'd ordered first. The IIS receptionist's voice cleared that up. "Good morning, Inter-American Industrial Services."

"Hi, Rebecca. This is Sam Morris in Moscow."

"How ya doing, Sam! How is everything over there?"

"Fine. Is Mr. Davies available?" He waited as the receptionist connected him, again reflecting on the nice sounds from home.

"Hello, Sam. How are you?"

"So far, so good, Mr. Davies. Doing my best to keep warm. Just wanted to make a progress report."

"How are the negotiations proceeding?"

"Extremely well."

"I'm glad to hear that, Sam."

"I've succeeded in getting the Russians to concede to every single one of our preferences. I've gotten them to agree to everything we want."

"Congratulations, Sam," said Davies. "It sounds like you've really gotten the knack in how to do business over there. You're doing a fine job. Anything else going on?"

Sam paused. "Not much else, really. Maybe just one thing. I've noticed that the Russians have been acting...well, a little peculiar on occasion." Careful Morris. Let's not look like a wuss. "I guess they're just not used to dealing with Westerners."

"Probably so. This is new for them, too, you know."

"One question, Mr. Davies. Did Mr. Lukov and yourself ever discuss possible problems with the JV being registered by the Ministry of Finance?"

Davies paused. "No, that would be Mosteks' responsibility. We wouldn't be involved with that, so it never came up. Why? Is there a problem?"

Sam paused again. "No, I was just curious. Just something I wanted to look into. I'll give you another call in a few days."

"Very good, Sam," answered Davies. "Again, you're doing a fine job. Keep it up."

They disconnected. "Yes!" said Sam aloud, balling a fist. A fine job. He was pumped. Ready to complete his assignment. Ready for anything these Russkies might have in store for him.

219

Sam took a moment to look through the glass doors of the cubicle before pushing them open. There was Lyena, sitting confidently in the waiting area, her face now hidden behind a book. He saw the swell of her large breasts beneath her sweater and briefly wondered what they might be like.

"Okey doke," he said as he walked toward her.

"Is boss okay?"

Sam smiled and nodded. "Boss okay. Lyena ready?" He extended a hand to her to help her up. He was definitely fascinated by her. Was it just because to him she was a foreigner?

"But you have second call, Sam."

How could he have forgotten? "Oh. You're right," he said with an embarrassed laugh. "I forgot about the one to my mother."

"Is shameful, Sam Morris," said Lyena playfully. "One should never to forget about Mamochka at home. She probably worrying about you all day."

"You're right, Lyena. Shh. Please don't tell her."

"Hello. This is Stacy Werner. I'm not available to take your call right now, but please leave a message after the tone, and I'll call you back as soon as possible, or press zero for an operator to have me paged. You may start your message now."

Sam heard the beeptone of Stacy's voice mail. "Hi, Stacy. Comrade Sam here. Just checking in. Nothing exciting to report, I've just been working my frozen butt off. I didn't want to bother you with a page. Miss you. See you soon. Bye."

Sam quickly hung up the receiver and turned his back to the phone, cursing himself for leaving the stupid message. He rubbed his eyes, ran a hand through his hair, and shoved the booth's door open.

Lyena stood to meet him and, as they turned to leave, unexpectedly linked her arm into his. They left the telephone station, silently braving the cold together on the way to a taxi stand in front of the building. Sam no longer felt upset about anything.

"Tell me what it's like working for Lukov," he suggested when they'd descended the building's steps. He couldn't feel the softness of her hand through their heavy clothing but was engrossed by its presence nonetheless.

"Oh, is quite good. He very nice to workers," answered Lyena. As before, she smiled and rubbed the thumb and fingers of her free hand together.

"But do you like the work? Do you feel like you're growing as an individual?" Maybe too profound, but it seemed like an appropriate question for such a cerebral woman.

Lyena nodded her head slowly, without enthusiasm, then looked away. "I like work," she said, almost sheepishly.

"What do you do? I mean, besides serve tea and cookies?"

She suddenly became offended and removed her arm from Sam's. Her exotic eyebrows knitted into an expression of anger. "Is my job to serve tea and cookies. Secretary do all such favors for boss. Same in America, no? Why is problem?"

"I…I'm sorry, Lyena. I didn't mean anything, I was just asking. I really just wanted to know what else you do at Mosteks. That's all." He glanced at the now vacant space in his elbow.

Lyena looked up at him, the anger in her brow dissolving into uncertainty. Sam could almost feel her reading the sincerity in his eyes.

"Forgive me, Sam," she said solemnly, looking down. She sighed, a look of dismay replacing the confusion across her features. "Now you see, Sam, very difficult for Russian woman to grow as individual in job. You must to understand. Men very sexist here. Is very painful for us. At least for me." She gave him an embarrassed smile and again cast her gaze downward.

"What do you mean? Don't women have equal rights with men in Russia?" He waited anxiously for her to look back up at him. He met those entrancing eyes when she did.

"In principle, yes. But not in reality. There are of course successful Russian women, but very few. You see, Sam, I am engineer, like Misha. I having same credentials. But I not find job as engineer because companies not trusting young woman to do this work. So instead I am secretary.

"Of course I like Ilya Konstantinovich. He good man. He treating workers fair and paying us well. This very rare for Russian boss. So we are happy to work hard for him. In general, I must say am happy at Mosteks. But no. I not growing as individual." She gave another painful smile. "This is answer to your question."

Sam reflexively touched Lyena's cheek with a gloved forefinger and watched with delight as her face brightened at his gesture. He might have kissed her had a taxi not pulled up at that moment.

Sam opened the door for Lyena. When they were both inside, she gave the driver instructions.

"If it makes you feel any better, it's the same in the States, Lyena," said Sam. "I mean, it's often much harder for women to do well at the same thing men do. It's probably the same everywhere."

"Yes. But is much worse here, Sam. I am forced into role of servant simply because I am woman. I am fortunate to have job at good private company with high pay, but this is all my fortune." She took off her gloves, showing Sam the hand that had captivated him a few minutes earlier.

"Is that why you're so quiet when you're with the Mosteks brass—uh, bosses?" he asked, resisting the urge to take that hand into his own.

She nodded silently. "Women supposed to be quiet at job, Sam. It is our role, and I not wanting to risk losing good job. But no feel sorry for me, Sam. I know how to live in Russia. Maybe some day our culture change. For now, women like me must only survive." She smiled warmly. "You are good man, Sam. I

think I see this on first day we meet. I am glad to have met you."
She kissed his cheek lightly, causing a chill to descend his back.

The taxi arrived at Hotel Novgorod, and Sam moved to get out, but Lyena stopped him by putting a hand on his shoulder. "Sam, Misha and I coming for you at seven o'clock tonight. We going to *tusovka*. To party. You will enjoy. Okay?" She smiled with renewed enthusiasm.

"Fantastic! I'm looking forward to it. See you then." He returned the smile, then opened the car door.

She leaned over and again kissed him affectionately, this time on the lips. Her perfume shot a twinge through his nose that warmed it despite the stinging air.

Sam had gotten out of the cab and was about to close the door when Lyena beckoned him toward her once more. When he leaned into the car, she gave him a folded piece of paper. He opened it, revealing her phone number. "Until soon, Sam," she said smiling, her voice almost a whisper.

Sam was still a bit jet lagged and was ready for a nap as he stood in the hotel elevator. He fondled the slip of paper Lyena had given him, wondering what she had in mind, what the gesture had meant. He was curious. He'd think about it later.

He'd gotten somewhat used to sleeping in the narrow bed, although he was definitely looking forward to his queen-size back at home. Just a few more days, he thought as he opened the door to his room.

Sam stripped and washed his face before heading to the flimsy mattress. He carefully lay down on his side, negotiating his body in search of a comfortable position.

Something inside the covers scratched his leg.

Sam reached under the blanket and felt around until he found a small piece of sturdy, flat plastic. He drew it out and gazed quizzically at it. A photograph. Polaroid. As the picture came into focus, he gasped, nearly jumping out of the bed in panic. His scalp tingled when he saw the picture's purpose.

It was him, standing in front of the Mosteks facility. The photograph was of poor quality, the colors somewhat yellow, which only added to its macabre effect. But the snapshot unmistakably depicted Sam Morris with a hatchet sketched into his head. And what may have been real blood around the wound.

Sam took a moment to catch his breath before examining the photograph more closely. He then saw the words *Go home Amerikan!* inscribed on the bottom.

SIXTEEN

"What time will you be back, Misha?" asked Marina, cutting an apple for dessert.

Misha was just finishing his dinner. "I'm not sure, Marinka. Don't wait up. I have to entertain the American tonight with the Mosteks directorate, and it may get late." He didn't want to upset her by telling her he was going with Sam to a *tusovka* at Dalya's place. Marina didn't like that circle; it was a bit too unruly for her. Besides, he knew he might get laid that night and didn't want to worry about a curfew.

"I'd like to meet your American friend sometime," said Marina, handing a slice of apple across the table to him. "He sounds interesting."

"Maybe you will, then." He was tired of keeping so many things from her. How much did she know, or at least suspect? he wondered. Marina wasn't stupid. Meek and modest maybe, as a proper woman should be, but not stupid. Sooner or later everything would come out into the open about him and Petya and the Gagarintsi. What would her reaction be? Hopefully he'd find a way to work everything out without her ever having to know. But the devil knows it'd better be soon.

"Would you like to have him over for dinner one night this week?" she asked.

She didn't give her pleasant little raising of the eyebrows when suggesting it. Was she probing him? Testing him to see how he'd react? Maybe he was just paranoid. What could Sam have to do with Petya and the mafia? "Uh, sure, Marina," Misha said. "I'll ask him about his schedule."

Marina looked up at him, the pretty slanted eyes he'd always found so irresistible revealing more than a hint of trepidation. He found he couldn't meet those eyes for long.

Why should he feel this way? He put his fork down and impetuously stood from the table. Wasn't he giving her a wonderful life? Shouldn't she be happy with all she has? He appreciated the fact that she was worried about him, but wasn't a man's business his own concern? He walked to Marina and kissed her cheek. "I'll see you tomorrow morning," he said before putting on his coat and heading out the door.

"Drive on! Quick, Misha, go! Find a side street and pull off, okay? *Go!*" Sam had frantically jumped into the Zhiguli, looking around him anxiously.

"What is matter, Sam?"

"Just go, okay? *Go!*"

Misha drove out of Hotel Novgorod's parking lot. After riding a short distance, he turned off the thoroughfare onto a small access road and pulled over. He turned to Sam, his eyes wide.

"Look at this!" said Sam, shoving the photograph at Misha. "I found it in the bed in my room. Someone's been following me. Look! And they must have access to my hotel."

Misha studied the picture, then closed his eyes and sighed. He squeezed his hands together to avoid slamming a fist onto the dashboard. It didn't take him long to decide what to do; it was his gut instinct that would guide him here. His budding friendship with Sam was too valuable not to tell him at least part of the truth. He owed him that much. "Is probably mafia, Sam." His voice had gone hoarse. "They trying to scare you away."

"What! The mafia! Why?"

It was actually a good question. The picture really didn't make sense. The Gagarintsi wouldn't be so stupid as to leave hard evidence of their business. And Petya had promised there'd be no violence at Mosteks, ever!

But Misha hadn't told Petya much about Sam, about how they'd grown to be friends in the few days they'd known each other. Had Svetov somehow convinced Petya that Sam wasn't really a part of Mosteks and was therefore fair game? "I not know," he answered, forcing himself to look at Sam.

"Wait a minute, Misha. Hold on. What do you mean mafia? Here? In Moscow? Why would the mafia be worried about a joint venture?"

Again Misha sighed and said, "I not know."

Sam rolled his head against the back of his seat. "Come on, Misha! You can do better than that!"

"There is many mafias in Moscow, Sam. Maybe thirty big families. Not just like in States, but similar. They always been in Russia, but stronger now since reforms."

"But why would the mafia be worried about me?"

Misha shrugged.

"Should I get out of Russia? Do you think I'm in danger here?"

"Maybe we talk about this death threat with Ilya Konstantinovich tomorrow. Then we can call police or arrange early flight for you out of Moscow, if necessary, Sam. Is difficult to do this, but Ilya have good connections at Aeroflot airline."

"Ah, shit!" muttered Sam, shaking his head incredulously. "I can't believe this." He leaned back in his seat and closed his eyes. "What do you think I should do?"

"For now, I think you are safe, Sam. Trust me. Mafia knowing that is very difficult for foreigner to leave Russia on earlier date than planned, so they not expecting you to be gone immediately." Sam still had his eyes closed, his head pressed against the car seat. Suddenly the American smiled dubiously, then grinned, then almost began to laugh. "What is funny?" asked Misha, smiling himself.

"You're right," said Sam. "The Russian mob isn't like what we have back home. This photograph is like something from a bad TV crime show. If the mob in the States didn't like me," he chuckled, "I'd be wearing cement shoes. I'd be rubbed out in front of some restaurant or in a back alley!"

Misha took a moment to figure out what Sam was saying. "Is obvious they just wanting to scare you, Sam." He placed a hand on Sam's shoulder. "I'm sure is safe for now. I call Ilya Konstantinovich tonight and tell him we must to handle this problem tomorrow. In worst case, we get you back to New York quickly as possible. Okay?" He watched Sam nod, then started the car, again considering an unsettling question.

Would the Gagarintsi really be so stupid?

But Sam couldn't quite shake it off as he struggled to study the photograph again in the darkness of the car. Maybe he should tell Davies about it. It would probably mean the end of the project, of course. The boss wouldn't want to continue doing business in Russia if there was danger here—and rightly so.

He looked at the empty Moscow sidewalks as the car sped along.

Moscow.

It was supposed to be Sam's big opportunity, his chance to be at the helm of Old Virginia's rebirth. Maybe he should just sit tight and see what happens, let the damned thing play itself out. It could be dangerous, but hell, sometimes risks were necessary.

Just ask Hyman Morris, who'd risked all he had to set up Old V in the first place. Would he have dropped his plans because of some bullshit threat?

Sam sighed. Get a grip, he told himself, ashamed of how he'd freaked out in front of his new friend.

He put the picture back into his jacket pocket and forced his attention away from it. "So where are you taking me, bud?" he asked. They'd been traveling in an unfamiliar direction.

"We going to my friend Dalya. You met her at dinner on night you arrive," said Misha, who seemed to be occupied with thoughts of his own.

"I remember her. The actress, right?"

"Yes. She having *tusovka* tonight. Lyena meeting us there. Will be food. Lots of nice girls. And…" Misha flicked the side of his neck with his middle finger.

"What's that?"

"Oh, my friend. You have so much to learn about Russia! Whenever Russian making this sign with finger on neck, it mean drink vodka. Much of vodka." He raised his eyebrows.

"Gotcha." Sam raised an opened palm at Misha expectantly and waited for him to slap it.

Misha smiled and tapped Sam's hand lightly. "You know, Sam, this is first time I seeing you without suit."

Sam was wearing blue jeans, a flannel shirt, and a denim jacket. "I'm here on business during the days, Misha. I don't always wear monkey suits, especially to parties."

"I know. But you looking so different in jeans."

Misha laughed, embarrassing Sam, who'd never liked being classified as just another vapid young careerist. Now the Russkies were categorizing him as such, without even knowing it. "Misha, how come your wife never goes out with you?" he asked, changing the subject.

"What you mean? I'm often with wife when out. I spending most evenings with Marina. Just sometimes good to be apart."

"Of course. But I haven't even met her yet. Why didn't you bring her along tonight?"

"In Russia we have saying, Sam. 'When going to Tula, don't bring your own *samovar*.'"

"Your own *samovar*?"

"You see, Tula is Russian city famous for its big selection of beautiful samovars. *Samovar*, you know, is decorative Russian tea kettle. People coming from all over world to buy them in Tula."

Sam laughed in spite of himself. "You're too much," he said. He was beginning to relax and actually look forward to the party. The death threat still lurked in his mind, but there was nothing he could do about it now. The hell with it.

They arrived at Dalya's apartment, which was very similar to Yasha's, except that in place of bookshelves, the walls were covered with pictures and posters. The flat obviously belonged to Dalya's parents—there was a distinctly middle-aged air to the apartment's design and order—but the parental unit-skies, Sam figured, were away. Some of the same faces he'd seen at his welcoming dinner were among the ten or so at the *tusovka*. A table was arranged with plates of sliced sausage and cheeses and other now-familiar hors d'oeuvres. Bottles of vodka were also waiting to be imbibed. Sam was beginning to think that Russians apparently ate and drank the same things at every meal.

To his delight, a boom box sat on the floor blaring American music. Sam was by no means a Madonna fan, but the Material Girl sounded pretty good to him now. He'd barely taken a seat on the sofa when Misha presented him with a shot glass of vodka, which Sam took and swallowed without hesitation. He could use a good time tonight. "You becoming real Russian," he heard from behind him. He turned to see Lyena looking down at him.

"Hi!" he said, nearly jumping from the couch. "Come sit down," he said, pointing to an empty seat next to his. "Would you like something to drink? Or eat?"

"Some champagne, please." She walked around the couch and sat down.

Sam went to the refreshment table and returned with two glasses of champagne and some cheese, which he set on the coffee table in front of them.

"So. How are you, Sam?" asked Lyena.

What was it about this woman? Sure, there was a mysterious appeal about Lyena, the way she peered at him with those discerning but unrevealing eyes. The way she inexplicably understood him so well. But she wasn't beautiful or flawlessly built. She didn't carry herself in that sexy way that made some less pretty women enticing nonetheless. So what was it? Her large, shapely breasts? He liked them, but Sam usually preferred slimmer women. Maybe it was because she was a foreigner, unlike any woman he'd ever been close to. What would a Russian woman be like in bed? he wondered. Aloud, in answer to her question, he said, "I'm pretty much used to Moscow time now, so I guess that's one victory."

She laughed softly. "I am glad. You will enjoy Moscow better when full awake."

"I think so. Life's so much easier to enjoy when you can keep your eyes open long enough to see it." Brilliant, Morris.

"Is good your eyes open, because one must sometimes look hard to see Moscow's beauty. But this beauty, you will see, is biggest beauty in all of world, Sam. It is beauty of Russian soul."

Sam marveled for a moment at Lyena's style, how she melded light talk with profundity without sounding stupid, even when her words were spoken in response to a stupid remark. All of her thoughts and expressions seemed loaded with varying degrees of passion, of feminine spirit. Sam stopped himself from raising a hand to touch her face. "Even with jet lag I could see that beauty, Lyena."

She leaned toward him, beckoning him to lower his head, as if to hear a secret. The gesture alone was exciting. Sam felt the firmness of Lyena's breast against his shoulder, followed immediately by her warm breath in his ear, and the electric sensations overpowered the sound of her light whisper. "Huh?" he said, feeling his lungs fill with air. He glanced at her smooth face, her smile, and couldn't wait for her to repeat the message. Again he inhaled, slowly this time and through his nose. She approached to repeat her whisper.

"I'd like to visit you in America some day."

Sam first felt disappointment for some reason, but then looked at her again and saw a romantic passion, a gentle fervor he'd never before seen in a woman. "It'll be great," he whispered in reply, his eyes locked on hers.

Lyena smiled warmly again, then turned her head to reach for a slice of cheese.

"Well," said Sam, clearing his throat, "since I'm on my way to becoming a Russian, let me try my hand at making a toast."

"Okay," she replied, tilting her head, her smile playful. She joined Sam in raising her glass.

"Here's to my meeting Lyena. The beauty of her soul is matched only by the beauty of her company. And here's to many happy times, now and in the future. May you be happy and successful in all you do, Lyena." He tapped glasses with her and threw back the vodka.

Sam spent most of the evening with Lyena. She made him feel at home at the *tusovka,* introducing him to the other guests, translating for him, explaining various elements of Russian culture. He drank several hearty shots of vodka and enjoyed an inebriated camaraderie with the Russians, having all but forgotten his previous worries.

Meanwhile, Misha had been ensconced on a large armchair with Dalya for hours, their public display like that of young teens at a high school party. Misha was even wearing his wedding band on the same hand that toyed with Dalya's bleached hair! Too much! thought Sam.

At about midnight, Misha stood up, leaving a frisky Dalya alone in the chair, a listless expression on her overly made-up face. He staggered up to Sam and summoned him quickly to a nearby corner.

"Sam," he whispered, the alcohol on his breath causing Sam to jerk his head back. "I getting pussy tonight. I want staying here with Dalya, okay? Can you take taxi back to hotel?"

Sam smiled. "Sure, Misha," he said.

"Lyena give you directions, okay? I pick you up tomorrow morning for meeting." Misha then ambled back to Dalya, who was waiting patiently on the armchair.

Sam returned to Lyena, still smiling and shaking his head.

"I take care of you, Sam," she said, apparently guessing what Misha must have said. "Hotel Novgorod on way to my apartment. We take taxi together."

It was about one o'clock when the guests finally began to leave the *tusovka.* Sam didn't want to go, but the nagging reminder of business and how he'd have to handle the photograph thing tomorrow were beginning to wear him down. He was also a bit tipsy, and more vodka would probably put him over the edge.

As if she'd read his thoughts, Lyena said, "Shall we leave?"

He nodded and followed her out of the apartment into the freezing night air. They walked along silently, Lyena's arm linked into his. Sam began to wonder what she really thought of him. Was he misreading her gestures?

He glanced to his left and saw Lyena turn her head, bundled in a white cotton hat, simultaneously up toward his. She met his gaze.

No way. There was no misunderstanding here, the language between them was crystal clear.

Fortunately, a cab was waiting across the street at a taxi stand. Sam opened the door for Lyena and followed her in. He listened to her give directions in Russian to the driver, her voice as delightfully sonorous as when she spoke to him in his own language.

"That was lots of fun," he said.

"For me, too, Sam," she replied, gazing at him with her penetrating brown eyes, her face completely still.

Sam felt a stirring in his pants as he looked into the magnetism of those eyes. She wanted him, he'd seen the look in its varying forms on enough women to recognize it anywhere.

She put her hand on his, both now ungloved, causing a chill to run up his arm and down his spine. He felt his arms wrap themselves around her shoulders and had to restrain his mouth from lunging onto hers. Instead, he lowered his head slowly, taking one last look at her expectant face before meeting her full lips.

The tip of her tongue moved slowly against his, then a bit faster. He felt her hand travel sluggishly up his back, then to his neck. She caressed him diffidently, teasingly, heightening his desire for her. For a moment, he expected her to heave a sigh, but unlike Stacy, Lyena only breathed silently.

He gently lowered her back onto the car's back seat, never breaking the kiss, then put his hand under her knit pullover. The skin on her belly was smooth and soft. He'd suspected that. He slowly moved his hand upward until it came to her bra, tight and sturdy to accommodate her size. He reached under her toward the hook—

"Gostinitsa Novgorod," announced the driver. The cab came to a stop.

"We here," whispered Lyena softly, not attempting to push him off of her, renewing her penetrating gaze.

She wanted an invitation. Sam wanted to give her one. His finger was on the metal clasp of her bra when he kissed her on the lips once more. "I have a big day tomorrow," he said, removing his hand. "But I can't wait to see you in the morning." He helped her sit up and straightened her sweater. "I really can't."

She gave him a half smile.

"Good night, Lyena," he said.

Lyena stayed silent until Sam had almost closed the cab door behind him, then said, "Good night, Sam."

Misha had to be sure that Dalya was asleep. When she didn't respond to a light shake of her bare shoulder, he carefully slid out of the creaky bed and crept silently on his bare feet into the living room.

The apartment was cluttered with the evidence of *tusovka,* empty vodka bottles and shot glasses littered throughout the room. He stepped around a tray of leftover cheese and made his way toward the side table where Dalya's parents kept their telephone. It was one of those new push-button models, although you still heard rotary clicks after pressing the numbers. Not yet on par with the West, he decided, but it was definitely progress. He picked up the receiver and dialed.

"Hello. Petya? Petya, this is Misha. Misha! Wake up!" He waited impatiently for his brother to become coherent.

"What's the matter, Misha? What's going on?" said Petya, his voice muddled.

"I have to talk to you. It's important."

"Okay, little brother. My ears are on the crown of my head. What is it?"

"Sam, the American, got a death threat today. It ordered him to go back to America. What's going on, Petya? Why is this happening? You said that if I helped out the Gagarintsi at Mosteks, there'd never be any violence!"

Petya paused. "Well, has there been any violence, little brother? Was the American harmed?" He was still a bit muddled.

"No, but he was very shaken. And understandably so."

Petya paused again, then said, "I don't know anything about it, Misha. Honestly. What was his response? Did he say anything about his plans?"

"Look, Petya, that's not fair. You're not keeping your word. I told you I didn't want to get involved in any kind of violence. You said you never hurt anyone, anyway! You said it was never necessary to harm people!"

"And I don't, Misha. There's no reason to be upset. I promise. And I promise I know nothing about any death threat. It's not from us."

Misha felt his heart begin to race. "Then what is to happen with the girl!" He'd spoken loudly and had to check to see if he'd wakened Dalya.

"What girl, little brother?"

"The girl in the photograph, fuck your mother! In the pictures you had on the table yesterday! Is she a target? Is her father a kooperator who refused to pay the Gagarintsi protection money?" Misha put the receiver to his other ear, trying to control his surging anger. "You plan to have her raped, don't you, fuck your mother!"

"Misha, calm down, little brother. The girl has nothing to do with you or Mosteks, believe me."

"That's not the point, Petya! What are you in to? What are you doing? What have you become!"

"Misha, please. Please calm down. I assure you I have done no harm to anyone. And as you can see, no one at Mosteks has been hurt. That was our agreement, and it hasn't been violated. Now, do you want to continue receiving two hundred thousand rubles a month just to keep your ears open at Mosteks, or should I inform Svetov you are no longer with us?"

Misha said nothing. He knew better than to impetuously make a decision of this magnitude while standing naked in the middle of the night at some *tiolka's* apartment. He pulled the receiver away from his ear, looked down it, and heard Petya's muffled voice, "Little brother? Little brother?" What had become of his sibling, the man he'd emulated all of his life? Had Misha been a fool all these years?

236

Suddenly his frantic thoughts were interrupted. "Misha? What's the matter?" It was Dalya, naked, strolling out of the bedroom and into the living area. "Who are you calling?" she asked.

Misha quickly hung up. He looked at the woman, the body he usually found so irresistible not tempting him in the least. He shrugged. "Oh, no one, Dalya. Let's go back to bed."

SEVENTEEN

The next morning, Sam followed Misha into Mosteks' conference room. There waited the usual crew, as well as a stone-faced man in uniform Sam hadn't seen before. No Boris Shturkin. Also noticeably absent was Ilya's smile. Everyone was standing.

"Hello, Sam," began Ilya in an uncharacteristically somber voice. "On behalf of Mosteks and City of Moscow, please accept my sincere apologies for unfortunate incident you were suffering yesterday." His face showed genuine concern.

"Thanks," said Sam, hanging up his overcoat on the standing coat rack. Everyone but Ilya, Sam, and Stone Face migrated to the far end of the room, as if on cue.

"Please be assured we already taken successful measures to see to safety of you and our relationship," continued the chairman, his head hung slightly. "I would like to introduce you to Lieutenant Dmitri Ivanov of Moscow militia."

Ivanov stood in military attention, his austere face unflinching. His blond, crew-cut hair stood as straight as his posture, and his stolid expression clearly affected everyone in the room. Sam noticed that Ivanov's rugged eyes were tough, seasoned, like those of many New York City detectives. The man extended a large hand to Sam and said, "How do you do?" with a slight nod. He reached into his breast pocket to display an official-looking identification card.

"I'm fine, thanks. It's a pleasure," responded Sam uncomfortably. A former KGB agent, he thought, recalling the stereotypical description given in countless spy novels he'd read. This man just had to be. What experiences had shaped those eyes?

"Misha informed me of threat you received last night, and I immediately contacted authorities," said Ilya, his voice still soft and solemn. "Fortunately, Lieutenant Ivanov and his men were able to quickly apprehend culprit. His department had already been investigating racketeers who operate like this and, I'm happy to say, have now put end to their activities." He tried to smile reassuringly.

"We have suspect in custody," confirmed Ivanov with a mechanical nod.

"Wait a minute," said Sam, feeling frustration replace his apprehension. "Who were these...racketeers? And why were they after me?"

"We cannot be sure," answered Ilya, shrugging.

Ivanov was silent. Sam turned to him and said, "Sir, the only dealings I have in Moscow are with Mosteks. Doesn't it seem likely that the death threat was somehow related to my business here?" He grew more confident in Ivanov's presence with each word he spoke.

"Is possible," answered the cop.

"Possible?" Sam turned to Ilya. "Do you have any idea why the mafia would want me to leave Russia, Ilya? Has this...mob approached the cooperative?"

Ilya made no reply.

Sam felt his eyes roll, then close tightly. "Why didn't you tell me Mosteks was having these difficulties, Ilya? Don't you think I have the right to know about something like that? Let alone the possible business implications!" He felt the anger seeping into his voice, so he toned it down. "How long has this been going on?"

Ilya approached Sam diplomatically. "Sam, such attacks on Russian private sector common these days. And authorities very effective in struggle with mafia. We not wishing to concern you or IIS with such trivial personal matter. As you see, the problem is minor and police has been effective." He raised his hands, palms up. "I ask for your forgiveness, my friend and partner, and hope this unfortunate event will not hinder our business affairs." The chairman again smiled at Sam, trying unsuccessfully to conceal his consternation.

Sam sighed. "How do we know there aren't more of these racketeers?"

"We have managed to arrest entire leadership of this mafia, Mr. Morris," responded Ivanov. "We are quite sure they not threatening you again. Besides, is unlikely that mafia will actually harm foreigner. Racketeers in awe of Russian authority's ability to track them down."

"They're obviously not too much in awe," said Sam, surprised by his own irreverence.

"Please understand, Mr. Morris, threats are all these criminals will do to foreigner," continued the cop. "Police make special effort to protect Western businessmen because is crucial to Russian interests. I can promise you will having no further trouble from this mafia. My department now conducting investigation to learn why these criminals threaten you. I must ask that you give me photograph you found so our detectives may using it in investigation."

Sam hesitated. He wasn't sure he wanted to part with the only hard evidence he had of the incident. But he realized there was no one else for him to turn to in Russia, and he didn't want to seem uncooperative with the only people who might help him. He reached into his briefcase, surrendered the picture, then said, "It concerns me that they know where I'm staying, Lieutenant. They also obviously had access to my hotel room while I was gone."

"We will take everything into account when making further investigation," replied Ivanov. "I must ask you few questions now."

The cop interviewed Sam about the previous day's events, leading up to his finding the photograph. While Sam responded to the man's inquiries, he noticed Lyena silently enter the conference room with her inevitable tray of tea and cookies. As usual, her face was expressionless as she served the men, but Sam knew her well enough by now to see she was absorbing every word said in the room.

"And you found the picture in your bed after returning to Hotel Novgorod from international telephone station?" asked Ivanov.

"Yes." Sam noticed Lyena steal a glance at him. It occurred to him that he hadn't told her about the death threat, even though he'd spent the entire party with her the night before. He immediately regretted not having been more open with Lyena and wondered what she was thinking.

"Did you tell anyone about it?" asked Ivanov.

"Uh, just Misha Grunshteyn. I didn't want to trouble anyone else," he said, finally catching Lyena's eye. "It didn't make sense to cause anyone else to worry."

"Thank you for your assistance, Mr. Morris. I will make report to my colleagues who are handling this case." With that, Ivanov began packing his things to leave, speaking with Ilya in Russian as he did.

"Lieutenant Ivanov, excuse me," interrupted Sam. "Being a newcomer to Russia, I have to rely on your experience and expertise in making my decisions in this matter. I hope you'll be frank in answering one question for me." He paused momentarily and fixed his gaze on the officer's rugged eyes. "Should I

242

remain in Moscow for the full extent of my planned stay? In other words, are you sure it's safe for me to be here?"

"Quite sure, Mr. Morris. You need not worry. We have taken all appropriate measures in your case." Sam was looking for a reassuring tone of voice as much as anything else. He didn't really detect one. But maybe the cop, like many American law-men, was incapable of sounding anything but official.

"And besides, Sam," interrupted Ilya, "I'm afraid it would be very difficult for you to leaving early. All flights out of Moscow are completely reserved weeks in advance. I not think we could get you flight before your scheduled date of departure, which anyway is in only three days from now."

Ivanov shook hands formally with Sam and Ilya. He again spoke for a moment with the chairman in Russian, then headed toward the door. "Uh, one last thing, Mr. Morris," he said before leaving. "I'm sorry, is of personal nature, but could be important to our investigation. Are you making personal relationship with any Russian citizens during short time you've been here?"

Sam paused, not sure how to answer. He deciphered a fleeting look of concern on Lyena's face as she continued with her chores at the far end of the table—he would ask her about it later. More importantly, he remembered Uncle Yasha's concern about keeping their contact secret. But did the police somehow already know about their meeting two days ago? Were they trying to trap him into admitting it? Nah, he decided. He'd read too damned many of those spy novels. This was the post-Soviet era. The hell with this guy. Leave Yasha out of it. "No," he answered.

"Thank you," replied Ivanov. He disappeared through the door.

"So," began Ilya, smiling again and slapping his hands together. "I hope we can put this unfortunate event behind us and push forward with our business."

Sam reflected on the situation for a moment and realized he was totally helpless to take further action on his own. He was completely in the hands of the Russians, of the Russian police, and would have to take his chances during the remaining days of his trip. He willed himself to put the predicament out of his thoughts. "I agree," he said, attempting to match the enthusiasm in Ilya's voice.

The group reassembled around the table for business talks. Sam breathed deeply, then began: "I managed to speak with Mr. Davies yesterday. We remain optimistic about the joint venture."

Sam watched the group express its delight as Misha translated the announcement into Russian. He realized how personally the Russians were taking the project and felt a sense of contentment in witnessing their reaction. He only wished he could understand the chattering comments they made among themselves.

The Mosteks representatives discussed several other business issues with Sam. Foremost on the list were tax issues and export licensing. But as before, Ilya and his team were very accommodating, and Sam's concerns were handled systematically. The meeting lasted only a few hours.

When they'd reached accord on the last issue, Ilya said, "Tomorrow we meeting to discuss few last logistical matters, which should complete our negotiations." His glee was readily apparent. "For the rest of today, Sam, we have wonderful cultural treat for you. Now Misha taking you on sight-see excursion of Moscow. Tonight we going together to magical Bolshoi Ballet. I think you should at least have opportunity to enjoy our beautiful city while here." His smile was back in full force.

"That sounds wonderful," said Sam. He wasn't much of a ballet enthusiast, but he figured it would be nice to go to the Bolshoi and see what the rave was about.

Sam looked across the room at Lyena after shaking Ilya's hand. She met his gaze this time, her eyes revealing apprehension, a distinct look of dilemma. The exchange made him wonder if he'd mishandled the interview with the Russian cop and somehow insulted her, but he decided she'd be perceptive enough to realize and understand his predicament. He turned away when he suddenly caught himself thinking about her intimately. She wouldn't need long to comprehend those thoughts. He'd wait until later to find out what was on her mind.

Boris was pacing the block on which he'd agreed to meet the thug. He'd never thought of a better word to describe the man, to refer to him, even in his own mind. It was probably better that way. What had he gotten himself into?

Finally, the stumpy character appeared from around the corner. He was dressed in the same bulky overcoat, his wide face peering out from under a large *ushanka* hat. He didn't remove his hands from his pockets as he approached—the pleasantry of a handshake wasn't in his manner. Nor was even a simple greeting, for that matter. "Don't be so upset, Boris Antonovich."

Boris knew his voice had sounded agitated over the phone when he'd spoken with the thug that morning to set up the meeting. But what difference did it make? "You haven't been effective," Boris said. "I received a call from Mosteks' chairman this morning inviting me to attend today's negotiation session with the American. Obviously your threat didn't work, and the joint venture is still being pursued."

"Relax, Boris Antonovich," said the man, his eyes staring and unsympathetic. "That was just our first approach. It is always best to try to handle these matters quietly, if possible. And I didn't want to deploy...sterner measures, without your prior consent."

Sterner measures. Boris wasn't sure he even wanted to know what that meant. He breathed deeply and asked, "What are my options?" Like before, his eyes went to the muddy snow at his feet.

"You could give Mosteks back the *valuta*," said the man indifferently.

Boris shook his head immediately. It wasn't an option. He'd sooner risk Lukov's ire by keeping the *valuta* and denying the JV registration at the same time.

"Or, we can step up our efforts to a more…persuasive level. This next level, in my experience, is quite effective with foreign businessmen, especially Westerners."

Boris looked up to see the man give a slight smile.

"Of course, a more involved effort will incur a higher fee," added the thug. "It would take an additional thousand dollars."

Boris looked back at the ground. Why should he have to go through this shit? Why was he the one to encounter such difficulties in getting what he deserved? Boris had long been convinced that the only way to enjoy any measure of success in Russia was to bend the law a little bit. Cut a few corners, turn a few things to one's advantage. But here he was with a vicious criminal, discussing violence against an innocent young man! How had this happened? How had it come to this?

"A decision should be made soon," continued the man. "The joint venture's negotiations are probably nearing completion, and our efforts will be useless if we're too late."

Boris was silent, looking up at the cloudy sky.

"Boris Antonovich?"

"Do what must be done," said Boris, startling himself with his own words. "Don't tell me what it is. Ever. I don't want to know about your…sterner measures. And I will pay your higher fee." He turned and walked away.

EIGHTEEN

After a few hours of driving around Moscow, of visiting the Kremlin and a few other tourist sights, Misha drove Sam to Hotel Novgorod to let him rest up before the ballet. He then sped to Petya's apartment and stormed into the living room, where he repeated last night's accusations.

"But I promise you, little brother, neither I nor Svetov had anything to do with that photograph!" replied Petya. "I just spoke with him an hour ago! We don't threaten foreigners to accomplish our goals! It's unnecessarily dangerous. You know that!"

Misha considered his brother's compelling words. It was true—he'd known it all along. Why would the Gagarintsi, with all their ministerial connections, risk involving higher levels of law enforcement by approaching a foreigner? There had to be another explanation for the photograph. Maybe it was a Mosteks competitor, or another band of racketeers Misha hadn't heard about in his snooping around at the cooperative. He sighed at his brother's persuasiveness and said, "I'm sorry, Petya. I guess I overreacted. But I still can't figure out what the hell's going on here."

"It *is* quite strange," said Petya shrugging. "I tell you what, little brother. Let me do some research. I'll talk to Svetov some more. Maybe he has some ideas about who might have made the threat. Agreed?"

"Sure, Petya. And thanks. I just don't want to see Sam face any danger here. We've become friends."

"Absolutely, little brother. You're such a good friend. I'm glad you're my brother."

Pyotr Olegovich Grunshteyn. What an incredible man he was! Petya always knew the right thing to say, the right way to act in a situation. How could Misha have thought that his brother was deceiving him?

Misha looked around his elder sibling's lavish apartment, at the expensive furniture, at the Western appliances and decorations. His brother's talents explained why things came so easily for him, why he was so rich. Rich in rubles now, and soon to be rich in real money, *valuta!* Maybe Misha would be lucky enough to share in some of Petya's lot.

Misha sighed. But what about Marina? What does she know?

As if he'd read Misha's mind, Petya said, "So tell me, little brother, how is darling Marina these days? I haven't seen her in a while. I've been so busy that I've neglected my little brother's wife. How terrible of me!"

"She's fine, as usual," Misha answered, smiling. "We're thinking of having children soon. She's quite excited about it."

"That's wonderful, little brother! It will be so nice to have a new generation of Grunshteyns with us. Papa would have loved to see his family grow, wouldn't he? But tell me. Is she healthy? Has she been taking good care of herself? Of her pretty face?"

Misha paused. "Sure, Petya. She looks great. Healthy as ever. Why?"

"Is she in good spirits? Is her mood still charming?"

"Charming as ever. I'm sure she'd like to see you sometime, too. Why?"

Petya stood up from the sofa and began to pace around the living room, looking down at the floor as he ambled. He crossed his thick arms and stopped in front of Misha. "I have a new project I'd like you to help us out with. You and Marina."

Marina? Marina! He must have misunderstood. Of course he had misunderstood.

"You see," continued Petya, "we need to lure the head of a fishing enterprise in Saint Petersburg up to an apartment. The man, you see, is old and lonely. We think a young, attractive woman would have no problem approaching him and…" He gave a short laugh. "Getting his attention! All she would have to do is get him into the apartment. Our people will be waiting there. Does she have a sexy dress, maybe one that's cut low in the front?"

"Marina?" said Misha, his voice lowered and controlled.

"The problem is, little brother, that we really don't have any other women for this task, at least ones who are pretty enough and able to travel to Saint Petersburg. Marina would be perfect for the job. She's so beautiful." He smiled, tilting his head. "All men think so, you know."

"Petya, Marina is my wife! My wife! You can't expect me to involve her in crime! She's innocent!"

Petya raised his hand, palm up, toward his brother. "But Misha, there's no danger here. All she has to do is get an old man into an apartment. The rest—"

"There is always danger, Petya! Have you really lost sight of that? This is crime! Suppose the police were alerted? Or suppose another mafia family became involved? Suppose the old man resisted? Are you fucked-in-the-mouth crazy?"

"Shh, Misha, relax. I understand your concern for Marina. It's very noble. But there's really nothing for you to worry about. Come on. Have I ever let you down?" He again extended his hand to Misha. "Would I involve my little brother and his wife in something that could possibly go wrong?"

Misha glared at Petya. "Absolutely not," he said, trying to maintain his composure. "And I ask you not to suggest such things to me again. Ever. Understand?" He looked away, realizing that he'd never before spoken to his brother in this tone of voice.

"Misha, please. It's really no big deal, little brother, I've told you. You haven't even heard the golden side of the proposal! You will receive one million rubles for Marina's one day of effort!" He seemed taken aback by Misha's response.

"Into the cunt with your money, Petya! I told you no! Now forget it!"

"Shh. Fine, Misha. Okay, okay. I'm sorry. Now, calm down. I'll find somebody else, then."

The two brothers looked at each other for a long moment, both at a loss for words. Finally, Petya smiled and, in a jovial voice, said, "Maybe some hooker at Hotel Galactica will—"

"What has become of you, Petya?" Misha's voice rattled as he spoke. "Hookers are women, too! You can't—"

"Women can make their own decisions, little brother."

Misha was now almost panting. "Go to the prick, Petya!" he said, then jumped to his feet and stormed out the door.

He was still fuming when he got home. He threw open the door of his apartment, went into the living room, and collapsed onto the couch. He felt like taking the red telephone and smashing it on the floor.

Marina glanced at him from inside the kitchen. "Feed me, Marina," he demanded. "I have to pick up Sam and meet the Mosteks directorate at the Bolshoi soon."

"How...are things at work?" she asked.

"It's none of your concern, Marina. You know, sometimes you act like an old *babushka!* Why don't you just do what you're supposed to do? Now, bring me some dinner before I'm late!"

Marina was silent for a moment, then came out of the kitchen to join Misha on the couch. She put a compassionate hand on his shoulder.

"What, Marina! Do I have to make my own dinner? Is my wife incapable of performing the most basic services for her husband?" He jumped up from the couch and headed into the kitchen, where he began slicing a sausage.

"Misha," said Marina from the living room, "what's the matter? What's going on? Why are you acting this way? Please tell me!"

"Oy!" he yelled, dropping the knife on the floor. He'd cut his finger. "Shit! Damn this knife! Why do you make the knives so sharp, Marina? Don't sharpen them so fine next time!"

"I'm sorry, Misha."

He took a plate of sausage with him to the table and began to eat, his breathing the only sound in the room. Marina sat on the couch for a moment, then stood and walked into the kitchen. She emerged with a pot of boiled potatoes, brought them to Misha, and put some on his plate.

"I didn't know you were in a hurry," she said. "I was making soup, but it won't be ready for a while."

Misha glanced up and watched Marina slowly take a deep breath, her brow anxiously furrowed. She crossed her arms in front of her. Misha, ignoring her, returned to his sausage and potatoes.

"Misha, tell me what you're doing with Petya," she said, her voice uncharacteristically loud and stern. "And the rest of the Gagarintsi. Please. I'd like to know."

Misha's mouth was full. He stopped chewing and looked up at her for a moment, then returned to his meal.

"Please, Misha! Don't I have a right to know? I'm your wife! I'm a person, too! I could be affected by these people! Something bad is going on, don't you think I know? Don't you think I can see it in my husband?"

"How do you know anything about the Gagarintsi? Where have you even heard that name? They're none of your business, Marina! Forget it!"

"It is my business, Misha. Can't you see that?"

"No! I am a good provider for you! A good husband! I love you dearly and give you a good life! I protect you! Now shut up, and leave me alone!"

"Protect me, Misha? Protect me by working with the mafia? How else do you protect me?"

"I said shut up, Marina! It's not your concern! I'm old enough to know how to take care of my wife. If it's ever necessary for you to know more about what I do, then I'll tell you!"

"But how can I feel safe, protected, when I don't know what my husband is out in the world doing?" Her voiced cracked on the last word.

She was beginning to cry, Misha saw. He closed his eyes for a moment and sighed, then threw a piece of sausage onto the plate. His teeth clenched, Misha quickly reached up to stop a tear before it could roll down Marina's cheek. He wanted to speak, to say something to comfort her, but nothing came out of his mouth. Instead he simply stood and embraced his wife.

Burdening her with his worries wouldn't be fair, would it? Wasn't his ample income all that should matter to her? Why did she have to concern herself with a man's business? Misha was still searching for something to say. He wanted words that would soothe Marina, make her feel safe in his arms. Feel safe in deferring to him. He could think of only one thing to say. "Have I ever let you down before, Marina?"

He watched her slowly shake her head. She even seemed somewhat reassured. But Misha knew he'd heard those same words before. From someone he loved but did not trust.

What's going on here? he thought, abruptly removing his arms from around Marina. What had Petya become? What was he leading him into? He looked around his spacious apartment, at all the luxuries made possible by earnings from the Gagarintsi. He reflected on how none of this would have been possible in Russia without the mafia. Everyone broke the law in some way or another here; it simply had to be done! It always had been and always would be the Russian way of life! How could he just give all of this up and live like Ivan Ivanovich? He deserved more than that. And so did Marina!

"The most important thing to me is for us to be safe and healthy," said Marina through her tears. "Not to have to worry about the police coming someday and taking you away. I'd give up everything else for that peace, Misha."

He couldn't even look at her.

"How can we consider having children when we don't know if our lives are safe?" she continued. "What will the future bring? Where are we headed?"

Misha forced himself to look into her reddened eyes, imploring him through their slanted lids. But they didn't beg him just for Marina's own sake. She was afraid for him as well. It was her soul that was calling out to him now, reminding him of how much he loved her and needed her. Yes, needed her.

Misha reached to touch her cheek again, then quickly pulled his hand back, suddenly haunted by the thought of Dalya's buxom body beneath him. He almost shook his head to dispel the memory of the *tiolka's* thick haunches and high-pitched squeals. How had he found that whore so appealing? How could he now touch Marina, with her magical soul and boundless love, after giving himself the evening before to such a woman?

"Please, Misha," continued Marina, her hands now clasped in front of her.

Misha wanted to leave the room. He wanted to go shower or change clothes, do something that might somehow make him worthy of Marina. Instead, he quietly sat back down and looked up at his wife, who then joined him at the table. For the first time in Marina's presence, he felt tears begin to well in his eyes, and he surprised himself by not even trying to fend them off. Finally, Misha put his head down and sobbed, seeking comfort in the soft hand that touched his neck so gently.

"Oh, Misha, don't cry," she said above him, her voice muddled and wet. "I just don't want to see you hurt, that's all. I love you."

A moment later, Misha's head and heart began to pound. He wiped his eyes with a napkin and took a deep breath, wondering what his voice would sound like when he spoke. "I'll end it with Petya," he said in a hoarse whisper. "As soon as possible, Marina, I promise. You don't have to live like this."

She looked at him, clearly at a loss for words. Only now did Misha realize how he'd made her suffer. And how strong she'd been to endure it. But the thought only strengthened his resolve. Dealing with Petya would be difficult, but he would find a way.

Misha stood up from the table and extended a hand to his wife, which she took, and then he led her to the couch. Their eyes and cheeks were wet. He lowered his lips to hers and kissed her, softly at first, then a bit more passionately, ignoring the tastes and sounds of their earlier dismay. She responded to him timidly at first, then surprised him by growing more passionate as well, returning his caresses more amorously than ever before. He began to unbutton her blouse, anxious to experience a raging, unchartered ocean of love.

Unexpectedly, she forced his hand away and quickly stood up from the couch.

"Marina!" he exclaimed, gasping.

She looked down at him, refastening her buttons and gaining control over her breathing. A smile appeared on her lips. "Not now, my dear Misha," she said. "You have a living to make. I don't want you to be late for your appointment tonight."

Misha watched her fix her hair, then leaned his head back over the couch to look up at the ceiling. He began to smile to himself, then he grinned outwardly. What a woman!

"Now, go get dressed before you're late."

NINETEEN

Sam and Misha were waiting in the foyer of the Bolshoi Theater, located across the street from Red Square. The Bolshoi was a majestic structure, both inside and out, contrasting sharply with the rather drab office and apartment buildings Sam had seen in Moscow. It was more ornate than even New York's theaters, with intricate detail painted and carved throughout the interior. This was truly a special place, Sam thought, a shining Russian cultural star that had managed to survive the grotesque assault of post-war Soviet architecture.

The vestibule undulated with masses of humanity pushing into the theater's various levels. Most of the people were Russians, although a good portion of the dressed-up theater-goers were foreigners. Designer clothes, Western furs, European suits, expensive jewelry, and the haughty air of well-to-do travelers collided with Ivan Ivanovich, who had obviously saved and waited months for an opportunity to visit the ballet.

"There they are," said Sam, having spotted Ilya and his two Mosteks directorate colleagues passing through the main entrance into the foyer. Misha and he quickly began weaving their way through the crowd toward them.

Misha reached the men first and began conversing with Ilya, who then presented Misha and Sam with theater tickets. Andrey Muravyev, the accountant, and Albert Denisov, Mosteks' manager, then greeted Sam with cordial handshakes. The four Russians then began to converse in their unintelligible language.

But Sam was occupied with his own thoughts. Where was Lyena? he wondered. He resisted the inclination to inquire, since his interest in her was something Mosteks didn't need to know about. Instead, he kept scanning the vestibule, searching for those piercing brown eyes.

"She be here shortly," whispered Misha unexpectedly from behind him. "She have to take taxi. Sometimes hard to get one this time of night."

"Okay," replied Sam, embarrassed.

Just then, Sam caught sight of Lyena in the doorway. It was snowing out, and, like most other Russian women, Lyena was wearing a floral scarf around her head. Sam had never thought that head scarves complemented a younger woman, but he was surprised to see she was as attractive as ever in the traditional garment. He enjoyed gazing at her, watching her take off her coat and begin searching for him and the Mosteks group among the crowd. She was wearing a white cotton pullover and a short red leather skirt. Her walk was sexier than ever; her hips swayed left and right just enough to be appealing, but not too much. And with each step, there was a hint of that luscious jiggle beneath her sweater.

"Lyena! Lyena!" he called as loudly as etiquette in the foyer would allow, pushing his way through the crowd toward her. "How are you?" he asked when he reached her finally. He leaned down and kissed her cheek.

"Very good, Sam," she answered, giving him her coat. "Is quite cold tonight."

"That's an understatement," he replied, nodding enthusiastically. It occurred to him how nice it was to see her, to be alone with her, even if just for a moment in the middle of a bustling crowd.

"Understatement?" she asked, her eyes puzzled.

He'd forgotten that verbal communication was not the easiest part of their...relationship. "Uh, if I say that Russians like to drink vodka, that's an understatement," he explained, smiling.

Lyena smiled her understanding back at him, then followed him through the crowd to the others.

He thought for a moment about how strangely she'd acted this morning at the meeting with Ivanov. She seemed warm enough now, though. Forget it, he told himself, directing his thoughts to last night's cab ride home instead.

The two moved toward the coat check where the others were waiting, and, to Sam's disappointment, Lyena joined in the Russians' jumbled conversation. He was trying to find an excuse to butt in when a bell rang, apparently signalling show time.

The group headed into the main auditorium. As they approached the entrance, which was guarded by an elderly man taking tickets, Misha nudged Sam slightly and leaned his head toward him.

"Take, Sam. Take!" he whispered urgently, handing Sam his ticket. "Now give me your. Quick!"

"What?"

"Just do, Sam!" said Misha, yanking the ticket out of Sam's hand.

When they reached their seats, Misha's intentions became clear: Sam's seat was now located next to Lyena's, while Misha had seated himself between Ilya and Andrey Muravyev further down the row. Misha confirmed the successful maneuver with a wink. After the bookkeeper whispered something into his ear, Misha said, "Sam, Andrey wanting to tell you that this is very special performance. He sure you will like it."

"Tell him I'm looking forward to it," replied Sam with a gracious smile at the accountant. Sam's smile erupted into a chuckle when he caught a glimpse of the accountant's sweatshirt, which was visible under his mismatched sportcoat. It read *Same Shit, Different Day*. The theater lights dimmed before Sam could comment.

The performance of *Romeo and Juliet,* Sam had learned, was one of Moscow's hottest tickets. He understood why. The beautiful sets, amazing choreography, and talented dancers were nothing less than astounding. After watching the spellbinding performance for a short while, he leaned toward Lyena and said, "They're incredible, huh?" Her eyes were also locked on the ballet.

"Quite good," she replied cheerfully.

But despite the captivating events on stage, Sam found himself lost in a sea of thoughts about the feminine presence seated beside him. He wondered about Lyena's life and what it would be like to become close to her, to really get to know her. Then he fantasized about her. He could almost feel the velvet-soft skin he'd touched briefly the night before. He envisioned her piercing eyes cutting through the ceiling over his back as he made love to her. How would she sound? And what would those magnificent breasts be like up close? Were her nipples large, or small and pert?

Two hours later, the theater lights brightened for intermission. The Mosteks group got up and headed toward a large chamber containing a buffet of various pastries, tea, and juice. Fortunately, Andrey had buttoned his sportcoat.

Sam's diet had been too limited during his stay in Moscow, and he was looking forward to trying something new. The group took their seats around a table and, as expected, each of the Russian men quickly lit up a cigarette. Misha left for the buffet to get refreshments.

When Albert Denisov leaned forward to speak to Sam, Lyena poised to translate. "He ask how you liking ballet," she said.

"Tell him I'd never paid much attention before to the ballet. Now I see what I've been missing. It's beautiful, and I'm really enjoying it. Thanks for taking me."

She translated for the Russian men, who beamed proudly upon hearing Sam's response.

Misha soon returned with several pastries and a few glasses of an apricot beverage. It was a bit too sweet and would probably work on his stomach, but the juice was a welcome break from the metallic mineral water Sam had drunk with every meal so far. The four Russian men began conversing among themselves, so Sam took the opportunity to speak with Lyena.

"How often do you come to the ballet?" he asked.

"Not so often. Difficult to get ticket. Ilya Konstantinovich have many friends, but he only using connections to get tickets to help business. Is big treat for me tonight. I must to thank you," she explained, quickly glancing at her boss at the other end of the table.

Sam thought he saw her start to put her hand on his, but then pull it back.

"Why don't you go to ballet in New York?" she asked, taking a bite of pastry.

He shrugged and said, "I don't know. None of my friends do. I guess we're just more into movies, concerts, and—Wait a minute!" He gave a surprised but delighted smile. "You're not smoking! In fact, I don't think I've seen you with a cigarette since we were in the telephone station. Did you give it up?"

Lyena nodded her head flirtatiously.

Sam threw up his arms. "I'm shocked! This is big international news! Is there a reason, or did you just decide to die healthy?"

Lyena supported her tilted head with one hand and said, "You not like smokers, right? Well. I not wanting you to lick ashtray when you kissing me." She gave another coquettish smile and immediately rose from her seat. "Excuse me, Sam. I come right back. I going to certain place."

Sam followed her with his eyes as she left the table. He then turned to Misha and interrupted the latter's conversation.

"Misha, what does 'a certain place' mean?"

Misha laughed. "She say she going to certain place?"

Sam nodded expectantly.

"She going to ladies' room, Sam. Russian lady never say 'toilet.' She be right back."

Sam joined in a conversation with the Russian men through Misha's translation, discussing New York City and Virginia. Shortly after Lyena returned, the bell sounded again, and the six headed back into the auditorium.

Sam got completely caught up in the second half of the ballet, which was as enchanting as the first, although his thoughts wandered more than once back to the shapely woman beside him. Would she be energetic or passive in bed? Would she be full of surprises? Had she ever been with an American? The ballet was over before he knew it.

As the group put on their coats and prepared to leave the theater, Misha leaned toward Sam with his clandestine expression and whispered, "You, Lyena, and I now going to restaurant to drink little vodka. Good?"

"Sure," replied Sam with a nod. Clearly the directorate officers were not to be privy to the gathering. Probably a good idea. They were "company men," Sam thought. He shook hands with Ilya, Albert, and Andrey, thanking them and bidding them good night through Misha's interpretation.

Lyena, Misha, and Sam then took a cab to a nearby restaurant.

"Here's to Sam's first experience of incredible Bolshoi Ballet! May the memory be pleasant reminder to him of his stay in Moscow, and be first of many such performances our friend from New York will enjoy with us," toasted Misha with his usual jaunty suave.

The three raised their vodka shots in unison, knocking the three glasses on the table after they'd swallowed the fiery liquor. Sam noted with pride that he'd become rather accomplished at drinking straight vodka. Too bad Eric wasn't here to do a few, he thought.

More shots followed, and Sam joined Misha in sharing a few anecdotes about their youth. They were partying Russian style, sharing stories and experiences, thoughts and attitudes, all with a bottle of colorless liquid as emcee. Lyena joined in their raucous laughter when they discussed their more embarrassing moments on the soccer field. She seemed to enjoy their discussion, although many women Sam knew might be uncomfortable sitting in on such a session. And yet she was as appealing as ever, her hand supporting her tilted head, her captivating eyes absorbing everything in the room. There were many sides to this woman, Sam thought, and he realized how much he wanted to see them. All of them.

Sam soon began to feel the mild dizziness of vodka inebriation, although Misha, and even Lyena, seemed unaffected. He'd just cautioned himself to slow down when Misha said, "And now, my friends, I must to go home."

"What for, Misha? It's not even midnight yet. What happened to that Russky party animal I thought I knew?"

"Not tonight, Sam."

"That's the story of my life."

"I have lovely Russky wife waiting alone for me in Russky apartment." He stood up. "I not want to be late. I picking you up tomorrow morning, good?"

Sam stood up and shook hands with his friend, realizing he hadn't quite figured the Russian out. But one thing was for certain. Misha sure loved women.

Sam and Lyena sat for a short while longer, discussing their families. It was about one o'clock in the morning when the bar's lights began to flicker on and off, and the two put on their coats and left the warm building. Thankfully, the numbing effect of several shots of vodka allayed the sting of the penetrating Russian air on Sam's face and body.

They walked to a nearby taxi stand, Lyena's arm again linked in Sam's. A cab soon pulled up and, when Sam turned to open the door for her, he noticed her looking up at him. There was an expression there he hadn't seen before. Was it…suggestion? Invitation? Who knows, he thought, trying to shrug away the notion. But he couldn't help but contemplate those full red lips.

Neither said a word as they got in, and Sam wondered if she was thinking about the last time they were in a cab together. It was certainly on his mind. Again he remembered touching her, caressing her beneath her sweater, wanting desperately to move his hand farther up, but then having to stop. Right when they'd reached the same destination they were headed to now. He listened to Lyena give instructions to the driver in Russian, just as before, and tried to decipher if she'd said the same thing as she had last night. She didn't speak as long, it seemed. And the last thing she'd said sounded something like Gostinitsa Novgorod, with no subsequent destination.

His thoughts ran riot as he again imagined taking Lyena to bed, kissing her, removing her clothes, warming her up…

But then he stopped. Stacy's face had suddenly appeared before him. He couldn't shake the vision; he'd already focused on her pretty smile, so white against her olive skin. He braced himself for the rush of guilt that was sure to follow.

No! He forced himself away from it, almost shaking his head in doing so. Stacy isn't here now, he told himself. He looked down to see Lyena's hand holding his own tightly.

The taxi pulled into the Hotel Novgorod parking lot. All questions were answered when Lyena paid the driver and got out of the cab ahead of Sam. He followed her up the stairs and into the hotel lobby. As they headed toward the main entrance together, he looked down at her, engrossed for the thousandth time by her eyes. She gave him that look again, that luring expression. Definitely, he thought. It was more than just suggestion or invitation, it was almost demand. His curiosity was soaring.

"Nyet" was the only word the elderly doorman spoke to Lyena that Sam understood. The man was obviously unwilling to allow her to pass into the hotel, even refusing a thousand-ruble note she'd tried to slip into his hand. She immediately motioned Sam aside and whispered into his ear.

"You have dollars?" she asked.

"Uh, yes," replied Sam.

She motioned with her fingers for him to take out his wallet quickly. He did, then flipped through it until he found a five-dollar bill. He hesitated before handing it over, then gasped when she snatched it from him.

"But Ly—"

"Wait here," she said, then darted off toward the doorman.

Sam did without protest, realizing he was completely under the woman's spell, her domination. He cursed himself for getting drunk and falling into a situation where he wasn't in full control. Was this a good idea?

Of course it was!

But what about the JV? What about…Stacy?

He wondered how much the alcohol was really responsible for his predicament. Don't worry about it, he ordered himself.

Lyena waved at him from behind the doorman's post, telling him to quickly follow her into the elevator. He didn't look at her once on the way up to his floor, or down the hall to his room.

"What is matter, Sam?" she asked after he'd safely closed the room door behind him. She took off her coat.

Sam paused and did likewise.

He'd forgotten it was impossible to hide his emotions from her, especially when he was buzzed. Damn! She was sitting by a small desk near the window with an inquisitive expression on her face. "Nothing," he replied with a feigned smile. He sat down on the narrow bed. "I reckon I just had a little too much to drink, that's all."

"You enjoy evening?"

"Very much."

"Wasn't ballet beautiful?"

"It was. Really."

"Misha make good toast, no? He always good company at *tusovka*."

"He's a wildman. Reminds me of a friend of mine back home."

Sam's movements were almost reflexive. He'd never made a conscious decision about what to do, one way or the other. But he stood up from the bed and extended a hand to Lyena, which she accepted before standing and walking toward him slowly. He put his hands on her shoulders and helped himself to her eyes, losing himself in their mystery. What are you doing, Morris? This is a business trip!

But it was too late. He was already kissing her, savoring the intimacy, exploring her responses. She was a timid kisser, as shy now as she'd been in the cab. Maybe she was just uneasy being with him.

He guided her carefully onto the narrow bed. Might this hurt the joint venture? he wondered once more. Was he being foolish, careless?

But her soft, full lips felt and tasted delicious. Sam soon realized he'd been prolonging the kiss so as to avoid the decision which confronted him.

What about...Stacy? He broke the kiss.

But Lyena would not allow such thoughts to persist in his mind. She moved closer, and he felt her full chest push against him. Never mind. He'd worry about Stacy...and the joint venture...later. He pressed his mouth back onto hers.

Sam soon found himself removing Lyena's thin sweater, pulling it slowly out of her skirt, over her breasts, over her head, off of her arms. He quickly unclasped and pulled off her bra. "Oh," he muttered softly. There they were. He took a moment before touching them, satisfying the burning curiosity which had raged inside him for nearly a week. He extended his hand to gently caress them, marveling at their perfect shape and texture. Then his mouth investigated her large nipples.

Sam stood up and removed his suit impetuously, nearly falling down as he stepped out of his trousers. When he returned to the bed, he was surprised to see that Lyena's usually self-confident demeanor was now somewhat perplexed, maybe even bewildered. Just her reaction to her excitement, he decided.

He kissed and fondled her, moving up and down her body, gauging her reactions, seeking out what she liked best. He was slightly disappointed when Lyena remained silent and motionless no matter what he did. Did Russian women prefer something with which he was unfamiliar? Again, he looked at her face. Once more just to be sure. Confusion was written across her features.

He slid off Lyena's skirt and panties and lowered his head between her thighs. This should liven you up, babe, he thought, anxious to see how a Russian woman would respond. But the moment his tongue touched her, Lyena's back arched up from the bed.

"What you doing?" she demanded loudly, startled.

Sam jerked his head back. "Are you all right? Did I hurt you?"

Lyena didn't respond. She was looking down at Sam's head, still poised between her legs. Her expression had changed from perplexity to near distress.

For a long moment, Sam looked into her eyes. "Has…a man ever…done this for you, Lyena?" he asked.

She hesitated, then shook her head slowly, almost sheepishly. She opened her mouth to speak.

"Shh," he whispered. "I won't hurt you, Lyena, I promise. Okay?"

He moved slowly and carefully, making sure she was comfortable with him, secretly enjoying his unexpected role. He was teaching her, guiding her. He marveled when his tongue caused her first quiver, savoring her dependence on his experience, on him. He relished her every response, from the first twitches of her pelvis to the increasingly accentuated gasps in her breathing. It was all his doing, and he knew she'd remember him forever.

Sam saw that Lyena's eyes were locked on his face as he moved to position himself over her. She was asking for direction, for approval that she was performing correctly and adequately. "Shh," he repeated when she tried to speak.

His passion was piqued when his thrusts invigorated her. Her pleasure slowly manifested itself in groans and beads of sweat, and her eyes grew unfocused as she experienced him. He made love to her, controlling his own pleasure until he could no longer.

They were uncomfortably cramped on the confined space of the mattress, so that both had to lay on their sides in order to fit. Their faces were only inches apart.

"You are fascinating for me, Sam," said Lyena unexpectedly, her voice delightfully raspy. "You so different than Russian men."

"Really? Why?"

She tried to shift to a better angle. "You remember when I telling you that Russian men are sexist?"

Sam nodded.

"You see, this attitude going to sex as well. I never have man doing so much for me before. It make me feel so good. I mean..." She seemed embarrassed.

"I know what you meant," said Sam. He kissed her cheek lightly.

"Only once did I have man who care at all about me in bed. I married him." She giggled playfully.

Sam also laughed. "Why do you think Russian men are like that?" he asked.

"I think because they simply don't know. I explain. Why are you so skillful? Why you care so much about woman's pleasure?"

"I don't know. I guess I enjoy pleasing a woman as much as I like being pleased. It's only fair, I guess."

"But why? How do you know what to do? Do women tell you?"

"Sometimes."

"This is big difference, Sam. Russian woman never telling man what she like. Is not comfortable for us. Is not proper."

"But even if a woman doesn't tell me, I still know what she'd probably like. From what I've learned."

"And where would you learn?"

Sam shrugged. "I don't know. From experience, from other guys, books and movies, from magazines..."

"You see, Sam, here, at least until very recently, we not having literature and movies which dealing with this subject. And here you not learn from friends because they also not raised to care about woman."

"You mean it's like a taboo subject, uh, a subject society agrees is not to be discussed?"

Lyena nodded. "Russian men never change because there is nothing to change them. Is in their roots. Women here to serve men, they think. We just for having their babies. Of course they love us. They want us to be a part of them. But not equal part. I think Russian marriages much different than American."

"All Russian men can't be like that," said Sam incredulously.

"Not all. But by far most, Sam. I think is because attitudes toward women in Russia still like in feudal times. It never develop. Men still thinking women lower people."

"Russian women should boycott sex or something until the men get their act together," joked Sam.

Lyena laughed. "I not think so, Sam. We not so unhappy with men here. Besides, Russian women do like sex. Closeness always nice. I bring you to hotel tonight, remember?" She laughed again and snuggled closer to Sam, stroking the back of his head.

He kissed her playfully.

A moment later, she looked at him and said, "We should to get married, Sam. I make you wonderful wife."

Sam laughed. "You got it, Lyena. We'll have a country wedding in Newport News, Virginia with plenty of vodka and Budweiser."

"Is my dream."

"We'll find a band that can play both top forty and Russian polkas."

"I love all music."

"We'll buy a log cabin outside of town and decorate it with *palekh* boxes and Russian icons."

"And we will have much children together. I always wanting to have son and name him Vladimir."

"Vladimir Sam-ovich."

Lyena was quiet, still toying with the back of Sam's head, now looking at the wall behind him.

"Speaking of betrothal, why did you get divorced?" asked Sam, breaking the momentary silence.

"Huh? Oh." She shifted in the narrow bed. "Because my husband become alcoholic. Was impossible to live with him. He not concerned about life. This is another big problem in Russia, Sam. Life so difficult here that it making people drink. Vodka ruin many marriages. Maybe we should not have it at our wedding."

"So you live alone now?"

"I live with parents. Is only place for me."

Sam nodded, trying to look unaffected. He knew the more he learned about Lyena, the sorrier he would feel for her. He decided to change the subject. "Let me ask you something. Why did you give me that look when I was explaining to Ivanov, the militia officer, about the death threat? Were you mad I didn't tell you about it at the party?"

Lyena paused, looking away. A moment later, she said, "No. Not mad. Maybe little confused. Should I be mad?"

"No, I reckon not. I just thought you might have been hurt that we'd had such deep discussions, and I never even told you what had been on my mind."

Lyena paused, then shrugged. "Maybe at meeting I just concerned for you, Sam."

Again, Sam decided not to press the issue. He leaned forward and kissed her lightly on the lips, but Lyena suddenly returned his gesture passionately. She met his tongue more confidently this time, and a moment later Sam felt her hand lower to stroke his butt. He opened his eyes when she broke the kiss and saw that she wanted him to show her more, to teach her something new.

TWENTY

Sam hadn't slept much. Parts of his body—his knees, back, neck, even his arms—were aching. As if he'd played soccer last night for the first time in years. He tried to remember how many times they'd done it (was it three, or four?), and in how many different positions. But God, it had been great.

He'd wanted Lyena to spend the night with him at the hotel, but they'd decided against it, mainly because there just wasn't enough room in the bed for two people. What time did she leave, anyway? Was it four o'clock? Later? He stifled a yawn.

"...we believe is fair. If you disagree, IIS should give us counter-proposal..."

He heard Ilya's voice rambling on. It was hardly worth paying attention, he thought, since the chairman had agreed to virtually anything Sam had wanted all week. Boris Shturkin had shown up for a few minutes this morning to "guarantee" IIS there would be no problems getting the JV registered with Min-Fin. Big deal. No one had been worried about that in the first place. It was odd that the husky, disheveled bureaucrat had come to announce it, but even odder that he'd packed up and left immediately after making the point.

Maybe Sam should call Davies and let him know how friggin' strange things seemed here.

Nah. What the hell for? The more he did by himself in Russia without assistance from the brass, the better. He'd already decided that at a more pressing time than this, right? Might as well stick it out. It was a piece of cake now, anyway. All he had to do was wrap this sucker up and go home to claim the prize. He even decided not to call Davies again unless—

But what about Stacy? Stacy. He'd told her he'd give her a ring today, too. Damn. Maybe he should run back to the telephone station this afternoon and give her a call. Especially after leaving that idiotic message last time.

No. No way! Not from Moscow, where Lyena would see him squirm. And why should he feel ashamed, anyway? He would've been a fool not to have gone for it last night. What red-blooded American wouldn't have? Besides, he'd only been dating Stacy for three months! What she don't know won't hurt her! His thoughts returned to Lyena and last night.

"Sam? Is that acceptable?" asked Ilya, looking across the conference table at him.

"Huh? I'm sorry Ilya, could you repeat that? I was reading my notes." The group was in the union building conference room again, reviewing logistical details of the joint venture. There were a few technicalities that needed attention before the documents could be signed and presented to the authorities.

Ilya repeated his last statement without a trace of impatience. "The joint venture charter fund will be financing shipment to Russia of all equipment IIS provides, but should there be necessary replacement or spare part shipments because of faulty machinery, IIS agreeing to finance shipment of them personally. Is this acceptable?"

"Uh, yes, Ilya. That's acceptable."

Lyena leaned over the conference table in front of Sam to pour Albert Denisov a second cup of tea. Sam caught himself scrutinizing her body, reliving last night. His memory was somewhat befuddled—he'd tossed down at least five shots of vodka before they'd gotten to the hotel—but he could clearly remember the various expressions on her face, the progressive stages from insecurity to burning ecstacy. He had been her teacher, her leader. She might as well have been a virgin last night. And he knew she would remember him, no matter who else—

Sam shook his head, trying to will himself back to the meeting.

Ilya reviewed several other points, and Sam ceded them almost thoughtlessly. Once he caught Lyena studying his face—she must've realized that he was preoccupied. It made him feel awkward, and he immediately looked down at his note pad.

"And so, Sam," continued Ilya. "Our next issue concerns assembly of IIS equipment. We feel that because equipment constituting American partner's capital investment to JV, and since, of course, equipment is useless without proper assembly, that IIS should individually bear all expenses associated with installation, including sending of American technicians to Moscow for this purpose." The chairman smiled as he awaited Sam's response.

"No, Ilya. That's not equitable. The equipment becomes JV property as soon as it reaches Moscow, so the JV should take responsibility for it from that point."

"But as I said, Sam, equipment is virtually useless to JV without proper assembly and installation. And, I must add, it is conventional in Russia for supplier of machinery to take responsibility for its initial use. Authorities may not accept different arrangement."

"All right," agreed Sam after a pause, nodding apathetically. "We'll take responsibility for installation of the equipment." He was spaced, but at least it occurred to him to cover his ass. "I'll have to confirm that with Mr. Davies, though." When would this be over? He took refuge in the fact that the present subjects of negotiation were minor.

A short while later, Lyena interrupted the meeting by saying something to Ilya in Russian. Sam figured that the cars must have arrived and were waiting to take them to lunch when he saw the Russian men extinguish their cigarettes and begin packing their briefcases. He was relieved to hear Misha confirm that it was indeed lunchtime.

"We going to very fine restaurant in Hotel Volgograd for lunch today. You will enjoy," said Misha.

"Sounds great," replied Sam. "I just hope I don't enjoy it as much as I have all the other lunches and dinners we've had, Misha. I could use a break!" He joined Misha in a chuckle and put on his overcoat. Before he walked out of the room, he glanced back at Lyena and gave her a secret smile. And this time, she raised her shoulders and smiled back.

Sam listened impatiently to Ilya's lengthy luncheon toast. He knew he wouldn't be able to escape the lunch without at least one shot, so he might as well accept the fact in good humor. There was something about just sitting around a table with Russians that made indulgence almost mandatory. After tossing back a shot, they ordered lunch.

"Excuse me, Sam," said Misha after the group had consumed its bowls of soup. "I must go to call wife. I return in moment." He stood up and walked toward the pay phone in the nearby lobby.

Sam watched Misha's body language as he conversed on the telephone, presumably with his wife. He noted that the Russian apparently had no problem screwing around, despite being happily married. And this was the rule with men around the world, not the exception! Misha was right at home living a lie. With his wife! So why should Sam be upset about a little fling? All he'd done was have a one-night stand, even though he had a girl-friend of only a few months.

The Russians had reached a lull in their repetitious libations, so Sam took it upon himself to fill the table's six shot glasses. When Misha returned, he rose with a shot in each hand and gave one to his friend.

"I would like to make a toast," said Sam, watching the men's attention focus on him. "Here's to my wonderful experience in Moscow. It's been a tremendous pleasure to meet and work with such hospitable partners." He paused, regarding the Russians while Misha translated. "I look forward to a long, prosperous relationship with Mosteks." He joined the group in drinking the vodka, forgetting his concerns about another mid-day drunk.

"Very nice," said Misha with a smile.

"I'm catching on," replied Sam. The vodka had eased his aching muscles; a cup of Russian coffee and the group's banter was keeping him alert. He was feeling much better than he had at the meeting and was looking forward to filling his stomach with some hot food.

When he'd finished his Chicken Kiev, Sam rose and looked at Misha humorously. "I have to go to a certain place," he said.

"You already speaking good Russian, my friend," replied Misha, pointing in the direction of the restroom. "Is in hall through hotel lobby."

"Back in a jiff," said Sam, wondering if Misha could possibly know what a jiff was.

He found his way into the restroom, unzipped his fly, and relieved himself into the crude Russian urinal. No American Standard here, he noticed.

When he finished, he turned around and was faced with a large pistol pointed directly at his head. It was Sam's first encounter with a gun—his thoughts didn't even focus on danger for a full second. Instead, he simply stared into the barrel's open-ing, which was far wider than he would have expected.

There were two men. He wondered for a second if they had mistaken him for someone else. Or were perhaps playing a joke. They both wore bulky brown overcoats and *ushanka* hats, masking their builds and hair color. Even their hands were gloved. The taller of the two had a blue and yellow scarf wrapped around the lower part of his face, obscuring his mouth and nose and revealing only two vicious eyes. The shorter man, whose wide, hardened face was uncovered, was smiling over the pistol in his hand.

Sam felt his lungs fill with air, then force themselves empty—the first panicked, wheezing breath of what he feared would be many.

The taller assailant brandished a vicious-looking dagger and raised it to Sam's neck, while the other brought the handgun closer to Sam's head. Sam felt as if boiling water had been poured over his scalp, stinging his flesh as it ran down the length of his back. He fought desperately to maintain his composure.

"Sam Morris, American?" asked the one with the gun, his voice scratchy.

Sam's heart was racing—all he could do was nod. He looked again at the gun. The shorter man responded by moving the weapon closer to Sam's nose. As he did so, the thug's coat sleeve pulled back a bit, revealing a dark, hairy arm, and for some reason Sam quickly looked away, pretending he hadn't seen it.

"You do as we are telling you, understand?"

Again, Sam nodded. The two were muggers, he assumed. He tried to remember how much money was in his wallet. It would be best if he could give them a large plunder; they would more likely be satisfied and flee—

"You will not meet with Mosteks again," commanded the shorter man, his smile now gone. "You will no longer pursue joint venture you have been working on with cooperative. And after you leaving, you will never return to Russia."

Sam nodded again, struggling to ignore the frightening perceptions that inundated his mind and body. The eyes of both

276

men were burning through his skull. The large gun barrel was now at his forehead.

"We very powerful in Russia and will know if you disobeying us. If you do, you die. Understand?"

Sam continued to nod impulsively, his attention wavering from the cold steel near his neck to the now-invisible gun barrel pointed at his head.

"You already disobey us once. Why you ignore photograph you find, Mr. Morris?"

"I…I—" He was struggling to make himself speak. "I didn't know," he managed.

Sam felt an instant of relief when the gun lowered from his head, but his solace vanished when the gunman's free arm slammed into Sam's abdomen. He doubled over, the wind knocked out of him. As he gasped for each breath, he lost sight of the two men and their weapons.

"Do not lie, American!" hissed the shorter one, pushing Sam's shoulders back, forcing him to stand upright. The gun came back into Sam's view, but the knife was no longer visible; the taller man had moved it closer to Sam's right cheek. "It seems you needing lesson in Russian business, Sam Morris."

From the corner of his eye, Sam saw the taller man's hand move, but he couldn't tell what he was doing. He suddenly found the strength to speak. "I couldn't leave. There were no flights until—"

Sam saw blood splatter on the dirty white tiles of the floor beside his feet. He traced the source of the red drips to the right side of his face, where a warm trickle ran down his neck. He struggled to avoid fainting as the realization of what was happening came into focus.

"You will no longer meeting with Mosteks cooperative, understand?" said the gunman loudly.

"Yes," was all Sam could manage before the man's knee collided with his groin, causing him to double over again. But before Sam could even process what had happened, he was thrown back against the wall, his left elbow slamming into the urinal he'd just used. He slumped to the floor as the two men ran out of the restroom.

Sam put his hand to his face and found the bleeding cut. Only now did he feel pain from the three-inch wound, which ran from his right temple to his ear. He stumbled awkwardly to his feet, grabbed a handful of blue paper towels from the dispenser by the sink, and pressed them hard against his face. His abdomen and testicles ached, but he willed himself to remain standing. He staggered to the restroom door and locked it.

Get yourself together! he ordered himself. You're all right! It's nothing serious! Breathe!

He did breathe, and felt a little better. Hopefully this bleeding'll stop, he thought. Just have to get a bandage. Soon. Would the slash leave a scar? No matter.

Sam gasped when he heard someone come to the locked restroom door and try to open it. He saw the shadows of moving feet through the crack under the door. He wondered if the lock would hold, then held his breath until the intruder mercifully went away.

After a few minutes, he was able to gain control of himself. He grabbed some fresh paper towels and took several deep breaths, then opened the door. No one around. He walked out slowly, looking left and right for the two men, then ran through the lobby to the hotel's street exit.

The biting air penetrated his suit easily—his overcoat was still in the restaurant's wardrobe. He tried to turn the cold to his advantage by focusing his thoughts on it and away from his terror and pain.

Cops! Got to get to the cops! He raced aimlessly down the sidewalk, searching frantically for the familiar grayish-blue overcoat and *ushanka.* He reached an intersection and suddenly turned around, thinking, What am I going to do when I find a cop? I don't speak Russian! What good's a fucking cop going to do me? It was then that he saw the pay phone on the corner across the street.

There was a car approaching, but Sam ignored it and ran into the street. The car screeched and swerved to miss him, its horn blaring as it sped away.

Sam reached the phone booth and closed the glass door behind him. He struggled with his wallet, pulling out his list of phone numbers with one hand while still applying pressure to the slash on his face with the other. He fumbled with his change until he found a fifty-kopeck coin, deposited it into the pay phone, and carefully dialed with a trembling finger. Before the first ring, he crouched close to the floor of the phone booth to stay warm. And to hide.

Please be there, please be there, please be there, please be there! he thought to the hum of the Russian ring tone. His hand was inside his jacket, fondling his passport and airline ticket. Thank God he'd gotten them back from the hotel.

"Allo?" The woman's voice resounded through his head. It was Aunt Lilli.

He opened his mouth, but it took him a moment to speak. "Aunt Lilli, this is Sam," he said finally. "Can I speak to Uncle Yasha, please?" He tried not to sound desperate; it might disturb the old woman.

She began mumbling something in Russian, exasperating him, pushing him closer to the verge of panic. He grabbed control. "No, no, Aunt Lilli. It's me, Sam Morris. From New York. New York! From America! Gussie's grandson, Sam!"

"Ah!" said Lilli exuberantly. "Moment," she said, then left the line.

Be there, Yasha! He momentarily removed the paper towel from his face and saw that it was drenched with blood. He wondered if the wound was more serious than he'd originally thought—

"Hello, nephew! How has my relative from America been enjoying his stay in Moscow?"

Sam barely heard the words; he was too focused on the sound of Yasha's familiar voice. Again, he had to struggle to speak. "I...have a problem, Uncle Yasha." His voice came out a croak. "It's...kind of an emergency."

"At your service, young Sam. What's the matter, my nephew?"

TWENTY ONE

Sam crouched down in the phone booth for the eternity it took Yasha to arrive, shielding himself from the icy air. He kept raising his head high enough to see through the glass door, looking for the red sedan his uncle had told him to expect. The paper towels were almost useless by now, having been saturated to the point that compression on the wound only caused blood to stream down his cheek.

Finally, a dirty red vehicle approached with Yasha's familiar face peering anxiously through the passenger window. Thank God, Sam thought, closing his eyes and taking a moment to savor the relief. He forced himself to his feet, held his breath, pushed open the phone booth door with his shoulder, and stumbled through the freezing air toward the car.

As soon as he'd spotted Sam, Yasha had gotten out of the sedan and was now hurrying toward him as fast as his waddling legs and cane would allow. When he reached Sam halfway across the sidewalk, he silently guided him into the back seat of the car, then scurried back to the front passenger seat. "Lie down, nephew, quickly! And take this. Push it hard against the wound!" He gave Sam a cloth towel to replace the sopping paper.

Sam felt the car's warmth begin to soothe the chill that still gripped his body. His emotions were intensified by friendly assistance—he had to resist the throbbing urge to cry. He applied the fresh towel to his face and looked back up. Yasha was examining him.

"You'll be all right, young Sam," said Yasha, nodding. "We'll take care of the wound when we reach my apartment. Are you hurt anywhere else?"

Sam quickly surveyed the parts of his body the two men had assaulted. His groin still ached a bit, but the pain in his elbow and abdomen had lessened. "I think I'm okay," he replied.

Yasha said, "This is my friend and colleague, Grisha Zhdanov. He'll help us take care of you."

Sam nodded at the driver when he turned around. The elderly man had crooked yellow teeth and wore that same look of survival that Sam had seen on many older Russian faces.

They rode for what seemed like a long time, stopping and starting at traffic lights, riding slowly through congested areas and faster when the road was clear. Sam studied the car's tattered ceiling, occupying his mind by wondering how certain rips in the fabric might have been made. Who else had lain across the back seat to observe them? Occasionally he lifted his head to search for some landmark that might signal they were getting close to Yasha's building.

Finally, they pulled into the parking lot behind Yasha's apartment complex. Grisha gave Sam his coat, and the three headed quickly into the building, through the dank foyer, and into the small elevator. Yasha conversed unintelligibly with Grisha on the way up, his voice curt and deliberate. It was clear that he was taking control of the situation, apparently assuming a familiar role. Sam was about to ask what they were discussing when the elevator stopped with a jolting thud.

The three men entered Yasha's flat, where Lilli was waiting for them with a large pot of hot water and a tray of towels and bandages.

"Over here, my nephew," said Yasha, guiding Sam awkwardly onto the green sofa. Sam lay down and looked around the room. There was the unfinished manuscript on the table. The chess set rested on the bottom shelf of a book cabinet, ready for a match. Lilli's kind grey eyes were as expressive as they'd been a few days ago, although her concern for him was now also visible in them. He tried to ignore the clamorous Russian language which filled the air, concentrating on the familiar apartment's more comforting sights.

Lilli dutifully dressed his wound, cleaning the blood from his face and affixing adhesives tightly over the cotton strips she'd placed on the bleeding cut. She smiled at him when he met her eyes. Sam savored the feeling of sanctuary.

"Perhaps you'd be more comfortable if you removed your suit, young Sam," said Yasha after Lilli had finished bandaging his face. "Grisha brought some clothing that should fit you. You can change in the bedroom. Can you stand?"

Sam saw that his white shirt was stained with blood, and his suit had been soiled during his long wait on the phone booth floor. He groaned and stood slowly from the sofa, then took the clothes from Grisha. "'Preciate it," he said. He quietly went into the bedroom to change, his thoughts torn between wanting to leave Moscow immediately—and seeking revenge.

A few minutes later, he came out of the bedroom and saw Yasha motion him to sit at the table, which he did. Here goes nothing, he thought.

"We'll talk while you eat your soup," said Yasha, taking a seat next to his nephew.

Sam was dressed in a pair of brown polyester slacks and an old yellow shirt—he would have loathed them had he not been too preoccupied to even care. Lilli continued to comfort him silently, serving him a bowl of *shchi,* traditional Russian cabbage soup.

"I want you to tell me everything about this cooperative you're dealing with," said Yasha. "Everything you know, understand?" His untroubled expression was somehow not out of place under the circumstances, and Sam remembered his uncle's philosophy that one should never succumb to despair.

Sam cleared his throat, took a deep breath, and began to explain the joint venture project in detail, the meetings and his near-catastrophic tour of the facility. He also told Yasha about the threat against his life and the visit from the militia officer who'd assured him that the matter was under control.

Yasha sat calmly as Sam spoke, pensively nodding his head. On a few occasions, he interrupted Sam and translated for Grisha, who also sat attentively, taking down notes in a looseleaf notebook. They'd obviously played these roles before.

When Sam concluded his story, Yasha gave a loud sigh and patted him affectionately on the shoulder. "What I should tell you first, my nephew, is that the militia would not likely send a lone officer to interview you at Mosteks, especially in the presence of others. I believe this Lieutenant Ivanov was a fraud. And therefore, I'm afraid, so is your Ilya Lukov. I can't be sure, of course, but it's a good bet."

Sam gritted his teeth and jerked his head back. Fuck! he thought, barely catching the obscenity before it escaped his lips. He searched frantically for some way to refute Yasha's implication, but after reviewing the events of the past week in his mind, Sam conceded to himself that it made sense. He caught himself reaching under the cuff of the yellow shirt to grasp the Rolex.

"So," continued Yasha, "step two. Do you have any friends, so to speak, at Mosteks? Maybe someone whom you trust more than the others?"

Sam hesitated, then nodded slowly, tearing his thoughts away from his father and Old V. But if he brought Lyena or Misha into the picture, would he be putting them in danger? His head was in such turmoil, he couldn't figure out what their added presence might do. But he decided he'd best be honest with his uncle; there was no one else in Moscow for him to rely on. "Two, actually. They're both Mosteks employees."

"Do you know how to contact them at their homes?"

Sam remembered that Lyena had given him her phone number. He quickly reached into his wallet for the paper and gave it to Yasha. "I don't even know her last name," he said, then took a spoonful of soup.

Yasha said, "I want you to call her early tonight, nephew. If possible, we'll go visit her. What about the other?"

"I never got his home number, but I could probably get it from Mosteks."

Yasha shook his opened hand. "No, no, nephew. I think it best you not be in touch with the cooperative. It may be—"

"What about the cops?" interrupted Sam. "Don't you think we should contact the authorities? Maybe I should call the American embassy?"

"I don't think it wise to call the Russian police," said Yasha, shaking his head. "At least not yet. It may hinder our getting to the bottom of the matter. Here you must trust Uncle Yasha, young Sam. I'm familiar with my country. First we must do some work on our own." He put a hand on Sam's shoulder, turned to speak momentarily with Grisha, then went back to Sam. "You would also find the American embassy is both powerless and reluctant to take any real action here, my nephew. Such matters are not within their domain. I believe we should first do what we can on our own." He spoke as if he thought it might be difficult for an American to understand these things.

"Whatever you say, Uncle Yasha," Sam replied, taking another mouthful of soup.

Sam couldn't nap, despite Lilli's insistence that he try, and he spent much of the day pacing about the Edelmans' apartment.

He thought of Daddy and Grandpa and wondered what they would have said if they knew what he was going through for Old Virginia. Would they be proud, or would they think him a bumbling fool for having gotten himself into this mess in the first place? He looked at his Rolex several times, subtracting eight hours to determine the time on the east coast, and pictured Stacy sound asleep in her bed.

At about six o'clock, Yasha told Sam to call Lyena. He picked up the phone and dialed.

"Hello, Lyena? Is that you? Lyena? May I speak to Lyena, please?" Sam spoke succinctly, though not loudly, to the Russian voice. He gripped the phone tightly during the brief pause. How would Lyena respond to this? How did she really feel about him?

"Allo?"

Her voice had startled him. "Hi, Lyena, it's me, Sam."

"Sam! Where are you? Ilya Konstantinovich and Misha looking all over Moscow for you! Are you in order? What happened with you?"

"I need to talk to you, Lyena, soon. Tonight. Can we meet?"

"What is matter, Sam? I should to phone Ilya Konstantinovich and tell him you okay. They very worried when you disappearing from lunch."

"No, Lyena! Don't call anyone! It's important you keep it a secret that I've even contacted you! Promise me you won't tell anyone I called, all right?"

Lyena was silent on the other end.

Sam asked, "Can I come over tonight? With a friend? I really need to talk to you, Lyena."

"Not here, Sam," she said softly. "My parents here. I come to you. Tell me where you are."

He repeated what Lyena had said to Yasha, who shook his head violently at the suggestion that she come to his apartment. "Tell her to meet us at the Mayakovsky monument," he said.

"From there we'll go to the apartment used by SS writers for writing and meetings."

"It will be safe in this apartment," said Yasha as he opened the door and turned on the lights in the Sila Slova headquarters. "The authorities would never risk making a scene here, because SS is internationally known, and there would be bad press. But just to make sure, Grisha will wait downstairs until we're ready to leave."

Sam followed Lyena and Yasha into the apartment. The three took off their coats and hung them on wall pegs near the door. The room was filled with small chair-desks, the kind used in grade schools, which were covered with unfinished manuscripts, pens, dictionaries, and other books. The walls were lined with bookshelves, and a primitive-looking word processor sat on the floor under a window. Aesthetics were not an SS priority, Sam decided as he surveyed the filthy, ripped carpet and worn furniture.

"Many of our members come here to write. It's our clubhouse, you might say," said Yasha with a dash of pride. "Sit down, you two." He pointed to a frayed brown sofa against the cinder block wall. "I'll put up some tea." He waddled into the kitchen.

Sam sat down close to Lyena on the couch. What could she know that might shed light on what had happened? He saw her cower at his bandaged face, her usually impassive demeanor becoming more and more distressed. Did he read guilt in her expression?

"I'm so sorry, Sam," she said despondently, tears beginning to well in her eyes. "I—"

"So, my young friends," interrupted Yasha, returning from the kitchen. "Shall we get down to business?"

Lyena whimpered, her eyes cast downward, her hands writhing against each other. She stole a glance up at Sam and

Yasha, then paused for a long moment. "I wanted to tell you, Sam!" she said. "I try! I just too afraid…" She stopped speaking and broke into sobs, tears streaming down her contorted face.

Sam gave Lyena a moment to get herself together. "Lyena," he said softly, touching her arm lightly. "Shh. Listen. I knew about the mafia in Russia and what they do. I chose to stay here after getting that death threat, remember? It's not your fault I was hurt."

"But I knew, Sam," she continued, accepting a handkerchief from Yasha. "This man, Lieutenant Ivanov, not with Moscow militia. He used to be KGB agent who monitor old Soviet Ministry of Light Industries. He just friend of Ilya Konstantinovich. He having nothing to do with struggle against mafia crime. He never have." She paused and wiped her eyes and nose. "I knew it Sam. I knew he was just trick. I afraid to tell you because I not wanting to lose my job. Please forgive me, Sam! I not know this would happening to you!" She leaned her head over her lap and again broke into uncontrollable sobs.

Sam sighed, reaching under her head to take her hand. She should have told him. Definitely. But he could see how it might have been hard for her to do so. A job like hers was obviously very valuable in Russia. And career devotion was something he could easily relate to. He listened to her sobs for a moment and couldn't help but feel sorry for her. "It's okay, Lyena," he whispered. "Really. I understand."

She looked up at him slowly, her eyes red and pained, and Sam wiped the tears from her cheeks. She almost seemed bewildered that he'd forgiven her so easily.

"I just want you to tell me everything you know, okay?" said Sam. "Help me."

Lyena thought for a moment, then breathed deeply, trying to regain her composure. "The mafia…" She turned to Yasha for assistance with an English word.

"Extorting," Yasha supplied the term, nodding. As if he'd suspected it all along.

"Mafia extorting Mosteks for several weeks, since time when you first planning to come to Moscow. They making Mosteks pay them percent of monthly profit. Ilya Konstantinovich think that only way to stop them is to set up joint venture with IIS as quickly as possible so that Russian government will protect source of foreign currency."

Yasha continued nodding, as if he'd read the script.

"Ilya Konstantinovich's plan was to accept any terms you offer regarding joint venture so to make registration very fast. Before mafia can find out and stopping it."

Now Sam nodded. Everything was beginning to make sense. He only wished he'd been able to put it all together earlier. "I reckon the mafia found out about the JV soon enough," he added, touching the bandage on his face.

Lyena's eyes began to water, and soon she was crying again into her lap. Sam tried to comfort her by massaging the back of her neck. "Shh," he said softly. "It's all right. Everything's all right, Lyena."

She lifted her head and shook it at him hysterically, unable to speak through her renewed sobs. "Is not all, Sam," she finally managed, her voice now almost shrill.

Sam paused a moment. "What else, Lyena?" he asked compassionately, still massaging her neck.

"I tell you another lie."

He waited while she struggled to catch her breath.

Lyena removed Sam's hand from her neck and held it in both of her own. "Few days ago, you asking me how I get job with Mosteks. I tell you because my father knowing Ilya Konstantinovich. This not true."

"That's okay, Lyena," said Sam with a slight smile. "I may have told you a thing or two that wasn't true, also."

Again she shook her head, telling Sam he'd missed the point. "I get job because I know Misha's wife Marina, Sam. We friends for many years. I meet Misha through her, and he get me job."

Sam glanced at Yasha, who was also listening attentively.

"Sam...Sam..." She again had to struggle to regain her composure, and Sam put his arm around her back. "I think Misha connected with mafia! I think he inform to mafia about you and IIS joint venture. Marina tell me this in trust that I not tell no one else."

Sam sat speechless.

"Misha's brother, Petya, is big *mafioznik*," she continued. "It is his mafia what is extorting Mosteks. They called Gagarintsi. Misha very close to his brother, and I think that he doing crime with Gagarintsi, too."

"But...but he's not the type, Lyena," said Sam incredulously, finally finding the words. "He's...such a nice guy! Are you sure? How well do you know Misha and Petya?"

"It would make sense, Sam," interrupted Yasha. "Misha would have known exactly where you've been at every moment since you arrived in Moscow."

Lyena said, "There is big rumor among Mosteks workers that Misha informing for Gagarintsi. They very fearing Misha. And they all afraid to go to Ilya Konstantinovich because they not want trouble with mafia."

Sam remembered how the plant workers, including the woman in the red scarf, had fled in fear when he tried to speak with them during his tour of the facility. They must have seen him walking around with Misha and thought he was with the mob as well.

Sam leaned back into the sofa and sighed, the realization of what was happening having lodged in his gut. He recalled all the fun he'd had with Misha, how he'd begun to think of him as a real friend. But now the image of Misha Grunshteyn's face in his mind brought only rage. He felt himself begin to breathe more deeply. "Do you know where Misha lives?" he asked, staring at the far wall.

Lyena nodded silently. She looked up at Sam as if to ask, What are you going to do?—but he didn't reply.

Instead, he quickly stood and grabbed the coat that Grisha had loaned him.

"No, Sam!" said Yasha, struggling to his feet and shaking his head, his eyes closed tightly. "I don't think it's a good idea! You don't know what this Misha may be into, or what he might be capable of doing if you sneak up on him! I don't think you should go there!"

"I have to go, Uncle Yasha, there's no two ways about it," replied Sam sternly, putting on the coat and taking down the other two. "You're welcome to come along."

Yasha remained silent for a moment, looking at his nephew, then at Lyena, then back at Sam. The tea kettle he'd put up in the kitchen began to whistle, as if it were an alarm signalling imminent danger. Yasha tapped his cane a few times on the floor and said, "You are a headstrong young man, Sam Morris. And you have my blessings." He walked clumsily into the kitchen and turned off the stove, then waddled back toward Sam, who was holding open his uncle's overcoat. He struggled to get his arms into it, then said, "However, I cannot go with you. As you can see, I'm in no physical condition for a possible confrontation, and I have responsibilities here which prohibit me from becoming entangled with criminals." He straightened his coat and said, "All I can offer you, I'm afraid, is a ride to this man's apartment and my congratulations for your purpose and resolve."

Yasha waited for Sam to help Lyena into her coat, then opened the door and followed them out into the cold Moscow night.

TWENTY TWO

"He living in apartment 526," said Lyena to Sam after Yasha and Grisha had dropped them off at Misha's building. The two were standing in a small foyer on the ground floor. A telephone was attached to the left wall above a metal box with numbered buttons. To pass through the set of doors leading to the elevators, they had to enter a coded sequence on the buttons. "I not know correct code," said Lyena, examining the device. "We can call him to let us in."

"No," said Sam. "If he finds out we're here, he might take off."

"Wait, then," said Lyena. "Just a minute. Maybe I find out code numbers." She began searching around the foyer, running her hand along the concrete walls as she went. "All apartment buildings in Moscow having code written somewhere in entrance. Tenants also forgetting numbers, and someone always writing them somewhere.

"Ah! Here is. It may be in backward order or something, but these numbers should be code." Lyena punched the numbers in different sequences and managed to open the doors. After the two had boarded the elevator inside, she pushed the button marked "5." They stood in the noisy lift, looking at each other but not speaking, the intensity in the air increasing as they ascended.

Sam had been unable to tear his thoughts away from Misha. He thought about the Russian's suave toasts and how they'd gotten drunk together. He remembered their conversations about anti-Semitism and women. He'd been looking forward to playing more soccer with Misha, to evening the score, next time maybe in Central Park.

But he'd been brutally betrayed.

When the elevator abruptly stopped, his heart began to hammer inside his chest. He walked straight to apartment 526, as if he'd been there before, and banged on the door.

He waited. He heard footsteps. The locks turned on the other side of the door, which swung open a moment later. Suddenly the two men were face to face.

Sam felt his hand curl into a tight fist, then rise above his shoulder and slam into the Russian's mouth. He felt the pliant softness of Misha's lip collide with the rigidity of his teeth, Misha's shrill yelp confirming the accuracy of Sam's punch. Misha's back slammed into the wall behind him, and he slumped to the floor in pain.

Sam expected Misha to retaliate and braced himself for a return, but then saw that Misha had no intention of even getting to his feet. Sam was astounded at the impact of his own blow, causing him to look down at his still-closed fist.

"No, Sam!" exclaimed Lyena suddenly, grabbing Sam's arm from behind and moving to stand in front of him. He'd somehow forgotten about her. He stood silently, catching his breath, looking first at the injured Russian, then at Lyena's pleading face. The day's events repeated themselves in his mind, beginning with the assault he'd suffered in the restroom and ending with the strike at Misha's mouth.

Sam looked down at Misha and saw fear and confusion in the eyes staring back up at him. The Russian lay on the floor, supporting himself on one elbow, a rivulet of blood trailing from the corner of his mouth, his chest heaving.

Lyena filled Sam's hand with the softness of her own. She looked up at him, silently imploring him not to continue the violence. Her expressive eyes, and the memories they elicited, were enough to stem the tide of Sam's fury.

He looked around her to make eye contact with Misha. A moment later, he said, "You're lucky I don't kill you, Grunshteyn." His voice was hoarse.

"I not understand, Sam!" said Misha, panting.

The denial was enough to renew the rage that had just been tempered in Sam's chest. Only Lyena standing between the two men kept Sam from a second attack. "Please, Sam," she said, her own voice shaken. "Let's sit. We talk. Will be better than this. Please!"

Misha stood up slowly and stumbled into the living room, where he sat on an armchair, nursing his bleeding mouth. Lyena took a seat on the sofa, but Sam found it impossible to sit and remained standing across the room. He scowled at Misha and said, "Now, tell me what the fuck's going on with the mafia, asshole! What're you doing for them?"

Misha was dazed, as if Sam's words had somehow caused him to forget about the pain in his mouth. He looked as if he were about to ask Sam how he'd learned of his activities, but then changed his mind. Perhaps answering the question would be more prudent. "I just making some errands for my brother, who work with Gagarinskaya mafia, Sam. Nothing more. Sometime he asking me about Mosteks. I make report. This is all. You see, mafia can control cooperative through their connections in government. They not needing my help to make Mosteks pay them money."

Misha's eyes widened with apprehension when Sam stomped toward the armchair where he sat. He stopped a few feet from

Misha and leaned over. "You see this, asshole?" he demanded, pointing to the bandage on his temple. "Your friends did this to me! One of your little errands was to set me up, wasn't it, asshole?" He glanced back at Lyena, who had stood from the sofa, and he had to fight the urge to strike Misha again. "When you made a call from the restaurant this afternoon, it was to those fucking goons, wasn't it? You said you were going to call Marina, but you called them and told them where we were for lunch!"

"No! Is not true!"

"Then all they had to do was wait for me to go take a piss! They knew what I looked like, of course, because you pointed me out to them one day in front of the fucking factory! You knew all along that the mafia was trying to stop the joint venture from going through, to protect their plan to extort money from Lukov, didn't you, asshole?"

"No, Sam! Is not true! All I ever doing was report to Petya about what I hear at Mosteks! Usually sales and business problems! Everything else they do through threats and connections with government! They would never attack foreigner! I promise! Is not necessary!"

"Sam!" interrupted Lyena from behind. "I think Misha telling truth."

Misha visibly forced himself to catch his breath, then said, "The day after you getting death threat in the photograph, I call my brother Petya. He not know nothing about this. Mafia have nothing to do with it, Sam. I very sure. This not how they working. I went to Petya myself. If they want to hurt somebody, they would never leave photograph that can be found by police."

Suddenly, the door leading to the bedroom opened, and Marina, dressed in a white nightgown, walked warily into the living room. Her hair was disheveled, and her eyes hadn't adjusted to the light, but she was clearly confused and frightened by the disturbance. She began speaking anxiously to Misha and Lyena in Russian.

Sam watched Marina as she spoke. He thought it curious that Misha's wife had slightly Asian features, but as he'd expected, she was an attractive, pleasant looking woman. Her timid manner contrasted sharply with her husband's.

But then Marina noticed the blood on Misha's mouth. She gasped and raised her hands to her face, then ran into the kitchen. After a moment, she brought back a wet towel, which she applied to Misha's mouth, all the while mumbling in Russian.

Shortly, Misha gently bade Marina to stop. He stood up and walked over to a small wooden end table next to the sofa and withdrew a brown package from its single drawer. He drew a deep breath and said, "I do this both for you, Sam, who I still call my friend, and for my beloved wife." He opened the package, revealing thousands of colorful ruble notes, all neatly stacked and arranged in folded groupings. There was a letter on top of the money and a photograph of a grey-haired man dressed in typical Russian business attire. "For me to show you this is to risk anger of mafia. A very big risk. If they catch me, it be very unpleasant. But I taking this risk for you and for Marina, to whom I already promise stopping business with my brother." He paused for a moment, allowing the seriousness of his words to sink in.

"This is delivery I am to make tomorrow, Sam. It not related to Mosteks. This for other privatized business. Package is payment to chinovnik in Ministry of Agriculture whose picture is also here." Misha gave the letter to Lyena, who began reading it. He then walked back to Marina and comforted her, putting his arm around her shoulders.

Lyena finished reading and said, "This man is officer in ministry. But it seem he also working for mafia. Ministry of Agriculture regulate distribution of fertilizers to farms. This man taking bribe for favors he doing for Misha's brother."

Misha said, "I show you this, Sam, because is proof that my brother not needing to attack foreigner to stop joint venture."

Sam considered Misha's gesture, nodding his head.

"Please, Sam. Petya is my brother. All my life he is what every Russian man wanting to be. He having money, *valuta* money. He having girls and contacts with foreigners. You have seen how hard life is in Russia, so am I really so terrible for doing just this little business with him? He make mafia sound so easy, so normal. Can't you see that I do this only because of circumstances? And now I ready to stop this business forever."

Again, Sam nodded.

"There is another thing I wish to tell you, Sam," continued Misha. He exhaled loudly. "I overhear Ilya Konstantinovich speaking with Boris Shturkin about bribe payments Mosteks making to him. You were right this week when you feel strange about Shturkin at meeting. Shturkin agree to give JV immediate registration with MinFin only after Mosteks making corrupt arrangement with him. They paying him dollars.

"Sam, you must to believe me. I supposed to tell Gagarintsi everything I hear, and this information very important. You like to know why? Petya would want to know about Shturkin and Mosteks' business, because Gagarintsi also paying to Shturkin. For very long time, just like to this man at Ministry of Agriculture. Mafia order Shturkin not to allow JV to have registration, at all. They not want JV to be created, as you have learned, because this would stop their business with Mosteks." Misha stood from his chair and took a few steps toward Sam. "But Sam. I not tell Petya this. Or any other of Gagarintsi. Never. I not tell them because I am promising Marina to quit this mafia business." He slowly moved closer to Sam, stopping a few feet before him. "I also not tell them because of my friendship with you. I very much not wanting you in any way to be involved with these people, Sam. I see I have failed, but please believe that my soul is right."

Lyena had taken Misha's seat next to Marina and was translating for her. Marina looked at Sam from across the room, her face as contorted as Lyena's had been an hour earlier. She couldn't speak to Sam, but she nodded at him solemnly, imploringly.

"Then what the hell's going on here?" demanded Sam in a quiet voice, exasperated, throwing up his hands and slapping them against his sides. "Who would go to such lengths to stop the IIS-Mosteks deal? I'd always thought the textile business is about as boring as it gets," he added with a wry laugh.

Misha returned to the arm of Marina's chair and sat pensively for a moment, then shook his head. "Nobody at Mosteks was opposed to JV," he said. "Ilya Konstantinovich convince directorate that JV with IIS our only chance to survive mafia problems. He say is important to break into international market immediately."

Sam began to pace the room. "So Mosteks is paying bribes, hard currency bribes, to Shturkin. That makes sense. Sounds like Ilya Konstantinovich is no angel after all. But while Mosteks is paying Shturkin a kickback to provide immediate registration of a JV, the mafia is paying him to make sure the joint venture doesn't get registered. At all." He stopped pacing abruptly. He gave Misha a communicative look.

"Shturkin never risk making mafia angry, Sam, I assure you," said Misha wide-eyed, reading Sam's thoughts.

"But he wouldn't want to piss off Lukov, either, after he'd already been paid." The room fell silent.

"In *valuta*," they said together.

Misha said, "Is possible Sam. Very possible. The only way both mafia and Ilya Konstantinovich to be happy with Shturkin is for joint venture to fail for reason other than Shturkin." His eyes grew wider still.

"Shturkin," said Sam, shaking his head slowly, his voice nearly a whisper. "Who the fuck else could it be? I knew there was something wrong with that guy from the very beginning!" He sighed, stopped pacing, and walked over to Misha, who was translating softly for Marina. "We have to call the cops, Misha. And I want you to help me. I want to take this whole mess to the authorities."

Misha was silent for a moment, a look of trepidation returning to his face. He spoke in Russian to Marina, his voice almost cracking, and Lyena translated for Sam. "I don't think the Gagarintsi would ever let me go, Marina! I know too much. Am I really to betray my brother to the police? And if we did go to MVD, what about what I've done? Won't the police hold me accountable for having worked with the Gagarintsi? What am I going to do, Marina?"

"Give Petya a chance, Misha," interrupted Sam. "Call him and tell him to come clean. I don't know how Russian cops operate, but in the States the authorities usually grant immunity to someone who helps them catch harder criminals. Who knows? Maybe we can even get the police to agree not to go after Petya if he testifies against the rest of the Gagarintsi. And with the incriminating evidence you have against the mafia, I'm sure the cops would be willing to overlook the few errands you ran for them if you come forward. I'm a lawyer, remember? I know about these things."

Misha translated for Marina, confusion and despondence still visible in his eyes. Sam watched the couple converse for a few minutes, obviously discussing the dangers that going to the cops would impose. They'd never be safe anywhere in Russia if they did, ever again. Would I do it? Sam wondered.

Sam sighed and began to pace about the room, thinking about his life back in the States. His friends and family. Stacy. Old V. What he really wanted. Damn. He'd never before realized how confusing it all was. Or how good he had it.

Should he go for it? It was a big decision, and a very risky one. It might even be crazy. But wasn't it a risky move that had gotten him where he was in the first place? Hadn't his grandfather's decision to risk all and leave Russia been the real first step? Hyman certainly hadn't been afraid to take a chance.

Sam slowly formulated a plan in his mind, going over it, analyzing it, picturing each step. What might happen if this, what might go wrong with that. Cost, risk, benefit. Damned law school poisoning! He just wished he had a disinterested person with whom to discuss it.

"Misha," he said a few minutes later, interrupting the couple's conversation. "I have an idea. You won't have to worry about the Gagarintsi if you go with me to the cops." Misha and Marina stopped talking. Sam breathed deeply. "You and Marina will leave Russia. You'll move to the States with me. I'll get you out of here. Petya, too, if you can convince him to go."

Misha was taken aback by the suggestion. He was obviously searching for something to say, some way to respond. Marina saw how Misha was overwhelmed and begged for a translation, which Lyena provided energetically.

After an enchanted moment, Misha laughed nervously and shook his head. "Is such a wonderful offer, Sam, but unfortunately is not so easy. It taking much time to get visa and airline ticket for us to leave Russia. I afraid we would not have so much time. It be very dangerous for us even for one day here after going to police." Despair returned to his face as he spoke.

Sam said, "There's no way you can get visas and tickets in an emergency? There's got to be some way."

"Only on black market," said Misha. "And this cost much of money. Thousands of dollars. Not rubles."

Sam paused, closing his eyes tightly, then said, "I have it, Misha. Set it up, and I'll pay. Call your contacts or whatever."

Again Misha laughed nervously. "No call, Sam. This is still Russia, my friend. We must just to go to them. But only tomorrow. Now is too late." His face had become perplexed. "Why, Sam?" he asked. "Why you doing this?"

"I have my reasons, Misha." He tried to give a reassuring smile. "For now, let's just say I'm doing it to get a second chance at blocking your soccer shots. Next time, I'll have the home-field advantage."

Misha didn't smile. He was still confused, overwhelmed. "I should to call Petya, then?" he said, glancing at the red phone.

Sam looked at him silently.

"Sam, Petya is my brother. I—"

"Just do it, Misha! Just go to that fucking telephone and dial! Call Petya!"

Marina heard the names and understood what Sam had said. She stood and looked down at Misha, waiting for him to go to the phone.

Misha glanced at Sam and Lyena once more, then got up and walked to the red plastic telephone. He slowly removed the receiver and dialed, his eyes locked on Marina's.

"Hello, Petya. Misha."

"Hi, little brother. How is everything?"

Misha was silent as the gravity of the upcoming conversation settled in his belly, and he felt his hand grip the plastic receiver more firmly. "Uh, fine," he said. "Well…not so fine."

"I'm glad you called, Mishenka," said Petya. "Listen. I want you to run an errand for me next week. It just involves a pick-up near Arbat. We'll pay you fifty thousand rubles for a half-hour's work and…"

Misha stopped listening to his brother, feeling a bead of sweat break and roll down his brow. He felt the weak plastic of the receiver give somewhat under his tight grip. Moving to the West had always been his dream! He remembered almost forsaking Marina just to remain available for a Western woman! This was one of the reasons he'd decided to do business with Petya in the first place, he admitted to himself.

And here the West had fallen on him, like snow from a clear blue sky. It was so easy, yet so difficult! He almost asked himself what Petya would do in his shoes.

"…and if he is late, just hang out for a while, okay?"

Misha remained silent while Petya waited for an answer.

"Okay, little brother? Do you understand the plan?"

The younger Grunshteyn took a deep breath and said, "No. No, Petya."

"What do you mean, Misha? Is there a problem? Are you busy next week?"

Misha closed his eyes and said, "It's over, Petya. I'm not doing it anymore."

After a moment, Petya gave a confused laugh. "What do you mean, Mishenka? This is fifty thousand rubles for—"

"I'm not having anything more to do with the Gagarintsi, and…" Again Misha hesitated, his heart pounding in his chest. He quickly switched the phone to his other ear and said, "And I want you to quit, too. Give it up. We'll start our lives over without Svetov and his mafia."

Now Petya was silent. Finally he said, "Misha, what's the matter with you? Why are you acting this way? Do you know how much money I make, how much we make together? What are you afraid of? Listen, little brother. I'm sorry I suggested hiring Marina. You know I love her, and—"

"It's over Petya! Enough! I'm going to the MVD tomorrow! If you come along, I'm sure we can make a deal with the police. We'll trade your cooperation for a guarantee that you'll not be prosecuted. We'll have an American with us, so they'll take us seriously. And Sam will see to it that you get out of Russia immediately, to America. You've got to go with us, Petya. It's the only way."

Petya was again silent for a moment. "And what if I don't, Misha? What if I prefer to be a man? What if I want to go out and be somebody? To live like a human being, not like an ignorant, helpless peasant, or an unemployed immigrant in New York City? What are you going to do?" His voice had abandoned the affectionate tone it usually carried when speaking to Misha.

Misha looked at Marina, then at Sam and Lyena, then back at Marina. He knew that all three understood what was happening. How he was being forced to choose between the two dearest things in his life. He looked into his wife's eyes and thought about how Petya had wanted to involve her. It hadn't even occurred to his elder brother that she was special. Her soul, her spirit, were so important to Misha, but a woman's love was totally meaningless to Petya! Only the accumulation of wealth meant anything to him.

He looked back at the telephone and reminisced about his relationship with Pyotr. He thought of how he'd always wanted to be like him, to be as rich and smart and popular.

Misha was about to beg his brother to leave the mafia. He wanted to invoke their Papa's memory and remind him of their sickly Mama's wishes. But he didn't. Pyotr had heard these things all his life, and they'd never once fazed him. Instead, Misha breathed deeply and said, "Then you'll have to take your chances with the rest of the Gagarintsi when I tell the MVD everything I know."

Though Misha couldn't see him, he knew Petya was stunned. A long moment later, Petya said, "Misha, Misha! What are you saying, little brother? This is Petya! Surely you don't mean to say that..."

Misha heard his brother's feigned affection, but soon stopped listening to the words. What had Misha been doing for the last twenty years? How had he worshiped this man, this criminal, this monster for so long? How had he been such a fool? He briefly diverted his attention back to him one last time.

"...tomorrow, and we'll go to Arturio's restaurant. We'll talk, okay? Spend sometime together. Just you and me. And then we'll—"

"If you're not there when Sam and I go to MVD tomorrow," interrupted Misha, "then you are no longer my brother, Petya." His voice was steadier now. "Meet us in front of the statue on the building's front lawn at nine o'clock tomorrow morning. Do it, or you'll never see me again."

TWENTY THREE

Boris was waiting at the trolleybus stop a few blocks from his apartment building. It was a blustery morning. The ten or so people assembled by the stand were all crouched forward, shielding themselves from the cold. At 8:00 A.M., it was still dark in Moscow, but the early morning rush hour was already well under way. Finally, the trolleybus turned around the corner.

Suddenly, a Mercedes-Benz screeched a U-turn in front of the stand, cutting in front of the trolleybus, stopping right in front of Boris. Two bulky men sprang from the car, forcing the waiting commuters to cringe and jump backward. Boris shuddered when he saw the two men coming at him. Before he could move, they'd grabbed his arms and were dragging him to the car.

"What is this?" he managed before finding himself inside the Mercedes.

He was seated between the two men, both young and clean-shaven, both wearing conspicuously ordinary Russian overcoats and *ushankas,* both unfazed by their actions. "What is this?" repeated Boris over his panic. He looked up at the front passenger seat and saw a dark-haired man turn around to glare at him. Boris recognized the man immediately. The one with the familiar eyes.

"That's the question we have for you, Boris Antonovich," said the man casually, looking back at Boris. "What is this? Why has one of our most trustworthy associates betrayed us?" He rolled his familiar eyes imperiously, causing a twinge to descend Boris's spine.

Boris poised to defend himself, to demand he be released, but the man in the front seat put a finger to his lips. "Shh, Boris Antonovich. Later. We'll work it all out later."

They drove on in silence for nearly half an hour. Boris saw that he was being taken to one of Moscow's warehouse districts in the far eastern part of town. He occasionally glanced left and right at the two men who'd abducted him, but mostly he looked straight ahead, anxiously contemplating what might be in store for him. What had the Gagarintsi found out? From whom?

They reached the parking lot of a large rusty warehouse, apparently abandoned, and Boris watched as the faceless driver pulled into an empty, snow-covered field behind it.

The man in the front seat again turned around. It was at that moment that Boris remembered where he'd seen those eyes. They also belonged to the chief engineer at Mosteks. What was the kid's name? Grunshteyn. Boris leaned his head back against the seat, looking up at the car's interior light. "Who is the man at Mosteks? Your brother?" he asked.

"You're very observant, Boris Antonovich. Few people would ever guess that Misha and I are brothers. Except for our eyes, we really don't look much alike at all. But Misha has nothing, or at least very little, to do with my organization's recent revelations." He nodded at the sentry to Boris's left, who opened the door and savagely pulled Boris out with him. Then Grunshteyn got out of the car as well.

Boris's knees were shaking. He felt that his hat was tilted awkwardly on his head from the jostle, that his scarf was hanging loosely from his neck, but the cold was barely noticeable nonetheless. "The Mosteks joint venture will not go through!" he said. "It has not been registered, just as we agreed!" He glanced around the barren land behind the warehouse, but saw no one else.

"I know," replied Grunshteyn. "But not because you've been fulfilling your agreement with us, Boris Antonovich."

"That's not true! I have been doing everything Svetov instructed me to do!"

Grunshteyn had walked to the rear of the Mercedes. He opened the trunk and motioned Boris to look inside. When he did, Boris saw Mosteks' accountant, Andrey Muravyev, lying there, curled up, his hands and legs bound with lengths of brown rope. He'd been beaten; his scraped face was smudged with dried blood. Both eyes were purplish-blue. Muravyev looked up at the men outside, trying to adjust his vision to the morning light, and groaned.

Boris gaped at the wounded man. He was summoning the courage to protest, to make some effort at clearing the guilt and terror that now raged in his breast. Suddenly, the two *mafiozniki* grabbed the collar of his jacket and slammed him against the car.

"Your client here says otherwise," said Grunshteyn curtly. "He seems to recall arranging for transfers of *valuta* to you in exchange for guarantees that the JV would be registered immediately."

Boris was speechless and breathing loudly. He wondered how the *mafiozniki* would punish him. Would he be beaten? Would his family suffer? Worse? What was this Grunshteyn capable of?

"Did you really think we wouldn't monitor Mosteks, Boris Antonovich?" continued Grunshteyn. "Don't you realize we always know what's going on?" He released Boris's coat and looked up into the dawning sky for a moment, then nodded at his young cohort, bidding him to get back into the car. A moment later Grunshteyn said, "Ah, Boris Antonovich. How could you have been so stupid? You're not a fool. You're actually not a bad man at all. I rather like you, to be truthful." He smiled smugly. "In fact, I like you so much I'm going to give you a chance to make all this up. I'm going to allow you an opportunity to do a very big personal favor for me. Let's take a walk, shall we?"

Grunshteyn took Boris by the arm and headed into the snow-covered field. Boris hesitated at first, then walked on with him.

"Don't worry, Boris Antonovich," said Grunshteyn, "if I'd wanted to kill you, you'd have been dead an hour ago. And Muravyev will be fine, I promise. We'll take him home shortly."

They walked a short distance away from the car. "My brother Misha and I are having a...small family dispute," continued Grunshteyn. "For some reason, he doesn't seem to be in harmony with me anymore. In fact, he's threatened to turn me in to the MVD. I think he's just a bit upset, though, just confused by his meeting that American. Maybe the communist hardliners were right. Perhaps Russians do need to be isolated from Westerners to avoid...contamination." He stopped walking and glared into Boris's eyes. "I want you to stop my brother, Boris Antonovich. I want you to help me straighten him up." He gave Boris that *mafioznik* expression that said there was no refusing this *request.*

"What do you want me to do?" asked Boris shakily.

Grunshteyn explained his plan, his threatening gaze still fixed on Boris's eyes, which wavered from the dawning sky, to the white earth, and back to the familiar Grunshteyn eyes. When the *mafioznik* had finished giving his orders, Boris nodded. "Very well," he said.

Grunshteyn patted Boris on the back and motioned him back to the car. "Good, Boris Antonovich. Very good," he said, smiling. "We shouldn't have any problems, then, correct?" He smiled at Boris, again putting his arm around his back.

Sam glanced at Misha as the two ascended the stairs in the main building of the Ministry of Internal Affairs. He saw the pain in his friend's eyes and wondered what kind of past the Russian had shared with his degenerate brother. Sam couldn't even conceive what growing up here would be like, but he sympathized with Misha's grief over his loss. "I guess there was no way he could have done it, Misha," he said. "The mafia has become his life. You probably lost him a long time ago."

"I know this, Sam. I think I always knowing this. But it not making this easier for me."

Sam nodded silently. There was nothing more he could say to ease his friend's pain.

They reached the office of Major Nikita Aleksandrovich Kulishev at MVD's Department for the Struggle with Organized Crime. He was the officer whom Ilya had called when Svetov first approached Mosteks. Misha had learned of the major while snooping around Ilya's office as part of his assignment for the Gagarintsi. Sam and Misha had decided it would probably be best to go directly to Kulishev, who was already familiar with the Mosteks situation. They stood silently in front of the door a few seconds before Sam finally reached to open it.

Kulishev stood behind his desk, his face expressionless as he peered down at the two young men. He wasn't as tough-looking as Sam expected, with his thick brown hair and broad, somewhat flattened features. Nothing like that Ivanov guy, or whatever his real name was. But Sam could tell by Kulishev's mien that he wasn't a wimp, either.

The stacks of ruble notes were in front of him, along with the picture of the corrupt ministerial official for whom the money was intended. Misha and Sam had just concluded their story, which by necessity implicated Misha as a mafia runner. Or at least a former one. Kulishev walked around his desk. "You have done horrible thing, Mikhail," he said. "You have contributed to your country's suffering. You have made victim of every Russian.

"But you are also very brave and honest man, Mikhail. For this, I commend you. I'm sure you understand dangers of your coming to me." He was speaking in English for Sam's sake.

"Of course am aware, Nikita Aleksandrovich. This is why I wish to leaving Russia tomorrow with my wife. I hope to have your assistance in obtaining exit visas and airline tickets."

Kulishev paused uncomfortably, then said, "I'm afraid my abilities to show thanks for your services have big limits, Mikhail. Is impossible to arrange travel documents so quickly. However, I am happy to provide you with protection for time necessary to obtain documents. I can provide safe quarters for you and your wife for week or two. This should be sufficient time."

The conversation was interrupted by a loud rap on the door. Two uniformed cops rushed in, one of whom carried a small leather satchel. Sam didn't understand them, but Misha translated almost simultaneously: "Major Kulishev. I apologize for interrupting. But we have just been advised by Ministry of Finance that Mikhail Olegovich Grunshteyn and American Samuel Morris submitted incorrect data and false documents to Ministry of Finance in order to obtain approvals for JV registration. Is believed that the two intend to flee country in short time. We are requested by MinFin to detain suspects until proper hearing can be arranged." The officer then reached into the satchel and removed a written report, which he handed to Kulishev.

Misha and Sam looked up at the major anxiously.

"Is convenient, isn't it, Mikhail?" said Kulishev in English, nodding. He then turned to the officers and bade them to leave.

Sam glanced at Misha and saw the same consternation that he himself felt. They were both waiting to hear what kind of trouble they were in.

Kulishev walked back around his desk and sat down. "Like I said, I not able to get you visas and travel documents so quickly. And now, I'm afraid, would even be difficult for me to offer you protection. All I can suggest—"

"You don't believe that son of a bitch do you?" said Sam, cutting into the officer's words. "That report—"

"Of course I not believe it, Mr. Morris," returned Kulishev, unflinching. "If anything, it confirms in my mind truth of your story. I know enough about how mafia works in this country to see it in front of my nose. Gagarintsi clearly not wanting you to leave Moscow so they can continue to intimidate you and make sure you not destroy them. I'm sure their next step is threat that if you not retract your reports to MVD, that terrible consequence will result."

Sam felt better, although he still had no idea what would happen next. He waited for Kulishev to continue.

"I also think that this Shturkin was ordered by Gagarintsi to file report and is probably making documents right now to support it." He tossed the paper aside indifferently and sighed. "Now, then. Officially, I am obligated to detain you until investigation of charges made by government agency against you. In fact, this is my only allowable action. You are suspected in serious violations of Russian law." He looked at Misha and Sam for a long moment, then lowered his voice and said, "But I am beyond all else committed to fight against corruption in Russia. With my knowledge about circumstances here, I must to take other action. In name of justice. Understand?"

Misha and Sam nodded.

"Let's go, then," said Kulishev.

He went to the door and opened it, waiting for Misha and Sam to lead the way. Sam hesitated, wanting to ask a thousand questions, but decided not to. What else mattered now, except that they get to the airport and onto a plane?

The MVD officer followed Misha and Sam out of the office, and out of the building. Surprisingly, Kulishev accompanied them all the way to Misha's car in the parking lot.

"Good luck," said Kulishev as the two got into the filthy Zhiguli. "I'm sorry am unable to do more for you as law enforcement officer." He turned to Sam and said, "As you can see, Mr.

Morris, my country having long way to go. Unfortunately, we already received negatives of a free society. Positives are yet to come. I am hoping situation will change in near future." He extended his hand to Misha and then to Sam, and they bade Kulishev farewell.

Misha pulled the car out of the MVD lot. Sam looked back at Marina, who sat silently in the back seat. He was sure she'd spent the entire hour they were with Kulishev crouched down on the floor of the Zhiguli, wondering if her husband would be all right, whether going to the police was the best decision after all, whether the Gagarintsi were right outside the car waiting to pounce on them. "Where to now, bud?" he asked Misha.

"To get travel documents for tomorrow," replied Misha, meeting Marina's eyes in the rearview mirror. His tone of voice was far too casual.

They drove for a short while before Misha pulled into the lot of a large apartment building. As if following some kind of standard procedure, he parked a good distance from the building's entrance and got out of the car. "Wait here," he said. "I be back in few minutes." He closed the door, walked quickly across the lot and disappeared into the building.

Sam again looked back at Marina, wondering what she saw in his own eyes. He was frustrated that he couldn't speak with her, but he knew she felt the same bond with him as he did with her, regardless of the cultural and language barriers that separated them, regardless of the fact that they'd just met a few hours earlier. He wanted to comfort her, to reach back and offer her his hand, but thought better of it. She seemed shy—reserved—and he didn't want to offend her.

Finally Misha returned, accompanied with a heavyset man a few years older than he and Sam. He was pleasant-looking, dressed in tight-fitting Calvin Klein jeans and a Rolling Stones tee shirt, his lips set in a perpetual smile on a thinly bearded face. He sat in the back next to Marina, and Misha returned to the driver's seat.

Misha said, "Sam, please meet Dima, my old friend from engineering institute."

Sam leaned back to accept Dima's outstretched hand and shook it. Dima wasn't what Sam was expecting. He'd thought a scowling, underworld type would be making the deal.

Dima said, "Is nice meet you, Sam. Please excuse my mistakes of English. Is long time since I speaking."

"No problem," replied Sam, keeping a straight face. He wasn't sure he wanted to buddy up with a black marketeer.

"So, Sam," began Misha with a deep breath, "Dima tell me that is very difficult to get airline ticket and exit visa in one day notice. But is possible."

Dima nodded apologetically. "Is true, Sam. You must to forgive me, but my contacts only do such work for much of money. For much of *valuta.*" He shrugged his shoulders sheepishly.

"How much?" asked Sam.

"For two will be eight thousand dollars." He remained apologetic. "Is not for me, Sam. Please understand. I must to pay this to contact working in Ministry of Foreign Affairs visa department. Is big risk for this contact. Exit visa in big demand now. He get airline tickets, too, which is also very difficult. This is why so expensive. I taking nothing of this sum. There is no percent for me."

Sam wasn't sure he believed the man, though he found he was inclined to trust someone Misha trusted. He looked at Misha to gauge his reaction, but there was nothing there.

But what the fuck difference did it make? Sam only had one bargaining tool to pay for the documents regardless of what the price tag was. He nodded his head in agreement.

"You are interested in this?" asked Dima, incredulously. "You are able to pay such money?"

"Yes. I think so."

Misha turned to Sam and said, "Sam, so to be sure you understand. You must having this money now. You bring this many dollars with you to Moscow?"

"Yes," he replied. His mouth had gone dry and he felt sweat forming on his brow. "I think so."

Dima and Misha looked at Sam, confused. After a moment, Sam pulled up his shirt sleeve and removed his gold Rolex watch. He clutched it tightly in one hand, then brought it to his face for one last look. He kissed the watch, then quickly held it out to Dima. "It's pure gold," he said. "And worth at least eight thousand dollars. Probably more. You can also have all my clothes and stuff in the room at Hotel Novgorod. Take it."

Dima took the watch slowly. He was apparently familiar with Rolexes and knew this piece was authentic. "Is very dear to you, no?" he said sympathetically.

Sam nodded.

"I am sorry to take such thing from you. Please forgive me." He hung his head slightly, still holding the watch.

"Are the documents and tickets you'll get us all we need to leave the country?" asked Sam.

"Yes," replied Dima. "When you reach States you will have to take Misha and Marina to chamber to request special refugee status. This can be difficult, but American authorities will grant if Russians having you with them as sponsor."

Sam nodded. "When do we get the tickets and visas? The flight is tomorrow at noon. We should be ready to leave for the airport at nine in the morning. No later."

Dima nodded. "It will be done, Sam. Misha and Marina my dear friends. I not let you nor them have problem with it. I have them for you early tonight. Is my promise."

"See you then, Dima." He reached back and shook the Russian's hand sincerely. "'Preciate it."

TWENTY FOUR

Yasha and Lyena were waiting anxiously at the Sila Slova head-quarters when Sam, Marina, and Misha arrived. Sam came through the door first with both thumbs up. Lyena rushed to the door to greet him with a hug. Even Yasha managed to stand and give a spirited smile.

The group sat on the threadbare sofa and the battered chairs, and Grisha set a kettle of hot tea on the table before them. Sam recounted the morning's events while Lyena sat beside him and translated for Marina.

"Ah, what a predictably unpredictable world we live in, young Sam," began Yasha, still smiling triumphantly. "You know, it's really the one thing that makes life tolerable for an old man like me." A writer sitting in one of the chair-desks looked up at him, so Yasha lowered his voice. "Sam, my nephew, after a life-time of making a stink in the Soviet Union, one develops a keen sense of smell for what's going on here. I had my suspicions about that cooperative from the first moment you described to me your business with it. Remember?" He put his hands behind his head.

"You mean you could see what was happening from the very beginning?" asked Sam, suppressing a smile.

"Quite so," answered Yasha. "Not in the specifics of the crime, mind you, but in the nature of it. Although I don't consider this kind of thing characteristic of present-day Russian society, it's definitely a symptom of our generally impractical social system. There's nothing unusual about it. Nothing at all."

Yasha assumed his familiar didactic posture, and Sam braced himself for the forthcoming oration. He couldn't quite tell what the old man was taking credit for, but why not let him enjoy the moment?

"In fact, my nephew," he continued, "if I might be allowed to ambush you with my iconoclastic ideology, I believe that it is to some extent healthy that Russia suffers from the presence of men such as Messrs. Lukov and Shturkin. At least given our current state of affairs."

"What do you mean?"

"I am a realist, young Sam. I have conditioned myself to ignore the hardships of the present in order to concentrate my thoughts and efforts on what my country is becoming. I believe Russia is on a path toward democracy and freedom, following the example of the rest of the modern world." Yasha leaned forward slightly, getting to the gist of his point.

"Let's take Mr. Shturkin, for example. His actions were based on principles of free enterprise and capitalism, right? He was following his natural proclivity to capitalize on an advantage he held by virtue of his position with MinFin. Of course, I don't condone his criminal behavior. But look at the broader picture, at the implications of his actions. Are they not demonstrations of man's natural inclination to better his position in life? And isn't that the foundation of capitalism? Marxism and Leninism, you see, never provided for or even allowed this inclination. So what would have been a true disaster—in the broader picture, mind you—would be if the red banners around Moscow of the last seventy years had succeeded in depriving the Russian people of this most basic of human characteristics." He sighed again contentedly.

Lyena raised her eyebrows, as if to say, *Makes sense to me.*

"There will always be criminals, my nephew," continued Yasha. "In every society. But Russia needs more typical criminals. It needs drug dealers, my nephew. Yes, drug dealers! People who unscrupulously commit more malicious crime for what crime really is, thereby contrasting with the benign black marketeers who are simply victimized by their circumstances." Yasha poured himself a cup of tea and took a sip.

Misha nodded his agreement with Yasha's philosophy as well. "I think he right, Sam," he said. "Here is not always clear what is criminal. With ordinary drug dealers like you have in States, we would be knowing."

"I don't think your joint venture with Mosteks could ever have worked out," said Yasha. "Cooperatives are able to base their activities on the natural inclinations of the kooperator to seek profit, but those inclinations, at least at this point in time, are often unrefined. It's a natural result of the environment in which entrepreneurs like Ilya Lukov grew up. If the JV had been registered, Lukov may very well have been tempted to reap an immediate profit and run. He quite likely would have asked himself, 'With all that's going on in Russia today, why should I risk a long-term arrangement?' And he may have answered the question by saying, 'The hell with Sam Morris and Inter-American Industrial Services. This is a once-in-a-lifetime opportunity for Ilya Lukov.' And it probably would have been a simple choice." Yasha raised his eyebrows to say, *understand?* "Only with time will such men see the value of integrity in business and the need to make a life out of free enterprise and, as you Americans say, 'the pursuit of happiness,' instead of a quick, selfish buck." He gave a short laugh.

Sam wasn't sure he agreed, but he took Yasha's point.

"But look at it on the bright side, my nephew. Your boss in America should be quite pleased that his young attorney saved IIS from what could have been a disastrous business relationship."

Sam noticed Misha look away, his face a bit flushed at Yasha's comments. "I guess that's a good point," said Sam.

"I can't say Mr. Shturkin is an evil man," continued Yasha. "He's not. His attitudes were molded by his society. Unfortunately, he was left with a warped sense of direction. And I think Lukov is honest, but only by a definition of honesty bestowed upon him by a confused society."

Sam wondered what Ilya would have been like in New York City, which recognizes—indeed thrives on—the human inclination to excel. He was looking forward to seeing how Misha would adapt to living there. "It's hard for me to see it from your perspective, Uncle Yasha, but I think I understand. What you're talking about is the basis for the revolution that's coming, isn't it?"

Yasha winked, pointing his finger into the air. He then took another sip of tea, his lined face revealing his contentment. "Our problems are profound," he said. "And they will take generations to solve. It will take patience and forbearing on the part of the Russian people. Our lives are difficult, but I think we have much to look forward to." Yasha smiled and looked at Lyena, who had been sitting silently. He then slapped his hands together, stood clumsily from the couch and summoned Misha and Marina to a chair-desk to discuss tomorrow's plan.

Lyena looked up at Sam solemnly after the others had that them alone. He felt the familiar maelstrom of emotion which her presence always generated in his belly, now heightened by the events of the past twenty-four hours. He looked into her eyes and recalled the mysterious spell they'd cast upon him from the very beginning. He thought of the intimacy they'd shared and all the confusion it had created in him. And then he thought of the gratitude he'd felt when she helped him finally straighten everything out.

She, too, had been through a lot, and signs of the ordeal were visible in her exotically attractive face. His affection for her surged once again, but this time on a deeper level than before. He was trying to think of a way to express his sentiments when she spoke.

"He right, Sam," she said softly, looking away.

"What do you mean?" She seemed to be apologizing again.

"I mean Yasha right when he say that life difficult in Russia. We have many problems here. We always facing impossible choices, it seems." She shrugged.

"I know that," replied Sam compassionately. "And it's okay, Lyena. Really." He put his hand on hers, ignoring the recurring vision of Stacy's smile as he toyed with her fingers. "We're all faced with hard choices."

She breathed deeply and said, "Sam, I was not making joke when I asking you to marry me. You were, but not me. Do you remember?"

Sam paused, then nodded.

Lyena looked at him, her eyes suddenly torn between shame and pain. And perhaps a hint of hope. Sam searched his mind desperately for something to say, something that might comfort her, ease her struggle, even for just a minute...

But Lyena turned her knitted brow downward, giving an embarrassed laugh. "Was stupid idea, Sam, I know. I am sorry to trouble you."

He still couldn't find anything to say. She was a product of her culture. And he of his. He felt his teeth grit.

"Your girlfriend is such lucky woman."

Sam's scalp tingled. How could she have found out?

"Was easy for me to feel your concern, Sam. I could tell you not really opening your soul to me. I knew you must having favorite woman in America."

He nodded, looking down at his lap.

"But she so fortunate to have man like you, Sam. How I envy her so! I not think you dishonorable, Sam."

Sam smiled, his eyes closed.

"Is wonderful that you so very moral, Sam," she continued. "You see, is impossible for most Russians to have high morals. Or at least to live by them. I not think one can understand this until he living here himself. The catastrophe with Mosteks not surprising me. Is nothing new. Russians living with such people and such things every day. Is part of who we are."

"I do understand, Lyena," said Sam. "If there's one thing I've learned in the short time I've been here, it's that people have to adapt to their surroundings as best they can. And if there's a second thing I've learned, it's that you, Lyena, have very high morals."

She looked down again, her hand tightening its grip around Sam's. "Thank you," she whispered, her voice barely audible. "You are wonderful man."

"What are you going to do now? I don't think Ilya knows you were involved in what happened. You could probably keep working for him if Mosteks stays in business."

Lyena hesitated before answering. "I not think so, Sam. Maybe is difficult to live by high morals in Russia, but every person must have certain line which they must never crossing. I not think I can work at Mosteks anymore. I not want to be part of this—this attitude there. I believe it is for me that I should make life out of trying to become engineer. Real engineer. On my own. Despite being woman." She gave an embarrassed smile. "Mosteks was good for me, but for bad reasons. I not live life like that, Sam. I think I probably quit tomorrow."

Sam found himself reflexively leaning forward to kiss the Russian woman's cheek. "I'll never forget you, Lyena. And I'm sure we'll see each other again."

"Soon, I hope."

The next morning, Sam hunched down in the back seat of Grisha's red sedan, holding his head just high enough to see out the window. To his left, Marina was crouched down on the floor, with Misha leaning uncomfortably over her. It was Yasha's idea for the three to be concealed on the way to the airport. Although Yasha and Misha said it was unlikely that the Gagarintsi would try anything on the highway, it was always better to be safe.

Grisha pulled the car out of the apartment building's parking lot, with Yasha seated to his right, and he headed for Sheremetyevo Airport. As before, Sam saw husky *babushkas* treading through filthy snow, a look of invincible steadfastness on their weathered faces, which, along with their loud kerchiefs and clashing garb, reminded him of the severity of Russian life. He saw the few remaining placards feebly attempting to assert the people's dedication to the causes of communism, and the car passed several long lines of humanity waiting tenaciously in line. Do Russians accept such conditions as simply the way life is, he wondered, or are they just too passive, too tired, to be frustrated? As Grisha turned off onto a side road to lose any possible followers, Sam recalled the alien sense he'd felt when first entering Moscow, the discomfiture of not knowing what the place would be like or what would follow. He remembered the sensation as being akin to mild fear—apprehension at dealing with a country and a people he'd been conditioned all his life to disdain. But then he looked down at Marina, a woman with whom he'd never verbally communicated, and he intuitively sensed her warmth, her soul. The feminine spirit that Misha found so irresistible. Then he thought of the silent old men in the front and of their essential beauty. And he pictured Lyena. Indeed, there was an almost palpable charm in these Russians' love for humanity and its qualities, and Sam realized that his earlier prejudices about Russia were completely unfounded.

Yasha interrupted Sam's reverie when he yelled something unintelligibly at Grisha, who responded by quickly stepping on the gas. A loud Russian dialogue followed between the old men, and Sam stole a glance through the rear window.

A white Mercedes-Benz was behind them.

Grisha made a quick turn onto a windy road lined with smaller buildings under construction. He made several other maneuvers, but he clearly wasn't skilled at driving an automobile under these conditions. The white Mercedes was still behind them.

After several more awkward turns in the neighborhood, Grisha screeched into a lot behind one of the construction sites. Both he and Yasha began searching frantically for the Mercedes, their eyes desperately scanning the road in all directions.

"What's up?" whispered Sam, realizing immediately that his attempt at being quiet was senseless.

"Probably nothing, nephew. There are a fair number of expensive cars in Moscow, but when seeing a Mercedes, we have to be careful nonetheless." Yasha leaned back to Misha, who was still on the floor of the back seat, and asked, "Do your brother and his cronies drive a white Mercedes?"

"I not know," replied Misha anxiously. "They having many Mercedes. Is only kind of car they driving. I never see white one, but is possible they having."

Yasha again looked around for a few minutes, his head bobbing as he scanned. "Well," he said finally, "we seem to have lost it, if it was theirs." He nodded at Grisha, and the battered red sedan pulled back onto the road.

Sam felt relieved, though he was somehow sure they weren't out of the woods yet. He lowered his head for the rest of the trip, only occasionally looking up to check for a landmark.

Soon he saw Sheremetyevo Airport coming up. Grisha maneuvered the car up a long ramp and into a parking lot in front of the airport complex. Here goes nothing, Sam thought.

Yasha said, "We'll get out here and walk directly to the terminal. When we get inside—"

"Wait a minute, Uncle Yasha," interrupted Sam, no longer whispering. "You're not going anywhere. Neither is Grisha.

There's no reason for y'all to get involved in all of this. Besides, we might have to run, and you wouldn't be able to keep up."

Yasha was anxiously silent. He was about to speak when Sam again cut him off.

"You have too many more battles to fight here, Uncle Yasha. Remember? You told me so yourself."

Yasha hesitated, then sighed and nodded. "I'll be waiting for letters from you, young Sam. Regularly. I'll expect pictures, too. And someday, soon perhaps, I expect to see you again. Agreed?"

"I promise."

Yasha Edelman leaned over and took Sam's head in his hands, kissing him fervently on the cheek. He looked at him solemnly for a long moment, then said, "Good luck, my nephew. Give Gussie my love."

Sam, Misha, and Marina got out of the car and quickly headed toward the terminal, Misha carrying a suitcase and Marina a small handbag. It was all the Russian couple were able to gather together before hastily leaving their apartment the night before. They were refugees in every sense of the word, Sam realized, a status he hoped they'd be able to demonstrate to the American authorities at JFK. Sam followed the couple, looking around for signs of unwanted company. He was glad he was dressed in Grisha's old clothing; the outfit was less conspicuous than his suit would have been.

The group pushed through the glass doors leading into Sheremetyevo's main chamber. Sam remembered being rather disconcerted here a week ago, feeling a bit uncomfortable, but his earlier trepidation was no comparison to what raged inside him now. He followed Misha and Marina to the line of people waiting at the customs checkpoint, and, per Yasha's instructions, all three turned their heads in the same direction. It would be more difficult for them to be spotted that way.

Sam checked the clock every minute, though it felt like every half hour. The Delta\Aeroflot flight was scheduled to depart at noon; it was now only nine o'clock. Plenty of time. Too much time, Sam thought. The line moved slowly, each passenger presenting customs declarations and luggage to the stoic officers who mechanically examined both before stamping the documents. Sam looked around for suspicious characters, although he didn't know what any of the Gagarintsi, including Petya Grunshteyn, actually looked like. He never spoke to anyone, his only communication being occasional, silent eye contact with Marina and Misha.

Finally, it was Misha's turn at customs, and he presented his documents and suitcase to the officer, a young official with boyish features and a scrawny build, but with a look of conviction that could match the severity of the most seasoned KGB agent. Misha's deepest fears about the extent of Russian corruption were confirmed when the young customs officer suddenly pushed a suspicious-looking button and stood silently, his arms folded.

Misha looked back at Marina and Sam, breathing deeply. He wiped the sweat from his brow as he waited for the ensuing encounter. Would armed militiamen appear and wrestle him to the ground? Would he be sent to prison? And what would happen to Marina? Marina! He looked at his wife, who still clutched her small handbag. Her gaze was cast downward, but Misha could almost feel her anguish. She looked the same way she had on the night he'd proposed to her, when that *svoloch* had tried to mug them. He tore his thoughts away from the memory to glance at Sam, who was also quiet, but more energetic in his apprehension.

Finally, an older officer in full uniform approached. He, too, wore a grave expression, but there was no boyish innocence to be found anywhere on his face. He approached Misha and said, "I am Captain Satrovskiy, Russian Federation Customs. You are being detained. Your wife and the American Samuel Morris are also under arrest."

"Why my wife?" snapped Misha in return, meeting the officer's eyes. But he understood, of course. The Gagarintsi had ordered them all detained, even though the story about MinFin having been supplied with false information only implicated Sam and Misha.

Satrovskiy then repeated the statement for Sam in English.

The three were led away from the customs inspection point by the captain and two armed guards, the eyes of other passengers following them curiously. When Misha took a quick look at the crowd, he saw a dozen heads turn away collectively, as if the people were afraid to be associated with the detainees in any way whatsoever. The reaction heightened Misha's feeling of helpless isolation.

They were taken through a nearby door and down a corridor containing a number of small detention rooms. The captain walked to their right, the guards marched to their left, all three in rigid military formation. From the synchronous squeaking sound of their boots, one would have thought it was only one man traversing the corridor.

The group stopped at the first of the small rooms, where Satrovskiy unlocked the door and conducted Marina inside. Misha saw her terrified eyes open as wide as her narrow lids would allow. He wanted to say something to her, to beg her forgiveness. This was his doing, he realized; he'd ended his corrupt dealings too late. She held her hands clasped in front of her as she looked at him, her lower lip beginning to quiver, her silky smooth brow now creased with worry. Misha clenched his eyes shut when the captain closed the door, leaving his wife alone in the detention room.

The customs officials then turned to continue down the corridor, a guard pushing Misha's shoulder when he hesitated to move. Misha turned to walk on, taking one last look back at the room where Marina was being held.

Suddenly, he stopped short.

He'd seen something familiar. A pale, *nagliy* man standing at the far end of the corridor, wearing American jeans and a black leather jacket.

Svetov.

Misha looked back at the *mafioznik* and saw the criminal's harsh eyes return a vicious gaze. We got you, those eyes said. Misha quickly turned back around when the guard nudged his shoulder again.

The group stopped a few feet down the corridor, and Satrovskiy fumbled with the keys to open a second room, this time apparently for Sam. The American said to Satrovskiy, "I demand to see a representative from the United States embassy before—"

"You will have opportunity later, Mr. Morris," interrupted the captain. "Right now, you must obeying my orders." The official's voice, as well as his face, made it clear there would be no negotiations on the matter.

Misha looked over at Sam, hoping to somehow silently communicate an apology to him. Suddenly, a bustle erupted at the end of the corridor. From where Svetov had just been standing. It was the sound of someone being forced to the floor, struggling, with several men trying to subdue him. Men shouting. A slap. Satrovskiy jerked his head at his two armed guards, who ran off to investigate.

The noise escalated with the sound of more shouting, apparently from Satrovskiy's two cronies. At whom? Misha wondered. But soon it stopped, and Misha thought he heard the sounds of weapons being cocked.

A few seconds later, Major Kulishev appeared from around the corner, flanked on both sides by six uniformed officers of the Ministry of Internal Affairs. The steadfast MVD major walked resolutely toward Satrovskiy. "I understand that these two men, and one woman, are being detained by your customs detachment," he announced. "May I ask why, Captain?"

"For violations of Russian Federation law, major," answered Satrovskiy nervously.

"May I ask what law they are accused of violating?" Kulishev waited patiently, staring coldly at the customs officer.

Satrovskiy was silent.

"As I thought," said Kulishev. "You are under arrest, Captain Satrovskiy, for exploitation of your office for personal ends. You will release your three prisoners immediately."

Misha immediately ran back to the opposite end of the corridor, wanting to take pleasure in Svetov's long-overdue downfall. The *mafioznik* now sat awkwardly on the floor, his arms handcuffed behind him. For a fraction of a second, Misha expected the man to look pitiful, like a caged animal in a zoo. But Svetov behaved more like a snake in a glass jar, with nothing in his face but spite and venom. There was nothing there to pity.

Kulishev and four other MVD officers accompanied Sam, Misha, and Marina through passport control and took seats with them in the Aeroflot/Delta waiting area. Sam had been silent since departing company with Satrovskiy, but could no longer contain his curiosity. "How did you know?" he asked Kulishev.

The major was expressionless, as usual. "It seem, Mr. Morris, that Boris Antonovich Shturkin not worst kind of Russian criminal," he said. "His soul not able to allow innocent person to be harmed at his fault."

Sam leaned back in his chair as Misha translated for Marina, Yasha's words returning vividly in his mind.

"Shturkin learn that mafia plan to meet you here at airport. He call MVD this morning and tell us everything, even telephone number of men who harmed you. We will arrest them this afternoon."

Sam wanted to shout, wanted to somehow express his delight. But under the circumstances, it didn't seem appropriate.

Instead, he suppressed his glee, simply nodded, and said, "I'm glad to hear that, Major."

"With information from Mikhail Grunshteyn and Boris Shturkin, we have no problem putting end to this Gagarinskaya mafia," continued Kulishev. "Forever."

And somehow, Sam knew it was true. He could tell that Kulishev, much like Lukov, had retained some Soviet tactics in his approach to his job.

TWENTY FIVE

"Sam, you did a fine job. I can't say I'm glad about the way things turned out, but you saved IIS from what could have been a disastrous affair," said Jonathan Davies from across his huge desk. "The company is indebted to you greatly."

Sam had just explained to the CEO and Benjamin Kaplan what had happened in Moscow. He looked at the company's top man with a self-confidence he'd never before experienced and nodded silently. Just wait till I drop this bombshell, Jonny, he thought.

"In fact, Sam, I think it's fair to say that your future with IIS is as bright as the North Star on a clear Virginia evening. I'm looking forward to taking advantage of your legal skills here for a long time to come." He gave Sam an energetic smile and leaned back in his chair.

Sam wondered what any of this had to do with his legal skills. The CEO was obviously looking to wheedle him, just to avoid the subject both men had in mind. It was unusual to be in charge of the situation, but it felt good. "Thank you very much, Mr.

Davies," he said. "I'm glad to have had an opportunity to serve the company, especially with respect to Old Virginia Mills."

Davies smiled. "There's nothing like family loyalty, Sam. I'm always glad to see it in my troops. It was through a family business that I got started. Did you know that?"

Sam nodded, a feigned smile upon his lips, just enough to let the CEO know that he was being polite. He wondered when would be the proper time to sock it to the bossman. Should he drag it out? How would he break the news? He reached down and pulled his briefcase closer to his chair, thinking of the arsenal that waited inside.

Davies paused, then said, "I understand how attached you are to our Old Virginia facilities, Sam. So I'm going to see to it that you receive all legal assignments related to that division from now on."

Ha! Now he's squirming. Sam allowed himself to smile genuinely this time. "Thank you very much, Mr. Davies." Maybe he should wait. There really was no reason for him to come forward today, was there? Why not enjoy the spotlight?

"Well. We both have work to do. You'll find a ten percent raise in your next paycheck, Sam, as compensation for your ordeal and as a symbol of IIS's appreciation for your fine work." The CEO clasped his hands in front of him and again smiled through his beard.

Kaplan, in the monotonic voice Sam had almost forgotten, said, "And you will be receiving new business cards this week, Sam. They will indicate that you are now an assistant general counsel in IIS's legal office." He gave an uncharacteristic smile that almost made Sam laugh.

"Thanks, Mr. Kaplan." He stood to shake Kaplan's outstretched hand, wondering if the acquisitions exec might be needing a lawyer himself soon. He pictured Misha on the witness stand.

Davies said, "And by the way, Sam, don't worry about your two Russian friends. We'll take good care of them. In fact, I can think of a few of our own operations that could use a skilled mechanical engineer. I'll send you information on the best available positions this afternoon."

"Misha will be happy to hear that, Mr. Davies. I'll bring him in to meet you this week. Thanks very much."

Sam paused, then picked up his briefcase and left Davies' office. He walked straight to his Uncle Ned's. On the way, he reflexively felt under his shirt sleeve, only to find his bare wrist, and he wondered how long it would take him to get used to not having his father's Rolex. No matter, he figured. What he'd gained in exchange was well worth the loss. And he was sure that Daddy would have agreed.

"Hello, my boy," said Ned, rising from his seat. "How was the trip? Whoa! What happened to your face?"

Sam kissed his uncle, sat down, and sighed. He was already getting tired of talking about it. "I guess the trip had its ups and downs, Uncle Ned," he said. He explained what had happened, barely paying attention to his own words. Maybe he shouldn't have delayed blowing the whistle on Davies. He still hadn't decided whether he should tell Ned what he'd learned. About how Old V was being run by a company as corrupt as anything he'd encountered in Russia.

When Sam had finished recounting his trip, Ned suddenly became flustered, unable to look up at him. Something was wrong. Had the old man somehow figured out on his own that Davies had given dollars to Lukov to bribe Shturkin? Ned, after all, had been involved in the early negotiations—

Ned's hand slammed down on his desk with as much force as the elderly man could muster. He snorted loudly, then stood to close the door. "It weren't supposed to happen like that," he said quietly, sitting back down.

Sam again wondered if Ned had figured it out on his own. Could he have known all along? No way, he decided. He would've told his nephew. His brother's son. Uncle Ned would never have allowed bribery and corruption to play a role in Old V. Of course not. Besides, it had only been a fluke that Sam himself had been able to figure out what had happened.

"Davies and Kaplan could've gotten me killed, Uncle Ned," he said. "I thought something was strange about the way they sent me off alone on this project. I guess they were just protecting themselves. But when I found out that Mosteks was paying hard-currency bribes to the Ministry of Finance, I realized that the only source of dollars Mosteks had was IIS!" He felt the pride of a sleuth who'd cracked a case. "So this morning, right after we got through immigration at the airport, I dropped Misha and Marina off and went to the law library to do a little research. And guess what happens to be against American law! I—"

Sam stopped short when he saw his uncle begin to weep, shaking his head slowly.

In a quivering voice, Ned said, "Jonathan and Ben had nothin' to do with it, Samuel. It was me. I gave the Russians the money 'cause they told me in privacy they needed dollars to make the deal work."

It took a moment for Sam to comprehend what he'd just heard. He felt the same as when he'd first heard of his father's death. He looked at his old uncle, the last of Hyman's sons, his only living relative who'd actually been a part of Old V. Sam couldn't speak. He could barely think. "What did you say?"

Ned took a moment to catch his breath, then looked at Sam with wet, red eyes. "Ilya said the JV wouldn't work without it," he repeated. "It was my last chance to see somethin' come of Ol' V, Samuel. Do somethin' on my own for the mills." He started to sob. "I'm seventy-three years old, Sam. I ain't got many years left." It came out almost as a plea.

Sam was still too shocked to speak, let alone tell Ned that what he had done was a felony. He had a folder in his briefcase containing the text of the Foreign Corrupt Practices Act, the "FCPA," which he'd been planning to shove up Davies' ass. The

Act made bribing foreign officials, or having anything to do with such bribes, strictly illegal and punishable by imprisonment.

"Oh, God," cried Ned, his voice hoarse. He rubbed his wet eyes and covered his face with both hands. "What would Papa say?"

Sam sighed. He'd even brought back a witness, someone who would help prove that IIS was corrupt! He'd worked out the plan a hundred times in his mind, in Misha's living room, at Yasha's, on the plane home. And all along it was his own uncle who could have gotten him killed!

But only now did he ask himself what he'd ever hoped to accomplish. What good would sending IIS up the creek do? Was it all just revenge? How fucking stupid! Thank God he hadn't said anything in the CEO's office!

Sam stood and went around the desk to comfort his uncle. "He'd say you did your best, Uncle Ned. Now come on. You couldn't have known what was going to happen to me." He kissed Ned's cheek, trying to offer his uncle reassurance and forgiveness.

Sam caught himself walking hastily, almost running along the sidewalk to Stacy's brownstone apartment, a novel feeling of excitement resonating from his knees up to his throat and back down again. He refused to think about what had happened at the office today. He'd deal with that later.

She'd probably find it strange that he was so wild about seeing her—they'd only been apart a week!—but that didn't matter. He could almost see her smile already, those white teeth shining brightly against her olive skin. He couldn't wait to press his lips against hers. He clutched the bouquet of roses and his travel bag more tightly, trotted the last few steps to her building and pressed the buzzer.

"Yes?" sounded Stacy's voice immediately.

"Comrade Sam, here," he responded.

"Who? Who? This wouldn't be the same Comrade Sam who was supposed to call me regularly from Moscow, is it?"

Sam smiled, not allowing the reason for his neglect to surface in his mind. "No, not that one, Stacy. It's another Sam. The one who wants to take his girlfriend on vacation to the Cayman Islands next month."

Without another word from the microphone, Sam heard the door unlock. He entered the building and quickly climbed the stairs to Stacy's apartment. She was waiting for him in the opened doorway.

"Did I hear you correctly?" she asked, her smile beaming at Sam. "Is Samuel Morris, the quintessential yuppy and career devotee, going to find perhaps a *week* to enjoy alone with his girlfriend? Call the *New York Times!* Get Ted Koppel over here! This is a major news event!"

"Where's my shovel?" asked Sam through a smile, wrapping his arms tightly around Stacy. He kissed her, pushing her back into the apartment as he did. He dropped his travel bag and the flowers onto the antique trunk before lowering her onto the couch.

"Hey, what happened to your face?" she asked, pushing him back.

"I'll tell you later." He kissed her again.

"And what's with the suitcase? You moving in?"

"Yes."

"What?"

"I'll explain later!"

He lost himself in her mouth, savoring her familiar replies. For a brief moment, he couldn't help but remember Lyena, whose fuller body contrasted sharply with Stacy's, and who was so timid a lover in comparison with the energetic woman beneath him now. He'd contemplated telling Stacy about the Russian woman, maybe at some later time, because he wanted Stacy to know him completely, even if such knowledge would reveal his weaknesses. But not now, of course. For the time being, Sam's experience with Lyena would remain his secret.

Stacy took that first deep breath, that exciting musical gasp, and Sam's distractions vanished completely. He was almost too forceful when he pulled her sweater up, constraining himself when he heard the fabric rip. He began to undress her more gingerly, absorbing her music. He didn't even notice Jimmy Dean on the wall…

When they'd finished making love, they sat up on the couch, and Sam told Stacy about his trip, about Misha and Marina, including all the appropriate details, leaving out those that weren't. Her enthusiasm for his story made him realize for the first time what an adventure it had been—it put the terror he'd experienced into a different perspective. She listened to him wide-eyed, her mouth opening in awe at the more lurid parts of the story, looking at him reverently when he explained how he'd helped to break the Russian mob.

When Sam had finished, Stacy said, "So you're a real James Bond, I guess. 007 with a southern accent!"

Sam smiled to himself, dismissing the smart-ass replies that came to mind. "You got it, M. Hey! Are you going to have any problem getting time off from work for the Caymans?"

Stacy was silent for a moment, then looked down and shook her head. Sam could almost feel her spirits evaporate.

"It wasn't that tough a question, was it?"

"Oh, Sam, do we have to talk about that now? I was going to wait till later. You just got home. Why don't we just hang loose for a while?"

"Sure, Stacy."

She took a deep breath. "All right, they gave the job, the head stylist position, to some blond bimbo. She's probably been fooling around with Colby, the head of the company, for months. She's the only one who walks out of his office every time with a disgusting smile on her face."

"Sorry, Stacy. What are you going to do?"

"You really want to have a heavy, Sam? Right now? One hour after you came home?"

Sam shrugged.

Stacy sighed, then said, "Okay, I quit. I mean, who needs that shit? Everyone at Hobgoode knows I was the best one for that job. I guess I should just be grateful I'm in a position to quit. If I didn't have—Sam! What are you doing?"

Sam had encircled Stacy with both arms, pulling her head back down onto the couch. Perhaps a bit too roughly. But before she could continue her protest, he'd pressed his mouth onto hers, looking forward to finding that boomerang tongue of hers. And savoring it when he did.

A while later, Stacy broke the kiss. "I never knew that a chick's career problems were such a turn-on for you, Morris."

"You're the turn-on, Werner." He kissed her again, lightly this time.

"So where are Misha and Marina now?" she asked.

"That's actually why I brought my bag here. They're going to stay at my place until they can get an apartment of their own. You'll meet them tomorrow."

"Great!"

Sam looked at his girlfriend again, wondering if he should say something, if he should somehow express...how much he...had missed her during the past week. He was again looking for words, some way to express his feelings for this incredible woman...

"The Cayman Islands, huh?" she said, cocking her head coquettishly.

Sam touched her cheek, then reached into his jacket on the floor. He removed and opened an envelope containing airline tickets and a colorful brochure. "I thought this looked like fun," he said.

"I think I'm going to send you to Russia more often, comrade," said Stacy, taking the tickets and examining them. She looked like a little girl who'd just gotten a new bicycle. "The Grand Caymans, huh?"

Sam marveled at Stacy's excitement over the trip and wished he'd scheduled the vacation for a closer date. He leaned down to kiss her again, partly because he found her so irresistible, but partly because he was stalling. When he realized this, he broke away from her.

"So how'd the workaholic become such a romantic?" whispered Stacy.

"I guess...he just figured..." He breathed deeply. "Because he's got it bad for you."

Sam was unable to sleep that night because of jet lag. Stacy was sound asleep, however, so he quietly got out of bed and went into the living room. He took a notepad from the telephone stand and jotted down a letter.

Dear Ilya,

By now you will have learned what happened to me because of your deal with Boris Shturkin. Obviously, the joint venture with IIS will not be possible. You may be interested to hear that Misha and Marina Grunshteyn will be settling down in New York City, where I'm sure they'll have wonderful lives together.

During our first business meeting, Andrey Muravyev delivered a toast at the Firefly restaurant. I remember him intoning about how lucky Mosteks was for having IIS as a partner, and how Russia had so far to go to be on a par with the West. He said that business with companies like IIS was the beginning of Russia's "conversion."

What comes to my mind first, Ilya, and what I'd originally intended to tell you in this letter, was that Russia, and people like you, Shturkin, and the Gagarinskaya criminals, have far more to go to reach the West than Andrey could possibly imagine. But I'm not sure that addressing such thoughts to you, or any of the other individuals I just mentioned, would be appropriate. My ideas may be inaccurate, anyway. Perhaps you Russians are already on a par with us and just don't know it.

I don't want to leave you with some kind of patronizing lecture or a plea for change of your situation. Rather, I'd just like you to know that Russia must be careful. Very careful. As I see it, you and your countrymen have traveled down a long, difficult road and have now reached a fork. You must choose one of two directions. One direction will lead to catastrophe, and the other to prosperity. The former will be easier to travel, it doesn't require any sacrifice. But the latter leads to a much better destination, for all concerned.

When we had our first business meeting, you gave me a palekh box to "remember my Russian friends." Because of my rather tumultuous departure, I was unable to retrieve the box from my hotel room before leaving Moscow. It's presumably now in the hands of a black marketeer who arranged to get Misha and Marina exit documents.

Maybe one day I'll return to Russia. I hope you'll have the occasion to give me another box.

Meanwhile, best wishes in your travels, Ilya.

Sincerely,

Sam Morris